MARVEL

AN ANTHOLOGY OF THE MARVEL UNIVERSE

BLACK PANTHER

TALES OF WAKANDA

AN ANTHOLOGY OF THE MARVEL UNIVERSE

BLACK PANTHER

TALES OF WAKANDA

Original short stories edited by

JESSE J. HOLLAND

TITAN BOOKS

MARVEL

BLACK PANTHER: TALES OF WAKANDA
Hardback edition ISBN: 9781789095678
Electronic edition ISBN: 9781789095692

Published by Titan Books
A division of Titan Publishing Group Ltd
144 Southwark Street, London SE1 0UP
www.titanbooks.com

First hardback edition: February 2021
10 9 8 7 6 5 4 3 2 1

FOR MARVEL PUBLISHING
Jeff Youngquist, VP Production and Special Projects
Caitlin O'Connell, Assistant Editor, Special Projects
Sven Larsen, VP, Licensed Publishing
David Gabriel, SVP of Sales & Marketing, Publishing
C.B. Cebulski, Editor in Chief

This is a work of fiction. Names, places and incidents are either products of the author's imagination or used fictitiously. Any resemblance to actual persons, living or dead (except for satirical purposes), is entirely coincidental.

Special thanks to Wil Moss & Brian Overton

Black Panther created by Stan Lee & Jack Kirby

A CIP catalogue record for this title is available from the British Library.

Printed and bound in the United States.

This work is lovingly dedicated to our Forever King
Chadwick Boseman

Long May He Reign

TABLE OF CONTENTS

Introduction by Jesse J. Holland | **9**

Kindred Spirits by Maurice Broaddus | **17**
Heart of A Panther by Sheree Renée Thomas | **37**
Killmonger Rising by Cadwell Turnbull | **75**
I, Shuri by Christopher Chambers | **97**
Of Rights and Passage by Danian Darrell Jerry | **127**
And I Shall See the Sun Rise by Alex Simmons | **149**
Faith by Jesse J. Holland | **165**
Ukubamba by Kyoko M | **193**
What's Done in the Dark by Troy L. Wiggins | **211**
The Underside of Darkness by Glenn Parris | **243**
Return of the Queen by Tananarive Due | **273**
Immaculate Conception by Nikki Giovanni | **297**
Legacy by L.L. McKinney | **331**
The Monsters of Mena Ngai by Milton J. Davis | **351**
Shadow Dreams by Linda D. Addison | **375**
Bon Temps by Harlan James | **401**
Stronger in Spirit by Suyi Davies Okungbowa | **447**
Zoya the Deserter by Temi Oh | **469**

About the Authors | **491**
About the Editor | **501**
Acknowledgements | **503**

INTRODUCTION

AN UNEXPECTED GIFT

AS A child, I began constructing my Wakandan soul.

You see, one of my first comic books—if not the first—was a copy of *The Avengers* #177. Inside was a collection of heroes, some my adolescent and comics-obsessed mind knew, and some I didn't. In particular, I discovered a soft-spoken man in black who didn't have a magic hammer, an indestructible shield, or a red-and-gold suit of solar-charged armor, yet somehow was respected by everyone from the Invincible Iron Man to the Mighty Thor and Captain America. Even the issue's villain noted how noble, how honorable, how regal this man was.

This was my first time laying eyes on T'Challa, the Black Panther, and I was hooked.

Here was a character who wasn't a sidekick or assistant, wasn't a Blaxploitation-style stereotype talking "street" character or wearing discotheque-style clothing, wasn't in awe of the godlike white men with whom he associated. In fact, he was richer and more powerful than Tony Stark, on par with geniuses like Bruce Banner, Henry Pym, and Reed Richards, and was just as royal as Thor, Doctor Doom, or Prince Namor. Best of all, he looked like me! (Or at least what I hoped I would look like whenever I made it to adulthood.)

There, on the pages of a comic book, was an unapologetic,

proud, intelligent paragon of Blackness, our personal King Arthur. In addition to saving the world alongside the Avengers and other super heroes, the Panther took on issues that we personally cared about, like the Klan, apartheid, racism, colorism, anti-Africa hatred. He walked the mean-yet-majestic streets of Harlem, and he called the most advanced country in the world—which happened to be in Africa, no less—his home.

From that day forward, I absorbed as many tales of the Black Panther as I could find, whether it was as a supporting character in *The Fantastic Four*, a member of the Avengers, the star of his own tales in the unfortunately titled comic *Jungle Action*, or in his own *Black Panther* series. Eventually he would move into other media in a 2010–11 Black Entertainment Television cartoon series, and finally the eponymous record-breaking movie.

Indeed, many of us have been constructing our Wakanda souls for years.

We know every twist and bend in Serpent Valley and the heights of Warrior Falls. We know his uniform is a kingly habit, not a "cat costume." We sat with T'Challa and Monica Lynne as they bonded overlooking scenic Wakandan countryside. We cried when Bast blessed the union of Ororo and T'Challa, and we raged when the world wouldn't allow them to remain together as they were destined to be.

We feared the coming of Killmonger, the one man T'Challa has never entirely beaten.

Our fascination with the character gave us a head start on Wakandan lore, and for a long time it was a relatively exclusive group. In recent days that's changed. The Black Panther has joined the ranks of cultural icons, and we're ecstatic that so many other people—many of whom had never heard or cared about the Panther before the movie—have figured out what so many of us always knew.

T'Challa is THE man, and we are Wakandan.

With the Panther's ascension, many of us found the courage to define for ourselves who our heroes would be, what they would look like, and what they represented, not only to us but to the world. This is the true gift that the Black Panther gave the world: an opportunity to embrace his or her own personal heritage, each unique, each worthy, each distinctive to his or her own nation, culture, ethnicity, and even neighborhood.

Yet this legend is more than just a mythology told by modern-day griots around an electronic fire. Wakanda is more than the ancestral plains to which we may aspire, and T'Challa is more than a dream-king meant to inspire greatness. The Black Panther has long represented genuine change in the comic book industry, and a step forward by the men and women who crafted these modern-day morality tales.

WHEN STAN Lee and Jack Kirby created T'Challa, Wakanda, and the Panther mythos, they weren't creating just another supporting character for a popular comic book series. Appearing in *Fantastic Four* #52 (dated July 1966), T'Challa was the first major Black comic book character to appear in a mainstream comic. By introducing him, they made a declaration—that all men are equal, that every man and woman could prove worthy of being a king, a queen, and a hero.

It didn't stop there. In his editorial "Stan's Soapbox," which appeared in all of the Marvel titles, Lee proposed, "racism and bigotry are among the deadliest social ills plaguing the world today," that we should, "judge each other on our own merits," and not on the color of our skin, our gender, or religion, or any other artificial barrier that mankind has invented.

I don't claim to know what was going through their minds when Stan and Jack came up with the Panther. (It feels right to call them "Stan and Jack," instead of Mr. Lee and Mr. Kirby, given the sheer number of their comic books I devoured.) What I do know is that their work revolutionized the industry, and shattered a glass ceiling for comic books and all popular culture storytelling. The Panther was first, but in his wake came a whole new world. Other characters followed, including the Falcon (Marvel's first major African-*American* hero) and Luke Cage.

With the Black comic book characters there came another world-changing concept—Black comic book writers and artists! They had existed before, as with the lauded artist Matt Baker of the 1940s and 1950s, and even George Herriman, creator of *Krazy Kat*, but few readers knew their ethnic origins. Suddenly we discovered illustrators such as Billy Graham, who worked on both *Black Panther* and *Luke Cage*, Keith Pollard, Arvell Jones, and Ron Wilson.

Black innovators became prominent in other media, as well. There were Floyd Norman, an animator for Disney, and Martin R. Delaney, author of *Blake; or, The Huts of America*, considered one of, if not the, father of African-American speculative fiction. Other such prose superstars have included the incomparable Octavia Butler, whose work opened the eyes of so many in my generation, Nalo Hopkinson, N. K. Jemisin, Tananarive Due, and Nikki Giovanni.

Back in comics, innovation continued as Marvel brought on board a pioneering African-American editor, Christopher Priest, who went on to write the *Black Panther* series. The great Dwayne McDuffie, my own personal griot and one of the first comic book writers I ever met, helped to found an entire imprint dedicated to African-American characters and creators. Their legacy continued through creators like Aaron McGruder, Ta-Nehisi Coates, Reginald Hudlin, and more.

WHY SHORT stories?

I've loved these characters my entire life. I've loved comic books my entire life, but I've also loved books and, in the early days, wondered why there weren't more books that featured my favorite comic book characters.

In my mind, super heroes translated well to the printed page: great heroic characters, tragic situations, massive sacrifices, happy endings, romance, heartbreak, loneliness, despair and triumph, all wrapped up in characters who have a strong belief in the righteousness of their actions and the idea that someone should do something when a person needs help.

What better characters to feature in a novel?

But when I was beginning my reading journey, those books didn't really exist. Oh, there were the Big Little Books, but those were baby comics and didn't have enough story in them to satisfy me. (I came along before the easy availability of collected editions, and I still own my copy of the first Marvel graphic novels, *The Death of Captain Marvel* and *The New Mutants*.) I wanted more story than I was getting from the monthly comic books, and to me, novels were the best option.

This is actually how I personally started writing, because I couldn't wait until next month to see what happened to Luke Cage, the Avengers, or the Black Panther, so I started plotting the stories for myself at home to fill the time in-between issues. And of course, being crazy happy when one of my ideas showed up on the page (Great minds think alike, I thought!), and setting my ideas aside when the writer and artists went in other directions. But those days sitting at home, coming up with stories around what Jim Rhodes, Sam Wilson, Misty Knight, Ororo Munroe, and other Marvel characters would do in the situations that I would put them in is still a fond memory.

And then the Distinguished Competition had its breakthrough.

I loved that first Batman movie with Michael Keaton and Jack Nicholson, but what was even better was that after that movie came out, there was a line of anthologies that allowed writers to write their own version of Batman stories. They weren't just about Batman, either: there were Robin stories, Catwoman stories, Penguin stories, and Alfred stories. This wasn't just *The Further Adventures of Batman*, these were tales of Gotham, these were stories about the World of Batman.

I still have my three tattered *The Further Adventures of Batman* anthologies, edited by Martin H. Greenberg, here in my bedroom, dog-eared, tattered, well-read and absolutely loved. I consumed them over and over, and when I finished my own Black Panther novel, *Black Panther: Who is the Black Panther?*, I looked at those anthologies and thought back.

The 2018 Black Panther movie was just as or even more influential than the 1989 Batman movie. The Black Panther is just as if not more influential than Batman is today. Therefore, T'Challa's world needs, nay *deserves*, the same kind of exploration in prose form as Bruce Wayne's did, told by writers who appreciate and admire the world of Wakanda in the same way writers adored the world of Gotham a couple of decades ago.

And the idea was born.

IN YOUR hands you hold a first—an anthology of Wakandan stories told specifically by authors of African heritage who have been inspired by the Black Panther. Tales told in a variety of voices, revealing a variety of concepts, yet all coming from the same place—their Wakandan souls.

With this book, our goal is to take the spirit of what Stan and Jack started, combine it with what so many writers and artists continued over the years, and reveal the inspiration instilled in readers like me, who discovered T'Challa and suddenly felt connected with something greater. In these tales, we hope you find the passport into a world where African colonization failed, Afrofuturism rules supreme, Wakanda is forever, and the Panther stalks those who would threaten the innocent. Come sit with us around the fire, feel the arid wind and the unforgiving sun, as we pledge honor to the Panther God and her disciple by keeping their legend alive with some of the newest and most exciting talent to come from Mother Africa.

Somewhere, I hope there is a young child—like me—sitting alone in their room, learning that the world is a lot larger than he or she thinks. And that for them, with this anthology and Bast's blessing, the first spark of their own Wakandan soul ignites.

KINDRED SPIRITS

MAURICE BROADDUS

WATCHING WAKANDAN people through a series of cameras and satellites is not exactly spying if they're family.

Sort of. Well, maybe the whole idea's fried. The thing about being a *Dora Milaje*—the royal protectorate gathered from various tribes for the Wakandan king and, well, his personal bodyguards (not that he needs either)—is that I have access to all sorts of technology and surveillance. Not that studying a fisherman ranks high on anyone else's priority list.

Just outside of the Crystal Forest, home of the Jabari cult, an old man gathers his catch. Still strong and able, though he's seen his share of days, he hops out of his boat onto the white sands of the beach and heads to his village. Passing farmers tending to their fields, that's life in my home village.

One I couldn't enjoy, because of the politics of who I am. Queen of the Jabari cult. Since T'Challa keeps the peace between the tribes of Wakanda with the chosen *Dora Milaje*, I'm a walking international incident waiting to happen. The spying thing probably doesn't help, but this is the village where the family I never knew comes from.

Until recently, as far as I knew, I was born Chante Giovannie Brown. I gave myself the name Queen Divine Justice. Come to find out that my true Wakandan parents named me Ce'Athauna

Asira Davin, meaning "the Peace of God." But ever since I was sent away, I've known anything except peace. Or, for that matter, divine justice.

I pan the camera back toward the unspoiled Nyanza Bay and stare out at the water for a while. That's when I see it.

A fish bobs to the surface of the water. Then another. And another. Soon, a hundred or so float in the bay, their lifeless eyes staring up at the sun. Not sure if this is a thing, I hesitate, uncertain of the protocol in this situation. This is one of those moments when I try to talk to my mom and dad. Anywhere else, I'd probably be labeled crazy, since they were killed when I was a baby and I don't even remember them. I only have a vague impression of who they were. But here in Wakanda, they're all about talking to their ancestors. Heck, I work for a guy who talks to spirit cats that date back to the dawn of time, so I'm in good company.

My gut tells me this is a spy vs spy situation, so there is only one person to contact.

"You summoned me, my Lady?" I recognize the voice before I turn around. Hunter. Also known as the White Wolf, chieftain of the *Hatut Zeraze*, literally "the Dogs of War." Figuratively, he's the head of Wakanda's secret intelligence forces.

And the Black Panther's half-brother. The king trusts him as much as Thor trusts Loki.

"I ain't down with that 'my Lady' ish." I fix my eyes on him the way I would any dude who cat-called me while I was trying to take a stroll minding my own business. That hard "don't test me" stare flashes to bear like breathing at this point.

"Just showing the respect due a queen." Hunter leans against the doorframe without a worry about getting the slightest bit of dirt on his perfectly white, perfectly tailored business suit. But everything about him is a lie. His suit is actually his White Wolf uniform made to appear as a suit, with the same advanced technology that allows him to sneak in here and pose dramatically.

That's the thing about Hunter: he's like the uncle that is always up to something.

"I can get with that." I shut off my display. "Though I hadn't actually summoned you. Yet."

"Yes, you had, though you may not have realized it. Perhaps now would be a good time to caution you that when you use our defense monitors to spy on a restricted area, someone's going to notice."

"Okay, I kinda thought my *Dora Milaje* status gave me clearance. Anyway, I wanted your opinion on something." I point to the fish clustered on the water. "What do you make of this?"

"A fish kill." His wry grin betrays amusement at his own smug response.

"That much I figured out on my own."

"What do you think it means?" Hunter's eyes constantly size me up.

I hate how everyone around here treats every opportunity like it's a teaching moment. "Someone's dumping something they shouldn't."

"What do you plan to do about it?"

"I don't know. It needs to be investigated. Maybe take it to the king."

"This is nothing to bother the king about. He already mopes about in his malaise."

The ever-present shadow of the king looms long, with few ever escaping it. No one ever wants to trouble him.

"Then would you check it out? Investigate and learn more? Those are my… I don't know what those people are to me, but I'm protective of them."

"Very well." Hunter steps to the console and produces a series of holographic images. "In the meantime, I'm to brief you on the gala tonight."

"Where's…" I glanced about for my *Dora Milaje* instructor.

"This is a state function and a security matter. You'll be escorting the king as he meets with the Chinese business delegates as part of the Build and Railway Forum soiree."

"A… BARF party?" I yell louder than I intended. I can't hide the snicker in my voice.

"Queen…" his voice trails in admonishing disapproval.

"Don't get mad at me for calling it what it is. They spend all that money, and no one had an extra $50 to chip in for better branding?"

"I assure you, this is a matter of grave import to the Chinese. Their larger agenda involves building a railroad from Azania that will eventually extend to Narobia and Niganda, replacing the line built during British colonial rule. The better to transport wealth out of the countries more efficiently."

"Cynical much?" My eyebrows arch, but I also have a resting skeptical face.

"Merely a student of history. Colonizers are like addicts."

"I know my share of addicts. They don't see people. They only see resources to be consumed. Once they have, you cease to exist and they move on." Rotating back to the monitors, I see the fish drift to the shore to rot in the sun. "They dump whatever they want, destroying our rivers. Our quality of life.

"As long as we continue to be the object of their irresponsibility, injustice, and inhumanity, our entire continent and way of life is in jeopardy."

"Welcome to the new colonialism: plundering nations with a checkbook." I talk with my full chest now.

Hunter tilts his head like he's surprised by my answer. "And the Black Panther sits idly by while it happens."

"You could at least try to hide your resentment of the king."

"It's not resentment. I simply hate the lies and hypocrisy of Wakanda. I have one motive: to defend and serve the kingdom of Wakanda. And its king. I do the dirty jobs so that my brother and his father before him could keep their hands clean. And blameless."

"You're a white dude, trying to speak on our behalf."

"I am the son of its king." When he was a baby, the plane carrying him and his family crashed in an outlying area of Wakanda. T'Chaka, T'Challa's father, adopted him. Hunter's been sort of overcompensated on the loyalty thing ever since. His *Hatut Zeraze* are reputed to be the most loyal of the many secret services operating on behalf of Wakanda. Almost fanatically so. He never let little things like torture, assassination, and brutality slow his roll any. Which was why T'Challa eventually dismissed him. Hunter's been slowly working his way back into his brother's good graces, from freelancer back to player in the game.

"For a decade, I was the lone son of King T'Chaka and Queen N'Yami. Until T'Challa, the king's biological son, arrived. N'Yami died in childbirth. T'Challa's birth…"

"…and you lost your parents all over again."

Hunter stared at her. "You have no idea what it's like to be colonized within your own family."

"We have a lot in common…" My voice trails off as I catch myself with the observation. I hate it when bits of accidental truth slip out. A moment passes between us, the communion of loss in the silence.

Being adopted into royalty doesn't make up for being dealt a rough hand. I'm just as lost and lonely surrounded by all the trappings of wealth and power. Always struggling to fit in, to find my footing, to be accepted.

"You need to get ready for the gala." Hunter shifts noisily. "You don't want to be late for the gathering."

"Aren't you coming with me?"

"No. My brother, the king, does not require me there."

I understand Hunter giving this shindig a hard pass. People only knew of Hunter in relation to T'Challa or his father. It's difficult to find your place in a family with a celebrity in it. Everyone approaches you interested only in your famous relative. It may take half a dozen questions before they even notice you exist as your own person. It's got to be doubly tough when you are the older brother, and the younger is king. The favored one. The wanted one.

Without another word, Hunter activates his cloaking technology and fades into the background like an annoying ghost, remaining unseen.

LIFE IN Wakanda always feels like part pageant. Life as celebration, using any event as an excuse to showcase our culture. The drummers announce the entrance of the *Dora Milaje*, falling into rhythm so we can step in a choreographed dance, like Alpha Kappa Alphas on steroids. Though there's something extra to it, like I'm tapping into the source of the very spirit of our dance. Only once our performance has ended do I settle down to business.

For once, it's fitting that the *Dora Milaje* have me outfitted in my standard dress like a dinner party might break out at any moment. People look through me as I walk, at best cognizant of my position. A businessman approaches me with an appraising gleam in his eye. I wave him off with a snarl and my hand reaching for a weapon. After grabbing a plateful of those bacon-wrapped shrimp things, I withdraw into my thoughts.

China is the big player in Africa, while the U.S. still thinks of it as just one big country, too far away and too poor to care about. China sends delegates and corporate representatives to the capital of every nation in Africa every year to be hosted at a (I refuse to call it by that ridiculous name) party. All to secure various infrastructure projects. Over ten thousand Chinese firms are doing business in Africa.

None in Wakanda.

That's why the surrounding nations from Azania to Niganda quietly resented T'Challa. Not that the king expected to be celebrated for ending Wakandan isolation, but as far as the surrounding countries were concerned, it was like growing up hungry only to find out your next-door neighbor had been gorging on burgers the entire time.

Then, without fanfare, the king arrives. I know he's here the way you knew any cat was in the room. The way my bladder suddenly felt full as if I might be potential prey. An indefinable sense of presence. Watching you. Tracking you. Hunting you.

His black cutaway coat—with Wakandan patterns embroidered at each cuff and about his collar—has a regal drape. King T'Challa glides through the room like a shark unhampered by water. No, that's not quite right. He's free, in the truest sense of the word. No one here holds any leverage over him. No one can control him. No one binds him. Not by chains. Not by favor. Not by money. Yet there's still a heaviness to him, like he carries the responsibility to his entire nation. When you're king, the weight of the world rests on your shoulders—and he has big-ass shoulders.

"Why am I here?" Without heat, genuinely curious, I assume my position at his side.

"To watch. To learn." T'Challa only speaks to me in Hausa, his default language of and that of the *Dora Milaje*. Any given citizen of Wakanda speaks three or four languages. At least.

I was born in Chicago. I still don't know much Hausa. Even less Wakandan. "I need you to speak American. Preferably in the dialect of hood."

The corner of his mouth twitches, practically a beaming smile for him. "Consider this a practicum in your study of international affairs. Part of your training as *Dora Milaje*, if you are to one day lead."

Hunter's warning flits through my head, but I need to bother a brother.

"King T'Challa, a matter has come to my attention. There's been a fish kill at Nyanza, on the outskirts of the Crystal Forest. I… asked the White Wolf to check it out." I close my eyes, waiting for the yelling about overstepping my bounds to start. At least, that's what my life in Chicago taught me to expect. When it doesn't come, I open them again.

"My brother is not to be trusted," T'Challa intones, low and serious.

"What's the deal with you two? If he can't be trusted, why put him in charge of anything more important than toast?"

"He's still family. He's still loyal to Wakanda."

His childhood—already constrained by being the heir to an ancient and unbroken dynasty—ended when he was about my age, when his father was killed in front of him. His life, all duty and sacrifice, measured in discipline, drive, and focus. I'm doing good to get my Corn Flakes in the morning. It might be the king thing or the hero thing or the inner teenage boy whose dad was taken away from him thing, but he's closed himself off. Rarely letting anyone in, the man's in need of a hobby.

"Good evening, King T'Challa." Jiang, the chief executive officer of one of Asia's largest corporations, sidles up to us. Though the king towers over a foot taller than him, the CEO of the East Asia Corp. carries himself with the confidence and unassuming power of someone used to being underestimated. "It is still 'King', correct?"

This jumped-up real estate mogul trying to be slick with his shade. T'Challa recently thwarted a challenge from Erik Killmonger. As part of his strategy, King T'Challa dissolved Wakanda's political government and crashed its economy. One of his typically convoluted plans that pitted everyone against each other so that folks couldn't see what he was up to. U.S. State Department liaison Everett Ross once told me, "If you learn nothing else about my client, learn this: whatever you think he's doing, he's doing something else."

But like all actions, it had its share of consequences. He's still technically king, but no longer chieftain. The way I understand it, the rule of law became tribal over political. One of the reasons I was brought here from my safehouse in Chicago was to quell some of the tribal council tensions.

"I am Wakanda's king." Though he spoke without a hint of annoyance, T'Challa's voice always had the undercurrent of "Tread lightly or I'll take grandmomma's switch to your behind."

"We hope to be Wakanda's friend. The East Asia Corp. of course hopes only to help Africa stand by themselves." Jiang's face lit up, all warmth and charm. "Our government, and our business concerns, have always backed African liberation movements, since Wakanda won't."

"A velvet glove does not make the yoke of colonialism any less brutal. If you've come to exploit us, it only makes you someone new to resist." T'Challa meets his eyes. It's a dark and terrible thing to stare into the eyes of a panther up close.

Jiang takes a half-step backward. "We have learned much from the way of those who would oppress us."

"That is the fear: that you believe that it's China's turn to exploit us. A new colonizer looking to grow its power on our wealth."

Jiang presses his hand to his chest in mock injury. "Our corporation pursues a different path. After all, after the death of our founding father, our more progressive leaders chose to invest in business, science, and technology. Now we simply do business. We're offering trade and aid. For example, we're building a $1.7 billion-dollar hydropower dam in Niganda."

Jiang leads the way to the center stage. With a hand flourish, a three-dimensional holographic rendering of the edge of Niganda appears. An ancient shoreline on the far side of the Nyanza. Once that image settles, Jiang overlays it with the image of the proposed project: a tourist park, residential area, industrial zone, commercial zone, tech park, art district, all terminating at the dam in progress.

"We want to turn the city into a high-tech hub. One of the world's largest cities with the largest port." Jiang all but beams with pride. "It's all about responsible investment."

"Responsible foreign investment is an oxymoron." At the sudden silence, I glance around. Everyone shifts toward me. I had accidentally used my outside voice.

"Go on," T'Challa says.

"When I first read the proposal, it looked generous," I begin, hiding the quiver of uncertainty in my voice. "The deals and loans weren't profitable for China's Commercial Holdings International bank."

"Why do we listen to the naïve prattling of a child?" Jiang's umbrage sears as a visible scar of a sneer across his face.

"The way you talk to the youngest of our citizens is emblematic of how you see all of us. This 'child' is a valued member of my inner circle. The children of Wakanda are trained as leaders from the time they can speak. And are free to share their thoughts." T'Challa nods for me to continue.

"But," I emphasize the word for good measure, "when you read the fine print, should a country fail to meet the terms of the loan, Chinese corporations and, by extension, the government of China will control those projects for their interests. Outright."

"The finer points of international commerce may be lost on you. We pay our fair share in taxes to the countries we do business in. Azania. Canaan. Narobia. Niganda. We promote African autonomy and independence because we need more trading partners. Again, we only want to be a friend to the *hei ren*."

That means "black people." The way he says it, I hear a hard "r."

"Africa has no friends. Only exploiters. The history of empty promises and condescension from the West has made us wary. We know when we're addressed as equals. After all, we, too, are a nation of banks."

This is exactly why I hate political intrigue. There are simply times you need to just straight cuss someone out to their face. Speaking of, T'Challa's face devolves beyond a poker face. Like he's able to hide even his, I don't know, *spirit* from me. There's just a wall where a man should be. Ruling seems to be about managed paranoia. Calculating what your enemies are up to, even what your friends are up to, since everyone moves according to their own self-interest. An outsider can only know T'Challa from his actions, and even those are layers within schemes. A lonely place within the halls of power.

A flutter in the hologram draws my attention.

"Is this a live feed?" I ask.

"Yes it is." Jiang relaxes, sounding entirely pleased with himself.

"My king…" I nod toward a shimmer on the screen. The slightest ripple, but to those who know what they were looking at, it's the signature distortion effect produced by the way *Hatut Zeraze*'s cloaking technology bends light. Hunter. The king surely saw it, though his face didn't betray a flicker of recognition. Then I wonder if I was supposed to alert anyone to it at all, and curse my big mouth. Jiang squints, but he doesn't know what to look for.

"If one of your operatives sabotages our work," the businessman blusters, his assumptions filling in the blanks of what he can't see, "we will hold you personally responsible."

"As a measure of our commitment to building our relationship, I will personally see to any rogue elements of my kingdom."

"No." A heightened measure of alarm fills Jiang's voice. "We will see it as an intrusion of our sovereignty."

"And, yet, you have no standing here. Niganda is not your nation."

"Nor yours." Jiang straightens his suit as if unruffled. The elephant crapping in the pool being that Niganda is a kleptocracy on its best day. Its loyalty bought by whoever has the largest check at the moment. "Besides, we have sensitive corporate intelligence issues in play here. We would not want to put Your Highness in a position to be accused of espionage."

"If there are any rogue elements, I shall gather them before anyone is compromised."

"Your Highness, there is simply no need. We…" Jiang's voice trails off as he considers his words. It must be important, because he usually flows with no kind of filter. "Such an egregious trespass will not be tolerated. You'll be wise not to meddle in our business affairs."

"This was not a request." T'Challa whirls on his heel with the ease and power of a hurricane changing course. Pity any who got in his way.

"WHERE TO?" Preparing to punch coordinates into the Talon, a Wakandan stealth jet, I glance back toward the king.

"To the Nigandan site, Beloved." T'Challa's suit transforms, his jacket fading into the ceremonial vestments of his tribal rank. 'Cause, seriously, who was going to take that suit from him. Vibranium soles. Energy daggers. Built-in night vision. Claws made of anti-metal, a Vibranium alloy that destabilizes the molecular structure of other metal it comes in contact with. No longer chieftain in title, he was still the Black Panther.

And he must mean business, because he's not wearing the cape.

(I'm not one to judge another's drip, but I never felt the cape.)

He focuses his scrutiny on me. I don't know if it's the odd tilt of his head or what, but it's like his steady gaze takes in the entirety of who I am. "What's troubling you?"

I hate it when he does that, like a doctor diagnosing you before you're ready to admit that you're sick. "How many Wakandans are out there as part of the Diaspora?"

"None."

"None?" Even my voice arches in skepticism.

"None of our people were ever enslaved."

"I wonder what Killmonger would have to say about that." I regret my words as they leave my mouth. "I'm so sorry, my King. I chose my words poorly."

Funny how I get all "my King" whenever I remember he's not the typical member of the long underwear club. He's actual royalty. It's within his discretion to order my execution as a matter of state. I might slip and catch a case for treason. No, that's not what fuels it. It's more that I am reminded of the fundamental respect I have for the man. The title comes along for the ride, but it's the man I never want to disappoint. Or hurt.

"Say your piece, Beloved," his tone gentle and inviting.

Flying over mud hut villages with thatched roofs, coconut groves along the beach, reminds me how close we are to the villages of the Crystal Forest.

"It's just that while even Ghana welcomes those of us from the Diaspora home, it feels like Wakanda has turned its back on us." I feel myself getting heated. Like all the years away from my tribe, hidden away in Chicago—all the things I'd seen, all the moments I lost—bubble up as… anger. "What have you invested in your brothers and sisters? I shouldn't have to convince you that all Black lives matter."

For what felt like years, silence sits between us.

"Did I offend you, my King?" I am so conscious of my words I tread extra lightly.

"I read your assessment regarding the banking deal." His voice as inscrutable as his face, he taps his Kimoyo card. "Kimoyo" is Bantu for "of the spirit" and is the name of the Wakandan tech that works like a supercomputing tablet. "You have some observations. Remember, we do not play their game on their terms. I am adjusting your suggested protocols." He pulls his mask into place. "We are almost there. Be sharp."

The White Wolf skulks in the shadows of the castle remains. He's plainly up to something I just can't tell from up here. T'Challa doesn't wait for me to land. He opens the Talon's window above him and leaps out. With no parachute.

I'd like to say that I'm used to this sort of action, but my heart nearly squeezes my throat shut. I know enough not to cry out in concern, and search for the nearest landing spot instead.

Though I manage to land ahead of him, he passes me without acknowledgement. The wind blows through the leaves like the whispers of ghosts, louder than any sound marking his passage. The scariest thing about T'Challa when he's in Black Panther hunting mode is his eyes. Unknowable black mirrors. Everything becomes prey to him, always stalking, always three steps ahead. It's exhausting to watch, so I can't imagine what it was like to live like that.

Fun fact: the Castelo de Sao Jorge de Mina in Elmina, Ghana, was the first trading post built on the Gulf of Guinea, the oldest European building south of the Sahara. It became a key stop on the Atlantic slave trade. It wasn't the only slave fort built. Slave traders constructed the forts in the most defensible positions, fortified against pirates and other European nations they were at war with. The Portuguese demolished the homes of villagers to make room for them, the same way folks tore up our neighborhoods back in Chicago to make way for the highway.

One such fort occupied the bay on Nyanza.

A dry, double moat surrounds a huge rectangular castle along a rocky perch above a dam. A white-washed fortress, five stories high, surrounding a stone courtyard. The ruins of the inner façade of the bastions built from lime, stone, and bricks. From the remains of the towers, windows like empty eyes stare over the ground-level warehouses that once stored gold, brandy, tobacco, weapons. Below them, the dungeons. In the eerie silence, I can hear the wailing of my ancestors. People left to languish in those prisons waiting for slave ships to collect them. Their food passed to them through iron gates. No toilets. No bed berths. Only the small holes at either end of the ceiling for light or fresh air. Untold hundreds died there in the oppressive heat, left to an existence of terror, death, and darkness. Until one day, the fortunate survivors passed through an unassuming gate—the gate of no return—where they were loaded into ships, never to be seen by their kinsmen again.

In the slave fort's shadow was the dam.

"Hunter, stand down," the Black Panther shouts with the authoritative voice of someone used to being obeyed.

"My King, the last charge is almost in place." Hunter doesn't look up.

"Do not do this thing. This trespass is a matter of state."

"Command me in all things, my King. Tell me not to reveal the truth and I will submit."

T'Challa pauses an extra heartbeat. There is an unspoken language between siblings. The knowing nods and furtive eye glances. The deep nuance of understanding. But this may be one of those "better to ask forgiveness than permission" sort of situations. Hunter taps his Kimoyo card.

The entire courtyard trembles as a series of explosions erupt all about us. I cover my head and duck behind the remains of a tower. None of the explosions shudder near us, but rather along key points of the dam's structure. Dropping the outer concrete wall like a heavy stage curtain. The water slowly drains from the lock within the bay.

"What have you done?" the Black Panther asks.

As the water continues to empty from the man-made lake, it reveals more of the cliffside of the fort. I'm not sure what I'm looking at. Machinery, at first looking like mechanized scaffolding until the entire picture coalesces in my brain. A warship, easily as large as a N'Yami-class mothership. A battle cruiser.

"That's not all." Hunter gestures for the king. "The station is stocked with experimental magnetic-powered Reverbium weapons. Ballistic weapons. Electromagnetic pulse-based weapons. It's an entire first-strike operation for a private army. I suspect similar Chinese-built stations at each hub in all of the nations surrounding Wakanda."

"This is why they are being so aggressive with their 'aid,'" I say.

"Why didn't we know about this before now?" the Black Panther asks.

"It was an underwater operation. I would need authorization for such observation without violating agreements with our neighbors."

"But, Hunter…" Older brothers can't help themselves sometimes. Like, no matter what, they have this baseline instinct to be protective of their younger siblings. I start doing the math. And eventually carry the one. True to form, I realize that White Wolf manipulated me to maneuver the king here. Probably sabotaged the system by the Crystal Forest on the Nyanza himself to lure me in. With the dawning understanding sweeping my face, Hunter all but winks at me.

"Your xenophobic isolationism was a dangerous provocation. We have to take steps to protect ourselves and our interests." Hunter stands, his arms held out as he nears the king. "These Chinese corporations, and by proxy their central government, will use its African territories to fight the West. Establish a base of operations for future wars. A war on African soil, drawing Africans into the conflict."

The *Dora Milaje* train in a variety of subjects, especially those involving human behavior. There's a theory of thought called family systems that describes how when two people are in conflict, sometimes people triangulate. That's when, rather than resolving their disagreement, they involve or entangle a third person in an attempt to avoid or diffuse their own conflict.

The Black Panther and White Wolf are about to triangulate the mess out of the Chinese.

"You cannot act in the name of Wakanda without my leave." T'Challa raises his voice.

"You could have funded, even built, a clean-energy infrastructure. Propelled all of Africa, not even just our neighbors, past any other first-world nation. With reforms and opportunities in education and employment, you could transform entire developing economies. You squander your rule by betraying your own people."

Anger is a gift. I understand because I'm like the Santa of rage. All that diplomatic training and big picture thinking has trained T'Challa to be a miasma of repressed emotions. Internal pain always comes out. Stuck in patterns, cut off, stuck in conflict, and played by politics, be it family or governmental. All those hurts, insecurities, slights, resentments, anger all welling up. Using their fists to sort out their feelings, everyone pays the price. In that, maybe the Black Panther is not so different from the regular spandex set.

"You... dare?"

The Black Panther never hesitates. He leaps into the air, going into full flip mode. Dodging. Cartwheeling. The way his body moves makes no sense. Clawing at the White Wolf, then diving away, not allowing the dude to draw a bead on him. I duck behind a pile of fallen stones.

Hunter skulks about the shadows, casually blasting away like that's what people do. He strikes without a sound, noiselessly passing with brutal efficiency. Every bit the king's rival. And brother.

"Y'all can't just hug this ish out?" I scream over the weapons fire.

One of the White Wolf's blasts ruptures a pipe of some sort. There's another explosion. Smoke fills the spot where Black Panther once was. My heart can't help but pause worrying after him. King or no, he is my family. Maybe the only family I have left. I suppose they both are.

Through the swirl a shadow moves. Faster than my eye can track, the Black Panther dashes from the smoke, and in a mighty leap lands a kick that sends the White Wolf across the room. Staggering to his feet, the White Wolf looks so lost. Like a dutiful son desperate to please a father who would never love him. A man in search of purpose and mission. Something to accomplish to fill the hole in him. A missing part of himself.

Like his brother, trying to be strong in a world that tears at that strength. Not wanting them to be great.

I love T'Challa, I really do, but he has the emotional intelligence of a goldfish. It occurs to me that maybe one of the reasons he went to America, to eventually join the Avengers, was to become more connected, to learn our story.

"Stop!" As I come out from behind the stones, I raise my hands in a "don't shoot" pose. "In all your time together, did you ever learn his story? Or were you too busy becoming your father's son? Forgetting and leaving behind the man who was your brother. Everyone just wants to find a place in their family. Even Hunter."

White Wolf continues to circle, but some steam has been taken out of his movements. T'Challa lifts his hand to stop him. Black Panther pauses, tilting his head again like he's taking in every aspect of his brother for the first time.

"*Sawubona*, Hunter," T'Challa says, low and measured.

Back in Chicago, I was in a summer program called the Sawubona Lab. The word is a Zulu greeting that literally means, "I see you and by seeing you I bring you into being." It's a beautiful way to say "hello."

"*Yebo, sawubona*," Hunter replies, the customary "yes, we see you, too," but looks like a man trying to figure out a way home. "For a self-described man of peace, many of your conflicts end with violence."

"Why do so many of your attempts to snap me out of my supposed malaise look like attempts on my life?" T'Challa asks.

"Sibling reparations," Hunter says.

"Which are not a thing." His voice as calm as ever, like he's on a pleasant stroll through the park, T'Challa smirks. "Beloved, if you would deal with our friend, the CEO."

My Kimoyo card dings. On cue, Jiang's image pops up in all his holographic glory from it.

"You are encroaching on private property. Uninvited. Violating our agreements with Niganda. Guilty of industrial espionage." His clipped speech builds up a head of steam.

"We had reason to believe that there were other... actors who might engage in military aggression. Wakanda does not interfere with the affairs of other governments; however, foreign corporations pitting allies against each other in a costly military conflict is a game we won't abide."

"We are cautioning you, Your Highness..." Jiang begins.

"Caution all you wish. We cannot allow such a gesture to go unanswered." The Black Panther removes his mask so that Jiang stares into his eyes. "Beloved, can you illustrate for him what a nation of banks can do?"

"Yes, my King." I activate my protocols... which T'Challa revised. He knew. Of course, he knew. It's not about us. It's about Wakanda. Always Wakanda first. Sometimes I feel like we're all— me, Hunter, Jiang—always playing catch up with him.

"Through a series of international shell corporations," King T'Challa begins, "the nation of Wakanda has purchased all available shares in the bank handling the financing of your deals. Enough to initiate a proxy battle for Wakanda to assume all African loans. At the very least, this will bog down this hostile incursion for years."

"You really don't want to see Wakanda flex," I add.

"This..." Jiang studies his unseen screen. "You can't."

"This could all be a misunderstanding," the king continues. "Elements of your corporation not informing other elements of such pre-emptive military escalation. No one should misinterpret our... restraint... as weakness. Our next response shall be equally... pre-emptive."

"I am... shocked that I was not looped into such a military escalation effort by my underlings." Jiang strokes his chin. "If I were to advise my board about how best to de-escalate the situation, what could I pass along?"

"That this installation, and all such first strike stations, cease operations. My brother will oversee this." Black Panther nods to

White Wolf. "Though you are encouraged to follow a course of rebuilding the infrastructure you promised."

Jiang's face acquiesces before his image disappears. Without another word, the White Wolf turns to find whatever transport he took here. T'Challa leads the way back to the Talon, but pauses. Without quite turning around, he says, "You should report to your home… the palace, when you get back."

Hunter angles his head in consideration. And nods.

"Are you two good?" I ask.

"We are brothers," T'Challa says. "We both serve the land of our fathers. Our home, now as it ever was, is Wakanda."

Sometimes, with family, that's as good as things get.

HEART OF A PANTHER

SHEREE RENÉE THOMAS

THE HERBS were dying.

An elder, Adisa, held a wilted, bruise-stained blossom in shaking hands. Black soil, thick and fragrant, rested in her palms. Dirt lined her nails, dark half-moons. The sorrow in her eyes matched the shock in T'Challa's own.

He had not visited the ancient groves hidden in the great mountain since the shamans brought him there years ago. It was the weeping time when his father, T'Chaka, had joined the ancestors, the time when T'Challa had to prove that he was worthy to wear the sacred mantle, worthy to follow in the steps of the great Panther King.

The path of a panther was arduous and long. The prospect of the throne twisted the mind of his half-brother, Hunter, and tempted his best friend, B'Tumba, to betray him. Only T'Challa—the Black Panther—and his younger sister Shuri remained, but Bast's favor created a distance between them. T'Challa had long been prepared for the burdens of ruling, but loneliness gnawed at him and now strange dreams haunted his sleep.

He stood in a barren field that faced the rising sun, then darkness fell down all around him. Huge stalks burst from the earth, imprisoned him in a wall of thorns. Covered in a thousand wings, he was no longer a king, a panther, or a man. He could not leap, climb, or crush. He could not see, hear, or breathe. When he opened his mouth to scream, he found the field was on fire, but the land was no longer beneath his feet.

T'Challa was ashamed to wake with the fears of a child. Though the dreams made no sense, he woke with something else, something close to clarity. Even before his father was killed, still arrogant with youth, T'Challa wasn't sure if he could be king. And now, when there was no longer any doubt, T'Challa wasn't sure he still wanted to be.

A DAMP, earthy scent filled the cavern's still air. Faint green lights flickered across the darkness, with bioluminescent beetles and glowworms scuttling across the ground, leaving trails of breathtaking blue. T'Challa brushed his palm against the craggy wall, maintaining balance as he leapt down the treacherous rocks, each step as graceful as the next. His enhanced vision adjusted easily to the cave's darkness. The sweet musk of cave moss intensified as the murmurs of the underground river echoed off high, jagged ceilings. Halfway there, he wound his way to the center of Mount Kanda, home of the Heart-Shaped Herb.

As one of Wakanda's most sacred symbols, the rare plant was nearly as mysterious as Vibranium, the element that provided the herb with its strength and power. Together, the two secret resources had made Wakanda invincible to its enemies over the millennia. But while Vibranium fueled his kingdom's economic and technological success, it was the Heart-Shaped Herb and its connection to the Goddess Bast that was the origin of the Black Panther's most impressive powers—and in this moment, his deepest fear.

Shadows danced along the damp, earthen walls carved in the signs and symbols of the earliest Wakandan script.

"The language of the ancestors," his father once said.

T'Chaka, a fiercely loved leader whose reign was still sung by griots, had told a very young T'Challa the story of the mysterious meteor that crashed into the mountain. The Vibranium had set off a chain of reactions buried deep within the earth. The arrival of the extraterrestrial element heralded a new age for their people, one that would see them prosper and emerge far more advanced than their neighbors over many long years.

○――――――○

"HOW LONG?" T'Challa asked.

Guilt flashed across shifting eyes. An elder and yet a child of Nganga, Adisa's line had tended the sacred herb for generations. No crop before had ever failed. The shame was as palpable as the cloying wet heat in the air.

"The answer would not please, Your Majesty," Adisa said.

Her purple robes billowed around her as giant fans spun slowly up above. She had the noble stature and melodious, calming voice of her family. Shamans spoke and sang to the flowering herbs, with spells and ancient magics that guarded them well.

"We have been monitoring these developments for some time," she said carefully. "Our family uses the best practices, perfected by tests and culled over a thousand years. We have tested and we have prayed. We sang the old songs and we danced. The soil health is strong, the water is pure, but the seeds, the roots and the flowers… they deteriorate."

"But how can this be?" T'Challa asked.

He reached for the wilted herb, held its leafy heart-shaped blossom in his hand. Light as a butterfly's wing, as soft as a feather, the herb smelled overly sweet, almost putrid. Its beautiful color, once vibrant and lush, was faded in some spots, darkened in others. It looked as if poison had seeped through its taproot and filled every vein.

"Soil samples are Vibranium-rich, the minerals and nutrient levels normal. No weeds or intruder species apparent. Your Highness, there are no known parasites—at least none that we can perceive."

The elder's fear was understandable but the question in her voice troubled T'Challa more.

"What do you mean, 'none that we can perceive'?" He held the

Heart-Shaped Herb up, allowed the artificial sunlight to pierce the thin petal.

Adisa chose her words carefully. "Without a new harvest…" she began.

"Wakanda risks being unable to pass the Black Panther's powers on to the next king."

"Without a king… the Black Panther…" Adisa whispered.

"Wakanda is lost." T'Challa stared at rows upon rows of shriveled-up herbs, sacred plants stunted on the vine.

Worry darkened his face. His jaw set, his eyes narrowed as he remembered the bittersweet taste of the herbal tea the shamans urged him to drink. The Rite of the Panther was one of Wakanda's oldest traditions, but there were few traditions without sacrifice.

Phantom pain rippled through the muscles in his neck and chest. Memories rained down on him, a sharpness that ran up along his throat to gather at his temples.

Adisa watched him. Fear etched itself across her whole presence. Even the Kimoyo beads on her wrist, the shaman's necklace around her neck, vibrated with the hope for their nation. She motioned at the groves that filled the cavern. Rough and calloused, she had a gardener's hands, but she spoke with the concern and softness of a healer.

"My King, perhaps we are looking in the wrong place."

"What do you mean?" T'Challa asked.

She bowed her head.

"Don't be afraid, Adisa. You may always speak plainly to me."

She hesitated. "Perhaps the problem is spiritual. The herbs are connected to you, my King. You are joined in ways that neither you nor any of us, your shamans, fully understand."

When she finished, Adisa looked as if she wanted to disappear, hide beneath the many folds of her priestess robes. She clasped her hands the way Queen Mother Ramonda did. The small motion reminded him of the comfort he felt with the quiet force that was his stepmother at his side. T'Challa stood silent, his questions resting in his throat.

He understood Adisa's discomfort. During his reign, his father once banished all sorcery and magic. The shamans had a difficult time. Such a suggestion might have elicited a different response from the former Panther King, but T'Challa's thoughts led him down a road he would rather not travel.

"My King, I fear there are few answers here. But perhaps a solution lies in the City of Knowledge, or the lands beyond, or—"

"Thank you, Adisa." T'Challa waved her aside. "You have served our people well. I am grateful I may trust you and the other shamans to hold these mysteries in the safety of your healing hands."

"Of course, my King. There is no kingdom greater than Wakanda."

"And there is no bond greater than the love we have for our people."

T'Challa turned and knelt in the spiral of rich black soil that formed the grove. Each plant lay limp, the heart-shaped leaves shrunken and bent. He ran his fingers through the wet earth. In the silence he could hear the drum-like drip from the cavernous ceiling above, the hum of the river below.

The shaman struggled to share news that might further distress the Panther King. "There is enough to pierce the veil, but even the dried teas have lost their potency." She handed him a vial. The dark amber liquid looked dull and lifeless.

Pain narrowed T'Challa's eyes, made Adisa avert her own. The elder hastened to lessen the blow.

"If we are frugal, my King, we may have enough of the Heart-Shaped Herb to anoint one future victor."

A keening sound, wailing chains sinking in angry waters, filled T'Challa's head.

T'Challa crushed the rotten blossom and let it fall to the ground.

AS HE walked past the River of Grace and Wisdom, a heaviness weighed in T'Challa's spirit. The sleepless nights, throbbing headaches that assaulted without warning, and the sporadic visions had plagued him for a number of days. Now it made sense. If the Heart-Shaped Herb was failing, perhaps there was a chance that the Black Panther might fail, too.

But T'Challa did not fear for himself. He feared for his people, for the future that rested upon all the panther dynasties that came before. He thought of Bashenga, the shaman warrior the goddess Bast had chosen as her vessel, a worthy keeper of the holiest of secrets. A mighty force, the ancestor wielded his war-spear and bore the crimson mark of the goddess herself.

But no shield or spear would protect his people now. The enemy was an unknown entity, a foe that could not be defeated by battle, blessings, incantations, or spells. A shaman's dance would not help him. T'Challa needed higher counsel.

In search of answers, he had left Adisa, whispering prayers to the dying plants in the grove. Her voice had echoed through the great mountain's caves, haunting him as he departed. First, he would seek the wisdom of the elders, reach across the veil of time to enter Djalia, the Ancestral Plane. If need be, he would appeal to divine authority, the Goddess Bast—that is, if she agreed to see him again.

The river was calm and placid. T'Challa wished the old stories were true, that he could drown his troubles in the waters and emerge, wiser and at peace. But a war waged inside his spirit. Strange visions darkened his days, spilled over into his sleep.

A thousand years ago the river had grown angry. Currents swelled its banks, whole villages swept away on the waves of rage. The people of Wakanda fled to the mountains, up to the Panther God's temples, but the elders said the people had lost their way, with bickering tribes unable to set a course together. They left the temples unattended.

The goddess was angry as the river, her priests insisted. She turned her back on them as rageful waters rose, sweeping the way for a new era in the kingdom. The tribes huddled beneath the stone statues of the great panthers, prayers unanswered. Broken limbs of homes dotted the land like scattered bones. The Panther God had taken the livelihoods of the people—and crushed them between her teeth.

The next day when the sun rose, a blazing witness, wild animals and livestock hung from the trees. Their bloated bodies were a reminder of the dangers of infidelity. The Panther God demanded loyalty and devotion. To offer less risked her wrath, or worse, indifference.

T'Challa climbed the great, grass-covered terraces. The giant steps curved like a green scarf across the shoulder of the mountain. Only Djalia, the mystical Ancestral Plane, could return his mother's voice and face to him. The Queen Mother would speak sweet words of comfort and insight. She had a quiet way of calming fears he never expressed. T'Challa took out the vial and held it up in the fingers of sunlight that drenched the sky and fell like a blanket at his feet. He had climbed to the tallest of the terraces, to perch under a many-limbed tree.

The liquid was not one you would drink for pleasure. Its Vibranium-laced aftertaste left his tongue numb, his head spinning. He chewed on the precious few leaves Adisa had saved for him as an extra precaution. The bitter herbs got caught in his throat, in his teeth. No time for ceremony or the boiling of leaves and tea. He needed to consume the precious plant in its purest form, a direct connection to divinity. The Panther God no longer answered when he called her name. Wakanda had thrived under his leadership, but while the kingdom prospered, T'Challa felt his passion for leading diminish. He wanted to build upon his father's legacy, but lately, each day, he found himself thinking of the person he might have been if he had never become king.

When T'Challa reached the top of the last grass-covered tier, he was out of breath, something unheard of since he had become the Black Panther. Lightheaded, T'Challa's thoughts were like birds levitating. Each idea took flight but the meaning landed somewhere else. He sat in a grassy spot on the highest tier and let the setting Wakandan sun cast burnished gold light across his

44

face and shoulders. The fate of a legacy hung in the balance, a kingdom protected by the rich, powerful deposits of Vibranium and the Heart-Shaped Herb that changed mortals into myths. What would his beloved nation do if death took him and there were no herbs left to ensure the ascension of another Panther King?

As birdsong trilled in the distance, T'Challa did not fear death. It haunted him all his years, even as a child. How many times had he sprinkled the sacred ancestral dust over loved ones lost? Loved ones returned to Djalia, to join the Ancestral Plane? T'Challa learned to embrace dust at an early age. It was the dust that taught him how to live through grief, and it was dust that his body would return to, to nourish the earth while his spirit joined the realm of the ancestors. So many passages witnessed. He accepted it as a natural cost of his royal lineage. But now grief that he didn't know he held and dark visions he could not comprehend accompanied him like unwelcomed shadows.

T'Challa quieted his thoughts and centered himself, focused on the beautiful vista before him. Few places captured the wonder of the Wakanda kingdom as well as the dazzling heights that led to the Ancestral Plane. He took out the rest of the precious herbs the shaman Adisa gave him. A bittersweet numbness stung his tongue and then a warming sensation spread down his throat to rest in his chest. The golden-orange sky shimmered. When he opened his eyes again he found himself sitting beneath a banyan tree.

Grass tall enough to hide behind bent and swayed in fanning waves before him. The wind felt soft against his cheek. He rose and wiped the soil from his palms. No sooner did he rise, than he heard a low growl behind him. T'Challa turned in time to see a black panther transform into his beloved mother.

"Mother," he said. She embraced him.

"T'Challa, there is no time." Seven panthers emerged from the tall grass behind her. Their eyes glittered, green jewels in the night.

"The shamans do not know why the Heart-Shaped Herb is—"

"Dying," N'Yami finished. "It is not for them to know, T'Challa, but for you, the king."

"The Panther God," T'Challa began. Shame cracked his voice. "I cannot feel her spirit."

Queen N'Yami stroked T'Challa's cheek. "My son, the gods have their work, and we have ours. The elders have waited for you."

She gestured at the seven men and women who stood behind her. They wore garments like none T'Challa had ever seen. Strange skins from beasts that no longer existed. They spoke in a tongue he did not understand.

"These are the elders who came of age in the time of Bashenga," N'Yami said. "Bast's first shaman warrior king. They are the Mena Ngai, the oldest among us. They remember his spear and the mark on his face. They remember the songs of the water, the songs of the mother of water, and their memory is wide and deep as the River of Grace and Wisdom."

The elders gathered around him, eyes hungry as if they could taste his thoughts.

"What are they saying?" T'Challa asked and stepped back. Wet blades of grass smacked his calves. Fireflies circled around his ankles. One by one the elders placed their hands on his shoulders, pleading with him.

"You must concentrate on their meaning, T'Challa, not their words. The longer you are here in Djalia, the more you will understand. Focus on their eyes," N'Yami said, "then you will hear."

The elders' voices rose in amber waves. T'Challa could follow only a few words as their voices lifted, their speech quickened. Pain and fear filled their faces. One gnashed his teeth. Another tugged her hair. They pressed closer to him. A scent like warm spice rose from their skin. N'Yami watched. Offered no further guidance. Even with his enhanced hearing, T'Challa strained to hear the other words spoken beneath the wind.

"They say I must cross the big water. Ride the Great River to its mouth."

T'Challa strained to hear as the circle of elders edged closer, their voices conjoined to a song of mourning.

46 An elder with indigo and ochre dots covering his face burst

into tears. The circle of elders released a keening, wailing cry. The sound of anguish, the sound of his dreams. Dread rose in the Black Panther. T'Challa did not wish to be disrespectful, but in that moment the elders' touch was all he feared.

"Listen," N'Yami urged.

Above them the night sky shimmered and pulsed. T'Challa sensed storms and fire.

Find the stone that is free! Find the stone that is free!

The elders held out their palms, beseeching him, pleading. T'Challa looked for the Queen but she was gone.

Return what was lost! they cried. *Return what was lost! Return…! Wakanda will fall without the lost…*

They began to tremble and shake, their voices full of grief. First one, then two, then three. Blue-black fur blended with darkness. One by one they transformed before his eyes until seven panthers circled him. The voices changed from grief to growls. They hissed and roared, green jewel eyes burning in the night.

Cross the Big Water. Ride the mouth of the Great River. Find the stone that is free. Return what was lost!

He had hoped to find clarity, clear vision, but the elders had left him with more questions than the answers received. What was lost, where it would be found, and how it would help avoid generational disaster were mysteries yet to be revealed. T'Challa left the beautiful tiered garden more uneasy than when he arrived. That night he slept with uneasy dreams. When he woke, he remembered what the seven elders had told him.

He was to cross the Big Water. *The Atlantic Ocean.* Ride the Great River to its mouth. Sitting upright in his bed, T'Challa scanned his memory. There were only so many great rivers in the world. One of them he knew well, known by the First Nations as the Great River. *The Mississippi River.* A stone that stands free. He tapped the AV Kimoyo bead on his wrist and searched for places that shared keywords from the elders' message. The supercomputer revealed the House of Flowers Arboretum, located on a farm in a historic black town. T'Challa tapped the Navigation bead. A hologram of a dark green historical marker for Freestone, Mississippi, floated in the air. T'Challa tapped a few more times, then rose. He would need to speak with Shuri immediately.

○———————○

T'CHALLA FOUND his sister in a surprising place: Warrior Falls. The falls were isolated and rarely visited. The only time the idyllic place was occupied was during challenges to the throne. Shuri sat on the bank of rocks with her war-spear and the Ebony Blade resting at her side. Ever since T'Challa, disguised as an unknown challenger, defeated their uncle for the right to sit on the throne, his sister had started to distance herself from him. Over time the distance between them had decreased, but the throne still remained the root of something hidden, and the royal palace became a place full of solitudes.

"Shuri, what brings you here?" he asked, as the wind ruffled the tuft of bright feathers that rose from her braided hair.

"I could ask you the same, brother," she replied.

She did not turn to face him. Instead, she kicked her feet and let the cool water splash. A cerulean wall of silk threaded with silver spilled down the mountainside. Fragrant, plump lotus flowers floated by, leaving concentric circles before tumbling over the cliff. The loud roar of the water cascading over the staggered drops below drowned out the unspoken thoughts between them.

T'Challa watched his sister in silence. For a moment he could see the determined, ambitious little girl she used to be. The one who once adored her big brother and never left his side. There was love, always, but a sadness had touched the edges of it. His sister walked the way of the old world. She still struggled to find her place beyond it.

"I must travel to America, to investigate a lead."

"New York?" she asked, her voice disinterested. She focused on the waters, the cluster of orange flowers gathered around the lagoon's edge.

"No, Mississippi." That got her attention.

She turned. "What are you looking for there?"

T'Challa paused. "I'm not exactly sure, but while I'm gone, I would appreciate you taking over the throne. Are you willing?"

Shuri stiffened. A flock of blackbirds flew over her head. "I don't know, am I worthy?"

She swung her long legs out of the water. Her face had not yet gone stone-still. Apprehension lingered, just below the surface.

"Shuri, I know you are still hurt and angry."

"What do you mean, T'Challa? You are king and I am what I have always been. Your sister, a princess at your service. Why do you even ask?"

"I ask because I need you, and I trust no one above you. And…" He chose his next words carefully. "…I fear I no longer hold Bast's favor."

Shock broke the neutral expression on Shuri's face. The dejection in her brother's voice and demeanor told her the truth in his words. The self-doubt and confusion were familiar. Shuri knew all too well the sting of the Panther God's rebuke. She did not ask for an explanation, only a small request.

"Will you take Okoye with you? It is not wise for Wakanda's king to travel alone."

"Perhaps unwise," he said, "but necessary. I need some time to work this out on my own. I'll be fine in Mississippi. Don't worry, little sister."

Shuri rose and laughed, amusement on her face. "It is not Mississippi I worry about." She gathered her weapons and swung the dark blade through the air. He playfully blocked her, and for a while they enjoyed the carefree bond of their youth.

"I'll return as soon as I can," he said as he stopped at the winding path that led out of Warrior Falls. "And Shuri?"

"T'Challa?"

"Yes, you are worthy."

A SUN-BLEACHED American flag hung motionless from its metal pole on the front of the house. The air was humid, thick enough to step through. T'Challa marched as if walking through a closed door. This was not the comforting warmth of Wakanda, but a busier, mischievous kind of weather, the kind that smacked you in the face and dared you to do anything about it. With its postcard-perfect shade trees and huge wraparound front porch, equipped with a rocking chair, the property looked idyllic.

T'Challa was not fooled. He sensed gathering storms. More thunder. Fire.

"You must be Brother Flowers."

A raised eyebrow and silence were his only reply. T'Challa tilted his head, tried again. "You are…"

"Rickydoc." The man stared at T'Challa, appraised him with an expression the Black Panther could not quite make. His heartbeat was steady and sure. His breathing, smooth, efficient. Rickydoc, the Brother Flowers, took off his hat, revealed shoulder-length locks that spiraled across his shoulders. He sat the hat on a rusted hook and turned to gaze at T'Challa. Hardness set around his mouth and his narrowed eyes.

"Family calls me Rickydoc. Mr. Okonkwo, I presume." His was a voice that held secrets. T'Challa had heard such a voice before.

Ribbons of sound and anguish, grief that threatened to swallow a bursting heart whole…

"Why, yes," T'Challa said. The hairs on the back of his neck prickled. A coldness and a strange familiar scent wafted from Rickydoc, a wariness that underscored every word he said. T'Challa did not need his super-enhanced senses to know that the man distrusted him.

"New faces tend to get a lot of play here. We're a small town, Freestone's not used to… celebrities."

T'Challa's jaw tensed. A playful light flickered briefly in Rickydoc's eyes, then the shadows returned.

"I hear you're a big chef up in Harlem. You got one of those TV shows, or you just here… hunting?"

The way Rickydoc said the last word awoke the panther inside him. The great Panther Spirit paced inside T'Challa's mind, awaiting the moment when it could break free.

"Yes. I own a restaurant off 7th Avenue. I tried reaching you over the phone but I never got through."

Brother Flowers nodded his head. "Looks like you got through fine."

T'Challa shook his hand. The grip was strong, a greeting and a warning. "Back in Memphis, there was confusion about how to get here," the Black Panther said. "In fact, they weren't too sure you were here at all."

Brother Flowers laughed, his voice a gruff baritone.

"Well, you're here now. Welcome, o traveler. Come on inside," Rickydoc said and held the screen door. "Go on in before you let the cool air out."

A large nautilus-shaped skylight brought daylight inside. Bookshelves lined the walls. Tables covered in water-filled glass containers with sprouting plant specimens filled the room, more mad scientist lab than a Delta gift shop. Burlap feedbags sat piled in corners. A bowl of uneaten dog treats rested on the floor. A few spices and bottled herbs labeled with the House of Flowers winged gourd logo were tossed haphazardly on a wooden shelf. If Flowers was selling condiments, T'Challa couldn't tell.

"I don't skimp on my soil's health. You got to love the land or the land won't love you," Brother Flowers said, and pointed at a row of soil samples sealed in mason jars. The red, brown, black waves of earth were neatly labeled. "Mixed crops, compost instead of fertilizer, none of that peacetime poison. Not letting my land be fallow. You know how it is. Do you garden?" he asked.

T'Challa shook his head no, and followed Brother Flowers inside. He noticed a knotted root staff rested in a corner.

"I fear I am best with a skillet, a butcher knife, or stirring some spicy stew. You don't want me in your plants," the Black Panther said, laughing.

"A regular plant killer, huh?"

T'Challa's jaw stiffened. "Something like that."

"Well, you've seen the office. Let me give you what you came for. It's not every day someone flies from New York City just to get a taste of what we're cooking. We have one hundred acres. Used to be more. We've had to sell a little off over the years." It was the first time the Black Panther sensed an unguarded emotion in Brother Flowers. The fleeting expression in the man's eyes was pain.

"Times have been hard, but Freestone is still one of Mississippi's few remaining black century farms. Of course, we've been holding on longer than a hundred years. It ain't always been easy but we always been here."

T'Challa stepped through the back door and entered a wall of green. Rich, verdant land stretched ahead, a glimmering emerald road. Big leafy sunflowers, their heads wide as T'Challa's chest, lined the back porch like brightly colored shade trees—or sentinels.

"Outstanding," the Black Panther murmured. Yes, he was in the place in his dream. The land where the elders cautioned him to find what was lost and return it home.

Brother Flowers guided T'Challa past the most astonishing plants he had ever seen. Their beauty rivaled even the exotic plants in the Alkama Fields back in Wakanda.

"This is how we do," was all the man said when T'Challa shook his head in disbelief. As they walked, Brother Flowers proudly pointed out prized oversized plants, juicy melons, brightly colored squash, and other vegetables that appeared to grow effortlessly out of season.

"I was told if I wanted the best ingredients, I had to find a way to connect with you," T'Challa said. "But I had no idea the House of Flowers was an incredible Garden of Eden. Your bounty rivals even the famed hanging gardens of Babylon."

"Every now and then I manage to surprise myself. See, meet Big Luscious," he said, and pointed at what T'Challa thought at first was a small tree. It was a stalk of broccoli.

"I can spend most of my day deep-watering these babies. They drink so much, my water bill is about to touch the sky."

T'Challa admired the pride Brother Flowers took in his work.

It was clear he was born to be a leader, a protector, a role that T'Challa had begun to question. He led his people, loved them dearly, but he had begun to wonder what legacy he might leave. He had watched his father, T'Chaka, and knew that being king would be difficult, but T'Challa had not prepared himself for the loneliness. Uncertainty. Where would he lead his kingdom next? It was no longer enough to fight or settle scores. T'Challa had grown dissatisfied, restless, seeking something he was no longer certain resided in himself.

A woodpecker punctuated the air with its timpani drum song. Moths and butterflies flittered around the bank of bushes full of fragrant ripe blossoms. T'Challa peered over Brother Flowers' shoulders. He was nearly as tall as him, but his shoulders were wide, arms muscled, no doubt from laboring on the farm.

"What is that back there?" he asked. The Black Panther could hear the man's heartbeat slow down to near stillness. Hidden in plain sight, something was amiss.

"That's our pool," Brother Flowers said, wiping sweat off his brow. "Catfish farm. The lake has been there a while, figured we do something with it. You know you got to switch it up on 'em," Brother Flowers said. "We're about that agriculture and aquaculture. The game is to thrive, not just survive."

Though it was far away, T'Challa heard the splash. Too heavy to be a catfish. Something lurked in the clearwater ponds. Restless, the Panther rose up inside him.

They continued walking, touring the property. On the left was the huge lake that Brother Flowers claimed was his freshwater catfish pond, but T'Challa could hear the steady drumming of a heartbeat that could not belong to a single whiskered fish. The drumbeat was calm, though. Whatever the creature was, it felt safe.

The two examined soil samples, squash and okra, an unusual number of oversized gourds, and the many fruit-bearing trees on the property. But when T'Challa asked to see more of the arboretum, where he spied a remarkably advanced-looking greenhouse, the man steered them in the opposite direction, away from the surrounding swampland and back to the giant sunflowers that greeted him when he first walked through the door.

When they returned to the gift shop, Brother Flowers turned an eye on an old stove shoved in the corner of the room. "You lucky I like you," he said and poured hot water into a coffee mug. "Tell me this don't taste like the promised land."

He watched T'Challa from the corner of his eye as he added honey from Freestone's own beehives. "Best sun tea you'll ever have."

"No thank you," T'Challa said. "I don't drink tea."

Brother Flowers looked offended. "I don't trust nobody that don't like tea. Man, don't do me like this. What you think it is, soylent green?"

T'Challa chuckled and listened. Rickydoc's heart rhythm was steady, sure. He handed the Black Panther the beverage. T'Challa smelled fresh mint, chamomile, hibiscus flowers, and strong spices. He swallowed a few sips and politely placed the mug down.

Rickydoc watched him steadily for a few minutes, then shrugged. They chattered amicably, about the town's youth Agri shows, and the importance of offering young people daily connections to the natural world, but T'Challa could tell there was much more he was trying to hide. It wasn't a faster pulse or blinking eyes that were the telltale signs of deception. It was the man's sudden friendliness that confirmed for the Black Panther that the House of Flowers had far more to be seen. When Brother Flowers handed him a free sample of his garlic herb rub, T'Challa decided then the Black Panther would return for a private tour.

T'CHALLA PARKED the rental car off in a stand of woods, a couple miles down the road from Freestone. He knew now that if he wasn't the Black Panther, blessed with the Panther God's vision, he would not be able to see his way back down the winding road again. In the heart of Mississippi, the night was blacker than most. Fortunately, the Black Panther's visual acuity was sharpest at night. His ultraviolet vision helped distinguish prey and predators more accurately than the human eye. Even as he walked with only the faint glow of the moon, T'Challa could see the night unfold around him, the landscape nearly as detailed as the day. The Black Panther saw all, heard all, and could outrun most. As he jogged down the shoulder of the gravelly road, a neon streak shot past him. Ancient hunting instincts kicked in. White rabbit fur reflected in ultraviolet. He resisted the urge to chase it. He could smell the fear of the hare before it disappeared into the underbrush. The Black Panther had an idea of just where it was headed.

T'Challa sprang through a path in the woods. With his Vibranium claws he climbed up a swaybacked oak and leapt across the crown of trees. Over an ancient church he bounded, a few homes, neat respectable humble buildings, a gated cemetery with an ironwork fence, a school. Far away from the decorum and the diplomacy of the royal palace, T'Challa felt free and unencumbered. As he moved through the night, he felt closer to the way he was in his childhood, before he ascended the throne. When life was simple, and the burden to rule was his father's. The time when he was simply his father's son, his sister's brother, and not a kingdom's king.

Through the latticework of trees, he soared. This is what he missed. The thrill of leaping into nothingness, carried by the Panther God's grace. But he moved through the air slower than he was accustomed. Ever since the night visions disturbed his sleep, the Black Panther had noticed a change in his movements, a shifting of energies that his mind dared not call weakness.

There was little wonder why few found their way to Freestone. It was protected by a shifting wall of iridescent light that only rare ones could see. The shield was part spell, part natural phenomenon. So, T'Challa thought, Freestone has its own Northern Lights—or was it Southern Lights? Aurora borealis, aurora australis.

No, he thought as he climbed over a high-walled iron fence that bordered the Flowers property. *Aurora afromississippialis.*

He scaled the wall, did a backflip, and landed on his heels and palms. Back arched like the panthers who watch from the Great

Ancestor Tree, T'Challa raised his head and let the strange scent carry him to beyond the House of Flowers' back door.

The lights were out. Whatever Rickydoc, Brother Flowers, had been trying to hide that day, it now looked as if he was gone.

T'Challa raised his gloved palm and focused. A pulse of blue light, fluorescent carvings of the Black Panther's lifelines, disarmed the gate. The doors swung open and he crept inside. Eyes adjusting to the darkness beyond the wall. He walked down a dimly lit path to find what he had crossed the Ancestral Plane and the Big Water in search of.

Rows of black earth crisscrossed the land in intricate patterns that reminded T'Challa of his sister Shuri's elaborate braids. Fifty feet away he could feel the face of light on the surface of brackish water. Swamplands hidden in a thick wall of forest. Fireflies flickered like the luminescent life in Mount Kanda's most sacred caves. A heavy scent, sweet and fragrant, wafted on the wind. Familiar, startling. *Herbs.*

T'Challa glided down the path, into the old wide-trunked trees that guarded the greenhouse he'd seen earlier. He palmed the lock on the greenhouse doors. He'd never seen a garden that required such sophisticated security. He walked in and a strange, familiar scent washed over him. On either side, tall, leafy plants rose from the earth, their stalks as thick as sunflowers. Rows and rows of verdant crimson-colored heart-shaped blossoms, red as fire, tumbled over the ground. Anger tinged his senses. T'Challa could not believe the sight before him. He ripped one of the plants from the earth. Rootstrong, the counterfeit plant resisted. He held one of the oversized heart-shaped leaves up, inhaled a sweet musk. The leaves felt like velvet darkness in his hand. Disbelief filled his mind with questions. It was not his Heart-Shaped Herb, but something close, something else. A renegade species whose secrets were stolen from Wakanda. Thoughts of thieves, traitor flesh willing to trade the safety, the future of the kingdom for riches that would turn to ashes with time.

T'Challa wanted to crush the traitor's bones, reduce them to dust. But he needed these strange flowers, no matter their origin, and he had no intention of leaving a trace that they had ever existed. The Panther King would burn them down, every root, leaf, and stalk of them.

T'Challa gathered himself, focusing until the anger left him. He tapped his Kimoyo bead and began to photograph the forbidden foliage. He was collecting some of the plants when the glass on the greenhouse began to tremble and shake. His panther suit responded to the intense vibrations. A loud droning echoed through the room.

When Brother Flowers hit him, it felt like iron, bricks, fire, stone. T'Challa was not expecting the man to take him to the ground, but down the panther went. Deprived of the Panther God's blessing, perhaps because of his lingering ambivalence, T'Challa felt every bone-crushing blow. The king was accustomed to pain but this... was different. Perhaps his time on the throne, the interlude of peace, had made him soft and indolent. His mind was the portrait of unease. Now that indolence might cost him everything.

The two men rolled, plunged into darkness, crashed into the verdant tangle of wild ferns and vines. Around them the air suddenly grew eerily quiet. Hard breathing and even harder blows were the only sounds to pierce the silence of the night. Knotted flesh against flesh. Brother Flowers fought as if a tornado was in his skin. A shard of light shone down on them, a cloud passing over the moon. Brother Flowers worked T'Challa like human clay, but the vessel of a god cannot be broken by fists. Even a vessel that has lost his way. Remnants of the Panther Spirit remained. The blood rose up inside him. T'Challa held the impossibly strong man up, one vise-like hand around his throat, the other around his wrist.

For a moment, T'Challa had the best of the one whose family called him Rickydoc, but then a vision of the elders flashed before him. Sharp pain exploded in his skull, throwing his balance off. He saw the shadows take shape in the limbs of the trees. A memory, not his own, of blood painted on the walls of a cave-like structure, of cries so agonizing they made a soul long to return to the womb.

Brother Flowers took advantage of the reprieve and delivered a jaw-breaking blow to the Black Panther's skull. Pain. It had been a long time since T'Challa felt that kind of pain.

Head reeling, the Black Panther's heightened hearing alerted him to a stealthy enemy, danger.

A twisting, turning droning from above. A winged creature, the length of the Black Panther's arm, swooped over his head, missing T'Challa's scalp by inches. It swooped again, then jerked back, narrowly avoiding the Black Panther's claw. T'Challa leapt in the air and pummeled it with his fist. The creature collapsed to the floor, its wing bent like a broken bow. Brother Flowers yelped. With the blow the Black Panther had given the man his spine should have been broken in three places, but Brother Flowers rose up on his elbow, his root staff in hand, and let out a blood-curdling cry.

"No!"

The creature slumped and fell back into darkness. Brother Flowers shoved the Black Panther, slamming him into one of the greenhouse's raised flower beds. T'Challa bared his teeth as a sound like a hundred helicopters filled the air. Glass crashed and shattered. A battalion of giant winged beasts zigzagged through the room. Translucent wings with powerful fore- and hindlegs, a turquoise striated tail that balanced in the air. The only thing T'Challa could think of that resembled the beast was a giant dragonfly. *Meganeuropis permiana*. But nothing on earth had been that size for millennia. The evidence lay in fossils locked in glass cases, where Ivy League students could gawk at *M. americana*'s impossibly wide wings.

The creatures circled him. T'Challa waited for the first assault, crouched in a cat stance with dragon fists. If he was to fight off the dragonfly horde, he would have to rely on muscle memory and balance.

Wailing, Brother Flowers shouted orders to the hovering mass of dragonflies and ran to the creature the Black Panther had pummeled. Grief filled the man's voice, surprising T'Challa. This was not the sound of a killer. It was the kind of grief T'Challa and his sister Shuri had long come to understand. Loss.

T'Challa rose from his crouched position and walked past an upturned table. The moment he moved, two of the giant dragonflies attacked him. Their powerful toothed mandibles opened and released a blast of liquid that splashed over him. Drenched, the Black Panther cried out and grabbed one of the creatures' four translucent wings. It shrieked as he spun it in the air and knocked the beast from the sky. The creature scuttled across the floor on spiny front limbs, wings bent and twisted. The Black Panther's suit analyzed the liquid. Water.

Nothing was what it seemed in this forgotten place. The creatures were more like bombardier beetles, spitting and emitting fluids at their prey, than fire-breathing dragons. But Brother Flowers' arrhythmic, erratic heartbeat signaled deep distress, not fury. Each time T'Challa tackled and wrestled down one of the water dragons, Brother Flowers' serotonin levels tanked. If there was a scent to sadness, the gardener from Eden was covered in it.

"Rickydoc, what are these creatures?" T'Challa asked as another burst through the broken windows to hover over him.

"My alarm system," the man said. Grief deepening his gravelly voice.

"Call off your winged dogs," T'Challa said, "before I am forced to kill them. It's obvious they are of some bizarre importance to you."

T'Challa could hear the man's heartbeat slowly return to normal rhythms.

"They are Wild Ones, from the Wildseeds you are trying to steal from us, and they are our friends."

T'Challa had heard tales of the beasts that emerged from the ground when the meteor crashed into his ancestors' lands. They struggled against monsters and demon spirits that distorted some into grotesque shadows of themselves.

Had another meteor crashed here? T'Challa wondered. Did

that explain the creatures and the House of Flowers' superior growth and fecundity?

Brother Flowers carried the injured beast to one of the raised tables. He snapped off a few of the red heart-shaped flowers and fed it to the dragonfly.

"Oohlou, you rest now. It is time to heal."

He made a low whistling sound and the others spun in the air once, twice, then rose with a loud hum, sailing out through the broken windows and the open door. While T'Challa watched them flee, Brother Flowers ducked into a side room, then emerged carrying a firearm.

"Sorry brother, Mr. Okonkwo, but the only way you're getting out of here with those Wildseeds is if I plant you myself. My family has guarded their secret too long to let a jackleg like you take it all away."

Rickydoc produced a rusted ring of skeleton keys.

"Rootdoctor, I never chalked you off as a gunman," T'Challa said.

"Boy, you're in Mississippi. Everybody got a gun."

The barrel was pointed at the Black Panther's heart. T'Challa's Vibranium claws sprung out from his cybernetic suit. The Panther Spirit paced and growled inside his head.

"If you give me what I came for, I can leave you alive," T'Challa said. "It doesn't have to end this way. And no one need know about your... *M. americana* wildlings."

"End?" Rickydoc laughed. "I don't know how you managed to get through our defenses, but I see you got book smarts—too bad you don't have no country common sense. You break into my house to steal from me, but you think I'm not going to stop you?"

His gravelly voice was low and dangerous. He dispensed with all pretense that he believed the Black Panther was a Harlem chef. "I got your letters, all of them. The offers and the false promises. You're just a hustler like the rest. But you can't bribe me, Mr. Klaw, or whatever your real name is."

The Black Panther froze. "Klaw?"

"Don't play dumb." Brother Flowers walked over to a desk and pulled out a sheaf of letters. He waved them in the air and tossed them at T'Challa.

"First you claim you're some kind of music company. You signed that letter *U. Walk*. Ordering up my prize gourds left and right, saying you're going to make kora. We ship them off and then you stiff us on the funds. Next you send a different letter, from a real estate company. Signed that one *Ulysses Klaw the Third*. Now you show up here talking about you a restauranteur, cheffin', looking for ingredients. What you were looking for are our Wildseeds. You ain't the first but this will be your last," he said, pointing at the water dragon panting on the table. The creature lay on its side, and despite himself, T'Challa felt sorry for it. "Whoever you are, you've wasted enough of my time. Caused enough damage. Leave or I will make you leave."

The warning was familiar. Too much in this strange place felt like home to him.

"Look, I'm not Klaw, but I need to know everything you know about him," T'Challa said, retracting his Vibranium claws. "If it's who he says he is, you and this whole town are in more danger than you think."

"The only thing dangerous here is the business end of this gun. Go on in there," he said, pointing at a cellar door, "until I figure out what to do with you."

T'Challa ran through different scenarios in his head. Every single one of them was unacceptable. If Brother Flowers tried to force him into the cellar, the green man might end up dead. T'Challa had already decided that this was not an option. Instead, he snatched up some of the fallen red flowers on the floor and leapt in the air. He spun and twisted mid-flight, as a bullet shot past his ear. The Black Panther fled the shattered greenhouse, broken glass crushed beneath his padded feet.

Outside, the moon was a shimmering white disk etched in silver. The Black Panther staggered, then rolled, avoiding the gunfire that followed his steps. He raced through the tall sunflowers that now looked like guardian trees blocking the moonlight. The wind picked up around him. He stared. A huge dark figure swallowed the moon.

T'Challa lowered himself to the ground, advanced with quick, sharp movements. The shadow swooped down, shredding the thick sunflower stalks with huge, powerful talons. A screech tore through the night. The Black Panther turned, headed for the lake. Behind him, an orchestra of weta-sized crickets poured over the ground. Their chirping wind song was an unnerving tornado rapidly closing down on him. One leapt onto his shoulder. The Black Panther fell, but sprung up just in time for the largest owl he had ever seen to rake his shoulder with its tremendous claws. Its dark feathers were camouflaged in the night, and startled by the Black Panther's speed, it spun its no-neck head around to glare at him. T'Challa was surprised to feel the hint of heat glancing under the Vibranium steel mesh. The panther suit held up as T'Challa dove into the pond, narrowly avoiding another swipe from the screeching owl.

He plunged into dark waters. Swam beneath enormous lily pads and water lilies that floated above him like giant teacups. He emerged from the bottom water, rising up through aquatic plants until a strong current sent him reeling in the opposite direction. His panther suit vibrated and amplified the soundwaves in his skull. The heavy bones shook, then he heard the deep drumming of an enormous heartbeat. *Definitely not your regular catfish*, the Black Panther thought. His suspicion was confirmed when he was smacked in the back by the tail of a whale-sized catfish. The great creature opened its mouth to swallow him, but the Black Panther fought and wrestled him. There was no way he was going down like Jonah. He yanked the water-hose-wide whiskers, held open the great mouth, and his suit emitted a lightning bolt of electricity that stunned the fish. Protected by his suit, the Black Panther swam up through the crayfish and tadpoles that floated past him. Exhausted, he tried to catch his breath, resting on the bank, but the weta-crickets pounced. He bared his claws and swiped. The critters squeaked.

"Don't!" Brother Flowers cried. He stood with a dragonfly perched on one shoulder and the weta-crickets at his feet. The oversized owl screeched in the moonlight.

"Call them off!" T'Challa yelled. "We can do this all night, but I will survive and your wild things will not."

The man weighed these words carefully. He whistled then lowered his gun. "What are you? Why are you here?"

"I could ask you the same," T'Challa replied and stood up, his chest heaving. Behind him the wind rolled across the waters, making the lily pads drift and sway. A loud splash erupted, and the boat-sized catfish surfaced, shook its head, and sank back into the night.

"HOW DO you control such beasts?" T'Challa asked. His cybernetic suit was busy healing itself as he spoke. The damage was minimal, but the fact that the suit was impacted at all was a marvel to the Panther King.

"You cannot control what is wild," Brother Flowers said. They were now back inside the faux gift shop. "But if you are patient and respectful, you can commune. My family has had centuries to learn the language of the wild."

"Ours is the language of the forest."

"These wild ones live in the open waters of the river, breathe the open air. No cages here. They are free to go and come as they please. To answer my call or not. They are free. By honoring their freedom, they have ensured our own. And over the years they have never let us down."

"Is that how you have remained undetected?"

Brother Flowers considered silence, but the urgency in T'Challa's question spurred him on. When he spoke, his voice was just beyond a whisper.

"Oh, we have been detected, but few live to tell the tale. The Wild Ones grow as big as they please, swim deep into the dark crevices of the earth."

"The earth tainted by your seed, the Wildseed?"

"No, Panther, by this." Brother Flowers opened his palm and revealed an amulet, a heart-shaped metal with a dark bronze, purplish tint. Vibranium.

"Where did you get this?" T'Challa's voice was a low threat. The dragonfly stretched its wings in warning.

"The same place we got our seed."

"Wakanda," they said in unison.

Rickydoc picked up an overturned stool, swept glass into a dustpan, and picked up the larger shards from the floor. "The first one to come here and grow the food that would make us coveted was our ancestor, Djimoni. Her name is in the book. The *Book of Flowers*. In it she distilled what she learned of our world and passed down her hard-won knowledge. We hold the book and the ancestor in highest regard. We hold space for her memory on our altar and in our hearts. Her words have kept our crops and our spirits strong. Our minds sharp and our home safe. We maintain just a fraction of her magic."

"The cloaking shield," T'Challa said.

"Yes, but it was not always that way." He sat on a high stool. The water dragon he called Oohlou seemed to have recovered. It perched on Brother Flowers' extended arm.

"As long as we have been here, there have always been the tales. Of catfish with whiskers as big as bullwhips. Of dragon-like creatures that swallow fire instead of fleeing from it. When the others circled the wagons, tried to burn us out of our homes, the Wild Ones served as a fitting surprise. We protected them, then they protected us. As our great-grandparents once did. Refuge from the heat of fires, none of us wanting to be discovered, flushed out, erased."

"What are you hiding from?" T'Challa asked.

"Such a question from one who knows the answer all too well." The scorn in Rickydoc's eyes was twisted fire. "A poet once said, 'don't blame the masks, blame the smoke.' Our enemies weaponized both. White masks, hooded in the cover of night. Fire for eyes, they expected us to choke on the smoke of their hatred."

Rickydoc placed the healing Oohlou on what T'Challa at first mistook for a coat rack. Then he held his arm up, flicking his wrist. A buzz filled the air as a shadow darkened the room. The Black Panther looked up as one of the other water-breathing dragonflies landed on Rickydoc's leather cuff.

"But distant smoke plumes promised anonymity, not oblivion. They had burned down Tulsa, Cairo, Rosewood, pillaged Mound Bayou and terrorized Memphis. But not us. We turned their terror tactics back on them, and after some time, they learned to leave us alone."

"Not an easy lesson for some," the Black Panther replied.

"No. Don't start none, won't be none. That's our motto. It has served us well over these years."

"I didn't see that on your marker."

"The marker is a ruse. Half the truth don't never show up in those things."

"If you are constantly attacked here, why remain?" T'Challa asked. "No kingdom, no matter how small, can survive indefinitely under siege. At least, not without allies," he added.

Rickydoc took the meaning in the Black Panther's words, but the land was his greatest legacy. He had grown weary with those who only believed what was within their grasp, their vision. Brother Flowers' conviction was rooted in a story from a past he never lived, fostered by a faith in a future he was certain he would not live to see.

"We could never move," he said. "The risk would be too much, and besides, the soil is here. Djimoni's Wildseeds grow here. The Wild Ones are here. The earth has changed us as we changed it."

"It mutates..." T'Challa said, glancing at the dragonfly that perched on the lights overhead. The weta-crickets that gathered like small puppies at a bowl of pellets and other treats.

"It transforms," Rickydoc corrected him, "the way some trees have nuts that germinate after being burned. They grow like a phoenix from the ashes."

"Perhaps there is a path forward, a way we can both get what we want."

"What exactly is it that you want? Why do you need our seeds?"

T'Challa thought about the tradition that kept the Hidden Kingdom hidden. Something about this man told him that he could trust him. The care he showed the land and the strange life within it. The Panther King decided that, with so much at stake, to trust again was worth the risk.

"My people live in a land where there grows a similar seed. It came to us from the stars. That which you call Wildseed is ours."

Rickydoc's eyes narrowed then widened, anger and recognition spreading across his face. "It figures. You are from the nameless land, the place of our ancestor's origin."

T'Challa watched Brother Flowers warily as he scanned the pages of an oversized black leather-bound book. Gold filigree curved along the spine.

"Our ancestor, Djimoni, was said to be a master gardener. They named her gardener, but the truth was that she was a conjurewoman. She could grow anything, as if by magic. When she was first stolen and brought to this country, she worked on a tobacco farm. We believe it was somewhere in Maryland or Virginia. Slavery was outlawed where she was. All 'property' was to be sold. She and the others walked behind wagons from Virginia all the way to West Tennessee. Their own trail of tears, but no one mourned them. All the years she lived, she told one story. That she came from a wondrous place and that one day she would be free. She grew the Wildseeds so she could walk back across the ocean or fly away back to Africa. But she died here. The Wildseeds still growing, wilder and free. She waited for you, for your people. You never came. We kept the story and the seed. Now here you come, one hundred years too late, asking for something you think someone stole from you. Why should we trust you now? Those seeds are the only things worthwhile you've ever given us, and now you want to take it back?"

"Not given, taken. Your ancestor was a thief," T'Challa said. Anger roiled inside him.

Lightning blazed in Brother Flowers' eyes, but he was steady, controlled heat.

"Not a thief, a healer. She said she came from a golden city. Said she lived in a land of plenty, but her people—your people—were the only ones to eat. Djimoni, once a shaman and an herbalist, took the Heart-Shaped Herb to heal the suffering neighbors your fathers turned their backs against. It seems this is a tradition in the family."

T'Challa felt the blow as if the man had punched him in the throat. The words stung but he could not deny their truth.

"It is against our laws to share what the Panther God has given us. It is for our safety. Your ancestor Djimoni made a choice. It is not our fault that she was forced to live out its consequences."

"Not your fault, perhaps, but the blame holds true. I see you have no shame, nor are you remorseful," Brother Flowers said, eyes filled with judgment. "You cannot grieve what has not left you, nor can you lose what you never missed."

"Had she honored the tradition, she would have been safe."

"If she honored your traditions, she would have been as culpable as you. Djimoni did what was right. While your kind sat high on the mountain eating nectar and fruit, Djimoni left the groves of the Hidden Kingdom to administer healing herbs to the neighbors you abandoned. She was no thief. She was a hero caught in a raid by treacherous slave catchers. From the same tribe she tried to help! Cut off from her own people, she suffered in the fortress they called Gorée Island. With only the seeds from your nation and the amulet she once wore openly on her chest, she wove a spell to cloak the precious items and even braided them into her hair."

A sharp pain pierced T'Challa's temples. Once again he saw the terrors from his dreams. He heard the elders' wailing cries and his mind was transported back into what he now knew was the belly of a slave ship. He had dreamed of Brother Flowers' ancestress. He had walked inside Djimoni's skin for some time, never knowing the grief and fear he felt was once all too real. Now he saw her face.

Covered in darkness, the stench of fear all around her, Djimoni's eyes were filled with determination. T'Challa could hear the songs of comfort Wakandan mothers sang to frightened children. She sang the songs to calm the cries of anguish. None spoke her tongue but they understood the strength she offered them. Djimoni did not know where the water would carry them, but she held the hope of a future hidden inside her braided ebony hair.

"You think you are the only one who has experienced loss and pain?" T'Challa asked the man. "The kingdom, the throne you envy so much, is the very thing that cost me what is most dear in my life. I may not know the terrors that your ancestors did, but I do know loss. I know what it means to have your parents die or be murdered. To lose your childhood best friend not through death but betrayal. To have them betray you in a way that only a blade through the heart can compare. To have your brothers-in-arms fall into the abyss, turning themselves into monsters created by their own hand. To have the only remaining kinsman you have left turn away from you because the one thing you never truly wanted is the only thing she ever asked for. I know pain. My whole life has been a litany of sorrow."

The two men stared at each other. Silence punctuated by the soft cooing of the great owl that peeped through the window.

"So, you are the one Djimoni waited for. You are the nameless, the Panther King." Brother Flowers studied T'Challa, his eyes examining the panther suit with interest. "You are the legend we could not know. What is your name, king?"

"T'Challa, son of T'Chaka, N'Yami, and Ramonda. Brother to Shuri and Hunter."

Brother Flowers stared at T'Challa steadily, his brown eyes looked as if he could see deep inside the Panther King's soul.

"Don't let grief and loss—or loneliness—make you turn your back on your destiny or work. Everyone carries a city inside them," Brother Flowers said. "A bit of the home or the place that shaped them." He stroked the water dragon. "Your city is just buried deeper than most. You can hide it from the world, but you can't hide from yourself."

"The fire in the vision was the crimson fruit of your scavenged Wildseed," T'Challa said.

"The fire in your vision, Panther King, is the reckoning that surely comes from injustice," Rickydoc replied, sadness softening his face. "We are all burning. Inseparable fires that only time can put out."

"The elders did not tell me," T'Challa said. Shame made him bow his head.

"Some things are never spoken of, even in dreams," was the conjureman's reply.

The rootman looked as if he was fighting a battle within himself. For the first time, he looked hesitant, unsure.

"The secrets we hold here have been protected for generations. My people have fought at great cost to keep Djimoni's gift safe. But now that I know who you are, King T'Challa, and you have helped shed light on why we are, I know how to proceed. Now that you are finally here, there is no doubt about what our ancestor Djimoni would want me to do."

Brother Flowers walked over to the wall of books and slid his palm behind the bookcase. The case swung open, revealing a hidden door. He stepped into darkness and returned with a carved wooden chest. Inside was a red-stained burlap bag.

With studied, deliberate motion, Rickydoc, Brother Flowers, wrapped the seeds and the precious taproot in red wax paper, tied it with string.

"T'Challa," he said, "this danger that you speak of. If you are not this Klaw man, then who is he?"

T'Challa frowned. "He could not be the same man I know. That one was transformed, as you say. But perhaps another of his line could have followed in his psychotic footsteps. He was obsessed with destroying my kingdom. His obsession costed him dearly."

"Unlike you, a son of the source of our ancestor's magic, this Klaw could never break through our defenses," Rickydoc said.

"Perhaps not, but if he is like the man I once knew, he will never stop trying. Freestone and all the people and life here may never be safe." T'Challa held the red bag tightly. The Wild Ones watched him, quiet as their friend and steward, Brother Flowers, began to speak.

"We have faced much here on this soil, for many long, hard years. But we are still here. We don't plan on ever leaving the place where so much of our blood and hope is shared. This is our land, too. We aim to keep it."

T'Challa nodded.

"But it seems you know something about pain and sacrifice, the loneliness of standing in one's truth. If you find that you ever need… time… know that this place is your place, humble as it is. Freestone is another shelter for you. Even a Panther King deserves a day of rest."

T'Challa heard the truth in those words and the unspoken warning. Care given from one brother to the next. One day he meant to return a kindness. But this day was not that. If he did not return with the new seeds of hope, someday there might not be a Wakanda for the Lost Ones to return to.

Rickydoc nodded assent. He took a piece of ancient driftwood from his herbal altar. Once gnarled but now ground smooth with time, someone had whittled the fist-sized branch into the shape of a pouncing cat.

"Brother Flowers, you have already given so much. I cannot accept this gift, too."

"No worries. This is not a gift but an offering. Our ancestor waited many years to return home. This is as good a time as any."

T'Challa placed both the bag of seeds and the treasured figure in his satchel. Then he shook his head. "I think you are meant to return it yourself. The ancestors said… the Cherished Ones will return to Wakanda." He placed Djimoni's panther sculpture back onto the altar. "Until then, you keep the faith. We will meet again."

"The Cherished, eh?" He stroked his beard. "I guess we can work with that, fellow traveler."

T'CHALLA TAPPED his Kimoyo bead. Shuri's responded from the throne room.

"Looks like you were right."

"You needed the *Dora Milaje*."

"I needed the *Dora Milaje*," T'Challa said, laughing. "But now I need you to do me a favor."

"What is this? You are acting so strangely, brother. First this mysterious trip, alone, and now you seem… different, almost giddy. You looked like the world was ending when you left."

"Perhaps it is," he said, staring out his aircraft's window. "A friend helped me see another way."

"A friend," Shuri said. "Now this is intriguing. You had to go all the way to Mississippi to make an actual friend. Is this a friend or a *friend-friend*?"

T'Challa sighed. "Shuri, I need you to keep the throne for a while. When I return I will explain everything, I promise. Meanwhile, draw up plans for a possible new compound. Large enough to house one hundred and thirty-seven people, if need be, and…" T'Challa struggled to think of the best way to say what came next. "…a large freshwater pond, big enough for a whale, and this should probably go near the Alkama Fields."

"Wait, what happened in Mississippi?"

"Thanks, Shuri! See you soon." T'Challa signed off.

"YOUR MAJESTY," Adisa said, and bowed when T'Challa ducked to enter the room. He was dressed in the ceremonial robes of royalty, his body tall, back straight. The past two weeks in Mississippi had been quiet. After T'Challa bid Brother Flowers goodbye, he stayed on, watching, waiting each night outside Freestone's perimeter to see if danger came, But the iridescent shield that protected the small town remained in place. With no intruders in sight, T'Challa returned to the throne. The operatives in the United States had already located the mysterious young man who shared Klaw's last name. Whoever he truly was, he would receive a nice surprise the next time he contacted Brother Flowers.

Adisa's eyes searched T'Challa's demeanor for visual clues. Her voice was quiet, water receding.

"I trust our king returns bearing good news."

"We have a future because we had a past," he said, and revealed the red pouch Brother Flowers had given him. "Not always a proud one, but ours nonetheless. There are certain wrongs that must be righted. What was lost must be returned. I know now what I must do," he said, remembering the rootdoctor's words. "Work to build a better kingdom. And that requires not just a king, but many hands."

"Your Highness, you know we are at your disposal," the shaman said. Adisa hid her confusion well.

T'Challa turned, the artificial sun in his eyes. "Yes. And I thank you. I will need your help to bring the Lost Ones and the Wild Ones…" He corrected himself. "…the *Cherished* Ones. I must chart a path that will finally bring those who wish to return home."

"My King, what exactly did you find?" Adisa asked. She watched him with interest. There was a certainty in his eyes, an assuredness in his voice that had not been there before his trip.

"A discovery and… a mystery." He handed her the shaman Rickydoc's red bag. "We will need to work swiftly to uncover both."

Confusion, then hope, surprise, and fear flickered across the elder's face, refracted light and memory. She studied the strange seeds and dried herbs, held the oversized heart-shaped petals in her shaking hand.

"But where did you find these?"

"Mississippi."

Her eyes widened.

"Extraordinary. This species derives from our sacred Heart-Shaped Herb," she said, "but it has returned much changed—and so have you." Her eyes were steady, unafraid as she watched him.

T'Challa nodded. "Shamans see all. I will tell you the story, as much as I can, but for now, let's say that a very old friend kept this secret safe for us. She did not know when we might need it, only that someday we would. It is my hope that her faith in us is deserved."

"My King, it is known that sometimes when a seed wanders far, moved by wind or by fate, its roots can grow strong in strange lands. The old seed can develop new powers that it never needed before."

She watched T'Challa closely, as if staring into a future only she could see. "It is no longer its old self, but something new and changed. And it will need new nourishment, if it is to survive."

She took the copy of the *Book of Flowers* Rickydoc had gifted him, flipped slowly through its pages. She paused at a few illustrations, whispering calculations. "Your Majesty," she said after a few moments. "Did you partake of this Mississippi heart-shaped flower?"

T'Challa folded his arms. The royal robes gathered around him. "Not exactly. I did have a few sips of tea."

He frowned, remembering the battle that followed. T'Challa wondered if he might be making a mistake.

"No, Your Highness, quite the opposite. You are a leader who loves his people more than he loves himself."

"Adisa, how did you know I—?" T'Challa asked.

"You just told me," she said. "I heard your voice in my head. It is good that you doubt, but you should not doubt so. Only a noble, brave leader would risk what you have, to return with this. And only someone who believes in you—a real friend—would trust you with such a treasure."

T'Challa stepped closer to the elder, shortening the distance between them. "Shaman, how do you know what I am thinking? I said not a word."

"But you did, Your Highness." The reflection of the cave's blue-green lights shimmered in her eyes. "Only a wise and loving king could compromise and rise above it all," Adisa said, her eyes following him. She held Djimoni's herbs to her chest.

T'Challa turned, felt a surge of energy rise inside him. The voice of the Panther God whispered in his head, her presence echoing through the cave.

Adisa watched, incredulous, as the Black Panther leapt over the spiral groves. His dark robes swirled, replaced with his suit as he climbed up the moss-covered walls as if gravity could not hold him.

Though strange, the journey had strengthened T'Challa's spirit, renewed hope. The new herbs would help safeguard the future of the kingdom. He knew now that he need not carry the burden alone. His sister Shuri would be at his side, the Panther God extended her grace. Relief and gratitude coursed through him, as once again, T'Challa heard the comforting voice of the Goddess Bast. She sang to him a praise song, one that reminded him of Djimoni's when she first journeyed across the waters. T'Challa vowed that Brother Flowers' ancestor would someday return home again to join her kindred in the Ancestral Plane. For now, T'Challa was lifted by his renewed commitment to the throne and his people—all of his people, the once lost and the newly found.

"No, Adisa," he said, laughing as he climbed even higher. He bounded onto a ledge, the craggy rocks glowing faintly as he hovered above her head. "I am not ill, elder. I am restored."

"Extra-sensory perception," Adisa said. "Kinesthetic bodily control. My King, you are even stronger than before. Once darkness held your spirit down, but now you *rise.*"

T'Challa, son of T'Chaka and Ramonda, brother to Shuri, friend of Rickydoc, the Wild Ones, the Cherished Ones, and the House of Flowers, vessel of the Panther God, looked down into the shaman's eyes from his perch, remembered the fire in his dreams— fiery red blossoms that would help seed a new future—and leapt into the air, the wind beneath his feet.

KILLMONGER RISING

CADWELL TURNBULL

"AND THAT'S it for this semester," Professor Stevens said, his deep voice reverberating with the slight African lilt he affected for his students. "Remember, your final projects are due a week from today. If anyone is running into problems, my office hours are available on the syllabus and posted on my door."

Zira, his student from Zimbabwe, gave him a quiet smile as she followed behind the stream of students exiting the lecture hall. He returned a smile, though it didn't reach his eyes. When everyone was gone, he slumped into his chair and sighed. Another semester over.

He heard Professor Callahan's footsteps before he saw her strolling down the center aisle of the lecture hall. She boldly propped herself up on top of Stevens's wooden desk. "Last class, huh?"

Stevens rubbed his head. "Thank the gods."

She laughed at his strange statement. "Erik—"

"It's N'Jadaka, please. N'Jadaka is my name."

She leaned over the desk so that she was almost at eye level with him. "You called yourself Erik when we met at the convention hotel bar. Erik is who I enjoyed meeting that weekend. It was Erik Stevens, the promising young MIT graduate student, who I introduced to Dean Cathey, who was so impressed by you at the end of the weekend that she slotted you into your first class here.

It's Erik that owes me a favor, and it's Erik that I'm cashing that favor in on now."

"What's this favor?"

She smiled. "Just dinner. And some drinks. I need it after the semester I've had. When are you available? Tonight? Sometime this week?"

"Rebecca—"

"It's Becca." She pointed at her chest. "Me Becca, you Erik."

Erik was flattered. Becca had that Jennifer Aniston look he crushed on when he was an impressionable teenager, against his father's stern warnings.

N'Jadaka was not interested but considered the valuable information she could offer on campus activities in realms he hadn't yet penetrated.

Killmonger's thoughts were more… disturbing.

N'Jadaka rubbed his head again. "I have plans every night this week, Becca. Sorry."

Becca got up off the desk. "It has been noticed that you're… friendly with all the African students, the women especially." She let the words hang there for a moment. "Don't worry, I just wanted to check in with you and make sure you're not—" She smiled at him. "—crossing any lines."

Erik and N'Jadaka frowned. Killmonger balled his hand into a tight fist and glanced up at one of the security cameras.

"I don't know what you're talking about, Becca," N'Jadaka said calmly. "But why don't we get that dinner in a couple weeks? I know a quiet remote place outside of the city where we can be alone."

Becca smiled. "I'm looking forward to it, Erik," she emphasized slightly and strolled back out of the room, leaving N'Jadaka to himself.

After another moment in the quiet classroom, N'Jadaka straightened, stood, and threw his stuff into his backpack. He had to do some surveillance before he visited Jewel tonight.

N'JADAKA RELAXED into the cushion of the leather couch and inhaled the strong bouquet from the glass of red wine. Jewel sipped from her own glass, tucking a wayward braid back behind her ear, and then reached out her glass for a toast.

"To the end of the semester, and the beginning of summer, Jackie."

"I'll drink to that," N'Jadaka replied, shaking his head. "You know, you're the only one who I let get away with calling me that gods-forsaken Americanism."

Erik loved it, because it made him fit in.

N'Jadaka hated it, because it made him fit in.

Killmonger didn't care.

"Oh, you love it," Jewel teased. "And call it payment for all the dinners you've eaten here at my house." She walked over to one of her wall-length mirrors in the hallway and smoothed out her thick dark eyebrows. Jewel was a former all-American volleyball player before her appointment at MIT and still had her tall and thin, yet muscular, physique from "those good old days" she reminisced about.

Walking back to the couch, she curled her legs underneath herself and watched N'Jadaka like a puzzle she'd be solving for the rest of her life. "You're not going to let it go, are you?"

N'Jadaka put his wineglass on the coffee table and sighed. "I can't. You know I can't."

"We've talked about this. I don't see why this is so interesting to you." Jewel sipped more wine. "I mean, I know why you're interested. Hell, I'm interested. A hidden African country in this day and age? And a rich one that was never colonized? That's an archaeologist's and a sociologist's dream.

"But we're engineers, Jackie," she leaned over and put her head on N'Jadaka's shoulder. "If they're as advanced as they seem, they're not going to need American engineers for a while." She kissed him lightly on the cheek and snuggled up against his warmth. "I know you think you're going to find some long-lost Ethiopian kin in Wakanda, but that's not going to be enough for them. We're gonna have to wait like everyone else until they open their borders."

All of his selves grimaced at the idea of waiting. There'd be no more waiting. For what was rightfully his. For truth. For vengeance.

N'Jadaka twirled one of her braids around his finger. "I've told you more about myself than anyone else alive. I've told you how I lost my parents. You know how I lived before I ended up with the Stevens. You know what happened in college."

"I know," she whispered. "But you need to let it go. You can't carry that kind of hatred around all your life."

"You're the one mad all the time."

"But your anger's different, Jackie. I look in your eyes sometimes and I see such rage. You've learned how to hide it like a lot of black men I know, presenting a bunch of different people, showing only a certain face at a certain time. But your anger, it's sitting right there beneath the surface. I see it when you don't think I'm looking, or in the mornings before you get your mask on, or whenever a police siren goes by, or at the airport when we're going through the security lines.

"You've got to let that go, or go see someone about it." Jewel cupped his chin tenderly. "You know my past. You know what my mom and I went through with my dad. I can't live like that, and more importantly, I can't love like that. I need more from you. I need you to be the special man I fell in love with."

It was a realization that had long eluded N'Jadaka—he felt special in Jewel's eyes. Since his father's death, he'd despaired of ever feeling that way again, but maybe with Jewel's love he could. Life could be more than the endless road to a bottomless pit called Wakanda.

Killmonger: Are you forgetting our parents? A girl smiles at you, and you give up years of training, of suffering, of scars, of hating them ALL? Our father N'Jobu and all of his ancestors would be ashamed you!

Erik and N'Jadaka had no reply.

N'Jadaka stood up suddenly. "If I give up my anger, what is that saying to the people out there who are suffering? I should sit here, sip wine, get married, go live in the suburbs, get a 401K, and just let all of this shit go?

"Let go of what happened to my parents, your parents, and

to black people here and around the world? Hell, no. I need to go there. I need to know why they stood by and let us all suffer."

Jewel was looking at him, fear in her eyes. "What's wrong with what we have here, Jackie? You and me, ride or die? Can't that be enough?"

It was the fear that forced N'Jadaka back down on the couch. Her fear of him. He didn't want her to be afraid of him. He pulled himself together. "Sorry, babe. You know how I get." He laid his head on her lap. "Let's just enjoy this moment. We have all summer to work this out."

"Are you going to stay tonight?" Jewel said, hopeful. "You know I sleep better when you stay."

He closed his eyes. "Let's see where it goes, okay?"

AT FOUR in the morning, N'Jadaka slipped out of bed. He wrote the text he'd send a couple hours later: Heading into the office early today to finish up some grading. Love you.

Jewel would be up before seven and would see the message. That placed him in bed for a couple more hours. More than enough time.

Once he'd finished all his preparations, Killmonger donned N'Jadaka's T-shirt and jeans, and slowly tiptoed out of the house to the silver-and-black chromed Mustang they shared to head out of town.

Killmonger carefully followed the speed limits and traffic laws. Getting pulled over for a traffic infraction would be less than ideal. N'Jadaka loved American sports cars. He often wondered what a purely African-designed sports convertible would look like. It would be years before the damage left behind by years of white colonizer rule subsided enough for a strong auto industry to arise in Africa. Until then, the colonizer's toys would do.

Killmonger took the freeway out of town, passing several exits before taking one that led him to the worn-down diner he sometimes used to meet the woman from Control.

She was already sitting at their usual booth, sipping her coffee. To an untrained eye, the lean woman with short gray hair could be an aging professor, calm with a quiet confidence. But Killmonger could see all that lay underneath: sharp awareness, cunning, and that same killer's instinct he had. When she looked at someone, she thought, "Could I kill them quickly?" Erik and N'Jadaka were wary of the woman. But Killmonger liked her.

She went by Anne. Not her real name, and definitely not the name she'd choose for herself. There was no sense of danger to a name like Anne.

He took his seat across from her and ordered himself a coffee and a pastry. He waited for the waitress to leave. "What you got for me?"

There was always work for an amoral wetwork specialist, especially one willing to work on home soil. Control had sniffed him out during his first tour, and a marriage of convenience ensued. After the academy, a couple of trips on their behalf added to his scar collection and paid for his MIT engineering degree in cash.

Anne, his handler, took a slow slip of her coffee before speaking. Her eyes moved around the room, even surveying the parking lot. "We want a group of gun-runners eliminated from Boston."

"Why?"

"They're putting guns on the street, and it has been fueling local gang activity."

"Bullshit. What's the real reason?"

Anne gave Killmonger her undivided attention. There was no indication of offense or amusement. She'd give him the truth or she wouldn't. It was this sort of straightforwardness that he liked about the woman.

The waitress returned with Killmonger's pastry and coffee. He took a bite of the pastry and waited for the waitress to leave. "Well?"

"We've confirmed that some of these runners are in Russian Intelligence. We think there's some long game at play. We want a firm and unambiguous response, but nothing that can be traced directly back to us."

That was certainly not bullshit. "Timeline?"

"You have three days if you want it. If you haven't done it by then, we'll pass it on to someone else."

The waitress returned and asked if they wanted anything. They both slipped their masks back in place and shook their heads, giving their best smiles. The waitress left again.

"We want this nice and clean. Quick if you need to, but we'd be grateful if you can extract some information from one of them."

Erik: We don't need this job.

N'Jadaka: We don't need this job.

"What's the offer?" Killmonger asked.

"Some leads on the secret location of Wakanda," Anne answered. "And payment, of course."

"And I bet you can't say what these leads are."

Anne gave her first real smile. "Do the job and find out. All I can say is that it's good intelligence."

Erik: We haven't had to kill anyone in over a year. We haven't needed to.

N'Jadaka: Sounds like another dead-end to me.

"Three days?" Killmonger asked.

"Three days," Anne confirmed.

ERIK: WE shouldn't be here.

Killmonger was standing in front of Zira Kaseke's door with a copy of her key in one hand and a Wakandan artifact in the other.

Killmonger: We do this or we take that job. Your choice.

Erik went silent.

Control often paid in cash, but occasionally they gave Killmonger a valuable piece of Wakandan technology for his efforts. This piece of technology—which Killmonger called Gods' Eye—was probably used by the Wakandans to perform full-body scans in any environment, from tissue and bone right down to the cellular level. Killmonger used it to scan buildings for hostiles, procure detailed images of people's fingerprints, and in this case, scan the backpacks of his African students to make copies of their keys.

Before putting the key in the lock, Killmonger used Gods' Eye to scan Zira's apartment from the outside. There was nothing alarming, just a regular empty apartment, but he was still suspicious. Wakandans must know the applications of their own technology. It would not be surprising if they had measures for counteracting Gods' Eye.

He put the key in and waited. After a few seconds, he turned the key and pushed. The door swung open. He released a breath. He knew a Wakandan wouldn't be foolish enough to booby-trap a front door, which would be a dead giveaway, but caution was still advisable. If there was a trap, however, it would likely be inside, protecting something valuable and hidden. If he survived the trap, he'd know he had his Wakandan.

Searching their apartments was the last thing he did. His preliminary work on Zira and the other African students was all typical spycraft. He meticulously checked into their backgrounds, looking for gaps or false information. He befriended them to learn as much about them as he could. Most importantly, he surveilled them. He developed a profile for each of his candidates, their likes and dislikes, their schedules, their habits, their relationships, and accounted for any gaps in their activities. He knew their histories going back three generations, knew many of their deepest, darkest secrets.

Zira Kaseke had no dark secrets. She was just homesick. He'd put in time talking to the young woman about her life back in Zimbabwe. He mostly listened in those conversations, trying to match her stories to the details he'd gathered himself. It always checked out, which meant she was incredibly honest and open, or she was a very good spy.

He knew from an earlier conversation that Zira would be watching a movie at Boston Commons. Her American roommate, Madeline, was already gone for the summer. Zira's movie started at six. She wouldn't be back until after nine, but Killmonger had placed a tracker on her just in case. He checked the app and found her exactly where she said she'd be.

Honest or spy. What a terrible game, Erik thought.

Once inside, Killmonger scanned the apartment again and found no oddly obscured spaces. In the artifact's viewfinder, layers of images sat on top of each other. From where he stood, he could see directly into her roommate's room through the walls and closed door. The American girl kept a gun in the back of her closet. A small pistol, nothing spectacular.

He went through Zira's shelf of books, flipping through each page. He went through every cabinet and drawer, taking everything out one at a time and returning the items just the way he'd found them. As he searched, a familiar argument was happening in Killmonger's head.

Erik: A wife, a family, a house, a career. What's so bad about all of those?

Killmonger: Vengeance against Wakanda and the ruling family takes priority. How does luxury get us any closer to vengeance? What N'Jadaka is doing, that helps.

Erik: Jewel's right. The best revenge is living well.

Killmonger: A life our father was denied. A life our mother was refused. Don't forget the dead and what they sacrificed.

Killmonger unscrewed a light bulb from the bedside lamp in Zira's bedroom and looked for anything strange. Nothing. He checked the backs of picture frames. Nothing. He hacked into Zira's laptop and searched for secret files. Her password was the name of her childhood dog: Pomegranate the Pomeranian. Moronic or spy was a variation of the same game. A clever Wakandan would do something like this to throw off a novice investigator. Killmonger was not a novice investigator.

Nonetheless, he'd found no secret files. No hidden compartments in her room. Nothing out of the ordinary. Zira had a collection of cards and letters from home, pictures of her brother and sister, her parents. Zira and her friends swimming in a pool, sitting on park benches, laughing and smiling in various poses. Her family was wealthy. She had been quite comfortable at home. She was smart, above average intelligence. She would probably get a comfortable job. When things got hard, she'd get support from her mom and dad.

The move to the United States was still hard on Zira. She kept her grades up, had even managed a social life, but she missed home and would likely return after graduation. In one of Zira's letters she told her mother she had a professor who was helping her through things. "Professor Stevens is so brilliant and kind. He really looks out for me."

Erik felt a sense of shame at this. What they were doing was a violation of every part of her life.

N'Jadaka considered it a necessary evil.

Killmonger did not need any rationalizations. For him, this was how the world worked. No one was safe from having their lives surveilled, their bodies threatened, their families killed before their eyes. Fortune was a precarious thing, balanced on a knife. A smart person, a strong person, prepared for the inevitable cutting.

Killmonger searched the living room. After a half hour, he slipped the couch back to its proper position, looked at it, and made a minor adjustment. The layout had to be perfect; sometimes people can spot a change on a subconscious level. He ran his hands along the living room walls and floor, checking for compartments. He checked the refrigerator. Someone had made spaghetti a few weeks back and it was growing fungus. Her roommate, Killmonger guessed. Zira's room was very clean.

The choice to infiltrate MIT over any other school was deliberate. Erik could remember conversations with his father about the legendary university and Wakanda's clever king, who had risked much to go undercover at the university as a prince. When T'Challa took the throne, MIT took on an almost mythical status within Wakanda, N'Jobu said, leading some of Wakanda's best scientists and mathematicians to study there with their king's blessing.

"If you want to find a Wakandan," N'Jobu had said jokingly to Erik one day, rubbing the boy's head, "just go to MIT and throw a rock at a black person.

"If they catch it, you got them," N'Jobu had said chuckling.

A young wide-eyed Erik took it seriously, post-college N'Jadaka took it seriously when it came time for school, and now Killmonger was taking it seriously. Getting information out of a live person, instead of trying to follow an ancient map or research ancient artifacts, was the easiest way to get to Wakanda. He'd learned much during his black-ops day, including the best way to extract information from a mark.

But it would not come to that with Zira. As it turned out, she was just a regular economics major at MIT. His search of her apartment had turned up only the trappings of a homesick girl. No surprises.

Honest. Not a spy.

There'd been more promising targets on campus before Zira, but they'd all turned up empty—Amdowa was from South Africa as she claimed, M'Kaba was a blue-blooded Ugandan, and K'Mumih really was born in Niger. Exhausted and frustrated, Killmonger began to feel his first shred of doubt. He glanced around the apartment looking for something he'd missed. There was nothing.

Erik: What now?

Killmonger didn't answer. N'Jadaka and Erik tried, but could get no answer out of him.

"OKAY, OKAY, you were right." N'Jadaka squeezed Jewel's hand as they strolled back from Castle Island's picnic grounds. "A picnic was the perfect place to unwind from the semester."

Jewel affectionately bumped him with her hip as they walked back toward the parking lot, holding hands and carrying their picnic supplies. "You'll learn to listen to me, buster. Jewel is all-knowing, Jewel is all-wise."

A couple of bottles of wine, some brie, some grapes—for her—a couple of cold chicken breasts and thighs, pound cake, and some Cruzian rum and Coke for him. A blanket for them to lounge on, some great conversation, and the setting sun serenaded by some old-school reggae from her phone.

She is so beautiful, N'Jadaka thought as he looked at her face, her braids blowing in the wind. N'Jobu had regaled him with his love for his wife, his mother, telling him of the warm glow just being around his mother inspired. How just walking hand-in-hand brought him such peace, such contentment, such love. How the rest of the world would just fall away and not matter, just as long as he could hold her hand and feel her love.

N'Jadaka finally understood. Feeling the warmth of Jewel's hand, N'Jadaka had never been so content.

Erik watched the planes coming in and out of nearby Logan, dreaming of his father's promise that they'd board one someday, heading home. Frolicking children in the park reminded him of his precious memories of romping and playing with N'Jobu, which always made him smile. He was happy.

Killmonger was nowhere to be seen or heard.

Walking back to her Range Rover, N'Jadaka placed the blanket and baskets in the back as Jewel stepped up into the driver's seat. Closing the door for her, he watched as she rolled down the SUV's windows to let the stagnant summer air escape. He bent down and kissed her gently once, and then again.

"Wow," she breathed. "I guess you did enjoy yourself."

"I did," he smiled gently. "For the first time in a long time, I'm at peace."

Jewel sat back and looked affectionately at N'Jadaka.

"This can be your all-the-time life, Jackie," she whispered. She reached out and squeezed his hand. "Look at the life you have here. Look at what we can build together: careers, love, a family, a future.

"This," she stroked his chin, "is a life that's yours, independent of your family's history in Africa, free of thoughts of revenge, of death. This can be a life you've made for yourself.

"I'm not asking you to forget your family. I can help, but our lives have to be about more than just you getting home. We have to make a home for ourselves, here, now, in America. That has to be our focus.

"Can you do that? For us?"

"Let me think it through," he said, cupping her chin in his hands and kissing her passionately. "I… love you, Jewel. All I know is that I want to try."

Killmonger was still silent.

Jewel smiled lovingly. "That's all I ask," she said as she rolled up her window. "Call me," she mouthed through the window as she pulled out of her parking spot.

N'Jadaka watched until he couldn't see her SUV anymore, his heart full, half-hoping she'd come back for another kiss. Inside, Erik was singing "Forever, My Lady," at the top of his lungs.

N'JADAKA PULLED out of Castle Island and accelerated toward I-93, smiling as he sang silently to himself. His black, freshly cleaned Mustang shone under the streetlamps as he decelerated under Copley Center and pulled onto Massachusetts Avenue.

He would not take the job from Control. He'd decided just then and found that his mind was quiet. No arguments. No rage.

After the appropriate paperwork and promises not to break cover ever again, they'd let him go back to campus and be the man Jewel wanted him to be. N'Jadaka felt a pang as he mentally shut the door on Wakanda and the Killmonger. This would be a rather ignoble end for his Killmonger identity, killed for love instead of in a foreign country or in a firefight in a revolution somewhere.

He did feel remorse as he envisioned his father fading in his head.

His father had remained young and strong in his mind's eye, calm and serene all these years, full of fatherly advice and righteous indignation. As Erik, the lost lonely foster child, he'd spent many a day talking with his father's image about anything and everything. When he didn't have anything else or when he had everything, it was his father who comforted him, his father who scolded him, his father who praised him.

He'd miss those conversations.

If N'Jadaka didn't need his father to move forward, he wouldn't need his experiences as Erik to hold him back, either. They'd all have to forge a new way.

N'Jadaka slowed and pulled onto Beacon Street. Not far now, he thought.

A shrieking siren and flashing red and blue lights pierced through N'Jadaka's calm. He looked in the rearview and saw the cop car. It's fine, he thought. He looked to see where he could pull over to let the authorities by. They couldn't be for him.

He hadn't been speeding; he wasn't on his phone; he wasn't weaving; he hadn't been tailgating. He kept his licenses and tags up-to-date and made sure all his lights worked. He kept his Mustang in tip-top shape.

But as he slowed, the patrol unit behind him slowed as well, and turned a searchlight on his car.

"Pull over," a voice barked out of the police car's loudspeaker.

Looking in the mirror, N'Jadaka could see the two white police officers looking intently back at him, one on the car's CB radio, calling in his license plate no doubt. He sighed, and pulled close to the curb.

The police car pulled up behind him and stopped, lights still flashing and the spotlight still burning at the back of his head. Keeping his eyes straight ahead, and his hands on the wheel, N'Jadaka rolled down the window and waited as he watched the two officers, one tall, white and broad, and dark blond, and the other, stocky, brunette and female, come up on opposite sides of the car.

The man, who N'Jadaka noticed wore a small mustache and carried flab on his stomach, leaned down and looked in the window. N'Jadaka noticed that his hand rested on his holster, and he looked over at the woman, who mirrored her partner's actions.

"License and registration, please," the officer ordered.

"I'm reaching into the glove compartment for the registration and insurance papers," N'Jadaka announced. He'd long figured out that you announce what you're doing to armed men before you do it. The woman, young and skittish like it was her first day on the job, flinched as he dropped open the compartment and pulled out the folder with his paperwork. "There are no weapons in the car."

"No weapons, huh?" the male officer watched carefully as N'Jadaka rifled through the papers, pulled out the appropriate documents, and handed them out of the car with his driver's license.

"We've had a report of some suspicious activities in this neighborhood recently, Mister…" The large officer gazed down at his driver's license. "Nah-Jack-A Stevens. Where you from?"

"South Boston by way of Oakland, officers."

"No, where are you from originally?" the woman said in a thick Boston accent. She was shining her flashlight over his passenger seat and into the back.

N'Jadaka quirked his eyebrow at her. "Oak-land," he said, stressing both syllables. "California? Maybe you've heard of it?"

Hewitt smirked. "Oh, we got a smart-ass. Okay. What African country did you call home before you got here?"

You wouldn't believe me anyway, N'Jadaka thought. "You've got my driver's license, Officer Hewitt, is it? Run it, and it'll tell you the same thing. Now, since my origins are in order, can you tell me why you pulled me over?"

Hewitt tapped on the car's roof. "This is a nice car. Who does it belong to?"

"It's mine," N'Jadaka said. "Bought and paid for through my own efforts."

"And what exactly would those efforts be?" Murph said. She was still shining her flashlight around his car. "Drugs? Prostitution?"

N'Jadaka put a growl in his voice when he spoke. "I'm a professor, and I don't appreciate your insinuations."

"Get out of the car now, sir," Hewitt barked, pulling the door open.

"Why?" N'Jadaka looked up at the officer.

"We're going to need to search your car."

N'Jadaka gripped his steering wheel tighter. "Unless you tell me what I'm being charged with, this is an unlawful detention and I do not give you permission to search my car."

Hewitt leaned down. He was close enough that N'Jadaka could feel the officer's breath on the side of his face. "Take a look at me. Do I look like I feel like putting up with your crap tonight, buddy? Get out of the car!"

N'Jadaka got louder. "My hands are on the steering wheel, okay? I haven't done anything wrong."

Hewitt's face was turning redder and redder, one hand flicking open his gun's holster. "You are going to get hurt if you don't do what I say," he threatened. "I'm going to give you one more chance."

"Just get out of the car, sir," Murph added reasonably. "We'll do a quick search and we'll be on our way."

"I do not consent to a search. I am not getting out," N'Jadaka repeated. "And you still haven't told me why you stopped me. And unless you're charging me, I would like to continue my evening."

Murph kept her voice low. "You want a charge? Here's a charge. We pulled you over for violating Massachusetts law Chapter 90, Section 7: 'Every motor vehicle shall be equipped with at least one mirror so placed and adjusted as to afford the operator a clear, reflected view of the highway to the rear and left side of the vehicle.' That pine-scented air freshener on your mirror? It looked to us like it was blocking your view of the rear of the car through the mirror. We were going to let you off with a warning. Now, it looks like you're obstructing an investigation and refusing a lawful order from law enforcement. Get out of the car, sir."

"That's a bogus charge and we both know it," N'Jadaka snorted. "I do not consent."

Hewitt took a step back and huffed loudly. "I'm tired of your lip." He pulled his gun out and pointed it at N'Jadaka. "GET OUT OF THE CAR, NOW."

Killmonger: This isn't the first time we've had a gun in our faces. Give me the word, and we'll feed these racists their own badges, and smile while doing it.

N'Jadaka: I'll handle it.

"Officers, let's calm things down here," N'Jadaka said, slowly rising out of his car. As soon as he stood up, Hewitt slammed him against the roof, and roughly bent his arms behind his back in an attempt to get handcuffs on him.

"Too late for that," Hewitt snarled and kicked N'Jadaka's legs apart as he repeatedly pushed him into the Mustang's hood. On the other side of the car, Murph rifled through his glove compartment and under the car seats, ignoring the two men.

"Hey, my hands are behind my back," N'Jadaka insisted as Hewitt slammed him again. "My hands are behind my back. I am not resisting. You are harming me! You are harming me!"

Killmonger: Why are we putting up with this? Give me a minute and this will be over.

Erik: Kill these cops and we lose Jewel, and MIT, and Boston, and everything.

"Hewitt?" Murph shook Hewitt's shoulder, as he slammed N'Jadaka again. "I've searched the car. There's nothing illegal in there."

"Let him go." She sounded disappointed. Hewitt looked at her, and then back at a furious N'Jadaka, and then back at her again.

"Let him go?" Hewitt looked confused as he backed away.

"Let him go," Murph said again, showing Hewitt N'Jadaka's MIT identification before unsnapping the handcuffs.

She stepped back from N'Jadaka, with her hands on her hips. "Thank you for your cooperation. Next time, watch your mouth, okay?"

"That's it?" N'Jadaka looked incredulous as he rubbed his wrists. "You stop me for no reason, you drag me out of my car, you accuse me of being a pimp or a drug dealer, and now it's, 'Thank you for your cooperation?'"

Hewitt and Murph sauntered back toward their patrol car. "Drive safe," Hewitt said before getting into the police car.

Another moment and they were pulling back out into traffic, a fuming and impotent N'Jadaka watching them leave.

KILLMONGER WIPED his blade on his leg, leaving a dark streak on his black camouflage. It wouldn't matter, because he planned to burn the clothes he had on anyway, but he'd keep the large knife and bleach it once he made it back to his garage.

Around him were littered several Russian bodies, all dead and in some form of dismemberment for disposal except one: a sandy-haired older man duct-taped to a chair in the middle of the floor.

Killmonger had spent the last few minutes dragging body parts into some diesel barrels he'd scouted out before entering the kill zone. Professionals not only planned the kill, but the disposal and escape as well, Control had once lectured. Sweat beaded on Killmonger's head as he dragged the bloody body parts across to the barrels. Disposal was sweaty work, more so than the killing. An unmarked cargo van was waiting outside, where he'd load the weapons and the barrels before heading to a disposal site managed by Control.

But there was a little more work to do before calling it a night, however. Killmonger glanced over at the terrified goon he'd duct-taped to the chair, knowing the man had watched every gruesome second of his chopping off heads, arms and legs, and mix-matching them in barrels to help throw off DNA identification, just in case.

Maybe a little conversation before entering the next phase.

"Whew." He bent over to catch his breath as he glanced at the terrified man. "Your friends were heavy, Misha!" He pulled out his knife as he walked over to the man, whose eyes teared up with terror. The blade shone in the darkness, reflecting the moonlight streaming in through the windows.

Killmonger laughed. "I'd bet you never thought you'd end up here when you woke up this morning, did you? At the mercy of a Black man, strapped to a chair in a warehouse surrounded by your dead friends."

The man moaned through the gray tape and dropped his head.

Killmonger lifted his chin with his knife.

"I want to be clear here." He knelt down in front of the chair, tapping his knife on the man's leg and staring into his eyes. "You're going to die. There's nothing that's going to change that. That's the job.

"But it can be quick and painless," Killmonger said as he

reached down and pulled a syringe from a pouch on his back. "Or it can be loud, messy and long." He brandished the knife in front of the man's face.

"Who do you work for in Russian Intelligence? Tell me, and you won't suffer. Don't tell me, you'll suffer and then tell me anyway." Killmonger ripped the tape from the man's mouth, eliciting a shout of pain from the immobilized man. "You choose."

Misha sucked in several breaths, and dropped his head. A savage look crossed his face, and he spit in Killmonger's face. "Delay svoje khudsheye," he snarled. Do your worst.

Killmonger just smiled. "Thank you for your cooperation."

JEWEL SIPPED her coffee worriedly, watching N'Jadaka pace. "Calm down, Jackie. You're going to wear a hole in my kitchen floor."

"Calm down? Your advice is to calm down?" N'Jadaka glared at her. "Someone slams me into my own car, and walks away, and you want me to 'calm down?' Someone dares to wave a gun in my face, and you think I should calm down?

"If that had happened to you, would you 'calm down?' Would you want me to tell you to 'calm down?'"

Jewel raised her hands in surrender. "Bad choice of words, Jackie. How about, 'get yourself under control.'"

"Get myself under control? Get myself under control?"

Jewel stood up, and dragged him into the neighboring chair at her kitchen table. "You're repeating yourself, babe. Breathe."

N'Jadaka took a deep breath and slumped back into the chair.

"They've got to pay," he decided. "You see that, right? They can't get away with this. They think they have power. They don't have true power."

Jewel frowned, not liking the look in N'Jadaka's eyes. "I don't like hearing you say that, Jackie. Let's think about this. We can file a complaint at the police station, we can go to administration…"

"A complaint? You know how seriously they'll take that." N'Jadaka snorted. "All the administration will do is put my name in a file that says, 'Do not promote.' The police will get a slap on the wrist, sit around the station for a week or so, and things will be back to normal for them by the end of the month. They probably do this shit to every brother coming down that block.

"No. They don't get away with it this time," he said as he envisioned Killmonger loading his rifle, sliding his knife into his leg holster, and strapping a garrote around his waist for easy access. "We need something a little stronger than a complaint."

"Jackie? I don't like how you're looking right now," Jewel said. "Don't do anything stupid. We… you've got too much to lose right now."

N'Jadaka pounded his chest, making Jewel jump. "Is it stupid to stand up for myself? Is it stupid to use my gifts to make sure some kind of justice is served? I've swallowed their shit all my life. I'm not swallowing any more. Especially since I don't have to."

Jewel sat back and looked in his eyes, wringing her hands. Tears welled up in her eyes.

"I've looked past a lot of things, Jackie. The disappearances, the wounds you bring over here on your body and soul, you shutting me out of your life when and where you feel like it.

"You know how I feel, and you know what I went through."

Jewel grabbed his hand, a pleading look on her face. "Let this go. If you can't, tell me now and walk out that door. Go find Wakanda. Get your vengeance. Live your life.

"But you don't get revenge… and me."

N'Jadaka looked stunned for a second, and then angry. "This is your 'ride or die?'"

Jewel wiped her eyes and crossed her arms. "You're going down a dark path, Jackie. My mom followed Daddy until we ended up sleeping in the back of the car, trying to find our way back to her parents," she sniffed. "His obsession over getting his family's land back ended with him swinging from a tree, and us growing up without a father.

"Can't you see? I can't go through that again. I've come so far, worked too hard."

N'Jadaka scoffed, feeling like he was seeing Jewel for the first time. "So that's how it is, huh? You're like all the rest of them, willing to turn the other cheek for a little respectability, for a few scraps off the table.

"I won't give up my pride, my hate, for a few dollars and a picket fence life," he said. "I need to know. Are you with me or are you going to abandon me, too?"

The kitchen was silent, with Jewel's sniffing the only sound.

N'Jadaka waited.

Slowly, Jewel began shaking her head. "I can't, N'Jadaka. I can't," she sighed, her voice breaking. She looked down at the table, refusing to meet his eyes.

"Maybe I'd better go," N'Jadaka said into the silence.

"Maybe you'd better."

N'Jadaka slowly walked over to the kitchen door and pulled it open. Before he stepped through, he hesitated and looked over at the now sobbing Jewel.

N'Jadaka closed his eyes.

But Killmonger opened his. "I was never here this morning," he said, emphasizing every word. "You haven't seen me since the picnic, right?"

Jewel sat up, her tear-rimmed eyes staring at the focused man in the door. She said nothing.

Killmonger took one step back into the room. "Right?"

She shrunk back unconsciously and nodded.

Killmonger walked out the door to his car.

He pulled his hoodie up and put on his sunglasses. He had a lot of work to do today, and not much time to do it in. After he obtained the information from Control, he would take care of a few things in town, and then he would get out of the country. If it all worked out, he'd be in Wakanda in a matter of days.

Erik and N'Jadaka hadn't said a word in protest. At least they were all on the same page.

Peace and quiet at last, Killmonger thought to himself.

I, SHURI

CHRISTOPHER CHAMBERS

"YOU MUST get your brother alone," old N'Gassi wheezes after a puff of oxygen and a squeeze from the palliative tube shunted to his vein. "If he's agreeable, together you can turn centuries of our *arrogance*... into a beacon leading the world from chaos. If he's not, then—"

"Then *forget* him!" Shuri snaps back.

"Mind what I've taught you, young lady!" N'Gassi rebukes. "*Control...*"

"I-I'm sorry... I shouldn't... it's just..."

"Ah, you wonder how this great mind could allow the cancer to grow."

"I-I refuse to wrap myself in the mourning shawl of your River Tribe, Teacher. I refuse to let you go."

"You must accept that my body rebelled because I did not listen to my soul. I put too much stock in *this*," his waxy brown finger points to his own head, "not *this*." N'Gassi places Shuri's and his own palm on his chest.

"Last night at dinner," Shuri groans, "Mother chided me for 'speaking rashly,' when all I said was that T'Challa was acting more like a politician than a leader."

"For shame," the old man mock-scolds.

98 "Hey, you taught me to draw people out, gauge them, right?

And my brother *nodded* at me like he understood! But Mother and your old fellows, Uncle S'yan and Zuri—they gaped at me as if I spoke *sedition*! General W'Kabi, oh my… and Okoye, imagine the freak-outs when I repeated that no one, including the *Dora Milaje*, is allowed in the lab when the King is giving a blood sample."

N'Gassi sighs and says, "Yes, Ramonda hints that our callow King winces at a physician's needles, and Okoye, with all delicacy, had to remind her, 'Respectfully, Queen Mother, the King does not wince.'"

Shuri's eyes are wide as the china plates on the huge mahogany table last night. "*You old goat!* You hacked the security drones—from a hospital bed? I'm vexed I told you about the codes!"

"Which you had previously thieved…"

"*Yes*. Because I'm *bored*. With schooling… with the role they wish me to play! I am Princess of *Nerds* as the Americans say… with AI synapses and test tubes as my subjects."

"Enough, Shuri. So tell me—why do you think they mock or question your genome project, eh? Yes, I watched the drone footage and some was the usual drek thrown at me for years, but this is different."

"*Meh*… Mother feels the work is waste of 'your time and potential as a princess.' S'yan must be watching the same Colonizer cinema they accuse me of bingeing when he teases that I'm 'cooking up a clone army' in the lab! W'Kabi… he says the research is extraneous for he can turn back any attack, squash any assassin or terrorist who dares soil the Kingdom. Zuri, I swear he thinks I am… I dunno… a girl, and like all the young, we are too *questioning* to the point of apostasy. Even heresy!" Shuri halts her rant as the old man's accompanying chuckles grow louder. "What? *You* tease me as well, Teacher?"

"Because you did not answer my question. And you did not because you are young, and the young can be excruciatingly self-centered while lovingly self-aware. Who did you leave off that list of parties who hurt your feelings, eh?"

Shuri twists away from N'Gassi's bedside, sinks her head so low the fluorescent stones of her necklace clack and clatter. "My brother."

"Indeed. And he has just been coronated. Everything is subordinate to that for now. They want no distractions. Neither for the Kingdom, or for he as paramount ruler who must learn to be both politician... and leader."

"I-I understand."

"Turn and look at me, child. *Now, that said*—this undertaking is either your passage, or your undoing... yours alone. Which shall it be? That is on the person you see in your mirror. Before my body is conveyed to dread Necropolis, Birnin Mutata, before my spirit answers to Bast, and joins your grandfather Azzuri the Swift and your father T'Chaka... I pray, girl, to see it be your passage. Not for the glory of Wakanda... but for all humanity. No *short cuts*, little one!"

Shuri nods. "I will get T'Challa's blessing. He has yet to be hardened by the pull of the throne, the weight of crown." When he pats her cheek, she rolls her eyes and huffs. "And I will *try* to live my life with control, Teacher."

Rather than grow the usual wry grin indulging her antics, N'Gassi is suddenly solemn, stone-faced. "As you know, your father authorized me to extract DNA from the tooth in my museum. Your brother does not know you possess the sample. The palace does not want the public to know that a Wakandan *may* have been taken as a slave to the Americas three hundred years ago. Knowledge is thus both a shield and a spear."

"Pentoh... The Traveler."

A pained cough wracks N'Gassi's body. Upon a sip of water he concludes, "But it is what Pentoh discovered... beneath the waves... that your brother must *truly heed*. You saw why... in that final volume of my notes, correct?"

She's nodding to ease his discomfort, knowing well she hasn't reviewed everything. And though a smile follows her kiss goodbye, inside she is grim, wrought-up. To steel herself she chants, inwardly, during the mere minutes of the mag-lev tram **100** ride to the bio-lab sublevels...

I can do it... I am Shuri... tell Einstein and Beyoncé... they got nothing on me!

And so in the lab she finds T'Challa is alone, as she hoped. They exchange hugs. The King requests a garish Zimbabwean reality TV show be streamed onto the huge plasma screens above, as background noise, for indeed he hates needles...

...and with the work complete, Shuri calls to her brother, still shirtless and sitting on the exam table, "I had to use the Adamantium-sheathed hypodermic this time, so I'm sorry it hurt."

"No, you aren't," the King scoffs. "Saw you giggle. Don't we have Vibranium needles?"

"I needed *sharp*, not superconductor, now that I'm your phlebotomist as well as your chief geneticist and—"

"*Naaaanh*... geneticist-in-training. Are you sure you finished your homework?"

"Whatever. Your skin and veins are tougher than rhinoceros hide."

"You took *five* vials, vampire girl," T'Challa mock-grouses. "Thought I'd have to call Blade to deal with you!"

Her peripheral vision catches the paramount King, the Black Panther... *swole* as the Americans say, pulsing his pecs, flexing his biceps, pursing his lips comically to provoke her. Alone in the bio-lab, they can be brother and sister. They can tease, be silly, be happy.

Yet now, she must make him *see* pictures of a world gone mad.

"I've not been... honest with you, Brother. There is... *more* to this project."

The King tugs his embroidered undershirt over his head, wraps his *agbada*, and tells her, "Shuri, I apologize. Affairs of state are relentless... sometimes my head's a drum-skin, beaten incessantly, or a cup, overflowing..."

"I mean... more than mapping the royal genome, or synthesizing antidotes to these poisons, these bio-weapons. The two are... related. Inviolate and inextricable."

"Studying vocabulary, too, I see," T'Challa answers with a chuckle.

Shuri's face hardens. "The latest attacks... London... Johannesburg... separatists in the Congo, the Horn of Africa... now New York. A super-potent form of Ricin, genetically-altered mutant anthrax, viruses. A chemical agent not even we in this lab can duplicate—dropped on a hundred thousand people in Syria. And I have ears, Brother... eavesdropping ears, I admit... and they hear of foes old and new harnessing weapons that can singe the very air we breathe, melt the bedrock on which our cities stand. Whilst this misery rakes the planet, all we do is deny and politick. Unlike you, there are heroes and mutants who are not immune to the poisons." Shuri pauses, manipulates images in the plasma floating above the lab floor. "Behold..."

There indeed is Storm... *Ororo*... eyes wet with grief as she briefs a phalanx of TV cameras and boom microphones in the aftermath of the anthrax attack on the New York subway to mask larceny at the Stark Tower. She vows to bring the unknown perpetrators to heel for murder.

The King sighs and asserts, "Shuri, she and I speak every day. When the crisis passes, we shall—"

"Shall what, Brother? Count the dead together when violence boils the world in blood?"

The plasma pops with animations of Shuri's research, applying old N'Gassi's favorite words: shield and spear.

Shuri narrates, "Any *wawa* can see that mapping a royal genome is conceit... when the goal must be a genetic capsule of every Wakandan alive now or ever born. Then coding and securing that information... creating a living matrix—the *shield*—so our people, our culture, our science, even our crops, husbandry, can survive a catastrophe, extinction."

"You calling me a *wawa*?" the King presses Shuri, the playfulness drained from his otherwise bright eyes. "This exceeds... wildly... the parameters of the experiments you described."

"Yes, you are *wawa* if you don't see how this relates to Wakanda and the world!" Shuri scoffs.

102

"Mind yourself," the King whispers, head lowered to hers.

"Brother... you are the *spear*. Your blood is infused with the heart-shaped flower. Without it, I cannot code the genome's *collective memories*, spirit... and secure it for centuries. Nor can I create a universal antidote against these exotic weapons—chemical, biological— horrors W'Kabi and Okoye could not begin to fathom yet you have seen with your own eyes..."

"Shuri... calm down before you say or do anything that—"

"*But listen!* You are the spear, yes, but the *key* unlocking everything—shield, spear—is rooted in the distant past—a branch of the royal tree—and the present. A common ancestor. Besides time, all we have is an ocean in between them. Without the key, the DNA of this common ancestor, the project fails and I cannot mold the shield and spear to protect Wakanda and all humanity." Shuri's countenance shifts from righteous fury to almost beaming pride. "All I need is your permission... tacit, no need to tell anyone... for an expedition..."

When she looks to T'Challa for affirmation, Shuri instead feels her spirits sink to her sandaled feet.

His look is stern, cold, as he tells her, "In the face of more immediate national priorities, I cannot even promise how much longer this project may continue."

"Y-You agreed at dinner..."

"*Let me finish*. I did not agree to all of *this*. You yourself admitted you have been dishonest. And whilst you do schoolwork, dabble, I am indeed preparing for future threats. Yes, some are microscopic, you are correct. Yet some are titanic, multidimensional, incomprehensible."

"*Brother!* Did not you see? The leaders of this world want protection only for themselves, for the wealthy and their possessions."

Shuri watches T'Challa move to her side, take her hand. But she yanks it away, points it to new images of war, privation, suspended in the plasma...

"I cannot meddle," T'Challa scolds, swiping in the air to kill the news feed.

"B-But my project will—"

"*No!* Don't even think about whatever you're thinking about." After a deep sigh he whispers, "Keep me informed of your progress with this new sample of blood serum. The universal antidote aspect is… promising."

"Y-Yes, my King…"

T'Challa busses her plump cheek, moves to the lift leading to the surface.

"Must we only battle monsters and madmen?" Shuri suddenly blurts, her eyelids quickly clenched as when she was little and Ramonda would scold her. "What about cruelty, chaos?"

"I'm neither a Messiah," she hears, "nor a policeman. I am an *adult*. Adults are strategic, Shuri… *Shuri, look at me when I speak to you!*"

She's afraid to open her eyes, lest they are moist and betray weakness. She wills them open, locking them with her brother's as she presses, "Did the spear of Bashenga splinter on the hides of the monsters that once feasted on oil and uranium, or before that gorged on gold, spices… *slaves*… when such monsters scratched at *our* doors?"

T'Challa backs into the lift. "You received a parcel from California… scanned and sterilized. And as you are princess of this realm, no one questioned its contents. Look on your desk. Give my love to Professor N'Gassi."

The lift doors hiss shut, and he's gone.

With her dagger she opens a box stamped with a San Francisco return address.

The inner package reveals the address of a laboratory in America's Silicon Valley. *FamilyGen DNA…*

The words in the cover letter steal Shuri's breath. "I *am* an adult," Shuri whispers inwardly. "And I'm doing this with or without you."

A shiny mini-disk comes with the kit. She pops it in, and immediately a blond Colonizer appears in the plasma… a fashion model's painted face, high heels and tight black dress, all incongruous with her white lab coat.

Shuri snickers at this default ambassador yet watches intently as the virtual tour guide orchestrates CGI-graphic maps and rays of blue, orange and red: colors and icons denoting chromosomal migration patterns and the journey of mitochondrial DNA from the Queen Mother, and Y-DNA from T'Chaka, her father.

The lines and glyphs interconnect Shuri's avatar with a handful of smaller faces on the African continent outside Wakanda. To be expected, given Ramonda's South African heritage.

Yet those tendrils fade as one face becomes as prominent as Shuri's. Now, she beholds a red line joining Wakanda with a spot in the States called Baltimore.

"Meet your genetic relative," the cheery guide relates. *"Correlating with the third sample extracted from the tooth…"*

Coretta Goins, age sixty-six. Her warm green eyes are a wonderful contrast to the dark skin. Wrinkles and lines tell a tale—but of what, Shuri can only guess. Her gray cornrows and braids stitch and cascade from her head, and Shuri feels bad for her as the style is so inadept when compared to hair artistry here in the city of Birnin Zana.

She is a nurse, the dossier explains, caring for the elderly parents of wealthy Americans, and thus had to give up a DNA sample as a condition of employment. She is a widow. Her only child, a son, died at age twenty-two, cause unknown. Shuri sighs, pondering the loss, yet with nothing to compare it to but her own life. As a teen, Shuri has already mastered physics and quantum mechanics, nano-engineering.

"I will call her 'Auntie,'" Shuri projects, and she does a dancer's pirouette and pantomime hug of this new relative. "All due to a sore molar… and she will save our people, all of humanity."

The technicians return; their banter cuts Shuri from her spinning thoughts. She ejects the disk, stuffs everything into her dyed sisal and leather carry-sack.

"Can barely keep my eyes open," she says with a yawn. "Might take a lie-down."

"That's new!" one technician jokes. "Usually you unwind by

kickboxing or running the Border Tribe's obstacle course!"

"I need blood-protein projections *now!*" Shuri huffs.

She ducks into the lavatory, leaving her people gossiping and gaping.

She finds neither Einstein nor Beyoncé in the mirror. Just an impertinent child—indulged only because she's a prodigy...

"*No!*" she battles back. She removes her handheld and swipes the hospital connection to N'Gassi's suite.

Still, she prays he's asleep, so she doesn't have to say goodbye again. An attendant is indeed changing his IV; he confirms that the old man slumbers.

"Tell him when he wakes that there is no room in the Necropolis until he hears of my passage."

With the codeword given, Shuri wraps her head and makes for the bubble-domed, colorfully painted EV taxis queued up along a boulevard thronged with workers heading home or to the markets of Steptown. Some cabbies are AI, some have human hacks as drivers. She jumps into a wheeled pod captained by an older woman sipping from a tea packet; sure enough, the human driver spends more time complaining about her husband's belly than divining the identity of the young woman in the back.

Even stiff Okoye knows of the *wageni soko*, where the taxi drops Shuri onto another boulevard boiling with people.

This is a crowd of chattering bohemians rather than hard-charging engineers, academics, and bureaucrats. These are Shuri's tribe: the young Wakandans congregating with exchange students, expats, and foreigners T'Challa had allowed visas. And within the district's beehive-shaped buildings, festooned with banners and strung with exotic fabrics shading the streets, Shuri isn't a princess. She's "Shani" to the tea server, or "Shurai" to her youthful cyber-followers on every continent.

She sips tea, bops to rhythmic music. Yet to her friends huddled atop the plush cushions, her revelations are bitter, jarring.

"The cancer has made our grandfather N'Gassi crazy," complains a thick-muscled teenager, off-duty yet still in his cadet's sash. "It's a commercial craft, but the codes are military, and W'Kabi himself would drop me headfirst into the Jabaris if they're compromised."

Shuri counters, "Do not speak of this as a crime."

A young woman, head shaven and adorned with red henna filigree and beads, counters, "I want to join the *Dora Milaje* when I finish school. I will never be accepted if I'm caught."

"Yes, the King is against me, and yet… I *persist*!"

A boy with huge oval black eyes and ropes of tinted locks twisting down his back nudges the young woman with his glowing tablet.

"We *must* persist… discover. This is from my mother… she's among the Colonizers, sent by the King. Read!"

The screen describes super-container-ship sinkings in the Atlantic. Billions in tonnage and money vanished, no wreckage. The few survivors rescued from lifeboats had no memory of the catastrophes.

"Professor N'Gassi says it has happened only twice before," the teen relates. "During the ugly world wars… then long ago, when the baobab tree lost her fruit to the sea…"

Shuri nods. "So many euphemisms for it, Kwami, as it didn't touch us. Her fruit was millions of our cousins, sent to die in mines, or fields of cane, indigo, tobacco and cotton. We, the young, shall illuminate this iconoclast who refused to be King, refused to be the Black Panther to serve knowledge. He beheld the holocaust and was consumed by the great beast."

"That Colonizer fable…" the young woman huffs. "People swallowed by a whale?"

"Stop!" the boy Kwami scolds. "I want to hear about the beast!"

Shuri tells him the "beast" is an allegory for the trading companies—English, Dutch, Portuguese, Spanish… and the Arabs who raided and bartered. "One Wakandan bore witness and might have stopped it. The one whose blood tints the Diaspora of today." Shuri pauses, as only young Kwami is transfixed. "Griot's programmed to cover your tracks," she assures the other two. "And erase mine. No one will think I've been kidnapped by terrorists.

I will transmit a message to the King mid-ocean. Now, who's helping for pre-flight?"

When the siblings shrug, Kwami stands and proclaims, "I'll be your *umncedisi*!"

At night, the hangar resembles a gargantuan, curving tortoise shell, twice the size of sports stadiums beyond the frontier. Border Tribespeople in western garb operate it in service to the sole runway Wakanda provides for primitive widebody airliners and smaller private jets. The "rim" of the shell, however, houses non-military mag-craft primed for global flight.

The moon and floodlights erase what little cover nighttime offers. Still, with VR images of the cockpit materializing from her handheld, Shuri goes through the pre-flight checklist with Kwami... in his mother's borrowed EV.

"I can't believe I'm in the back seat with a princess," he swoons.

"Concentrate, boy!" Shuri snaps, but she gives him a grin. At least someone's taken notice of her, his age notwithstanding. Indeed, his innocence soothes her guilt over what she's about to do.

"This person, Pentoh," Kwami asks as they come to the end of the protocol, "why did he leave?"

"He wanted to be an explorer... as I do. Used a tooth infection as cover for his escape. Because he was a descendant of Bashenga, that tooth had to remain in the Necropolis, the Birnin Mutata..."

"Do they save your baby teeth... toenail clippings?"

"Don't be gross! They stopped doing that. Lucky for us, the King opened the archive in the dead city. And lucky for Pentoh, his Vibranium replacement could communicate signals back home..."

"Lucky because he taught our vast knowledge to the outsiders?"

"No... because he *learned*. From the Jojof scholars and the scribes of Benin. Then from the peoples of the Gambia, where he served the Fulani viceroy who ruled from Timbuktu. He studied the plants and creatures of the estuary and ocean. Discovered a fossil that was the land parent of whales and dolphins. He published his findings a century before Charles Darwin, and scanned the deep in submersibles of pearl, iron, and massandawood."

"Cool! What happened?"

Shuri jumps out of the EV. "The viceroy may have sold him to the *tuabo* for gunpowder."

"*Tuabo?*"

"European slavers. The Jojof say they put him in a *barracoon*—a slave fort. Then he disappeared." She touches his chin. "Goodbye, my *umncedisi.*"

She activates the light-bending cloak on her clothing and vanishes. To the distortions that belie her path, Kwami calls, "*Tuabo* took the same route as container ships, you know."

Shuri is focused more on the guards, not Kwami's words. Still, security is geared to someone sneaking *into* Wakanda, not leaving…

…and when Kwami activates the engines, knives of blue light slice through the huge edifice's bays. The mag-craft rises then disappears long before scrambled fighters arrive to hover about the airfield like giant angry hornets.

"Auntie's coordinates are punched in," Shuri speaks to the voice-activated log. "Maintaining communication silence until over the Atlantic… I don't need nagging right now."

She engages the autopilot's telepathic interface… then fetches a mango popsicle from the galley. Sucking on her reward, she brings up N'Gassi's last notes, unread, on her handheld…

The Fulani, Jojof, and Benin scribes tell of the Aykoja [click for pictographs and morphology, minion of the "Sea-peoples" see, e.g. Atlantis.] The tentacled creature is similar to the red octopus, though factors of ten in metric tons larger. Thus, Pentoh's accounts were of a corporeal, not allegorical beast.

"*Umbono!*" Shuri scoffs as she winces from the popsicle's brain freeze.

A power-drain warning sounds from the cloaking-stealth generator. The autopilot senses a correction, so she reads on. The glitch can wait. This stuff is *sick*, as the American teenagers joke!

From the archives of the Royal Lisbóa Sugar Combine and the British West India Company, three schooners and two fast brigs were lost south of the Sargassum in the first six months of 1756 AD. A survivor—a priest who was also an interpreter—told of a leviathan with eyes as wide as a man's arm, and claims the creature tasted the filth leeching from the bilge owing to human cargo… translated from Portuguese: "…and the Negroes joyously sang above the screams of terror from the crew, as the masts cracked like twigs. 'Deliver us, your stolen children, from oblivion, so we may die free…'"

The survivor swore the monster was called away by a Lord of the Sea-peoples, a male though his captains were women. And while the mer-maidens were "sluggish out of the waves," he "flew above the wreckage… wings on his feet bearing him almost to the moonraker rigging."

"Must've been on painkillers when he wrote this," Shuri mutters. Yet every point cites documentary and tangible sources, not *nsangoma* spells…

…and soon the land-proximity alert sounds. Low clouds, good visibility over the shore, then the Chesapeake Bay… cloaking power to maximum yet nothing but local commercial air traffic to bother her.

From Wakanda comes a terse message. "*Sister, come home before you do damage.*"

The only damage Shuri's doing now is from the pad thrusters knocking over old bicycles, a refrigerator, and some wrecked furniture as she puts down the ship in a vacant lot. On her monitor, two cats are oddly nonplussed at the spectacle.

Shuri dons a hooded shawl to blend in. She has no weapon but for her body's training; the darting wand at her belt is meant only for immobilizing. It was N'Gassi's idea to pack it. "People will think you mad, or be afraid of you," he warned, "and thus need coaxing."

It's not a cat but a teetering elder—white hair, black skin, a tattered coat of wool—who surprises her. She uses her handheld as a bio-scanner. Sadly, there are narcotics in his tissue. Worse, he's running a slight fever. Before she can help him, he mutters, "West Side or East Side, hear me? If you West Side, that ain't the best side, and this here bus might be in pieces in an hour…"

"The power drain…" Shuri gasps in English. The ship's uncloaked, exposed! "Um… I am *East* Side tribe?"

"*Good!* You a Jamaican, li'l gurl? Y'daddy own the roti shop down on Orleans Street?"

"Um, *yes.* I am looking for the house of nurse Coretta Goins? I have something for her."

"Miss C? Bus' a leff at this corner, down to the bus stop. If y'all see Johns Hopkins y'all're too far…"

"The famous hospital! May I take you there? You need treatment and detoxification."

His face hardens. "Hunnerd years it be a scary place ta us. I be fine…"

He stumbles away, and Shuri's almost as wrought-up over the sight as she was with N'Gassi. She cannot relent; her prize is a brick home, white stone steps indistinguishable from the rows of others.

She presses the door buzzer. Hallway lights pop on…

"*G'won now…* I got a vicious guard dog!" Shuri hears.

"Mrs. Goins? May I speak?"

The dog that now menaces her through the parted outer door has the face of a gremlin and ears of a bat. The woman holding its snarling, wriggling little body is short and slight, gentle braids, dark skin, green eyes. She wears the blue togs of a healer.

"Child, I came off a double shift… so whatever y'all want me to boycott or buy, sorry."

"I am Shuri, I am a princess of Wakanda."

"The *hell?* G'night!"

Coretta doesn't shut the outer door fast enough. The dart hits her square in the shoulder, and Shuri catches the mini-beast just as Coretta drops it…

…and so Coretta wakes, shivering, gasping, on her sofa. Shuri sits beside her, stroking the ugly animal's little head.

"Y-You… gonna hurt me?"

"The dart… forgive. It's to make you… pliable, agreeable. *I love your dog…*"

"M-Millie? Millie hates everybody… *never mind…* am I dreaming?"

Shuri looks toward the primitive flat monitor hooked to

laughable Wi-Fi. "This cinema is so funny, Auntie: a prince and his friend come from a mythical African kingdom… so he may find a queen… in *Queens*! Ha!"

"Lord have mercy."

"I'm going to place a neural port on your temple. It will not hurt." She puts Millie down on the sofa with her human mother. With one hand she gives Coretta a silvery coin. With the other, she fastens a red device on Coretta's head. The coin hums in the woman's palm.

"Vibranium," Shuri explains. "You have heard of the Black Panther? The Avengers?"

"What use have any of 'em been lately?"

"I am here to change that."

Shuri activates the neural interface; Griot does the rest. Coretta goes limp again; she discerns Shuri as if a spectral guest is inside her head.

"Yeah, I know about an African in my past, *but past is past*," Coretta huffs to the image. "Right now, I'm worried about my patients if I leave… and I got no cash for overnightin' Millie at the dog place… rent's due in a week… they cut my pay, increase my hours…"

"Your blood might be the answer to everything," Shuri's avatar declares cryptically.

Once Shuri removes the interface, she escorts a woozy Coretta to the bedroom and finds a suitcase. "What would you like to pack?" she trills as if a dutiful granddaughter.

"Y-You put all this in my head," Coretta complains. "I don't doubt who you are… but—"

"The 'singing coin' is for your landlord," Shuri cuts her off, "payment to secure your home and items as Wakanda prepares."

"Prepares for *what*? Y'all gonna turn East B-more into Vegas, Wall Street? *Child*…"

Shuri nods as she folds a T-shirt. "Something better than what is here."

112   "What's here ain't much, but it's home, it's good people."

"There is violence, contagion coming, Auntie. It's inevitable. Just as inevitable is that our people will bear the brunt while your leaders feast and drink in their posh bunkers."

"So what else is new, li'l girl?" Coretta then sits at the foot of her bed, turns away from Shuri to peer at outlines on the wall where framed photographs must have hung. "What you didn't see in my head... was that I buried my Albert goin' on eight months now. Cancer. He died *hard*."

"There will be recompense, Auntie..."

"Don't want recompense and *stop* calling me that!"

Shuri's confused. Wouldn't Coretta be overwhelmed... grateful? "*I am sorry.*"

"That fancy smartphone tell ya what Potter's Field is?"

Shuri shakes her head, battling back tears.

"That's where my baby Andre lay, fifteen years this Christmas. Arrested at a party down south when he was visitin' his cousins... got too noisy, sheriff came. Say he was drunk, destroyed property... we didn't have bail so he had to work it off like a *slave* till his trial. Died in an accident, paving a road. Hadn't seen a judge or jury. County sent us a big bill, say it had to be paid in full before we'd get him back. Know how low it is when you outlive your baby? Lower still, when you can't bury him proper. That's why past is past."

"You are a daughter of Bast. You are a descendant of Bashenga."

"No, I'm plain ole *Mizz Goins*, Adult Care Specialist, Brookmead Assisted Living and Senior Center, and there's gotta be a better way to sort out this world than you kidnappin' me, like the reverse Middle Passage."

The words push Shuri next to Coretta on the bed. She dips her head to Coretta's shoulder, cursing inwardly because she cannot find her own words—words that flow so effortlessly from her brother when he inspires...

Coretta sighs, asks softly, "We goin' ta BWI? Reagan or Dulles?"

Renewed, Shuri gushes, "*Oh Auntie...* I mean Coretta... you will *love* this!"

She doesn't.

Lift-off rattles Coretta so much she allows Shuri to call her "Auntie" again.

Quickly, the twinkling Baltimore skyline and shimmery rivers and broad bay disappear, and all below them is clouds, open ocean… and the moving dots that are the lit-up hulls of great ships and tankers.

Millie soon frees herself from her crate and barks. Shuri's passenger now looks at the stars above, the sea below. Shuri's soul is warmed as she watches a smile of wonderment grow on Coretta's face.

"There's food in the galley, Auntie," Shuri shares, "or air-sickness meds."

Coretta frees herself from the cockpit straps and edges back to the cabin…

…when the first shockwave buffets the craft.

Coretta screams, scoops up a panting Millie, rushes back to her seat. Shuri will not let her see the panic; it must be the power drain again, this time crippling the magnetic-field propulsion keeping them airborne.

The second wave almost flips the craft over.

"L-Look!" Coretta calls, head tilting to the starboard monitor that scans below, in pinkish-green night vision. "Father God what is… *that?*"

Griot identifies a supertanker, the *Triton V*, inbound from Abu Dhabi to Norfolk, Virginia. Three hundred meters long… and now tossed like a bathtub toy by foaming bubbles the size of houses. Then Griot spits out the unthinkable. A methane hydrate plume is destroying the giant ship's buoyancy while raking the air with crackling ions… pulling Shuri, Coretta, and Millie closer to the waves.

Shuri wrestles with the helm, shouting, "The depth is over seven thousand meters here! The frozen methane could not… *no…*"

"*No* what?" Coretta demands.

"Our location… two thousand kilometers… over a thousand miles… southeast of the Sargasso Sea… Africa and South America at their closest… this was where… *the ship sinkings…*"

114

Coretta clutches Millie as she beholds the huge vessel sucked down in a heave, with lightning striking the bridge as a final insult. In an instant there's dark calm, and only two orange-painted covered lifeboats bobbing nearby.

"Griot is sending a maritime mayday," Shuri explains, struggling to stay composed. "The responses are registering."

"You droppin' down to help 'em anyway, right?"

"Charged particles, they hurt the engines... and Auntie, you are *indispensable* to the Diaspora..."

"*Help 'em!*"

The mag-craft hovers above the swells, shooting searchlight beams toward the capsule-like lifeboats. The power drain prevents Shuri from switching to autopilot. That and the survivors speaking many languages in her ear taxes her ability to coordinate a tug.

"I'm a nurse," Coretta calls. "Just get me close. Millie, you stay still for Mama, 'kay?"

But the eerie calm's disturbed once more.

This time, not from bubbles rising from the darkness.

This time, Millie barks and growls as a filmy, suckered arm corkscrews itself into the night sky, dozens of meters tall and thicker than the biggest acacia tree. The arm curls around one of the lifeboats.

"Y'all seein' this?" Coretta gasps.

"Yes... I have weapons stowed in the bulkhead!"

"N-Nah, hon'. Not *that* f-foolishness. I-I'm talkin'... *him*..."

Floating... indeed, suspended in the craft's light beyond the cockpit window is a man... *maybe?* His muscled chest heaves in the surface oxygen; his sinewy limbs glisten with seawater. He cocks his head, studying Shuri, and she matches his movement. His hair is black, shorn in a square, and shorn means civilized. Yet his ears are alien, elfish, and those eyes, opalescent, glimmer and cut right through her...

...and she sees the wings on his naked feet.

The figure drops back into the water, then leaps out again, dolphin-like, and slams into the tentacle gripping one of the lifeboats as if it's a crab morsel. The beast relents, and Shuri and Coretta gape as he lifts the boat from the waves, heaves it to safe a distance. With eel-like undulations, he pushes the second boat out of the monster's reach.

Shuri grunts in shock because the beast's attention is on her ship now.

A charge to the hull burns one tentacle, but the other seven yank the craft into the murk. Shuri shuts the air intakes at the last second… and all she sees as they go under are tentacles in the searchlight. Until the light dims…

"I should not have gotten you into this, Auntie," she whispers, for now the tears flow as the sinking craft's systems flicker, sputter. The red emergency-power lights cut on. "Griot, emergency beacon… *home*."

For once, Shuri prays for her brother's aid. Beacon or no, it will be too late. She takes Coretta's hand and squeezes… Millie whimpers… the craft rolls across suckered arms toward a chomping, parrot-like beak…

…there is a jolt, and the craft drifts loose.

"Look!" Coretta hollers, pointing to a flickering monitor.

The sea demon, big as the palace square in Birnin Zana, floats away into the abyss, limp.

There's another lurch, and there, in the cockpit window… he stares in.

Yet this time, his face is contorted and his teeth grit as he respires the saltwater just as he breathed the air above. With that seeming disdain, he points a finger toward the glow of a ridge of seamounts, seemingly cracked open like eggs, belching lava and hot chemical soup into the freezing water.

Shuri shakes her head, makes universal hand signs she hopes he will understand.

"Water goin' ta crush us like a soda can, hon'!" Coretta gasps.

"That's what I'm trying to tell him, but—"

She's silent because another disturbance rocks the craft.

116 The man is swimming around them now, blindingly fast. The

water heats into a glowing whirlpool. Griot confirms Shuri's wild speculation.

"H-His speed," Shuri stammers, aghast. "It sucks in the colder water, then strips its density!"

The last thing Shuri sees from the cockpit, through the white-hot turbulence, is the mighty *Triton V*, wedged in a canyon wall... its hull crushed... yet tended by strange craft, sucking its oil away like aphids on a juicy stem...

A blast of fresh air stirs her. She lay prone... cries out for the Queen Mother. She's answered by Millie's panting and wet tongue on her cheek.

I'm not dead...

Shuri reaches out, but her touch is retarded by a membrane between air and liquid... another state of matter much like the Vibranium-charged plasma that holds displays and images back home.

"Be still, grunion," she hears in a woman's voice, lilting and slight... *in English.*

The shock of that is nothing compared to what Shuri sees, beyond the membrane. The woman is blue skinned. Her eyes are yellow, her ears as pointed as those of the water-man. Her clothing is a form-fitting diaphanous material, stitched with shells, pearls, and strands of an iridescent purplish fabric. Her hair is a short, European-textured and a burnt-orange color, adorned with bits of coral.

"*Grunion?*" Shuri snarls. "How dare you! I am a princess of the realm!"

"Princess? *Realm?*" the blue woman huffs. "*Bah!*" Millie's now growling, and so the blue woman teases, "If you are hungry, we can cook this thing... or do you eat it live?"

"Don't you touch my Millie, Smurfette!" Shuri suddenly hears.

Shuri is suffused with joy and relief as Coretta lies on an adjacent pad, likewise enveloped in a membrane. With bizarre ease, the dog can wander between the two, pinching off small bubbles of the material as it walks a floor glittering with pearl inlay. Shuri looks up. Rather than lamps, she beholds sea creatures flashing with bioluminescence.

"Where did you learn English?"

"I know all the airling tongues, for I, not you, am a *princess of the realm*. The realm-eternal. We know everything."

"Are you his... wife?"

The blue woman laughs. "*No*, grunion. I am Dorma. I am his kin. I study and harvest the boiling ice at this outpost on his behalf."

Boiling ice—the methane hydrate? "I am a scientist as well. Girl magic, huh?"

The insolence prompts only a far-off look in this Dorma's yellow eyes—one Shuri's seen before. In a mirror.

Yet this blue woman's self-reflection doesn't last long. "M'Lord suffers you to inquisition. *Immediately.*"

"Why, because the surface navies will be gunning for you soon?"

"I wish it were so. Battle, I understand. M'Lord's incessant curiosity, I do not."

Coretta reaches for Shuri's hand. The membranes surrounding both women combine into a single envelope, allowing them to clutch, whisper encouragement. A massive cooled-lava tube—now a sloping tunnel—greets them.

"Closer," a booming yet unfriendly male voice calls in English.

The tube opens into a grand hall of shimmery metallic walls... and Shuri sees that it's not metal at all, but the vibrant linings of many millions of shells. Suddenly, the membranes evaporate and there sits the water-man on a throne chair of corals. Breathing chilly air.

He remains uncovered but for a material draping his loins and legs. Shuri glances at his bare feet. Ten toes like her. Yet... *wings*.

But this almighty being, this manipulator of physics and fluid dynamics... crosses his ankles shyly when he catches her looking at them...

"How do you speak English?" Shuri asks. "There have been no sightings of Atlanteans since the war the Colonizers called World War Two."

118   "Thee has no standing to make questions, *girl*."

"*Girl?*"

"Hon', not with him, not today," Coretta counsels, clutching Millie.

"Wise counsel, old one…"

"Who y'all calling *old*, you nekkid Mr. Spock!"

"I, sovereign! I, imperator! *I… Namor!*"

Shuri marvels as Coretta comes right back at him. "I'm from East Baltimore City, hon'! I nursed a dozen a my ol' folks back from the grave when the low-rent staff doctors say sickness had stolen 'em for sure! So you sellin' wolf tickets underwater don't scare me a damn side…"

Namor grins. "Lo, that thine wizened eyes have seen many things awful and arcane is the sole reason I do not feed you and that pet to *our* pets." He turns to Shuri. "Yea, you, girl, are the prize. Thy craft is unlike anything airlings possess. The power source and skin meld with the same substance."

Shuri's jaw goes slack when he presents a closed fist, opens it, and in his palm is a silvery nugget… in the form of a human molar.

"Like the singing coin!" Coretta calls.

"Aye, woman. As it *still* sings."

Shuri sees Dorma bend, whisper to her liege-lord. In English he rebukes her, "No! This interrogation supersedes any overstated danger. Heed me!"

As Dorma rises, she locks eyes with Shuri, then slowly lowers hers. For an instant, Shuri pities this young woman.

In Wakandan, Shuri offers, "*My noble N'Gassi taught me of the Traveler. Pentoh. Is that all that remains of him, water-man called Namor?*"

And she shudders when Namor replies, in her tongue, "*Aye. Verily, thou art a scion of the Traveler… black-skin airling who sank to Atlantis' bosom when wooden ships came to steal souls in return for rum and trinkets. 'Twas my grandfather who first saw him in his contraptions, bringing the light the depths…*" He switches to English. "So when my grandfather and his pets destroyed the slave ships— as I would do the U-boats and frigates and tankers when the paler among you warred 'round the planet—the Traveler offered, in exchange for his life, the singing metal... from his mouth."

Shuri's mind plays images of what may have happened. Namor's kin must have drilled Pentoh for the secrets of Wakanda, then betrayed him to the *tuabo*.

"You bastard. Your kind took what they wanted, then rendered him to slavery!"

Namor leans forward, fuming. "You were there, child? You read the mind and heart of my grandfather? *Yea*, he did learn tales of another great realm, on the continent from which all emerged. *Nay*, he did not betray a soul. He conveyed the Traveler to a swift dugout, yet not swift enough to elude a Yankee brigantine. And thine countryman was sold in the place called *the Carolinas*, for my grandfather, crestfallen, walked the surface and saw it done!"

"South Carolina?" Coretta suddenly speaks up.

"*Silence!* Verily, in these perilous times, I seek more of that metal. That knowledge."

In fury, Shuri hollers, "Vibranium is your rum and trinkets!"

He stands, and the opalescent eyes flash at both Coretta and Shuri. "My race is a kind spawned but one eon at a time... to bring peace and safety to those gathered around you. *They*... who are not immune to your garbage, your plagues, mutating as it sinks to them."

He plops the nugget of Vibranium into Shuri's hand, then strides, almost floating, to Coretta. Millie growls, bat ears stiff.

"She a French Bulldog," Coretta offers. "Best leave her be."

"Yea, as with your pets, ours, sadly, can be distempered, vicious." He then touches Coretta's braids, sniffs her skin. His cat-like eyes narrow. "Lo... thy blood is *clean*! Carries a *shield* against pestilence, disease within thee..."

"*He knows*," Shuri groans to herself.

Namor raises an eyebrow. "Rum and trinkets, Princess? *This* woman is but thine own *cargo*!"

Bewildered, Coretta looks to Shuri, who protests, "*No!* She is a symbol, she is *hope*!"

"Hope is porridge for the weak, girl. I desire weapons forged from the singing metal, which thou shall procure in barter for thy continued breath after we strip an initial supply from your craft." He returns to his throne. "Thee and thine are now wards of the realm-eternal."

Dorma intercedes. "The boiling ice is unstable, M'Lord. If we use more it will cause a chain reaction that will warm the surface, harm the waters…"

"Make way."

"M'Lord, I beseech… this was not what we agreed to in taking the surface ships."

"*Make way*… thy words stink of the impracticable. Grow up!"

"I know someone who sounds like you," Shuri shouts. "Refuses to answer the difficult question… *because he has not wrestled with it as he should*. Yet the man I know is no murderer, nor does he take hostages like a pirate. You are *not* a king!"

"*Insolent fry!* Lady Dorma… stow them for our journey, secure their craft for harvesting."

From a cell carved from lava rock, adjacent to a deck or bay for strange undersea craft, Shuri watches Namor's minions pack provisions, including prizes pilfered from ships' cargo.

Suddenly Coretta confronts her. "So, it wasn't just for love and history, eh, hon'? I was also y'all's science project… lab rat?"

"Auntie… I am… a girl. Not as strong as I want everyone to think."

"*Then be strong.* If your brother's gone… who becomes the Panther?"

"Maybe my uncle, S'yan… if there is a challenge, then we must—"

"Heck with that! *Who is the Black Panther?*"

"I, Shuri."

"Then say it!" And Millie barks up at Shuri to entreat, inspire. "*I, Shuri!*"

"Would you or your brother buy what Namor's sellin'?"

"No. It would mean… *war*."

"Uh-huh. And this world's suffering enough. Everything *right* starts small, hon'. Do what's right!"

Shuri grows a giant grin. She fingers the metal molar Namor so blithely remitted. "Introduced to active Vibranium—might be the jolt we need. But I must play a hunch."

Dorma is near, directing salvage of the mag-craft's hull and the evacuation of the base.

Shuri shouts from the cell as Dorma passes, "So, you do menial tasks whilst the methane hydrate goes critical?"

"Don't test me, airling."

"You are a maid, a turnkey. And your liege-lord damns you to a war. You have his ear, yet he never listens. I know how that feels. But I can give you advantage without price, victory without war."

"I can give you *death*."

"Then we are of no use to Namor."

Dorma's expression morphs from florid to tranquil. "Speak. You are unmonitored here."

"Get us to our craft, break us to the surface. I leave you with a weapon you can use to gain favor with Namor. In good faith, you give me the technology to the membrane you generate. You and I, no others, shall remain in contact… *strategically*."

"Contact? Why not rule if we have power?"

"Because we are not *silly*… like boys."

"Indeed…"

Quickly, Shuri's captor snatches a device from her waist, calls into it in her language. Two blue women appear, brandishing weapons along with a blue male toting a weird device that bristles with swaying anemones. The device seems to modulate the size of the membranes.

"Did you really think I would betray Namor over hurt feelings?" Dorma asks with a smirk. She tells her kinspeople, "Take them to their craft so we may torture them into saying which pieces to salvage first." She faces Shuri. "For a comical attempt at escape to have a chance, how would you have powered up your dead craft?"

Shuri exchanges a knowing look with Coretta. "With something small."

The guards bring Shuri, Coretta, and little Millie to the mag-craft, itself enveloped in another, thicker cavity that seems to hold back millions of metric tons of ocean. The blue people walk freely in the air, keeping only a pocket of water at their mouths, akin to water-spiders back home who keep gobs of air on their abdomens.

Dorma suddenly reappears, prompting quizzical, distracted looks and lowered weapons from the guards.

She shouts, "*Now!*"

Before the guards can react, Shuri's well-placed kicks and roundhouse punches pop the weapons from their arms and send the women to the floor.

The male backs right into Dorma's grasp, and he's stunned by the spine of a living creature in her delicate hand. She pricks her retainers as well.

"The venom renders sleep. Now—*dicker.*"

Shuri passes Dorma a pistol built into a dagger. Dorma plucks the device from the guarding anemone tentacles and pushes it through the membrane.

"This regulates the air-water interface. It also can communicate."

"As will this panel on the weapon."

Dorma sighs. "Did you just disable the kill setting?"

"And you, covalent bond disruptor?" Shuri replies with a giggle. "Aren't we a pair?"

"Goodbye... Princess Shuri."

"Goodbye, Princess Dorma."

"Auntie, strap in with Millie. Swipe the screens to your right. If you hear a hum, yell. If you don't... *scream!*"

Dorma watches as Shuri engages a small hatch that opens in the hull as if by magic, no seams.

In goes the Vibranium tooth of Pentoh the Traveler. Coretta shouts, "Bingo!"

The cavity in the ocean now pulses with blue light. Shuri straps in; the craft is rising so fast she can hear poor Coretta moan from the air pressure. In an explosion of light and compressed gasses, the craft breaks through the surface into the glorious sunshine!

Shuri must idle her ship until more systems come online, however.

"Punching in navi-computer. Hello, Griot!"

But Griot says the forward thrust is countered by something. And again, horror shrouds Shuri's face as giant tentacles seize the hull… and a familiar visage appears in the cockpit screen.

"Nay! I forbid this!" Namor hollers.

Yet his rant is cut short by the earsplitting sounds of incoming missiles. Taking direct hits, the tentacles wither back into the deep.

Smirking, Shuri points over Namor's shoulder, then up. Hover jets above… and, in the distance, gray-hulled battle cruisers. Not Wakandan, but welcome. Yet he still clings to the cockpit.

Coretta is a fast learner. She swipes a panel and chuckles, "This may sting a bit."

The hull charge loosens Namor's grip, but just before he falls back to his realm he twitches a grudging grin.

"*Slaves no more,*" Shuri hears him call in Wakandan, as he falls toward the waves…

…and when they land in Birnin Zana, there is no fanfare or feting at the hangar bay. There isn't even Ramonda with hugs and kisses. Or N'Gassi, for he was lain in the Necropolis hours after hearing of Shuri's adventure, and her passenger.

There is only T'Challa, flanked by Okoye and one of her fierce *Dora* retainers.

"You much finer a fella in person, sir, than on TV," Coretta gushes when she sees him whole. "I know I'd curse that past is past, but… it made what's *now*. See, my granmama in South Carolina tole me of her great-grandaddy, an African from a place none of the other bondsfolks had heard tell of, and they called him 'the conjure-man.' Led a big slave revolt down Charleston."

The King nods. "Welcome home."

Neither Okoye nor the other *Dora* stop Coretta as she rushes into T'Challa's arms, and they embrace, tightly. Sobbing, she says her son was just about the King's height. As if in agreement, little Millie douses the King's feet with sniffs and kisses. Even dread Okoye sighs, grins.

"But this person here," Coretta then whispers to T'Challa. "Bet you don't recognize her, eh? *Grown up.*"

Shuri backs away. Bashful, reticent.

"I do, Mrs. Goins," T'Challa acknowledges, eyes wet with pride. "She is the brain, heart, and soul of our people. And she is my sister."

Shuri's smile is as broad and beaming as the sun over the kingdom. But then she takes a solemn air. "There is much to be done, my King. The unrest abroad… and now this wing-footed fiend in the ocean."

"Indeed so. And portends of fell things coming from across the land, or across the cosmos… of friends who become enemies, of love postponed. *I need you*, Sister."

"I'll try not to order you around in front of everyone, Brother."

They embrace and laugh. For now…

OF RIGHTS
AND PASSAGE

DANIAN DARRELL JERRY

T'SWUNTU HATED the patriot's clothing.

The rough cotton itched his crotch and his back. He grumbled over the walking reed boats the patriots called shoes. The hobnails poked his heels, and he cursed the buckles fitted over his feet.

You have a left foot and a right foot, Bast spoke in T'Swuntu's mind, as she had since the day she saved his life and made him Wakanda's king. *These shoes make both your feet the same. Two left feet, two right feet, who knows?*

The Panther Goddess had complained from the moment T'Swuntu left Wakanda searching for his nephew N'Sekou.

T'Swuntu wanted to reply but communing with Bast in the open would draw unwanted attention. Instead, he watched the colonial rebels who called themselves patriots. The anger and curiosity the rebels hid in their downward gazes and covered whispers amused T'Swuntu. The idea of these mongrels hurting his nephew enraged the Black Panther. He wanted to press a knife blade against a patriot's throat. Gently, just enough to break the skin. He tipped his ridiculous felt hat at a young woman, who giggled behind a folding fan.

The Heart-Shaped Herb coursed through his veins. He walked in the spirit of a Panther Goddess that no one saw. He craved war, warm and wet, dripping from his spear. He stared past a large building the rebels called the Customs House, found comfort in the sunset. The honey-gold horizon recalled the sunsets at Alkama—his sister laughing when his nephew N'Sekou fell trying to climb a rhinoceros.

"My nephew, Crispus," T'Swuntu muttered his nephew's alias. He'd spent the day asking the Bostonians about Crispus, but every time he wanted to say N'Sekou.

Do you know N'Sekou from Wakanda—the last civilized kingdom? That is what you should say because that is the truth, the Panther Goddess chided.

N'Sekou had joined the War Dogs despite his uncle's wishes and followed Wakanda's spy network from the Golden City to the trade routes established in the west. As a practice, T'Swuntu avoided the foreigners and their war games. He kept Wakanda insular, but the War Dogs provided an invaluable service.

T'Swuntu had traveled three weeks at sea, two days along the coast, and half a day in the Boston streets. With morning and the afternoon spent, T'Swuntu smiled at the evening he saved for himself. He needed food and drink. After sunset, he would see his old friend, and he would find his nephew.

Wind brushed over the Boston streets. Warm air from the dense bush and the mountains in the west. A cool breeze carried the ocean from the east. The patriots, rebels if you asked T'Swuntu, bounced through the streets. Boston had shed its wig and slipped into a long gown tailored for partying. T'Swuntu remembered the festivals back home, where his people celebrated the blooming of the Heart-Shaped Herb. In his mind, Safia whipped her hair in a circle, rocked her hips, called him with her finger. The memory shut T'Swuntu's eyes, filled his nose with the ghost scents of sandalwood and musk.

He spied an inn two roads over from the Customs House. A man with a round belly and strong round arms opened a pair of double doors. The rebels, triumphant and gleeful, rushed past the round man as hearty laughter shook his stomach. He wore a pair of silver spectacles clamped around his nose. His bald head gleamed, and white fuzz sprouted along the sides. Thin lips, red and shiny, wrapped a half-moon smile. The round man bowed and waved T'Swuntu into the barroom. Red cursive painted over the door read *Smitty's City Tavern*.

T'Swuntu walked to the bar, surveyed the room as Smitty hurried to serve his customers. The barkeeper filled mugs and cups with beer and whiskey. Men in dusty coats and mud-caked boots, droopy hats and wrinkled shirts wiped sweat from their brows, unloaded their troubles. Women layered in stockings, long shirts, scarves, and petticoats sang outside the tavern, beckoned the sinners to give up the barroom and pick up the gospel.

Smitty sat a cup on the dark oak in front of T'Swuntu. The round man looked nervous, cutting his eyes at the door. The apprehension bothered T'Swuntu, but he sensed no immediate danger. Before he left Wakanda, the griots warned him about the slave traders, and the tension between the British and the rebels. Still, no one had attacked or bothered him since his arrival in Boston that morning.

But the sunset hasn't finished, the Panther Goddess answered.

"Beer or whiskey?" Smitty held up two pitchers.

"Beer." T'Swuntu reached in his bag, dropped a gold coin on the bar. "This should cover my expenses."

Beer worked for the moment. T'Swuntu would eat when he visited L'Musa.

T'Swuntu wondered if his childhood friend had kept the old ways. He looked around the tavern, pictured his subjects falling to the cannons and the bayonets of the interlopers.

By the will of Bast, Wakanda remained untouched. The sacrifice demanded isolation, and over time the solitude had worn his country's spirit.

No one has sacrificed more than Wakanda's king, the Panther Goddess consoled T'Swuntu, purring in his ear.

Four British soldiers stepped through the open doorway. The redcoats kept close to each other, and they kept their hands positioned on the straps of their rifles. The rebels stared at the soldiers with hatred and daggers in their gazes as one soldier with a blond ponytail and handlebar mustache approached the bar. He had a round face and a scar from his hairline to his jawbone. The blond soldier leaned on the bar and smiled.

"I don't want any trouble," Smitty said. He pulled a rag from his back pocket, wiped the wooden counter.

"You won't have any. My men and I need provisions. Give us a few rations. We'll be on our way. We don't need much." The soldier adjusted the rifle strap slung over his shoulder. His voice sank to bitter grit. "No need to worry, we won't be eating here."

Smitty disappeared through a door behind the bar. Metal crashed, and the barkeeper cursed behind the wall. The blond soldier approached T'Swuntu. The Black Panther smelled the soldier's sweat and the cheap soap used to clean his clothes. T'Swuntu sipped his beer, tapped the bar in time with the soldier's heartbeat.

"I saw you by the docks earlier." The blond soldier pointed at T'Swuntu. "Watch yourself. Boston is a slave city. They work your kind from sunup to sundown."

The blond soldier moved closer. "We don't own people in the Mother Country. If the rebels had their way, they would chain you to a plow or make you chop tobacco until your arms fall off. The Crown wants to protect your kind. Help us return the power of the throne to this kingless land before it's too late."

"I'm not here for war. I'm just passing through." T'Swuntu ignored the soldier's lie, stared at the patriots watching from the dark barroom. He wondered if they had known N'Sekou.

Remember to say Crispus, the Panther Goddess added.

Smitty hustled from the door behind the bar. He carried a wooden crate that took all the strength in his round arms. He set the package on the bar with a tired grunt. The blond soldier grabbed the box and stared at T'Swuntu.

"We set up camp at the edge of town. Drop by if you change your mind." The blond soldier walked to the open door, spoke over his shoulder. "You may be a freeman, but these men do not care. One minute they pour your drinks. Next minute they sell you at the auctions in Boston Harbor."

The soldier tipped his hat, led his men into the approaching nightfall. "Enjoy your beer," he called back.

Once clear, the barroom exploded in a mess of obscenities, flying hats, and threatening fists. T'Swuntu smiled. The sudden bravado amused the Black Panther and the Panther Goddess. He figured the Crown would send reinforcements and quash this motley rebellion. By then he planned to be back in Wakanda. He watched the barkeeper wipe the spot where the British soldier had rested his elbows.

"You avoid that one. It's best if no one sees you talking to him." Smitty cleaned the bar and shook his head. "People can get the wrong ideas."

Smitty filled another pitcher of ale for a broad-shouldered man in a mangy gray shirt, with the sleeves rolled to his elbows and the shirttail tucked into dirty brown trousers.

A man with a red beard and red curls combed sideways smiled with three missing teeth, a wide jaw, and a wiry beard. He worked a toothpick in the side of his mouth.

"Where you headed, friend?" The man had bone-dry peepers surrounded by dark patches.

"You count strangers as friends?" T'Swuntu raised his eyebrow.

"I meant no harm. For once I agree with His Royal Majesty. Most of your kind don't count for much, especially in a fight, but I know a warrior's heart when I feel one. Not all of your kind are slaves here. Boston is a place of new beginnings, a land with no kings, ruled by the people. We welcome freedmen in our city, and we need good fighters."

T'Swuntu counted fifty-two men and twelve holstered pistols in the barroom. He weighed the dull patriot firearms against the polished rifles carried by the British. T'Swuntu listened to the redbeard's heart. The steady drum betrayed a calm demeanor, no malice. The heartbeat sped when the redbeard talked about Boston, which T'Swuntu expected.

The Black Panther admired the patriot's heart but mistrusted the idea of nations without kings.

"Keep an open mind." The redbeard leaned close to T'Swuntu, so the scruffy tip of the patriot's moustache sat a hair's length from the Black Panther's cheek. "That greedy pig across the Atlantic bleeds us dry. They rejected us, so we left the so-called Crown. We're building a nation greater than anything they could imagine. Those ladies outside have good intentions, but the Good Book prophesied *us*. The last has become the first."

T'Swuntu glanced at the redbeard. The Black Panther noted hard forearms, muscles bulging under a dusty shirt. A strong jaw and eyes betrayed war and murder.

The Panther Goddess raged. *Cut his throat, right now. You are the King of Wakanda. You speak for Bast the Panther Goddess. We could kill a hundred of these men, and swim back to your throne before the first lifeless body hits the ground.*

"A land of no kings, you say?" T'Swuntu raised his eyebrows, sipped his beer. "In my country the king would destroy anyone, any group who challenged his throne."

Tension rose between the patriots and the Wakandan king. He considered the dirty clothes, unshaven faces, hands swollen from hard labor.

"This isn't your country." The redbeard lifted his shirt and revealed two machetes holstered against his stomach.

The patriots stood, but the redbeard held up his hand. He lowered his shirt, stood before T'Swuntu. Chest to chest, the redbeard spoke. T'Swuntu smelled whiskey and two rotten teeth.

"You look like a good man, but we'll see."

The redbeard grabbed a bottle from the bar. He returned to his seat with the patriots, filling the empty cups swarming like fireflies.

T'Swuntu finished his beer. He left another gold coin on the bar and started for the door. Smitty examined his pay and ran after T'Swuntu.

"Thanks for the gold, stranger." Smitty held the coins in the last traces of twilight. "This will feed my family for a month."

"I'm tracking a runaway from Virginia," the Black Panther said. "Perhaps you can help. He goes by Crispus, a young stud, half

Choctaw, half African. He wears a black ponytail like the Royal soldier. I must find him, dead or alive."

Lies! Tell the truth. You seek your nephew N'Sekou, treasured member of the Wakandan royal family, Bast commanded.

"Beg your pardon, but Crispus isn't a safe name to mention in Boston." Smitty covered his mouth and whispered, "There's trouble afoot, malevolent spirits at work. Keep moving if you can."

T'Swuntu wanted to smash Smitty's jaw, but the Panther Goddess protested. Such a worthless opponent spoiled the effort.

"I know that Crispus is here, and I won't leave without him." T'Swuntu tipped his hat to one of the women spreading the gospel.

She smiled at T'Swuntu but shook her Good Book at Smitty. The Black Panther headed west for the rising moon swinging over Boston.

T'SWUNTU FOUND the white Dutch mansion at the end of a long trail bordered by forest. Bone-tired workers, soiled and sweaty, lumbered from a tobacco field that stretched in neat green rows to dark trees that barricaded the distance.

Perched on a limb, he watched as the workers trudged to ragged log cabins arranged in a cove. T'Swuntu waited until the moon peaked and the stars trundled overhead. The wind carried whispers and praises, a night song worthy of the finest griot. He thought about his nephew, and the lies he heard at the tavern.

Either way, N'Sekou will receive his rites from his king, the Panther Goddess growled.

T'Swuntu leapt into the night and the wind. The voices called him, called the Panther Goddess that roared in his heart.

He slipped through the treetops and the warm night. The spirit song reminded him of the conjurers back home. Before long, the words took shape, called the Black Panther in the tongues of his ancestors. On his wedding night, his new queen Safia sang of her ancestors. She hummed and kissed T'Swuntu as a hundred arrows flew through their bedroom window.

Safia's cousin had led a rebellion for the throne and her hand, but T'Swuntu quashed the insurrection before it started. Safia watched her husband decapitate her cousin. Horrified, she fled Wakanda and took refuge in the Jabari Lands, becoming a priestess for the White Gorilla.

He'd been alone since.

T'Swuntu leapt into a clearing, found a ring of singers and dancers. A circle of women sang praises, threw their dark hands and their darker voices over their heads. A couple danced in the center of the circle. T'Swuntu had seen the tall man on horseback, escorting the weary laborers to their quarters. The Black Panther recognized the woman from the group of women preaching the gospel back at Smitty's. The couple thrust their hands out and jumped in unison.

All around them, the people danced and sang with all the passion and voice their bodies could muster. Their arms sliced the wind. They swung their heads and bounced on their heels. They praised Bast for her endless bounty, for giving them strong arms and legs, and for the health of their lost families.

Most of all, they thanked her for their king, the Avatar, who was prophesized to one day come and free them from their bondage.

The air shimmered. Each particle reflected moonlight. The conjure work reminded T'Swuntu of the ancient songs used to conceal the borders around Wakanda.

As T'Swuntu walked up, the tall man stopped dancing and approached him, carefully examining his face. As recognition dawned in his eyes, the man immediately dropped to his knees, crying, "Thank you, Bast. Thank you, Bast."

You see! Even in the west they know how to treat a deity, the Panther Goddess exclaimed.

T'Swuntu looked around the gathering as the worshippers kneeled and bowed their heads in recognition. Some wore rags and shoes made of bark and string. Others wore tight jackets and trousers that barely covered their knees. Some wore simple dresses and aprons. Others wore tattered gowns that hung in rags over their ankles.

Wakanda's distant cousins, Bast told T'Swuntu. *Blood in spirit, if not in body.*

The Black Panther raised his hands. Following their king's signal, the people rose. He hated kneeling Wakandans.

The familiar broad chest and shoulders, raven-dark skin, bowed legs that rode horses and praise—danced, parted the crowd, and embraced T'Swuntu. The man with raven skin stood seven feet tall. His long arms and hard muscles bulged under his sleeves. His thighs stretched his trousers. T'Swuntu marveled at the raven man's big boots, imagined his friend's dark rusty feet dancing on broken glass and hot coals.

"My king, I knew you would come." The tall man grabbed T'Swuntu's shoulders, scanned the treetops that surrounded the clearing. "Where are your *Dora Milaje*?"

"I have the Panther Goddess. Who else do I need?"

Now you need me? Bast roared in T'Swuntu's face.

"Give thanks and praises. The Panther Goddess has brought our king." The man smiled at T'Swuntu.

"I have traveled an impossible distance, L'Musa." T'Swuntu leaned toward his childhood friend. "We must speak alone."

L'Musa pointed at the trees that circled the clearing. He called two of the worshippers, a young man and woman. A frayed rope held the man's pants around his waist. Strong legs, chiseled stomach. He reminded T'Swuntu of the warriors back home. In his eyes, the Black Panther saw the darkness of human bondage and strength turned feral.

"My king," the young man bowed.

The woman had a pointed chin and high cheekbones, thick eyebrows, and feline eyes. She projected strength, a spirit tested by extreme thresholds of suffering.

The Panther Goddess roared. *I like this one!*

He expected her to bow, but she stared through T'Swuntu. Bast purred in the Black Panther's belly. He disliked the woman that stood before him. He recognized her from the group spreading

the good word in front of Smitty's.

"This is Benji and Gladys." L'Musa pointed to the brother and sister.

"I dreamed of this day," Benji said. His voice wavered. "L'Musa said that you would come to free your people."

"Are you Wakandan?" T'Swuntu waited for the young man to show the scars that would prove his lineage.

"We come from Charleston," Gladys interrupted. "North Carolina. My daddy was a planter, and my momma was a slave. That's how I blend in with the good ladies."

"Benji and Gladys were born here, my king." L'Musa grabbed Benji and Gladys by their shoulders. "Gather the worshippers. Our king needs provisions and lodging."

"Are you going past the trees? Is it safe?" Gladys balled her fists and straightened her back. "I will guard you, L'Musa."

"We need you watching over the worshippers," L'Musa said, his voice stern.

"The Panther Goddess protects us," T'Swuntu said.

"I'm sure she does, but over here, it seems like she needs a mite bit of help," Gladys snorted as she pulled Benji back toward the kinspeople. Benji scowled at his sister as they departed.

Wait! I may have spoken too soon. I will watch this one myself, the Panther Goddess growled.

T'Swuntu started for Gladys, but L'Musa directed his king toward the dark circle of forest. T'Swuntu felt the air shift as he left the clearing and the conjured wall that hid the worshippers. The darkness empowered the Black Panther, welcomed him to the wilderness. He wanted to run and leap through the trees.

"You want to know why I failed to report N'Sekou's disappearance?" L'Musa offered.

T'Swuntu searched his friend's eyes for treachery. "What happened to my sister's first born?"

The Panther Goddess grew impatient. *I want to find N'Sekou. His soul is trapped in this city.*

The Black Panther remembered the last day he'd seen his childhood friend. L'Musa had beaten him in combat training.

T'Swuntu's only loss enraged him. They avoided each other until L'Musa joined the War Dogs and disappeared. The spy network had taken L'Musa through the prison camps of neighboring tribes, across the Atlantic Ocean, through the plantations spreading up and down the coast of the so-called New World.

"I felt N'Sekou leave the temporal plane. I searched for him in Djalia but failed to sense his presence. He hasn't been buried."

T'Swuntu stepped closer to L'Musa. "His mother worried me for weeks about his transition rites."

"Is Kandika as strong as I remember?" L'Musa smiled, lost in a memory.

"My sister wants war against this country. I must send N'Sekou to Djalia, so he can commune with his ancestors before his mother burns your New World to the ground."

"The Sons of Freedom have N'Sekou." L'Musa stared at the ground. "They have his body."

"You call the dogs who enslave your countrymen Sons of Freedom?"

"They named themselves, my king. I've been in this country longer than I care to remember. Things look simple. You see land, resources, nations fighting—but this New World, this kingless land, is changing our people. I free as many as I can, and I help all who I encounter."

"L'Musa, you are one of my oldest friends, but the War Dogs' purpose is to gather information for your king." T'Swuntu watched a mouse scurry past his foot, through the grass. "Tell me everything."

"N'Sekou joined the Sons of Freedom." L'Musa rubbed his bald head and stared at the moon. "Gladys reported that you stopped in Smitty's. The British soldier you met at the tavern shot N'Sekou."

T'Swuntu balled his fist, remembered speaking with his nephew's murderer.

You should have ripped out his heart when you had the chance, the Panther Goddess snarled.

"N'Sekou renounced you. He renounced Wakanda. He even renounced the Panther Goddess. He cursed the absentee kings across the ocean. He spoke like the Sons of Freedom. I tried to reason with him. He wanted to abandon N'Sekou and become Crispus. He wanted to live the story we gave him."

T'Swuntu grabbed L'Musa's throat and slammed him against a tree. "None of this explains why I had to sail across an ocean to learn the truth."

"It started in the afternoon," L'Musa continued calmly. "With a young apprentice collecting a debt in front of the Customs House. The Royal soldier with the blond ponytail owed a bill for a shave. Instead of paying, the soldier slapped the young apprentice with his rifle. The crowd surrounded the Royals, but it was N'Sekou who struck the blond soldier and scarred the Royal's face. The soldier shot N'Sekou first, in the heart—the other Royal soldiers followed suit. Your nephew is the first man to shed blood for the patriots' rebellion, and yet their revolution cannot bear his black face."

"You let them kill my nephew. They took his blood and discarded his name. N'Sekou's trapped soul compromises Djalia. Kandika will not rest until her son crosses the plane." T'Swuntu held his grip, while L'Musa struggled. "I have to tell my sister her son is a traitor."

He threw his friend to the ground.

"I swore an oath to assist our people in the colonies and gather information that keeps the slave markets from penetrating Wakanda." L'Musa stood, rubbing his throat.

He stared at the moon, his eyes damp and shiny with failure. "I don't know what your griots told you, but my work is incredibly difficult. N'Sekou put our entire continent at risk for what? His Freedom brothers sold his body to the planters at the edge of town. The planters have dark powers, older than these colonies. You should have stayed in Wakanda."

Benji emerged from the clearing, where a bonfire blazed. The wind carried the scent of spiced meat. He fell to his knees before T'Swuntu.

"My king, your food and drink is ready. Tonight, we praise the Panther Goddess." Benji, oblivious to the somber attitudes of his companions, jumped and pointed as they walked back to the clearing. T'Swuntu stared at the flames licking the black sky and weighed the many troubles that arise in a land without kings.

Back in the clearing, the worshippers danced in circles. Filled with rage and grief, T'Swuntu tried to resist the drums and wailing that possessed his legs and spine, but L'Musa danced toward the middle of the circle. He threw his arms and jumped in unison with the rest of the dancers. He challenged Gladys, and she danced rings around L'Musa. Her strength and fluidity amazed T'Swuntu. Though she had never laid eyes on the Hidden Kingdom, she combined her rhythm with Wakandan history like no one the Black Panther had ever seen.

T'Swuntu refused to allow a foreigner to perform the sacred dances better than his own people. He did not care whether she praised the Panther Goddess or not. This Gladys was no Wakandan.

He slid toward her, swinging his arms and legs in intricate patterns that mimicked the birth of Wakanda and the arrival of their sacred Vibranium. Gladys enacted Bast marking Bashenga's face with the blood of the Heart-Shaped Herb.

Did L'Musa show this insolent one all of our steps? the Panther Goddess complained.

Back and forth, they danced for hours. T'Swuntu fought the anger and the pain of losing N'Sekou. He lost himself in sport and music, the Panther Goddess rising inside him.

After they danced, they ate and drank. T'Swuntu wondered how he had fallen for this woman so quickly and completely.

Is that all it takes, one dance? I could have married you off years ago, the Panther Goddess laughed.

T'Swuntu fell asleep beside Gladys and dreamed of his wedding night, with his bride diving between him and a flock of spears flying through their bedroom window.

Something exploded and he woke to the scents of smoke and bloody steel, muskets and screaming. Gladys scrambled under her pallet where she had just slept in angelic radiance and pulled out a musket, a bag of shot, and a hunting knife.

He heard a whistle and dove over Gladys. A cannonball crashed through the cabin, collapsed the quarters over the star-crossed companions. Gladys cursed, crawled through the mess of wood and debris.

"I should have known," she hissed. "Court a king, you get a king's problems."

She patted T'Swuntu's cheek and offered him the knife.

The Black Panther opened a pouch stitched in his pants' waist. One millipede crawled onto T'Swuntu's finger. The black bug had a flat, round shell made of Vibranium. The millipede scuttled over T'Swuntu's knuckles and split into two millipedes. The two millipedes split into four. T'Swuntu closed his eyes. The insects multiplied, spread their Vibranium armor over his skin. As the millipedes covered his face, he stared at Gladys, hoping for shock and reverence.

Instead, she looked aggravated, like she wanted to ask if he was finished. She loaded her musket with buckshot.

"We need to find L'Musa and Benji." Gladys crawled from the wreckage and disappeared through the smoke and burning tobacco leaves and flailing bodies.

T'Swuntu crouched near the ground, assessed his surroundings.

Someone had set fire to the tobacco field. The cove of ragged quarters had been destroyed.

Fire and more smoke leapt from the Dutch mansion. Patriots armed with muskets walked through the smoke, shooting at the flailing laborers. T'Swuntu spied Gladys marching through the confusion toward the Dutch mansion, screaming her brother's name.

A patriot ran toward her shouting obscenities, cursing the half-breed woman and all her kind. She dodged the man's blows, rammed her musket stock into his groin. The man crossed his legs, moaned, and fell on his face.

Another swore his allegiance to the Sons of Freedom and aimed a musket at her temple. As the patriot pulled the trigger, T'Swuntu grabbed the barrel's mouth, caught the buckshot racing from the hot musket. The Vibranium in his hand and arm sang. T'Swuntu loved when Vibranium chimed against his skin.

He snatched the weapon, smashed the man's jaw in one motion.

Voices clamored in the dark forest. Twelve men raced into the clearing and surrounded T'Swuntu.

The Black Panther leapt into the air. He laughed as the buckshot raced past him and scraped his insect armor. He leapt from the trees, pounced on each patriot. T'Swuntu slashed faces with his claws, broke bones with his Vibranium-laced hands and fists. He worked through the Sons of Freedom in a series of swift blurs and razor-sharp shadows.

Gladys and T'Swuntu shot and clawed their way through the dark trees and the clearing until they mounted the porch on the Dutch mansion. Gladys kicked the door and T'Swuntu peppered the room with the tiny darts he called "Panther's Teeth." Stepping over the bodies, they searched the house from the parlor to the master bedroom, and found L'Musa nailed to a wall next to the bed. His arms crossed his chest in Wakanda's ancient greeting, and someone had taken L'Musa's eyes, ears, and tongue.

On the wall next to a cherry oak chifforobe, someone had left a message written in L'Musa's blood:

The Planters are waiting, Your Majesty.
We have your nephew. We waited so long
for your arrival. You will be our greatest exhibition!

T'Swuntu reeled with memories of L'Musa. The Black Panther saw his friend dancing with Gladys and laughing with his sister Kandika as children. He saw every memory that he had of L'Musa in a single moment. He sat on the bed, covered his face with his hands, grieved for his childhood friend.

Gladys stumbled, sat on her rear, and stared at her dead mentor. "Baba." Tears streamed down her face. "You gave me everything. You helped so many." She held her musket against her chest, heaved through clenched jaws.

You must bury him. Give him his rites, the Panther Goddess moaned.

"If the goddess approves, I will retrieve N'Sekou and perform one ceremony."

"Who are you talking to?" Gladys asked.

"I know where to go. I feel my nephew's spirit, but I don't know the terrain." T'Swuntu turned to his new companion. "I need you to guide me. I will protect you."

"Have you heard of the Planters?" Gladys asked. After a moment of uncomfortable silence, she continued. "They own plantations in every state. They trade slaves, crops, boats, weapons. You name it, they sell it."

"These Planters took my nephew. As king, I owe him a proper burial."

"Is that all royal blood buys nowadays? A fancy funeral?" Gladys checked her gun.

This one is impetuous. Pay attention, the Panther Goddess advised.

"I know where we can go until nightfall." After a futile search for her brother, Gladys led T'Swuntu to the kitchen. She lit an oil lamp she found beside a door in the corner and led T'Swuntu down into a pantry. Pots and sacks lined the walls. Stocked shelves held jars of pickled vegetables. On the back wall they found an iron chest. Gladys pointed.

"Can you move this?"

"Who built this house?" T'Swuntu grunted. The metal moved like a solid block of iron. He imagined L'Musa moving the block with ease and cursed under his breath. He looked up and found Gladys admiring his arms. She pointed at a hole in the floor where the metal case had rested.

"This land belonged to my father's family since the first settlers." Gladys stood in front of the hole, faced T'Swuntu. "My father was the master of this house. My mother worked in the kitchen. My father called on her, knowing she could not refuse him. I grew up in the quarters and the kitchen, but I always liked the quarters. When I met L'Musa, I didn't see much. But he changed everything. Through this hole, he's freed so many. Only Baba, Benji, and I have seen this place with our naked eyes. Now, you've seen it too."

UNDER NIGHT'S veil, Gladys led T'Swuntu to a gray mansion with tall windows that turned the face into a glass pool. Sons of Freedom guarded the front yard. T'Swuntu estimated fifty men. The redbeard removed his shirt, as he strolled through the ranks. He carried the same pair of knives he had flashed at Smitty's. Raising the shiny blades, redbeard gathered the cheering militia by a row of cannons lined across the front yard.

They prepared a glorious party, the Panther Goddess and Gladys whispered in unison.

T'Swuntu saw the Panther Goddess in Gladys. He wanted to kneel and offer her his life. Instead, he took her hand. A thin black millipede jumped onto her arm. The bug multiplied until tiny scales of living Vibranium covered her body. Gladys tried to break T'Swuntu's grip, swatted the insects spreading over her chest.

"Hold still. Accept this gift from the Panther Goddess." T'Swuntu watched the insects cover Gladys to Bast's approval. "I know that you need to find your brother, but I want you to add my nephew to your search. You knew him as Crispus."

"N'Sekou." Gladys squeezed T'Swuntu's hand. The Vibranium shells hummed in their palms.

"N'Sekou," the Black Panther affirmed. "My nephew is in that house. I feel his soul burning."

By the origins! What have these monsters done to my child! the Panther Goddess screamed. T'Swuntu covered his ears.

"Your Majesty!" a voice bellowed from the mansion, mocking T'Swuntu. "Commune with us. Let us bask in your splendor, T'Swuntu."

Upon hearing his name, the Black Panther emerged from the dense bush that surrounded the mansion. He saw Smitty waving from a balcony that hung over the front door.

Below the balcony, a hunched behemoth with enormous forearms snarled on the front porch. The beast growled and smiled with sharp teeth that dripped saliva. Benji's face twisted. One eye twitched. He roared when he saw T'Swuntu.

144   Gladys screamed.

"Look what I've done to your brother," Smitty laughed. His voice shook the trees. "A little powder here, a few potions there. You'd be surprised at what we've picked up around the world.

"We thought Benji was boring, so I took it upon myself to spice him up. He can't wait to see his big sister."

Smitty leaned on the balcony's rail. "T'Swuntu, I want to talk about Wakanda. The Black Panther would fetch a king's ransom on the market, or you can guarantee us exclusive trade and exploration of your land."

He wants what from who? the Panther Goddess said, incredulous.

"I am the son of Bast and Bashenga. I am the rising sun of Wakanda," T'Swuntu and the Panther Goddess roared. "You place too much trust in gunpowder and witchcraft. You have taken my family's life. You bargain with my nephew's soul. You want my country, and you want to parade me in chains. You know my kingdom. You know my name. You should know that none of you will leave this place alive."

T'Swuntu felt the Panther Goddess grow. His hands ached for targets.

"Fire!" The redbeard pointed his machetes at T'Swuntu. Patriots stepped from the sides of the house, stepped into the windows, and stood on the roof of the mansion. The patriots pointed their muskets and shot at T'Swuntu. Patches of grass and smoke rose from the yard. The Black Panther laughed through the smoke and gunfire. The Panther Goddess roared through T'Swuntu's voice.

T'Swuntu charged the redbeard. The patriot swung his knives at T'Swuntu, who ducked the blades and slashed at the redbeard's face and chest. T'Swuntu admired the redbeard's speed, but the patriot threw a wide stab at T'Swuntu's throat. The Black Panther struck the exposed jaw with this fist and elbow. Vibranium buzzed across his arm as he stepped over the redbeard and fought his way through the crowd of patriots.

"You're going to make a wonderful specimen," Smitty laughed. "The Planters are going to sell you back to Wakanda one piece at a time."

Benji stepped through a smoke cloud and smacked T'Swuntu with a stone-hard backhand. The Vibranium rang. T'Swuntu tried to stand but Benji howled, smashed the Black Panther with both fists.

"You killed L'Musa?" The millipedes fell from T'Swuntu's head. His breath rattled, and blood dripped from his mouth, but the scent around Benji's body was unmistakable.

"He can't hear you." Smitty walked out of the front door and stood over T'Swuntu. "I used the same spells on your beloved Crispus, and yes, Benji killed your friend. Did you like the message we left for you? That was my special touch. Wakanda forever!"

Smitty imitated the ancient greeting and laughed. "All of Wakanda's neighbors work with us in some capacity, but never Wakanda, never the crowned heart of darkness. We want to change that. Let's see if this convinces you."

Benji grabbed his throat and squeezed. His fingers pressed through the Vibranium insects.

The Panther Goddess filled T'Swuntu's entire body. He closed his eyes, but Bast opened them.

Before he could move, T'Swuntu heard a gunshot. Benji fell and reverted to the round-faced boy that he met by the tobacco field. T'Swuntu knew that Benji had left the physical world, and Gladys had pulled the trigger herself.

T'Swuntu spoke, but it was Bast's voice mixed with his own. *You are a scourge to both the old world and the new. This land will not know peace until your empire falls. Leave my child now.*

T'Swuntu grabbed Smitty, who hurriedly began to bargain.

"Wakanda contains a treasure trove of natural resources. The Planters can show you how to profit from your resources. We can make you the richest king in Africa." Smitty covered his face with his arms.

"What do you think, Gladys? Should I accept his offer?" T'Swuntu dropped Smitty at Gladys's feet.

"Let's see how well he negotiates with Mr. Scratch," she said.

"Wait. I have something better." T'Swuntu produced a small

leaf of the Heart-Shaped Herb. He squeezed Smitty's throat, stuffed the leaf into the slaver's mouth. "Eat."

The Black Panther held on until Smitty swallowed. The barkeep's eyes bulged, and he cried with the suffering of all the souls he had stolen. T'Swuntu nodded. The ancestors had entered Smitty, and they would tear his mind apart.

T'Swuntu was about to walk away as Gladys aimed her musket and fired one shot into Smitty's head.

"He can suffer in hell," she spat.

T'Swuntu retrieved L'Musa's and N'Sekou's bodies and they later buried them with Benji in the secret tunnels under Gladys's pantry. He performed Wakanda's sacred rites and blessed the remains of the three men with a protection prayer.

A day later, after the burial rites and a special trip back into the city, he took Gladys to a private section on the beach where a small ship waited a short distance off. He took Gladys's hand, but she pulled away.

"This is as far as I go, T'Swuntu." She stared him in the eyes. "I have to continue the work I started with L'Musa."

"You have no family here, Gladys. I will be your family, and you will be my queen. There's a whole life waiting for us across these waters, a good life. A land with no king cannot flourish. You can free a few, but the majority must choose freedom on their own."

T'Swuntu held Gladys and kissed her. She leaned into his kiss with so much passion, he thought for a moment he had convinced her.

But she pulled away and gazed at him for a moment before turning and walking away into the darkness. She stopped, gave him one last longing look, and then vanished.

T'Swuntu knew he would never forget that moment. The light shining in her eyes, wishing him the wonderful life he wanted to share with her.

Instead, T'Swuntu sailed away from Boston, watching the spot where Gladys had vanished until he could no longer see the shore.

And then, the Black Panther sat down on the deck and cried.

Cheer up. You have too many wives anyway, the Panther Goddess consoled her king.

He stared at the waves and wondered how he would tell Kandika about her son, his nephew.

"I hope this gift eases your pain, sister." T'Swuntu closed his eyes as the ship sailed home. He reached into his pocket and pulled out a blond ponytail, the blood still dripping into the dark, endless sea.

AND I SHALL
SEE THE SUN RISE

ALEX SIMMONS

HOW CAN *death smell so sweet?*

N'Yami pressed against the bark of a tree hidden by vines, branches, and leaves adorned with the very pink and yellow flowers she'd loved so much as a child.

A glimpse of childhood innocence flickered before her eyes, just as the gleam of the machete yanked her back to the approaching doom. The man crept forward slowly, not out of fear or caution. More to extend his pleasure in stalking her. Mindlessly, he twirled the deadly weapon in his left hand. The large, flat blade hypnotically catching the blazing yellow sunlight, signaling a horrific death.

He was like an animal stalking its prey, and N'Yami felt blessed that he was not some jungle cat that could detect the scent of blood that trickled from the cuts and gashes on her arms and legs.

You should not have jumped from the Jeep, she scolded herself.

But it was my only chance, another part of her argued. *They'd planned to kill me. They'd planned to kill us both.* Her hand caressed the slight rise in her belly.

As the man moved closer to her, N'Yami held her breath and her mind snapped back to barely minutes before.

She was the wife of T'Chaka, King of Wakanda and the most

powerful warrior known, the Black Panther. She was the Queen of

Wakanda as well as its Chief Scientist. It was in this second capacity that she was traveling the road leading to the Vibranium mines.

It was customary to visit the mines once a week. She'd been working on a special project in relative secret, the culmination of years of theory and experimentation on her own. Even the men traveling with her—O'Kolu, second-in-command of the laboratory, and his two assistants, T'Baa and Ngabo—didn't know the true nature of her work.

At those times she was not the wife of T'Chaka, the reigning King and Black Panther. She was not the Queen of Wakanda. Instead, she played the role she enjoyed most: the scientist, the explorer of the unknown. And as such, she felt no need for bodyguards and fineries. Only the company of these three assistants.

She'd known O'Kolu since she first came to work in the labs. He'd welcomed her with open arms, smoothly drew her in, and she had discussed many of her ideas with him without reserve. So the words he uttered today came as more than a surprise. They were biting words of betrayal.

"You are unworthy to carry the seed of our King," O'Kolu threatened. He'd sat beside her in the back of the Jeep. The flat of his machete rested across her belly, and she shuddered at his intentions.

"You are the daughter of dirt farmers," he hissed through gritted teeth. "You are dirt itself, no matter your schooling. In spite of your childish knowledge of science, and experiments, your toys that you thought would be equal to men who have worked there for years."

N'Yami caught his unspoken bias. "Men like you?"

O'Kolu turned the blade on its edge and gently nicked the fabric of her garment. "We will take you to meet the others who have also sworn that no royal child of Wakanda will be born of dirt."

N'Yami blazed with fury. "Your King chose me!"

"He was tricked," O'Kolu snarled. "Blinded by your pretense at discovering new uses for our Vibranium. But no more."

He laughed as he raised the blade—perhaps to threaten, perhaps to kill. But she couldn't take the chance.

In one quick motion, N'Yami roughly knocked his hand away from her. The blade swung to the left, slicing into the driver's neck. As the man screamed, N'Yami whispered a prayer for her child and leaped from the vehicle.

The road was all rocks and gravel. They tore at her flesh hungrily, and the fall down the hill's grassy side was savage flips and drops before she came to a jarring halt amongst bushes. N'Yami had heard the Jeep crash up on the road. But that promised no safety. She managed to rise and stumble, and then to run. She'd kept running... until now.

N'Yami didn't know where O'Kolu might be, but the man holding the machete now was T'Baa, and he was closer. Now he was swinging the blade left, then right, cutting through the very foliage that protected her. Cutting down the very beauty that had once given her peace. Twice more he swung the blade; the tall grass, leaves, and flower petals fell like snowflakes.

He stopped, as if sensing her presence.

N'Yami bit down on her lip, stifling any sound. Holding her breath. *Why did I insist on no guards? The* Dora Milaje *would have dispatched these men before they'd gone six feet.*

T'Baa moved forward again, smiling, raising his blade as if ready to strike. He knew she was near. She knew he was eager to kill her. *Not just me*, she thought. *My child.*

As if to respond, the unborn baby stirred within her—the child of T'Chaka. The one-day King of the Wakandans. But most important, he was her child.

T'Baa was within two feet of her and would certainly have seen her through the leaves if she'd waited for him to turn.

N'Yami rushed out of hiding in a flash. T'Baa swirled to meet her, his blade thrust in her direction, but the young woman grabbed his arm and pulled him toward her. His momentum worked against him. Suddenly he was stumbling forward as she twisted away from him, then quickly back in the opposite direction. The move sent her attacker flipping backward, head over heels, with his spine smashing down across a large stone.

T'Baa screamed as his eyes filled with rage. He might have risen if the Queen hadn't dropped to one knee while driving three sharp blows to his throat. T'Baa gagged once, and then didn't move. The few moves the *Dora Milaje* taught her had served N'Yami well.

Still, she knew T'Baa's scream would bring the others. So N'Yami grabbed up the machete and ran.

They hate me, she thought as she raced through the underbrush. *But why?*

She stumbled as the answer suddenly came to her in memories of only a few years past.

She could see the remnants of her village, and the wounded men and shattered families. The tribal wars within Wakanda had ended. Her people never had a chance. She'd never understood why they needed to fight against the Wakandan ruler and his policies.

Yes, there were wars in other parts of the world. In East Germany, Iraq, the Falklands, in Somalia and Sudan. Even here in Wakanda, where no white man had ever ruled, there was dissension.

"Just speak with the King," she'd implored many of her friends. She'd been a believer in T'Chaka even back then.

But influential voices were so much louder. There had been a faction among her people who wanted *their* voices heard, their demands to be met. They'd insisted this was all "for the people!"

But in the final moments, the leaders of that faction had simply wanted to rule—to set the boundaries by which others would live. But they lacked the power the Wakandan king had; they lacked the technology, and of course they lacked the Vibranium.

And as if that were not enough, they were without the sacred spirit of the Black Panther. That was the true power the rebellion only glimpsed just before they were crushed.

N'Yami's memories shattered as white-hot pain shot through her abdomen. She fell to the ground, curled into a ball, and for what seemed like an eternity didn't move or breathe.

They will find me, she thought. *O'Kolu or perhaps the driver, if he was not badly hurt. They will find me here and slaughter me like a pig.*

No, they won't, her mind insisted. N'Yami placed her hands upon the ground and pushed with all her strength. The pain shot through her again, and tears ran down her face.

"We will not fall here," she declared through gritted teeth. "No, my child, we will stand."

She pushed again. Once, twice, again and again until finally she was on her knees. The pain subsided ever so slightly as she reached out and used a nearby tree to pull herself upright.

I can't keep running, she told herself. *They will overtake me, and this machete is not enough against men with guns.*

The young Queen took a deep breath and caressed her belly. "Do not worry," she said in a soothing voice. "I will fight for you, my child... and for my own life. But my strength is not in combat skills. My strength is in my mind."

She scanned the area as an idea began to form. "My mind... Yes, that is what I will use to save us both."

N'Yami knew their salvation was back in the Jeep, if it had not been destroyed. If she could make it back there, she had a chance... *They* had a chance.

Carefully, N'Yami determined where she was, then changed direction, swinging wide to circle out and back toward the scene of the crash. Once or twice she heard movement to her left or to her right. O'Kolu looking for her—maybe the driver? Or worse... was it some animal stalking its next meal? Panthers were not the only predators in Wakanda.

She needed to push the thought from her mind, so once again memories of the past rose to the forefront. She could see herself as she thought about leaving for the United States to study. Her people didn't understand, especially her parents, making her an outsider even in her own house.

"It is your duty to remain here!" Her mother's fist pounded the wicker table, punctuating every word. "You should marry, have children, to bring new life to our villages and to strengthen us so we may rise again!"

154   At least her mother had argued with her. Her father wouldn't

speak to her at all. He recognized N'Yami had skills and scientific abilities, but he was unbending in his opinion. She was abandoning all of their traditions, and her role as a woman in the tribe, to—as he saw it—waste away in another country. This was unforgivable.

She could still see him standing just outside their home after their last argument.

"My father, you know I love you. And I respect you," she pleaded, tears welling in her eyes. "But you have helped me become who I am. How can you deny me the right to seek out even more, so that I can become even better than I am?"

N'Yami tried to touch him, but he moved away. "I will return," she said. "I will learn all I can and come back, and maybe then…"

Her father wouldn't reply, and so she left that night for a walk carrying his silence and with her mother's harsh words weighing heavily on her heart. While it was her choice, she felt as if her parents, her village, had exiled her from their hearts, never to return.

They died soon after, and her choice to leave was made.

The memories faded briefly as N'Yami stopped by a pool of water. She sipped sparingly, then sought shelter among the bushes nearby. In the cool of the shade, surrounded by more of the natural beauty, the memories returned.

Europe had been her first stop. There her love and interest in earth sciences began to blossom.

Two years later she transferred to a university in New York, to pursue studies in molecular science. True, Wakandan technology was far more advanced—but coming from her background, she'd had no access to that. It was there N'Yami began to test her theories of the effects of vibrations on human physiology.

She reveled in the opportunity to learn, and then to take that knowledge back home to her people. She knew that her remaining family would not take her back. Despite that, she had tried.

Her heart broke when her uncle slammed the door of her ancestral home in her face the second he saw her. Her shouts, pleas, and entreaties brought nothing but silence from her uncle and tear-stained glares from her cousins before she gave up and walked away.

As she lugged her few bags through the small village, she could feel her once-neighbors whispering, judging, laughing at her—the exile who thought she could return home. By the time she made it to the village's sole taxi stand, she knew that she'd have to find a new home. One where her brains mattered more than a daughter's duty.

The Panther Goddess had been good to her, and things worked out better than she could have imagined. N'Yami had been back less than a year when she was called to the science hall of the royal palace. The former Chief Scientist had heard of her work and skills. He'd spoken to T'Chaka, and soon she was offered a position in the main laboratory.

At first she'd been conflicted. Memories of the war were still fresh in her people's minds. But N'Yami still cared, and knew the opportunity would bring stability to her family and allow her to grow her knowledge even more. There were so many exciting things she wanted to do, so many things she wanted to create. All she needed was the space and the resources. And the capital city of Birnin Zana, especially the science center, offered both.

For a while it had been perfect.

She performed her duties well, and slowly the others in the lab began to give her more responsibilities. They also listened to her ideas, and even explored aspects of her curiosity about the powers of vibrations.

Then the impossible happened. King T'Chaka noticed her. He seemed to like her mind and her enthusiasm. The more time they spent together, the more both had realized they were in love.

There had been some reluctance, on her part especially. But T'Chaka's patience and persistence won out over her concerns about being stuck in a palace as a prop, instead of using the mind she had suffered so much to exercise.

And after a proper courtship, they were married. Now their child's arrival in the world was only months away.

Only a few months away… That frightening realization brought her back to the reality of the moment.

She couldn't run forever. Not from these men, and not from the feelings they expressed. O'Kolu had said there were others who felt the way he did. It had just been unspoken. How could she fend them off? Would they come for her and the child?

She needed to face them, eventually. But for now, she needed to get back to the Jeep.

She didn't like the idea of using a blade or a gun. And her hand still hurt from striking T'Baa. She had one hope, and that was back in her satchel in that vehicle. That's where she had to go.

She moved on carefully. The savage pain had not returned, but what did it mean? She was eager to get back to the doctors at the palace so they could check the baby.

Still, N'Yami couldn't push herself as hard as she wanted to.

Her mind flashed back to images of when she used to run with T'Chaka. True, he often waited for her to catch up. And on one occasion, he even carried her on his back as he ran through the jungle with the grace of his namesake.

There was not a single indication that showed she was a burden in any way, as he ran just as smoothly with her as without. Was that what he really felt?

Once again, the child stirred.

"Yes, young king," she whispered to the wind. "You too will have your chance out here. You will become who you are meant to be. This I promise."

She smiled, and it was then she noticed where she was. Straight up the slope about a hundred feet was the road where she had abandoned the Jeep before it crashed.

Quickly but carefully, N'Yami scrambled up the steep embankment, all the time hoping that the Jeep had not been destroyed in fire or an explosion.

Until now, she hadn't wondered whether anyone would find her. She knew that when she didn't show up at the mines, as was her routine, word would spread, and soon T'Chaka would come looking for her. But it could be hours before he knew she was missing, and even more time before he found her.

She knew her husband had unique abilities. She had seen him in combat at least once. But this situation seemed so different, so insurmountable. Or maybe it was just that she had spent most of the past few hours worrying about herself and their unborn child.

Either way, until she knew otherwise, it was up to her to save them both.

That was her prime thought as she reached the road and saw the Jeep a few feet ahead of her. It had veered to the left toward the mountainside and run up onto a boulder. When she reached it, N'Yami saw one of her worries was pointless now.

The driver was still there, slumped in his seat. But she couldn't tell whether it was the blow from the machete or the crash that had killed him.

N'Yami quickly grabbed up her satchel from the backseat area, and was about to reach inside when she heard a noise coming from the trail behind her. Luckily, she dropped to the ground just as a bullet pinged into the vehicle right where she had been standing.

"I missed you that time," O'Kolu shouted. "But I will not miss again!"

N'Yami crawled into the small area where the front of the Jeep was propped up on the boulder. She could hear O'Kolu running up the trail toward her, just as her fingers closed on the object she sought.

O'Kolu came around the side of the vehicle and fired his gun into that crevice, but she was gone.

"Where are you!?" he cried out, quickly jumping up and whirling around.

He circled the Jeep from behind, certain that she was hiding on the other side. But she wasn't. "Where are you?!"

Not a sound. He looked under the Jeep, to see whether she had somehow crawled back in.

"You have nowhere to go." Once again, O'Kolu circled around the back of the Jeep.

"The road is open in both directions," he continued. "You

cannot scurry up the hill on this side. And there's the drop to the valley on the other."

There was no sign of her anywhere. He knew she must be nearby—he could feel it. But where?

O'Kolu quickly twisted left then right. Nothing… except a faint sound, like the buzzing of small flies. He felt someone behind him, whirled, and fired.

Again, no one was there.

"Your tricks will not save you!"

O'Kolu was not a nervous man, but still his skin crawled, as if he was in someone's gunsight. But there was no one to be seen in any direction.

The strange buzzing grew louder. Just as O'Kolu started to turn, he was struck from behind.

O'Kolu dropped to the ground, the gun clattering from his fingers. As he started to crawl toward it, he felt the machete blade press against his throat.

"You will not use that," he sneered. "You do not have the…" O'Kolu felt a sting as the blade of the machete nicked the skin just over the jugular vein.

"You threatened my child. You have no idea what I will do. Turn."

O'Kolu twisted his head slightly and looked up. He saw the blade floating next to his throat. A second later, N'Yami shimmered into existence. The blade never moved.

"How?"

"One of my… toys," N'Yami replied. "It's a prototype for a cloaking device, based on my *childish* experiments. Turns out if you can vibrate the human body at the right frequency, and have a special metal to absorb those vibrations long enough to keep a person from dying, they can simply vanish for a short time.

"Remember that thing we were going to the Great Mound for? If you'd been patient, you would have seen your Queen demonstrate it later today."

O'Kolu grimaced and spat on the ground defiantly. "You will never be…"

The blade pressed in, and O'Kolu froze.

"I may not take your life," N'Yami said calmly. "But I cannot speak for him."

High above them, two shimmering hovercrafts descended. But the Black Panther dropped to the ground before them, claws extended as he moved toward O'Kolu.

HOURS LATER, after receiving medical care, a still fuming N'Yami sat with King T'Chaka in the Great Conference Hall. Several members of the High Council sat opposite them.

"From what the Queen has told us, there are more of these dissidents here in the city," one of the advisors said as he referred to the notes on his tablet.

N'Yami nodded in agreement. "That's what they said."

"Then hunt them down, every last one of them," T'Chaka ordered. "And be creative about their punishment. I don't care, just be sure their deaths, for daring to endanger not only their Queen but their future King, are as excruciating as we can make them."

N'Yami reached over and touched her husband's hand. "My King, perhaps you could find them and bring them here before me."

She could feel T'Chaka's questioning look. Before now, she had cared little about Wakandan security, and rarely spoke in the council meetings if they weren't talking about the country's scientific and technological achievements. This incident, she thought, had changed all that.

"You wish to be the one to give the order for punishment?" T'Chaka asked hesitantly.

N'Yami stared out across the council room, a determined expression on her face. She could feel the room's silence as they waited for her word.

This, she thought suddenly, *is what it's truly like to be a queen.*

N'Yami cleared her throat and spoke without emotion.

"I wish to have them say to my face that I am not fit to be their

Queen." She felt the baby move. "I wish to have them say I'm unfit to give birth to our child."

"And then?" T'Chaka asked.

"And then," N'Yami replied, "I will laugh as you sentence them to exile."

T'Chaka rubbed his head and looked at his justice minister, who shrugged as if to say, "If that's what the Queen wants…"

"Exile has not been a traditional Wakandan punishment, my dear," the King replied. "The exiles would bring our enemies directly to the Golden City's gates. A sentence of exile is a sentence of death. That is not our way. "

Her voice was quiet, but firm. "Then perhaps it needs to change."

N'Yami turned to him. "I remember your words, my King, during the tribal wars against my people. No one is to question the rule of Wakanda. Ever."

The King rose from the table. "No matter what, our people understand that. Even those who challenge the throne know that in their hearts, the line of Bashenga are the rightful rulers of this land," he explained. "For millennia, we've had our own ways, our own beliefs, our own land. We own all of what we are.

"And no matter what, anyone who is a part of Wakanda is a Wakandan."

N'Yami faced him. "Not all of the people believe that," she spit at him, her anger at the day's events boiling over. "To some, because I am not of the Golden City, of a bloodline of court nobility, I am not seen as truly Wakandan. I am the outsider, the exile. Let them see what true exile really is, and live to know at least a piece of my pain."

"And if they speak of the Hidden Kingdom?" T'Chaka questioned.

"Wakandan tradition then holds true, my King," she whispered.

T'Chaka turned to face a balcony that looked out at the beautiful city before him. With his hands clasped behind his back, he stood proudly, pondering N'Yami's words for a moment, and then turned back to face her before gathering his wife in his arms.

"As usual, my Queen, your words prove you are the most intelligent person in my kingdom," he proclaimed. "In order to be the strength that we are, the unity, the very soul of this land, we must know *who* we are. And we must protect that at all cost."

"So then we silence anyone who tries to question our ways?" she asked.

"We remove anyone who tries to conquer us, who tries to make us what they want us to be."

"And if our own people refuse... question if your rules are right for them?"

"They are free to speak their minds, and then to leave," T'Chaka replied. "If they choose to do us harm, then they will pay the price. There is no other way."

"There could be." N'Yami rose and approached her husband.

"Should we leave, Your Highnesses?" one of the advisors asked.

T'Chaka shook his head, then turned back to N'Yami. "What do you mean?"

"I've been to the outer world," she replied. "There are wars everywhere. And someone always says the very same words you have. They use that as a justification for war and conquest. How is Wakanda different?"

"Because we do not use our powers, our science, to conquer others. But we fight to the death to protect what we have. That is the difference. Do you understand?"

"I do," N'Yami replied. "But..."

The King took her hand. "After what they did to you, and to our child... why do you insist they live?"

N'Yami took a deep breath, allowing her hatred of the day and its perpetrators to sink down into the pit of her soul. They would not change her, just as she refused to let her own personal exile change who she really was.

"Because I do not wish to have anyone else die in the name of our unborn child. Wakanda is about life and the promise of a magnificent future—not an inevitable death."

162   The King smiled, then turned to his advisors. "Find the others

and bring them to me... to *us*. In the name of our son to be, T'Challa, I... *we*, will decide."

N'Yami smiled as she gently placed T'Chaka's hand so he could feel his son *agree*.

FAITH

JESSE J. HOLLAND

WEDDINGS ARE *always horrible.*

The receptions, however, T'Challa thought to himself, now those made it all worth it.

Thumping music reverberated through the king's body as he sat back on his onyx throne and watched the cheering crowd throw themselves this way and that, as a scantily clad chanteuse sang what he had been assured was appropriately popular music. A wave of human-generated heat rolled across him carrying the scent of expensive perfume, rich food, alcohol, and the wonderful aroma of living, breathing, joyous human beings.

The festivities were taking place outside the Ifọkanbalẹ Tẹmpili, one of Wakanda's holiest sites. To each side his two *Dora Milaje* bodyguards, Okoye and Arnari, wearing strapless black formal dresses that did nothing to disguise their lethalness, scanned the writhing mass for trouble. Though if the Chosen One of Bast—the Panther God—couldn't be confident in his safety here, T'Challa thought, then he couldn't expect to be safe anywhere.

The whirling white dress of the newly married Dominique Namvadi was clearly visible as she whipped her long dark locks back and forth, dancing frenetically around her stiff uniformed husband, Obiejen Namvadi. Even after all these years, T'Challa thought with amusement, Obie still danced as if his pants were starched with iron.

Years ago, back at a boarding school dance, Obie had ignored the glares of his bodyguards, walked up, and asked one of them if they'd like to dance. T'Challa covered his smile with a hand and watched as the flustered woman—used to being ignored by the prince's friends and schoolmates—stammered a "n-no" before Obie looked over at the other one and asked her if *she* was interested.

This time he got a smile and a "no, thank you."

T'Challa decided anyone brave enough to approach his *Dora Milaje* warriors was someone worth knowing, so he and Obie became fast friends, then confidantes. Once he was crowned king, T'Challa promoted the bold Obie to one of his country's most important positions—that of American ambassador—and sent him to Washington, D.C.

Once there, it was only a matter of time before Obie walked up to *another* impressive woman, Howard University pre-med student Dominique Rutherford, and asked her for her telephone number. As often is the case between two people madly in love, things happened quickly, and Obie asked his friend, chieftain, and high priest if he would do them the honor of marrying them on Wakandan soil.

Of course, T'Challa agreed.

In all honesty, it wasn't often that he had the opportunity to perform formal duties as the High Priest of the Panther Clan, and when Obie asked if he could use the main temple for his marriage to the beautiful Dominique, T'Challa couldn't think of a single reason to deny his friend. If that meant he had to sit on an onyx throne wearing his uncomfortable black-beaded cossack for an evening, listening to an admittedly pleasing band and watching Dominique's American family attempt the latest Wakandan dances, well, that was the price of friendship.

After all, he thought, *kings don't dance.*

Just about everyone else did, however, and the luxurious tented reception hall they'd erected on the temple grounds was filled shoulder to shoulder with the combined families of the bride and the groom, many of them dancing around the oblivious newlyweds, who only had eyes for each other.

Everyone seemed to be having a good time, T'Challa noted, except for the bride's father. He sat alone at his table, arms crossed, glaring at his daughter.

T'Challa sighed inaudibly.

Weddings. It was always something.

The Rev. Dr. Wilberforce Rutherford of the state of Mississippi refused to attend his only daughter's wedding, despite the tears she'd shed standing on the Ifọkanbalẹ Tẹmpili's black marble steps. As T'Challa dressed in his priestly raiment in his private upstairs chambers, his hypersensitive ears picked up Dom's pleas, attempting to persuade her rotund father that the service would be interfaith. She assured him that the blessing of the Panther Clan's high priest wouldn't condemn her—and his grandchildren—to Hell.

Rev. Rutherford remained resolute, instead choosing to sit alone in the reception tent until after the ceremony had been completed. Even during the ceremony, however, T'Challa could hear the gray-bearded man's low, rolling growl condemning "paganism" and "heathen polytheism." He also saw the worry it caused the bride as he blessed their union in Bast's name.

Even now, with all of the frivolity around him, Rutherford still sat alone and angry, glaring at his own family and their new in-laws for having the temerity to enjoy the Wakandan hospitality, and to ignore his one-man boycott of what should have been the happiest day of his daughter's life. His hostility erected an invisible barricade around him.

T'Challa snorted, a very unkinglike sound, and considered the irony. The only two men with a direct connection to heaven were the only two who weren't enjoying the blessed union of these wonderful people.

Well, T'Challa decided as he pushed himself up and off his throne, *it is time for this to end.*

HIS PRIVATE Ifọkanbalẹ Tẹmpili quarters weren't as lavish as his
palace throne room. These suites were lined with black marble

and Ovangkol wood, and around the walls T'Challa himself had placed icons of Bast's rule—her Ankh of Eternal Life on one side and her Papyrus Wand on the other.

From below, the sounds of the celebration could still be heard.

There were shelves of ancient Wakandan and Egyptian carvings and friezes, some thousands of years old, with various representations of Bast from her she-lion manifestation to miniature cat dolls and Panther icons carved by some of his ancestors.

In the center of the main wall, instead of a throne, there stood a life-sized blue-black sandstone carving of Bast in her human form, standing in front of an Egyptian column, cat ears perked forward on top of her long, curled braids. Her elegant floor-length shift cascaded down to her feet, where a massive ebony panther bared his teeth. A close examination of the stone betrayed its Wakandan heritage, with the glittering veins of Vibranium streaking through the dark rock, easily seen by those brave enough to venture close.

Surrounding the shrine were multicolored silk pillows for when T'Challa wished to kneel directly before his god, and humble himself in front of her.

To the side of this statue, T'Challa kept his personal desk. The computer there was connected to the palace mainframe. A few personal mementos sat next to it—signed photos from Nelson Mandela, John Lewis, and others, knick-knacks picked up in Atlantis or gifted to him by his friends in the Baxter Building. Holos of his family and his father.

Whereas his throne room was meant to intimidate and impress, this room had a greater purpose. It was here that the king came when he wanted to be closer with his guiding spirit, or if he needed to muster the courage for an unpleasant task like the one that lay ahead of him today. This suite was as personal a space as T'Challa could afford, and few people were allowed inside. Its only nods to visitors were a black couch and a loveseat banished to a far corner of the room.

There was a knock at the door, and he opened it.

"Dr. Rutherford," he said, beckoning for his visitor to enter.

The heavy-set reverend hesitated at the double doorway, standing with his *Dora Milaje* escorts and gaping at the opulent room. T'Challa nodded to the *Dora Milaje*, who respectfully returned his acknowledgement before departing, closing the doors quietly behind. The king poured two glasses of his personal bottled water.

"Please, please, come join me." T'Challa waved the reverend toward the sofa as he placed the glasses on a tray and walked across the room. The reverend followed hesitantly, eyes darting around the artifacts before alighting on the statue. Tugging slightly at his clerical collar and straining to rebutton his black suit coat, Rutherford waddled his way toward the couch before falling backwards to a seated position on the cushions.

Breathing heavily, he pulled a handkerchief from an interior pocket and swiped at droplets of sweat beading on his head, then gulped down the proffered glass of cold water. T'Challa watched silently until the older man composed himself. As if to avoid losing some imagined advantage, Rutherford sat silently as well, his labored breathing sounding like snoring.

Finally, T'Challa broke the uncomfortable silence, picking what seemed to be a safe topic.

"Your daughter looked stunning at the ceremony," he offered quietly. Rutherford harrumphed loudly, and looked T'Challa straight in the eye.

"Though thou clothest thyself with crimson, though thou deckest thee with ornaments of gold, though thou rentest thy face with painting, in vain shalt thou make thyself fair; thy lovers will despise thee, they will seek thy life," he intoned.

T'Challa smiled at the older man.

"Jerimiah, Chapter 4, verse 20, King James version. I personally prefer First John, Chapter 4. 'Beloved, let us love one another, for love is from God, and whoever loves has been born of God and knows God. Anyone who does not love does not know God, because God is love.'"

Rutherford's eyes widened, and then narrowed, pointing his finger angrily before remembering himself.

"Do not deride me by misappropriating our Lord's word, sir." He waved his hand toward the doorway, through which they could hear the wedding music playing below. "The Good Book is clear. 'If your daughter entices you secretly, saying, "Let us go and serve other gods," which neither you nor your fathers have known, some of the gods of the peoples who are around you, you shall not yield to her or listen to her, nor shall your eye pity her, nor shall you spare her, nor shall you conceal her or...'"

Rutherford stopped, his words trailing off.

"'You shall kill her.'" T'Challa sipped from his glass calmly. "That's how the verse ends. 'You shall kill her.'"

Looking Rutherford in the eye, he set his glass down on the rug. "Is that why you came to Wakanda? To stop your daughter? Dom told me she had to entice you here with the promise of a trip to Israel, but surely she didn't know what you were planning?'

Rutherford's eyes widened and he began squirming in his seat. "My daughter's soul must be saved. Or else she will be lost."

"Saved? From what?" T'Challa stood up and began pacing back and forth in front of the reverend.

"From that!" Rutherford pointed an accusatory finger at T'Challa's Bast shrine. "That, that chicanerous paganism you and your African brethren are peddling to her, in the face of the one true God!"

T'Challa froze.

Suddenly he began to laugh.

"Chicanerous? By Bast, I remember loving the cadence and intonation of the American sermonic tradition when I was in the States." T'Challa got control of himself, and continued. "Anyway, you think Bast is false?"

"I will not be mocked by some pagan king, sir." As he grew angrier, Rutherford's eyes bulged and he hoisted himself off the deep-cushioned couch with a huff, popping the lone remaining button on his suit coat. "I am not some simple-minded country jackleg to be impressed by mammon. I have a flock to tend to, and no time to debate zoolatry with the likes of you."

"Peace, Reverend." T'Challa held up his hand in an attempt to placate the red-eyed man, and attempted to control his breathing. "No insult was meant to the father of the bride, particularly on this day. I was simply hoping to mend a rift between you and your daughter, as she was going to become one of my subjects. I truly do admire Dominique, and only wish for her happiness with my friend Obie."

"If you wish for her happiness," Rutherford huffed, "then send her back home with me."

"That I cannot do." T'Challa walked over to a small bar and poured himself another water. "It amazes me that a world that accepts gods like Thor and Hercules would doubt the existence of Bast."

Rutherford snorted again. "Those so-called super heroes are just using impressive-sounding names, like Mr. Dynamite and the Midnight Question or any of those other wrestlers on television. They're not actual gods, and no one worships them."

"Hercules would be amused at hearing that." T'Challa smiled to himself. "Besides which, my god is as real to me as your god is to you. Just as your god directs you and moves in mysterious ways, Bast does as much for me, and just like your god has an only begotten child, so does mine."

Rutherford crossed his arms and looked angrily at his host. "I've heard that line before, back at home, mortal men claiming divinity and leading their flock straight into Hell. Somehow, it doesn't surprise me that you're claiming to be a divine being, the son of God."

"Me, a child of Bast?" T'Challa chuckled aloud. "I can't claim that honor—but I've met her. In doing so, I found myself forced to face the future, and question my very faith in the most... direct way you can imagine."

T'CHALLA SAT in his throne room, being briefed by his security council, when the door opened.

His faithful war chief, W'Kabi, entered the room unusually

late and sat uncomfortably and silently against one wall. Unlike T'Challa, who was wearing a three-button silk business suit, *sans* tie, W'Kabi was in full traditional Wakandan garb: a brown loincloth with a loose green sash around his neck and torso. His customary red headdress held his long graying locks out of his frowning face.

Normally, the hot-tempered bear of a man would be pounding on the table at some imagined slight to Wakandan honor, T'Challa thought with a frown, instead of sitting silently with a grim look on his face. Though ill-tempered, W'Kabi was no alarmist, and anything that so distracted the foremost warrior on his council was worth attending to immediately.

The room had grown silent as T'Challa raised his hand. T'Challa stood and walked around the table to stand next to the brooding man.

"W'Kabi, speak your mind." T'Challa placed his hand on the man's muscular shoulder and gave it a slight squeeze.

"I think…" the man whispered, his voice hoarse. "We should talk about this in private, Your Highness."

T'Challa looked into the older man's eyes and saw despair, an expression that chilled him to the bone. He quickly dismissed the rest of the men and women, and then sat down at the table next to W'Kabi. The last time he had seen such pain in the man had been when the *Dora Milaje* brought the body of T'Challa's father into the palace, after his assassination at the hands of the criminal Klaw.

W'Kabi had been a rock that day, but T'Challa—during a late-night sustenance run—had found the older man slumped on one of the palace walls with tears streaming down his face.

Later that week, T'Challa had started his Panther training in earnest. W'Kabi's family long had been entrusted with preparing Wakandan kings, queens, princes, and princesses to ascend to the position of the Black Panther. There was no one who knew more of T'Challa's secrets, or had earned more of his trust.

That one instance had been the only time he had seen W'Kabi

cry. Now, however, when he looked in W'Kabi's face, it seemed as if tears would begin at any moment. He lifted a folder and placed it on the table in front of him. It held grainy photographs, as if taken from a long distance away.

"Speak your mind, old man."

W'Kabi sniffed, running his hand across his nose. He pulled out the top photo and floated it across the table.

"How long have you known, T'Challa?" W'Kabi emphasized the king's name, instead of his normal "Your Highness." T'Challa quirked his eyes at the war chief's unexpected familiarity.

"Known what, W'Kabi?" T'Challa picked up the blurry photograph and peered at the shadowy image of a cat-like woman, bounding across a city's skyline.

"That Bastet's daughter had taken human form." W'Kabi spat the words wearily, using Bast's formal title. "That our god's child was present on Earth, and lost without her kingdom and people."

"I don't understand," T'Challa said. "What makes you think that I knew about this, or even if I did, that this is Bastet's daughter, not a mutant, an Inhuman, or enhanced human being?"

"The goddess spoke to me, T'Challa," W'Kabi's eyes reflected betrayal. "She said my line would be entrusted to train her children, as well as her avatars, and that her children would rule Wakanda." He paused, then continued, his voice steadier. "Needless to say, the children of Bashenga—say, the current ruling family—would not want this known. So I say again, why haven't you brought her home, T'Challa?"

T'Challa put his hand on top of W'Kabi's, and squeezed.

His friend and mentor flinched.

"You know me better than that, W'Kabi," T'Challa said. "Any follower of Bast is welcome in the Golden City, and any child of hers truly belongs here in Wakanda, where she can be nurtured, loved, and revered in the way the goddess would approve."

T'Challa frowned. "The thing is, Bast has not… informed me of any child of hers—here in Wakanda, in Africa, or anywhere around the world. This, truly, is news to me."

174

Taking a deep breath, T'Challa leaned back in his chair.

"I can't speak to how she manifests to others, but with me Bast comes as she pleases, speaks when she wants, and says only what she wants to. I can spend a month on my knees, and she won't manifest. I can be in the middle of a speech at the United Nations, and she'll appear as a giant panther curled up on the desk of the Latverian ambassador, pantomiming as if she is eating his head. I can be at the Great Mound, speaking to the miners, and she'll appear as a child in the crowd.

"She's the quintessential cat and the quintessential woman," he continued, "all wrapped up in one. It doesn't surprise me that she's withholding information. I just can't figure out why."

Recognition dawned on W'Kabi's face.

"She knew if she told me, I'd tell you."

T'Challa nodded. "The question becomes, why was it import- ant for me to find out this way?"

"In the end, it does not matter, my king." W'Kabi stood. "Bastet's child must be brought home."

T'Challa stood, as well. "In that, my old friend, we agree." As he prepared to leave, however, he couldn't help but wonder if the woman in the picture heralded a much greater event than either of them dared say.

A FEW hours later, the king was navigating his way through a thunderstorm in his private Quinjet, heading toward the ancient ruins of Tell-Basta, Egypt. He had left behind his loyal *Dora Milaje* bodyguards, with the promise to call them at any sign of trouble.

Dark thunderclouds, ominous gusts, and sheets of rain that obscured the sight were somehow appropriate, T'Challa thought to himself as he skirted the coastline of Sudan. He navigated his way through the storm to land the vehicle at the edge of an oasis several miles outside of Tell-Basta.

Wearing boots, khakis, and a ridiculously unnecessary sun-resistant shirt, he placed a change of clothes and his panther habit into a simple knapsack, then activated the camouflage technology in his ship. Then he began walking toward the ruins.

Two steps in, the world faded away.

○———————○

T'CHALLA FOUND himself lying on the ground with his head resting on a short incline, in a field of brown grasses. In a distant haze he could just make out a lush jungle.

A feminine hand stroked his hair. He looked up and into Bast's eyes, which were filled with more joy and suffering than could be granted in a million lifetimes. Wearing a brown woolen shift, she appeared before him as a beautiful blue-black woman with piercing gray eyes and long braided white hair. T'Challa knew this was just one of her many forms, but it was the one he always found the most distracting—something he thought she was doing purposefully.

"Perhaps I am, my avatar," she purred, her voice silky smooth and melodic as she maneuvered his head into her lap. T'Challa frowned, never having liked Bast's ability to read his thoughts. She laughed again, and his displeasure was forgotten.

"You couldn't have told me first?" He glared up at her, an eyebrow quirked. "Before you told W'Kabi?"

"Why?" She smiled down on him. "Do you plan for your line to take over from his, and train my children on how to rule? Or is this jealousy, my avatar? Do you feel a little less special?"

T'Challa pushed himself up and onto his knees, where he could look directly into his god's cat-like eyes.

"My family has bled for you. My family has killed for you. My family has *been* killed for you, and now I find that we were just... what? Placeholders? Antecedents, mere heralds for your true children? What am I supposed to do with that?"

"What you must."

T'Challa sighed. "I know you are the god, and I am the mortal, but I would appreciate a little less inscrutability. What do you want me to do? Find your child? Fight your child? *Protect* your child?"

176   She smiled again, showing some very panther-like fangs.

"What do you think you should do?"

T'Challa stared in frustration. She wasn't going to come straight out and tell him what to do, and in that this situation was no different. He'd have to make his own decision, trusting his judgment and his knowledge of Bast to make the right call. Even if it meant stepping down and allowing his people to be led by her true child, instead of just her earthly avatar, the Black Panther.

"Hmmm," she purred, her form slowly shifting into that of a huge blue-black cat with glistening white fangs and a twitching pink nose. Her tail switched back and forth as she got into T'Challa's face, her hot breath tickling his nose. "You'd do that, instead of fighting for the right to represent me?" She pulled back, but held his gaze. "Interesting."

"You're toying with me."

"I am not." The panther began purring and coiled its way around the kneeling T'Challa. "I am trying to determine what's truly in your heart... and mine, o king. Of all my avatars, you are less steeped in the more... shall we say, 'mystical' parts of our relationship, than your predecessors—perhaps because of the early death of your father. But your 'superheroics' have spread my name far and wide, increasing my power. Yet how much more so would acts of heroism by the actual fruit of my loins?"

She looked off toward the sun, setting over the jungle.

"How many more people talk of Asgard and Odin because of Thor and Loki? Of Olympus because of Hercules and Ares? Yet they no longer have earthbound cultures dedicated to their glory, led by an unbroken line of mortal avatars—do they?" The panther yawned, its fangs clearly visible. "And yes, in answer to your unspoken question, even I don't know what I want. Not yet. We'll just have to wait and see, won't we?"

T'Challa began to speak.

"Yes, yes," Bast said, stopping him. "I've arranged for the two of you to meet in my city to 'hash this out,' as the humans would say." T'Challa quirked his eyebrow, causing the panther to smile. "You'll see."

She stalked seductively toward the jungle.

T'Challa watched the huge cat slowly fade into the darkness. Just as she slipped from sight, Bast turned around and looked at him, her gray eyes flashing in the darkness.

"Her name is Nefertiti, no matter *what* she prefers."

Then there was blackness.

T'CHALLA OPENED his eyes. It was late evening again, and he was in the courtyard of an ancient, open-air, sandstone temple, surrounded by towering columns covered with imagery of Bast in her different incarnations. The ruined walls had crumbled on one side, huge stone slabs turned on their sides, obscuring the crumbling stadium-style seating in the setting sun.

At the center of the football-sized field, directly opposite T'Challa, sat a girl, her arms curled around her legs. She was quietly rocking back and forth. At first glance he thought she was crying, her features hidden from him by her childlike posture. Slender but with powerful legs, she was dressed in a simple dual-strapped white sheath dress that contrasted with her dark-sable skin. Long, straight black hair cascaded around her shoulders. Despite her youthful appearance, she appeared tall, fit, and svelte, as if she ran down antelopes on a regular basis.

The one thing she doesn't look like, T'Challa thought, *is a god.* Could this be the one with whom Bast planned to replace his entire lineage? The very thought yielded a variety of conflicting emotions, which he tamped down.

Slowly he walked toward her, noticing that he was wearing his Panther habit. Bast's doing. Stopping within arm's length of the young woman, T'Challa took a deep breath, inhaling the rich, earthy scent she exuded and that his mind immediately connected with Bast on the Ancestral Plains, yet somehow lighter and more floral.

"Nefertiti?"

The girl ignored him, continuing to rock back and forth. A

low moan escaped from her throat, and sweat beaded on her brow.

T'Challa hesitated, his next move unclear. Was this how he looked when he was communing with Bast? He had never thought how his *Dora Milaje* or others might see him during the times he conversed with his god. Did he moan and rock like this?

He thought not.

If she was Bast's daughter, would it be the height of disrespect to touch the earthly manifestation of his god, especially while she was in this state? Bast wanted him here, that much was clear, but what were the protocols? Was there a ritual? Was this what Bast meant by reminding him that he had missed out on parts of his religious training because of his father's untimely death?

Nothing ventured, nothing gained.

T'Challa slowly lowered himself in front of her on one knee and gently placed his hand on her back.

"Nefertiti?" he whispered.

Without warning, the woman thrust her head straight up and into T'Challa's chin. He bit his tongue, and sparks of pain flooded his vision as she knocked him backward into the dirt onto his backside and away from her. Scrambling to recover, T'Challa licked the blood away from his mouth, and he felt some of it on the inside of his mask. As he did so, the woman came alive, bounding to her full height. She was as tall as he was, and she tensed as she maneuvered into a battle-ready stance.

"Faked ya out, didn't I?" she said. "And by the way, it's Neffie," she added, bouncing back and forth like a boxer.

T'Challa shook his head to clear it. It had been a while since someone, *anyone*, had gotten close enough to actually land a blow that hard. Faking a grace he did not feel, he stood as smoothly as he could manage and examined his opponent.

So much for the diplomatic approach...

She looked no older than eighteen, just in the first blush of her adulthood. Her weaving hands and fighting stance promised pain, but he could detect in her muscle patterns an unfamiliarity with the movements. It was a recognition years of studying body language with W'Kabi had taught him to detect.

T'Challa crossed his arms, looking down at her.

"Bastet told me it was Nefertiti."

She grinned, the picture of youthful confidence, and circled him.

"Mother knows best, huh?"

"When your mother is your god, yes, I presume she would know best," T'Challa replied, slowly turning in a circle to follow Nefertiti's movements.

Nefertiti frowned. "My mother is Angela DeLaroux of Cairo, Egypt, by way of New Orleans. Bast may be my creator and my god, but where was she when we were flooded out of the Ninth Ward during Katrina, and my mother had to send us to her parents in Egypt? Where was she when lung cancer took my father?

"Now that… things have happened," Nefertiti continued, "she wants me to be her daughter and rule her kingdom?" She shrugged. "She makes a convincing argument, and there are worse things than being an earthbound god, but I know who I am and where I come from, and I know what I have to do now." Her lips curled up into a snarl as she looked intently at the Black Panther.

"The only question is, are you in my way," she said, "or just a bump in the road on my way to my rightful position?"

She tensed, preparing to launch herself at him, and T'Challa waggled his finger at her as he set his back foot and readjusted his weight for battle.

"Uh-uh, young lady," he said. "You caught me by surprise the first time, but if you attack me again I will defend myself. Demigod or not, I will put you on *your* back this time."

Neffie grinned again.

"Yeah, Mom told me all about your 'Heart-Shaped Herbs' and the powers they give you," she snorted. "Don't you find it strange that a god who visits you regularly never shares any of her actual power? That you have to rely on chemistry and horticulture to do what she tells you to do?"

Suddenly her demeanor became darker, more menacing.

180

"Bastet is the Lady of Dread and the Lady of Slaughter, the feline defender of the innocent, the avenger of the wronged, and the goddess of justice," Nefertiti said. "She doesn't need some earthly plant to manifest her powers." She took a couple of steps back, and narrowed her eyes.

Patches of gray-black fur began to appear on her arms and legs, and her eyes changed from gray to a sickly yellow. She began making small jerking movements, and crouched down as her dress tore and fell to the ground, replaced by silky black fur sprouting all over her body.

A painful moan escaped her lips. With a grinding sound loud in the Panther's enhanced hearing, her bones began to twist and elongate, hissing and popping as muscles ripped away and reattached, and joints popped and shifted.

Her face transformed, a ridged brow protruding from her forehead as it slowly covered itself in glossy fur and her ears were lengthened and sharpened. Her jaw stretched and her nose shrank and turned pink, then new glistening fangs protruded from her mouth. At the end of each limb, nails became long, jagged claws, and once-taut muscles became bulged and sinewy. Behind her, a massive black tail sprouted. It began to whip back and forth in anticipation.

The transformed Nefertiti stood on two legs and peered at T'Challa with hooded eyes. A full-fledged human panther, she whipped her wild crown of hair behind her and attempted a smile, but the fangs made it look more like a snarl than a greeting.

"This is what a true child of Bastet would look like, o mighty king." Nefertiti's voice was raspy with pain yet still tinged with the earlier arrogance. "This is how I know who I am. When the transformation first occurred, Bastet came to me in a vision and explained my heritage and powers. She told me about her hidden kingdom, where I would be revered as a god and treated as a queen.

"She said her avatars had long prepared a place for her children," the young goddess continued. "Is this not true?"

T'Challa raised his hands. He had to de-escalate this, and quickly. The very fate of his kingdom might depend on it.

"Before today, I hadn't heard anything about this 'prophecy,'" he said, maintaining his calm. "The proud line of Bashenga has ruled Wakanda for millennia in Bastet's name, and the Black Panther is known the world around as her avatar and champion." He lowered his hands. "I, T'Challa, am her current champion, and it has been my honor to bring glory to Bast's name as Wakanda has stepped into the forefront of global affairs.

"The world is very delicate right now," he continued, "and a change in the ruling structure of our country may not be in the best interests of her people." He watched her carefully, not making any sudden moves. "Perhaps if we consulted—"

"Enough," Nefertiti growled softly, interrupting T'Challa's litany. "It sounds to me like you're defying your god's wishes, T'Challa." She was mocking him.

T'Challa was taken aback.

"My god has not made her wishes clear," T'Challa said, his own voice lowering into a dangerous whisper. "Whatever you say, I must do what I think is best for my people, and right now I don't think an immature deity on the throne of Wakanda is the best idea."

"Immature?" Nefertiti stalked forward, a rumbling growl underneath her voice. With one of her jagged claws, she poked T'Challa in the chest. Still he stood resolute.

"You are the immature one, *Black Panther*," she snarled. "It was you and your forefathers who assumed that Wakanda was yours. *Bast never said that.* You assumed. It was you, your father, and your grandfathers who assumed that you enjoyed Bast's favor, and that your god would always smile on your family. It was you, not Bast, who *came up with* the Heart-Shaped Herb and genetically engineered your line to be able to exploit it. And like any good parent, she let you be all that you could be.

"But guess what?" she said. "Your time's up. The Black Panther is obsolete, maxed out. You know it, and I think it's bothering you." Nefertiti gestured down toward her body. "The physical manifestation of Bast's approval is staring you right in the face, and I think you're a little jealous—aren't you, T'Challa?"

She narrowed her eyes and slowly made a show of extending the claws on her hands and feet.

"As my friends back home would say, you just found out that you're John the Baptist, not Jesus Christ, and you're having some feelings about that—but it doesn't change the fact that Wakanda belongs to Bast, and that it's *my* birthright, not yours.

"My mother—my *true* mother—left her entire pantheon here in Egypt to favor your kingdom, T'Challa. She was already worshipped here in Bubastis." Nefertiti gestured to the temple around her. "She didn't need another kingdom, but she had pity on your Bashenga; when he prayed to her, she led him to a promised land of milk, honey, and power. Without Bast, that history you're so proud of never would have existed in the first place."

She turned to him again, and her eyes were full of malice. "Now that she asks for you to place her true descendant on the throne, you want to, what... *consult*?" She growled again.

T'Challa just stared at her, standing still as a rock.

"Bast has told me no such thing," he replied, "but perhaps you can convince me that you're worthy."

"Convince... *you*?"

Nefertiti cried out and lunged toward T'Challa, claws and teeth flashing. He danced out of the way of her unschooled and emotional charge, watching as Nefertiti slid across the stone courtyard, obsidian claws sparking and grabbing at the dusty stones as she tried to halt her momentum. Recovering quickly, she crouched down like a true panther and bounded back across the open space, fangs flashing in the light.

At the last second, T'Challa leaped high in the air, feeling Nefertiti's claws rake the outside of his armor as she just barely miscalculated his jump. Flipping over the charging demigod, T'Challa landed perfectly and quickly hammered his fists down on the back of her head, causing her to yowl in pain.

Nefertiti rolled away from her assailant, and he leapt clear.

She shook her head, and then began to stalk around him in a circle, tail lashing. T'Challa set himself, adjusting his weight for the inevitable clash.

Nefertiti stood straight up and looked at him. Her features were full of disdain.

"You dance around like a ballerina, not a panther, T'Challa. What's wrong?" she taunted, running her tongue down her arm like a cat. "Afraid to face me, claw to claw? Are tricks and cleverness all you've got?"

"This entire exercise is one of futility, Nefertiti." Despite her taunts, T'Challa didn't drop his guard. He, more than anyone, knew how fast a jungle cat could be. "Bast knows what lies in my heart, as well as my mind. I would welcome you into my palace and my kingdom, but I will not let your rashness and inexperience lead my country into ruin—"

Nefertiti lunged at him.

T'Challa barely got his hands in front of him to catch her slashing claws as she bore him to the ground, straining to reach his neck. Maneuvering his feet, the Panther prepared to flip the great beast off of him. It was time to end this, and he would use the knockout gas in his armor's claws, meant for just this type of close-quarters combat. He just needed a moment to activate the canisters...

Nothing happened.

Nefertiti seemed to sense his surprise as she leveraged her strength to move the claws closer. Betrayed by technology, T'Challa flipped her high into the air and off his body. Like a cat, however, Nefertiti somersaulted in midair and landed on her feet. She wore a wide grin on her face.

"Ah-ah, T'Challa," she purred. "Remember, I said no tricks."

She gestured around them. "Here, science and technology—even in your famous battle armor—don't count as much as faith and belief. Here, your only weapons are your strength and your skill, not circuitry and gadgets. Your heart has to lead—and sadly, it seems to be lacking."

184   T'Challa narrowed his eyes.

Then, through one of the jagged cracks in the temple walls, he spied a hazy jungle in the distance.

"I'm still in the Ancestral Plains," he whispered to himself.

"What—did you think it was all jungle, savannah, and Okoume trees?" she taunted. "I may have only been here once or twice, but even I know it can be whatever Bast wants it to be."

Looking over at the wall of the temple, T'Challa saw Bast in panther form, lounging on top of a wall, grooming herself and lazily watching the commotion. She winked at him, and turned her attention back to her fur.

So that's how it is.

Taking a deep breath, T'Challa returned to his fighting stance.

"Regardless of where I am, Bast knows my heart," he said. "I, and my ancestors, have earned Bast's devotion through blood, sweat, and tears—through suffering and prayer, through war and peace. Everything we've done through the generations has been for the glory of our god, and the betterment of her people."

T'Challa narrowed his eyes as he stared.

"We don't demand to rule simply because of ancestry, or powers. We stand before our god and declare ourselves worthy to rule through ritual combat. Bast then judges us worthy—or not. I have suffered and bled for my god." He stared a challenge. "How about you?"

Nefertiti snorted.

"Blood is thicker than faith, king. You can pray on your knees all you want, but the fact is that I'm still the daughter of Bast. I'm still her living embodiment, the only daughter of the Lady of Dread, and the rightful ruler of Wakanda. I'm family." Again she grinned. "There's nothing you can do about that." Her tail lashing back and forth, Nefertiti stalked forward, ears going flat on her head.

"Would Odin hand Asgard to a human, instead of his son?" she challenged. "Would Zeus consider letting a mortal—or even a demigod like Hercules—rule Olympus? So why would you expect Bast to do something no other pantheon would do? You Black

Panthers, hiding from the world, marshaling your resources for a battle that never comes, instead of leading and ruling openly." Anger filled her voice. "How many suffer through diseases that your Heart-Shaped Herb might cure? How many have lived in poverty, in slavery, because you hid, believing you were special?

"What will you do now, now that you know your precious god favors another?" she continued. "Now that you know—*you know*—you're just a man, and not your god's heir?"

T'Challa locked eyes with Nefertiti.

"I will do what I have always done," he snarled. "I will serve my god to the best of my ability, whether as king or as Black Panther or simply as a man. My faith does not hinge on reward. I do as Bast instructs, as my conscience dictates, as my country needs and my heart demands. That will never change."

With a roar, Nefertiti lunged.

T'Challa braced himself.

"HALT."

Bast's voice rang deafeningly in their heads, locking them in place. T'Challa glanced over to where the massive panther had been lounging, but it was gone. Instead, Bast's human form strode across the courtyard, her brown shift swaying in the wind. A small smile graced Bast's beautiful face as she circled them slowly, her gaze seeming to pierce them to the core.

T'Challa dropped to one knee and looked down.

"Such respect," she whispered, smiling a broad smile.

Nefertiti sniffed with disdain and crossed her arms defiantly.

"It's where he should have been from the start."

Bast sighed.

"Take that off, dear." Bast's musical voice gave little hint of what she could do. She waved a hand and transformed Nefertiti back into her human form, white dress, sandals, and all. The young woman looked down and examined her hand, mouth wide open at the display of power.

"Let us all speak as equals, in an attempt to come to an… equitable agreement," Bast said, and she gestured for Neffie to sit.

The daughter dropped cross-legged on the ground, a sulky frown on her face. Then Bast reached over to touch T'Challa's shoulder. He gracefully joined his opponent on the ground, and she glared over at him.

With godly grace, Bast folded her legs under her, sat back on her heels, and looked at T'Challa and Neffie fondly before speaking.

"I enjoyed listening to you two debate, physically and verbally. If this is what results when you are pointed at each other, may the world beware if you are ever enjoined and aimed at the same target."

Neffie harrumphed, and rolled her eyes. T'Challa kept his eyes on Bast, whose smile only widened.

"Neffie, you are my only daughter, and therefore you are my heart," she said. "As an inheritor of my power, there is no doubt that one day all that is mine will be yours—here in Bubastis, in Wakanda, and in the Ancestral Plains and the Endless Deserts. You are my family and my heir, and nothing will ever change that."

Bast looked over at T'Challa. To his astonishment, a single tear formed in her eye.

"T'Challa, son of T'Chaka, the Black Panther. My avatar, my champion. The fruit of Bashenga is not the family with whom I was born, but the family I chose. Despite years of service, none of my Panthers have ever asked me for more land, more riches, more power. They have only asked to serve me and their Wakandan children. I can see no better model for my daughter than the men and women of your dynasty."

Neffie's back went stiff at her mother's words, and she looked over at T'Challa with a smirk. Bast caught her gaze and frowned.

The skies above darkened with clouds.

"I must agree with T'Challa, Neffie. You're not yet ready to lead. With the power you hold, and the divinity you'll inherit, it would be foolhardy to put millions of my worshippers—my base of power on the earthly realm—under your care. Not until you've matured."

Neffie stared at Bast, tears welling up in her eyes.

"You promised that Wakanda would be mine," she muttered. "You owe me two decades of loneliness, of not knowing why I was the way I was, of not being able to help the people closest to me despite having the power to change things."

She waved her hand at T'Challa.

"I'm not like them," she said. "They had power and chose not to use it. I didn't *know* I had power… and once I found out, I didn't know how to use it to help those I cared about."

"No, no, you didn't." Bast began to glow. "Which is why I have decided to spend some time with you personally, so that you can learn. We are eternal, child. We may have missed a time, but we have a millennia to make up for it. Wakanda will be there for you, someday, I promise."

She smiled proudly at T'Challa.

"The Black Panthers will keep it safe and ready for you."

T'Challa looked up into Bast's face.

"Do you have any idea when… Neffie's coronation might be?" he asked.

Nefertiti began to glow. The two women smiled, moving eerily together as Bast shrugged.

"Next year, next decade, next century, next millennium. Being immortal, we have time. Once she has gained the control that is required of her, Neffie will appear to you or your descendants in my temple in Wakanda. She will do so with my blessing."

"Will you show me how to dreamwalk?" Neffie said excitedly. "Oooo, I know some heads I need to get into."

Bast gently frowned at her daughter, then turned back to T'Challa.

"W'Kabi has some instructions, to prepare you for her coming," she said. "Nothing too extreme, and nothing that has to be done immediately, but you should begin to prepare. You and those who follow you."

Neffie stuck out her tongue, and T'Challa couldn't quite muffle the laugh that bubbled up inside him.

"Wakanda is yours today, T'Challa," the young woman said, and she grinned. "Tomorrow, it'll be mine."

"I can deal with that." He smiled back.

Bast closed her eyes, and then gave him a knowing look.

"Yes, T'Challa, I'll tell W'Kabi what we've agreed."

Neffie began bouncing on the ground. "Oooo, mindreading! Teachmeteachmeteachme!!"

T'Challa and Bast sighed in unison. She stood up, and T'Challa offered his hand to Neffie to help her to her feet. Bast quirked her eyebrow at him.

"You know, my avatar," she said pointedly, "there *is* a way we can all get what we want, right now." She peered at their briefly intertwined hands. "My daughter would make an impressive queen for a Black Panther…"

Neffie immediately jerked her hand away, turned her back, and flounced away. Yet T'Challa swore he could see a slight smile on her face and sway in her hips as she faded away into the light, leaving Bast and her champion alone in the temple.

"…someday," the god said. As a bright glow began to envelope the temple, she teasingly poked T'Challa with a finely manicured nail before morphing back into her panther form.

"Remember, the girl's mother can read your mind," she said. "Warn your children." Curling around his legs, purring, Bast cocked her head to allow T'Challa to scratch a particularly good spot under her ear.

"You'll see her again, my champion. Steadfast and forward, my Black Panther. Know that your god is pleased with you, and that your worship is both loved and appreciated. You are my family, T'Challa, and that I will never forget."

The panther walked into the glowing light.

"Wakanda forever, T'Challa."

"Wakanda forever, Bast."

A thought floated through the ether.

"Wakanda forever! Whoo, I got one in."

WHEN T'CHALLA blinked the light out of his eyes, he was still next to his Quinjet outside of Tell-Basta, dressed in his original clothes. He patted himself down, finding nothing missing or lost. But on his skin, he could still smell a hint of the panther's scent along with a newer, younger floral scent mixed in.

Climbing into the airship, T'Challa smiled to himself and headed home.

o———————o

THE REV. Dr. Wilberforce Rutherford sat back on the couch and expelled a breath. He looked surprised to find that he had been holding it during T'Challa's story.

"Have you seen her since?"

His throat parched, T'Challa poured himself another glass of water, and one for his guest.

"Not a word, not a thought, not a peep from Nefertiti. She's out there, somewhere, learning and waiting for her time to come home, to be with her people and to lead them."

"What of Bast?" the reverend questioned.

"Oh, she's always around." T'Challa looked at the panther curled up on top of his desk—a form only he could see.

"But... I don't understand your point," the reverend said. His earlier antagonistic stance seemed to have softened, though. "Why tell me all this?"

"Hmmm..." T'Challa said, walking over to his shrine before looking back at the seated reverend. "You wanted to know whether Bast is real. That is what you asked, but what you really wanted to know was about faith." He turned to the statue and continued. "I have faith in my god and her child. I have seen them. I have met them. I have touched them. I know they are real, because all of my senses tell me they are real.

"But even now, today, Reverend, your faith is just as strong and as powerful as mine," he continued. "Why do I know this? Because you, and your daughter, have faith in a god that cannot be seen, cannot be heard, cannot be touched. Your god can only be felt... here." He poked the man in the chest. "That's the kind of faith taught by fathers and mothers that is not easily given up, despite a change of continents, despite a new marriage, and despite living amongst those who believe differently."

T'Challa reached out to the reverend to give him a hand up.

"Perhaps you should give your daughter a chance to show you how well you've raised her in her faith. My only regret, Reverend, is that I can't show my father how well he instructed me in the few years we had together. Don't take that from your daughter."

"Well, perhaps I have been too hasty," the reverend suggested. "And she is my only child." He took the offered hand and pulled himself to his feet.

"If we hurry, I think we still have time for you to make the father-daughter dance," T'Challa replied. "A charming American tradition Dom insisted would be a part of their celebration."

The rotund man stretched his suit coat over his stomach, and allowed his host to escort him toward the door. Beckoning the waiting *Dora Milaje*, T'Challa sent Rev. Rutherford down toward the wedding reception, promising he would be along in a minute. Closing the door behind him, T'Challa smiled at the panther lounging on his desk.

"She asked about you the other day," Bast said in a musical sing-song voice.

"Tell her… her kingdom, and her avatar, will be waiting for her in Wakanda," he said with a smile. "Someday."

UKUBAMBA

KYOKO M

THERE IS no honor among thieves.

Okoye knew. She had always known. She had seen it for herself on the streets of Wakanda. She had seen it in the chaotic world outside their beloved city. She had seen how men were willing to betray each other, but most of all themselves, for want of profit. She had seen what became of men like Ulysses Klaue. It had stolen the life of King T'Chaka.

To her, there were few things on earth as low as a thief.

And King T'Challa knew it, too.

He stood facing the window in the throne room, hands folded behind his back, his posture perfect and straight, as it should have been, for he was royalty. T'Challa had suffered greatly throughout his life. He had been asked to wear a heavy burden as king and the leader of Wakanda's tribes. Yet that burden did not show in how he stood: regal, steady, and powerful. He was not simply a king, but a leader. He knew how to rally his people and how best to protect them, whether it was he alone or with the *Dora Milaje* or even the Avengers. Okoye valued his intelligence as much as his strength, for a true warrior needed both brain and brawn.

And he appreciated her the same way.

After saluting her fellow *Dora Milaje*, the general walked up to his right and gave her salute. "My king."

T'Challa nodded his head to her in respect. "General. I apologize for summoning you so suddenly, but we have an emergency."

The king faced her, his expression grave, but she could see hints of anger burning in his brown eyes. "A seven-year-old girl was taken from one of the border towns."

He touched the Kimoyo beads around his left wrist. A hologram of a smiling child with thick curls that fell around her dimpled cheeks appeared. "Her name is Nandi."

Okoye's eyes narrowed. "When?"

"Less than an hour ago. Her mother Liyana had brought her to the market. They were chased and then attacked in an alley. They snatched Nandi and broke Liyana's leg so she could not follow. She said they were headed south."

"How many men?"

"Three. She wasn't able to identify them; they wore masks. She heard two of them speaking Nigerian. She heard them say, 'the window is closing, hurry up.' The third one carried an unusual weapon: a pearl-handled pistol. American made, from what Liyana could tell. You have worked diligently with our border tribes to police the area for slavers and human traffickers. If anyone knows where Nandi is being taken, it's you."

Okoye paced the length of the window, her brow furrowed in thought. "With the local tribesmen alerted to the abduction, the kidnappers would not try to leave the city immediately. To cross outside of its borders, you would need the Ferryman. His name is Kamari. He transports illegal cargo in and out of East Africa, but if you pay him a substantial fee, he will allow human trafficking. The problem is we shut down his operation a month ago. All his assets have been seized and his associates were arrested. He is serving a ten-year sentence in Addis Ababa."

"Nature abhors a vacuum," T'Challa said. "If he is gone, then who would try to fill the void?"

"That is the question, my king," she said as she continued to pace. "I believe there are only two ways we can recover the child before she is taken out of Africa. One, we find the safehouse where she is being held. They will wait until nighttime and then remove her from there to take her to the border. Two, we intercept the exchange. More than likely, these men are just hired as spotters to abduct the girls when an opportunity presents itself. That is how it's been in the past. They remain here rather than taking the children to their final destination. However, are you certain Liyana and Nandi were not targets for another reason?"

"Not that we are aware of," T'Challa said. "She is a noblewoman of our courts but she does not hold a specific seat of power that they would be able to use. She received no word of a ransom, either."

"If she is not a target and this is truly a random kidnapping, then we must start with who would be able to transport her to the border. I will visit Kamari at the prison and find out who would try to fill his shoes in his absence. I will instruct the *Dora Milaje* to systematically search the border town and find any witnesses to the escape. If Kamari leads us to the new Ferryman, then we will set up a sting and rescue the child. If he does not, we must coordinate to shut down any way out of the town. If they cannot escape to complete the exchange, there is a chance they will instead try to ransom her back to Liyana. If that is the case, then we can recover Nandi once a time and date is set."

T'Challa nodded. "What do you need from me?"

"Unobstructed access to Kamari. He is in isolated imprisonment since his associations have made him infamous. There are many prisoners that would see him dead if given the chance."

"You will have it, General. By the time you land at the capital, he will be all yours." He lay one hand on her shoulder and squeezed it lightly. "Good luck, Okoye."

"Bast as my witness," Okoye said as she grasped his wrist in solidarity, "I will bring Nandi home."

TO OKOYE, Kamari was the very definition of scum.

He had been born in Ethiopia but had left it in his teenage years to go abroad. He'd tried his hand at petty crimes in New York

City, which had earned him nothing but broken bones and a nasty scar that bisected his forehead, ending at his ruined left eye. The Americans had found his tendency to betray his buyers if someone offered more money traitorous, and sent him packing. He'd barely escaped with his life. What he had brought home to East Africa was connections back to the States. He had coordinated with the local criminals to move illegal arms, stolen goods, and counterfeit money to the border and outside of Africa. It had taken months of investigating to secure any information that would allow the charges to stick. What had finally done Kamari in had been his ego. Okoye had approached him in disguise to set up a deal and he'd fallen for it thanks to his towering ego, for he knew little of the *Dora Milaje* aside from their reputation. It had filled her with spiteful satisfaction when she watched the authorities stuff him into the back of the car. Allegedly, he'd precipitated the transfer of at least a hundred young girls out of East Africa.

Therefore, Okoye was not terribly eager to be in his presence once again.

Heat pressed in on all sides as Okoye strode down the hallway to the isolated prison cells. Each one sat roughly twenty feet apart from the others and had wrought-iron bars, staggered so the inmates couldn't see each other. The stone floor hadn't been swept recently; her sandals left impressions in it as she walked toward Kamari's cell. The other inmates whooped and hollered at her appearance, making lewd suggestions or shouting insults as they recognized her uniform.

And Okoye simply smiled.

She'd put a lot of these men in here personally. It was one of her greatest accomplishments as a warrior.

Finally, she reached Kamari's cell.

He was a short man, around 5'6", and spindly like an underfed spider. His right arm had a cast from the elbow to his thumb, caked with dirt and lint from his prison uniform. He had a scraggly beard and unkempt hair. His brown eyes were lifeless and beady. He had two gold front teeth, not as a show of wealth, but rather because he'd gotten the original teeth knocked out by a New York mobster the same night he acquired the scar. She remembered he'd bragged to her that it had been none other than Wilson Fisk, the Kingpin, but she knew better. Kingpin didn't knock out front teeth; he caved men's skulls in with a single blow. But the story sounded good to other lowlife criminals, so he stuck with the lie to increase his reputation.

"How ironic," Kamari said, tilting his head up from his pillow as he spotted her. "My only visitor is the one who put me in here."

Okoye offered him a thin smile. "You should be grateful. Any visitors other than me would only visit with the intent to end your life."

Kamari flashed her his gold teeth. "You're not here to kill me? Lucky me."

"For once, you are more useful to me alive than dead," she said, rolling her eyes. "I need information."

"Oh, is that right?" Kamari said as he shoved himself up from his cot, levering a glare in her direction. "Why am I under any obligation to help you, witch?"

"If you don't, I will break your other arm."

Kamari scowled. "You already broke the first one."

Okoye's sharp smile widened. "I was feeling courteous that day."

Kamari spat on the ground. "Up yours. A little broken arm's not enough to make me snitch. You know what they do to snitches in here."

"Yes, exactly," she said. "And imagine trying to defend yourself from them with both your arms broken."

Kamari sneered. "You don't scare me."

Okoye shrugged. "Perhaps not. Perhaps your time here has forced you to become the kind of man who is unafraid of an elite warrior of my caliber."

She leaned back against the stone wall, lowering her lashes. "But what about Sturgess?"

198   Kamari stiffened. Okoye crossed her arms and watched the

gears whirring in the criminal's head. "Tell me, Kamari, what do you think Sturgess would do if he knew where you were?"

Kamari licked his cracked lips nervously. "He can't get me in here. He's back in New York."

Okoye leaned forward slightly. "Are you willing to bet your life on it?"

Anger pulled his sunken cheeks over his bones even tighter. "You're bluffing."

She let out a short laugh. "Why would I need to bluff? You're a bug under glass. I can squash you at any time. I have no need for lies. I will make this easy for you: answer my questions and I will not tell Sturgess where you are."

The feigned amusement fled her features, replaced with unflinching stone. "If you refuse, then I suspect I will be the last visitor you ever receive for the rest of your short life."

Kamari hurled his shoe at the bars. They clanged as it hit. He fumed for a few seconds and then threw up his good arm in defeat. "Fine, witch. What do you want to know?"

Okoye pushed off from the wall. "A girl named Nandi was taken from her mother when they were out shopping in one of our border towns. I need to know who your successor is."

He eyed her. "Why do you think I have a successor?"

"Because you don't want to die in here," she said flatly. "Even with you in poor health and less than sanitary conditions, you plan to survive it and return to business as soon as your sentence is up. In order to do that, you would have left someone in charge. Your successor was likely told to close up shop temporarily until the heat was off and then resume your illegal services, albeit in different sections of the city under a more watchful eye. However, they became impatient and decided to move sooner than you instructed, as evidenced by this kidnapping. Someone got greedy. Someone got sloppy. You will tell me who it is and where I can find them."

Kamari grumbled something under his breath as he scratched his unruly hair, and then sighed. "His name is Senai."

"How long has he been working for you?"

"He was a runner," Kamari said. "I used him to transport payments to my men, so that's why he didn't go down with the rest of us during the arrests. Kid knew enough about the illegal trading business to be left in charge while I'm in…" He let out an ugly chuckle, glancing at his dank surroundings. "…hibernation, as it were. I gave him instructions on what to do in the meantime. He must have jumped the gun. Stupid kid."

"Where can I find him?"

"Last time I checked, he was underground. No telling where."

"Then how have you been in contact with him?"

"I haven't," Kamari grunted. "I told him everything he needed to know before they put me on trial. I don't get calls, not with my record. Ain't got a family. Just me and these four walls."

"If Senai is coordinating the girl's transportation out of East Africa, where would they keep her?"

Kamari shrugged. "Can't help you there. Lots of spots."

"Two of the men who took her were possibly Nigerian. Does that make any difference?"

He paused. "It might. Did the mother get a description?"

"No, their faces were covered. The third man threatened her with a pearl-handled pistol."

Kamari snorted. "Oh, then I know who you're dealing with. That's Faruq, Habib, and Imam. They're all small-time crooks, usually theft or armed robbery. They work for cheap and they're always together to cover each other's backs to avoid getting caught. They're more likely to talk than Senai; you can never get those three to shut up. They're usually holed up at this recreation center by the river that runs a gambling ring out of the basement. That's why they take any job they can get; they piss away the money they earn on a frequent basis."

"If they're small-time, why escalate to kidnapping?"

"Pays better."

Okoye clenched her jaw. "You would know."

Kamari's lips curled up in a nasty grin. "Did I hit a sore spot, General?"

"Go to hell."

"Little late for that," he chuckled. "Everything has a price. Even human lives. Might as well capitalize on it."

"Yes," she said coldly, gesturing to the jail cell. "I can tell it's worth it."

Kamari let out a prickly laugh as he pushed to his feet and shambled over to the bars, his dead eyes fixed on her. "It will be. I'm gonna get out of here, General. And when I do, you're going to be my very first…"

His gold teeth gleamed. "…visit."

Okoye smiled again. "I hope that I am."

She leaned in toward him, lowering her voice, her onyx eyes boring holes into his. "But be careful. They don't make gold replacements for what I am going to remove off of you."

She left without looking back.

TO BE honest, Okoye felt strange without her armor. She'd gotten so used to the way it moved against her skin as she walked or how it swayed when she fought an enemy. She loved the bright contrast against her brown skin and the reputation she carried with her when she wore it. Everyone with eyes would know who she was: one of the *Dora Milaje*, the Adored Ones, the elite warriors charged with protecting the King of Wakanda.

But she was also a general. Generals had to know the best tactics for completing a mission.

The recreation center by the river was modest; just a large open space with tile floors and metal sheets for the roofing. Huge fans were plugged in at the corners of the room. There were families and old folks at the benches playing various games. Music played cheerfully from the speakers bolted into the overhead beams. She almost regretted that she could not join them. Had it not been for the kidnapping, it would be a nice day.

Okoye had changed into an emerald sundress and a black shawl as she strode past the friendly faces to the counter at the far end opposite the entrance. A bald, overweight man sat behind it flipping through a magazine, humming to himself. He glanced up as she approached, and she noted the appreciation of her beauty in his eyes as he stood to greet her.

"How can I help you?"

"I'm here to see friends," she said. "They're in the basement."

The man gave her a politely baffled look. "There is no basement."

Okoye smiled. "Oh. Perhaps I was mistaken."

She drew her wallet out of her small purse and withdrew a fat wad of money. "Can I leave this with you instead?"

The man stared at the money on the counter and then picked it up. "Yes, you can. If we had a basement, it would be down the hall and through the door to the right."

"Thank you," she said and swept past him.

It was darker and cooler in the hallway farther into the building. She kept an eye out to see if the man would do anything else, but she caught him counting the bills in her peripheral, so she felt confident he would be no bother to her. She passed the bathrooms and found a single door on the right. She tried the knob, but it didn't budge.

Okoye knocked. After a moment, a tall thin man with cornrows in his early thirties answered, his face already set in a scowl. It immediately switched to a skeezy smile upon the sight of her pretty face. "And just what can I do for you, beautiful?"

"Senai sent me," she said. "We need to talk."

His smile wavered. "Oh. Business, not pleasure, huh?"

"Sorry to say, but yes."

He heaved a sigh and opened the door completely to let her into the stairwell. It was a narrow space with only a bare bulb to light the way. Okoye kept him in her peripheral as well as she descended onto a landing and then turned right again to another set of stairs. She couldn't hear any hubbub from upstairs, which likely meant this basement had been soundproofed.

202   Good. That worked in her favor, for once.

At the bottom of the stairs, she found a wide basement with several tables set up and a full bar against the left wall. It was still late afternoon, so there weren't many gamblers around yet—just three men, the dealer, and the bartender. The bartender's features were similar enough to the man upstairs at the counter for her to assume they were brothers. The dealer at the table in the corner was female—a short, pretty girl with a neat afro pulled back into a puff. She wore a purple wrap dress and seemed unaffected by the loud laughter from the two men in front of her. They were playing some kind of card game from the looks of things.

"Ay," the thin man said, jerking his head to one side. "We got business."

The other two men were around the same age as him. One was lighter-skinned with a smattering of freckles on his nose and a fade haircut; the other was dark-skinned with short, beaded dreadlocks hanging above his broad shoulders. They both sized her up as they scooped up their winnings from the table and walked toward the stained couch in the left corner of the room. The tall man remained standing while the others sat and squabbled over what they'd won before addressing her.

"What's up, sis?" the one with the dreadlocks asked. "Senai's never sent someone so fine to our doorstep before."

She gave them a perfunctory smile. "Just to be sure I'm with the right men, I'm looking for Faruq, Habib, and Imam."

"In the flesh," the light-skinned one said. "I'm Faruq."

He gestured to the tall man. "That's Imam."

The one with dreadlocks grinned. "And I'm Habib. Nice to meet you."

"Good. Where is the girl?"

Habib adopted a confused look. "Where we said she'd be. Why?"

"There has been a change of plans," she said. "I will escort her to the border. It will raise less suspicion if she's with a woman than in a group of men. As you have seen, the authorities have spread out through the city quite thoroughly, so Senai thought it best to send me instead for better cover."

Imam pulled out his cell phone. "Sure, let's just confirm first."

"Are you questioning his authority?" she asked tartly.

Imam frowned. "No, I just—"

"Do you truly think he wants his time wasted with calls? Especially now? He's angry enough with you as it is."

"Angry?" Faruq asked. "Why?"

"You were sloppy," she snapped. "Grabbing a child in broad daylight. You did not think of the wrath that would come down upon your heads, nor his, with your impulsive actions. You had best not incite further ire and surrender the child before you make an even bigger mess."

"It's not like we knew things would go that bad," Habib groaned. "Imam was supposed to hit the mother on the head and we would snatch the kid, but she busted out some crazy Krav Maga moves and we had to fight her to get the kid. It wasn't our fault."

"Greed is the fault of all men," she sneered. "Unless you want to find out the punishment for that fault, give me the child."

"Fine, for Bast's sake," Habib grunted as he rose from the couch. "Can't believe he can't let us do one single thing without nagging."

He walked through the open doorway, hidden by beads, into another smaller room. Okoye drew in a breath as she waited for him to return.

He did. Only with a gun instead of Nandi.

"Who are you?" Habib demanded, pointing his pearl-handled pistol at her head.

"Bro, what the hell?" Faruq sputtered, his eyes wide. "Are you crazy?"

"Sis doesn't smell right," Habib said, glaring at her. "Look at the way she stands. Look at the quality of that dress. She maintains eye contact when she speaks. You know Senai hates that crap. She's not with him. She's a spy."

Imam and Faruq moved away from her to flank their partner on either side, both withdrawing switchblades. Okoye stared down the three of them as the bartender and the dealer both bolted up

the stairs without another word.

"Are you certain this is how you wish for things to go?" Okoye asked quietly. "If you surrender Nandi to me, this will be swift and painless. If you do not, then I will teach you the meaning of regret."

"It's three against one, Grace Jones," Habib sneered. "I like those odds."

Okoye nodded solemnly. "So be it."

She flicked her wrist. Her collapsible spear landed on her palm and extended itself just as Habib opened fire.

She slashed at the barrel of the gun, knocking it to one side. The bullet hit the wall behind her and his arm jerked to the side. Imam and Faruq lunged at her simultaneously. Okoye ducked their initial clumsy swipes and swiped their legs out from under them with the spear. Habib cursed and stumbled back, trying to keep the gun trained on her. Okoye bobbed and weaved as she darted toward him. The next three shots missed by inches. She stabbed him in the foot and he screamed, trying to pistol-whip her instead. She slammed the butt of the spear into his forehead and then grabbed his gun arm, snapping his wrist. The gun clattered to the floor between them, and she kicked it into the storeroom behind them before throwing him into his recovering partners in a vicious hip toss.

Imam recovered first and aimed for her throat with the switch-blade. Okoye threw her head back and then forward even harder, shattering his nose. He crumpled to the floor as blood splashed down his mouth and chin, clutching at his face as he wailed.

Faruq grabbed a chair and slung it at her. Okoye slashed it in half before it even came near her and then kicked him in the left kneecap. It dislocated with a sharp pop and he hit the floor on the other knee, shrieking. She brought her spear handle across the side of his temple hard and he flopped to the floor face-first, unconscious.

Habib tackled her. The spear hit the ground and rolled out of reach. He grabbed both ends of her shawl, strangling her with it. White spots popped into the edges of her vision as the enraged thief tried to crush her windpipe. She reached up and plunged her thumbs into his eye sockets. He screamed and the shawl slackened just enough for her to get a gulp of air. She twisted her legs up around his neck and shoved up from the floor, pinning him beneath her. He thrashed around underneath her, clawing at her as she knelt on top of him. She endured it and pressed harder and harder until his movements slowed, weakened, and then ceased. He passed out with a gurgle.

Imam had been trying to gather his feet underneath him to run when Okoye caught up to him. She kicked him flat onto his belly and lay the spear's razor-sharp edge to the side of his throat.

"I am not in the habit of repeating myself," Okoye murmured. "Now, tell me where the girl is or die here on this dirty floor."

OKOYE WEDGED the Vibranium blade of her spear into the padlock on the cellar door, which was around the corner from the basement storeroom, and snapped through the lock with an exertion of considerable strength. Her heart pounded against her sternum as she gripped the door and pried it open, spilling light into the small storage space.

And there, curled up in a ball, lay Nandi.

She had been bound with nylon ropes and gagged. The child lay with her back to the door and she flinched as she heard the door open. Her tiny shoulders shook and Okoye could hear muffled sobs that nearly crumbled her heart inside her chest.

"Shh, it's all right, little one," she whispered as she knelt. "I'm here to help. Hold still, okay?"

As delicately as she could, Okoye cut the restraints off and untied the gag. Nandi curled into an even smaller ball. The Wakandan warrior set her spear aside and rested one hand gently on the child's soft curls and the other on her back, rubbing in soothing circles.

"It's okay, Nandi. It's going to be okay. Your mother Liyana sent me."

At the sound of her mother's name, Nandi fell silent. Slowly, she craned her neck. Tears had crusted on her lashes and at the corners of her eyes. She wiped them and said in a small voice, "My mom sent you?"

Okoye smiled warmly. "Yes. It's time to go home, my child."

Nandi let out a joyous shout and threw herself into Okoye's arms, sobbing. Okoye held the little girl as she cried. She gave her comfort for as long as she needed it. Eventually, the little girl's tears dried and Okoye scooped her up in one arm, carrying her spear in the other to be sure no one would dare interfere as they left. She brought Nandi upstairs and out of the building. From there, she walked the city streets toward the outskirts, where the jet to take them back to Wakanda awaited.

"Who are you?" Nandi asked.

"My name is Okoye. I'm the general for the *Dora Milaje*, King T'Challa's royal guard."

Nandi's eyes grew wide. "Wow. You work for the king?"

Okoye chuckled. "Yes."

"So you can fight and stuff?"

"Yes, I can."

"How did you learn?"

"I was chosen to fight for Wakanda when I was young. I trained very hard for years and years."

"Oh." Nandi paused for a thoughtful moment. "Do you think I could be a *Dora* someday?"

"Absolutely, my child," Okoye said. "You are a very brave and special young girl. Every little girl is a warrior, after all. She must simply be given the tools to succeed in the battles she must face."

"I didn't feel very brave back there," Nandi mumbled sadly. "I was scared."

Okoye stopped and set the child down on the dirt path, squatting to meet her eye to eye. "I will tell you a secret, Nandi. You must promise not to tell anyone."

"I will!" Nandi stuck out her pinky. Okoye wrapped her pinky around it. "I promise."

Okoye gave her a soft smile. "I was scared, too. Being brave is not about being fearless. Being brave means doing the right thing in spite of how scared you feel. It's not easy, but you can do it. There are people who love you and will support you so that you can become stronger. Never forget it."

The little girl nodded. "I won't."

"Good girl." Okoye offered her hand and Nandi took it. Together, they headed home.

"OH, NANDI, my little flower!" Liyana fell to her knees and embraced her daughter, tears pouring down her cheeks.

"Mama!" Nandi hugged her mother fiercely.

Liyana pulled away and kissed her forehead and each cheek, stroking her curls lovingly. "Are you okay, baby?"

"Yes, Mama. Are you okay?"

"I am now, my darling. I love you so much."

"I love you too, Mama."

Okoye offered Liyana a hand up as she stood, balancing carefully on her crutches. Liyana clasped Okoye's hand hard. "Thank you so much, General. I am in your debt."

"You are in no such thing," Okoye chided. "I serve my country proudly. I am so glad I could return her to you safe and sound."

Liyana pressed her forehead to Okoye's hand in reverence. "Even so, from the bottom of my heart, I thank you. Nandi means the world to me."

She turned to T'Challa and bowed deeply. "Thank you for your help, Your Majesty."

T'Challa smiled and nodded to her in respect. "It was my honor."

He knelt in front of Nandi. "And I have a present for you, little warrior."

T'Challa held up a gold pin with the *Dora Milaje*'s insignia upon it. He clipped it to Nandi's dress. "There. Know that you are always welcome within the palace walls, Nandi. You are an honorary *Dora Milaje*."

"Yay! Thank you!" She threw her arms around him in a hug. He chuckled and hugged the girl.

Nandi hugged Okoye next. Okoye pinched the girl's cheek after she let go. "Until the next time we meet, little one."

"Come, Nandi, it's time to go home," Liyana said. "Say goodbye."

Nandi crossed her arms over her chest and beamed up at the pair. "Wakanda forever!"

Then she scurried to catch up with her mother as they left the throne room.

"I thank you for your hard work, General," T'Challa said. "It is good to see her returned home safely, and you as well."

"Thank you." They turned toward the window overlooking Wakanda as the sun began to set and night crept over the horizon. "But there is more work yet to be done."

"Always," T'Challa said, resting a hand on her shoulder. "At least we know one mother can sleep soundly tonight. That is enough for now."

She squeezed his fingers and stared into the sunset. "For now."

WHAT'S DONE IN THE DARK

TROY L. WIGGINS

I'M UP well before my strange Wakandan Vibranium clock alarm has a chance to interrupt my sleep. Alarm is set to go off at 5:00 a.m., Wakandan time, and I've been up since just after midnight, just looking at my apartment.

Everything's new, shiny. Glossy wood walls, covered in colorful Wakandan art. My furniture's all burnished and luxurious, much finer than anything I've sat on in my entire life. And most impressive, bay windows big enough to drive a semi-truck through, giving me a fantastic view of the Golden City's splendor and the Citadel in the distance. After so many years of scrabbling and scraping my way along as a desk jockey for the NYPD, where I am now is unbelievable... and it's not just because of the weird clock.

I catch a reflection of myself as I stare out into the Golden City: burnished brown skin, hair still cut low even after leaving the force. I've been running the streets busting low-level drug dealers and breaking up street-tier villain heists for years. All that hard work and no play is starting to show in the crow's feet at the corners of my eyes, the hard set to my mouth. Even though I've taken the Heart-Shaped Herb, the Wakandan catalyst for King T'Challa's superhuman abilities, I still can't hide the years on my face, or the yearning for my family, my girl and my child who are still in New York.

Yet here I am, in this fabulous apartment in Wakanda, awaiting King T'Challa's summons. I've been called up, called away from the streets and to King T'Challa's side.

For the millionth time, I ask myself: Who am I?

"Umoya," I call, grabbing a cup of coffee from the sleek silver automated brewing machine. Like the clock, and the apartment, the artificial-intelligence-powered personal assistant I've summoned is bought and purchased using money deposited in my account by the Royal Bank of Wakanda, signed off on by King T'Challa.

"*You called, Kevin?*" Umoya says, flaring to life as a hard-light representation of a young afroed woman composed of millions of lavender pixels. Her holographic voice has a Wakandan accent, and her image is dressed in the stylish patterned wrap, skirt, and sneakers that are popular with fashionable young Wakandan women. She's cute, in a disembodied way.

"Why won't you call me Kasper?"

"*That is not your name,*" she says matter-of-factly, and even has the nerve to quirk her head to one side like a curious puppy. "*Did you summon me?*"

"I did. Pull up today's news. Global and New York local, please."

"*Absolutely,*" she replies in her strange hollow voice.

My gargantuan holoscreen flicks to life on the wall and the uniformly grating voices of newscasters fill my living room in high definition surround sound that seems to come from everywhere. None of this makes *any* sense.

I take another deep sip of my coffee as I stand in my larger-than-life window, watching Wakanda transition from overnight into early morning. Big-ass apartment, and all this money to spend, but Gwen still won't talk to me. She'll take my money but won't talk to me. It makes me want to punch things. Hence, listening to worldwide news. This is what stepping up looks like.

"Three miners in coastal Chile happen upon huge meteorite in search of silver—"

"Yet another wave of bump and grab robberies in the Mog—"

"Luxury car owner racks up $750,000 in multi-vehicle crash—"

"Smoked hams experiencing a surge as spring looms—"

I absorb, filter, and eject information as it reaches me, moving around like an automaton as I get ready for my daily workout regimen. Robbers in the Mog—a cute name for a bad neighborhood that properly goes by Little Mogadishu—are nothing new. I stalked those streets for weeks, months at a time, both as a detective, and in my second life as a costumed substitute for Black Panther: the White Tiger.

The other stories don't grab my attention. I'm about to have Umoya turn on the shower when she pings, then appears directly in front of me.

"Kevin, you have a priority visitor."

"T'Challa?"

"Yes, King *T'Challa,"* she scolds.

Right. Manners.

"Please let him in."

The door to my apartment slides open and standing in the hallway in front of me is an imposing, stoic man with flint-hard eyes and a dangerous demeanor. Faster than I can blink, I find myself face to face with the King of the Dead. Haramu-Fal. The Lost King. The Sovereign Ruler of Wakanda. Unnecessarily, he waits for my nod before entering the apartment that he's provided for me. His dangerous, beautiful *Dora Milaje* guards stay outside, but I can feel their hard eyes on me even after the door slides shut.

The king and I stare at each other for a minute before I drop my eyes to the floor, and then head toward the kitchen, which is bigger than any apartment I had back home.

"Kevin," he greets me. His voice is calm, in control, as smooth as whiskey. "I trust that you're well."

I lean against my fridge, sweep my arm out over my beautifully lit apartment like a game show host showcasing a grand prize. "You know that I am. What can I do for you?"

"I've always thought that your talent for solving problems and finding lost things was unparalleled. It's why I provided you with the Heart-Shaped Herb, and why I called you here. I intend for you to be the tip of the spear for missions that require… a more delicate touch. Now is one of those times. I need your help."

I'm flattered, though I have to wonder what the king is about to ask me to do. I'm not into assassinations or wet work. I trained as a cop. Protect and serve and all that. Still, I give him a respectful nod. "Of course, my King. It *is* what you pay me for."

T'Challa fiddles with his Kimoyo beads and then points at my holoscreen, which shifts from the news into something different. The whole mood in the room changes as the image on-screen expands to fill the entire room, casting us both into a lifelike hologram representation of a nondescript warehouse space, the kind I've spent too much time inside busting druggies, criminals, and costumed freaks.

The video image is full of shadows cast over strangely lit bodies, all of which thrum and buzz with anxious anticipation. It's shot on a good camera: I can see very clearly the stains on one man's teeth, and the bead of sweat sliding down the back of a woman's neck. Part of this shadowy distortion is due to the intense globes of harsh light that could only come from the kinds of naked lightbulbs that hang in rooms where bad things happen. Lots of masked guys stand around brandishing guns, trying their best to look dangerous. In the middle of all these guys are two well-dressed prisoners, one man, one woman. The man's suit is rumpled, torn, and the right side of his forehead is sticky with dried blood that's been there at least through the night. The woman's hair is pulled back into a neat afro puff, and her dark suit and patterned sash are pristine, as if she just stepped out of the office to grab a cup of coffee. They both look angry enough to spit fire at their detainers.

"What's this?"

"You will see," T'Challa says, and nods at the screen.

Instantly, my room is filled with noise: the whooshing whir of factory fans, the soft whine of nearby trains, the rhythmic drip of water escaping old pipes, harsh breathing from the prisoners and goons alike. There's something else there, something whirring beneath all the other sounds. It's tech; I can tell by the low, uniform whine of optic cable, the whispery hiss of nanofans shooting coolant through mobility components. I unconsciously turn my head, searching for the sound.

"You hear it too," T'Challa says, and nods again.

If I didn't know any better I'd swear I sense... approval beneath that nod. My reverie is broken when one of the goons—dark-toothed, scruffy-bearded, wearing a stained dark flannel shirt—speaks.

"There is no more time for fear," he begins in a smooth, articulate baritone. I stifle a cough. I didn't expect this dude to sound so cultured.

"There is no more time for falseness, for baseless corruption and senseless cooperation. There is no more time for making spaces, safe or otherwise. There is no more time for anything... except the hunt."

His fellow goons whoop. The camera zooms in on the prisoners. Both of them stare fearlessly directly into the camera. The woman twists up her lips, spits in the direction of the camera. Someone's boot comes in from offscreen, blasts into the side of the man's head. He sags but hands lift him, and a deep moan escapes his lips. The boot has opened another gash, this time on his cheek. The woman continues to stare, her eyes blazing hatred.

The rage in her eyes makes me uneasy. "What is this?"

T'Challa remains his normal, stoic self, his expression unchanging. "Keep watching."

Apparently, the quick violence has satisfied the goon. He smirks, steps in front of the prisoners, and keeps talking.

"We are tired. We are hungry. We are poor. And we are forced to scrabble and scrape and make do with scraps while immigrant trash like these creatures feast on the fat that belongs to us! There is no more time. The hunt begins. Our prey: everyone who is not us. We are hunting, and we will not be stopped. Not by law enforcement, not by politicians, and—" The goon smirks, looks right into the camera like he *knows* T'Challa is watching. "—not by kings."

With a roar he rips his shirt open, exposing his chest, which is just a mass of scar tissue. The camera loses focus, then regains it and I can make out the scarring more clearly. It's a brand. A brand in the shape of… a lion?

"We are The Brave," the goon growls. "And the enemies of America are our prey. We will gnaw them and gnash them. And after we've had our fill?"

"We turn our sights on the world!" the goons yell in unison.

The screen goes dark. T'Challa silently steps out into the space left by the video and looks at me, waiting on me to say something.

"Those were Wakandans," I offer.

"Yes. Azzin Merkeba and J'kaya J'kina. Two of my most trusted diplomatic envoys to the United States. Impeccable service records. Azzin oversees support for Wakandans living and working in the United States. J'kaya manages all kinds of deals and our relationship with several foreign agencies, including your intelligence network here."

"Are both War Dogs?"

"No. Only J'kaya. Azzin is a civilian."

"Her assignment?"

"Classified."

"I thought you trusted me, my King."

"I am protecting you. Plausible deniability."

"Ah." I take a sip of coffee. It's cold. A bad sign for my day.

"Why call me? How can I help? This seems like a job for your other embedded War Dogs."

Wonder of wonders, T'Challa begins to *pace*.

"We have not been able to maintain our normal levels of intelligence in the United States these past few years. I can't use my local War Dogs, because discovery of any authorized activity on their behalf would likely interfere with local ongoing investigations and possibly expose my intelligence network to the Americans. It would take me at least two days to organize and deploy a War Dog detachment from here, and that is before we factor in my two most experienced foreign officers being kidnapped by a nativist terrorist cell. My people would be dead by then."

"Yeah." I pour my brick-cold coffee into the kitchen sink. "I can see how that's tough. So you're calling me because…"

"I would like for you to find them, yes. But that isn't all. This group, the 'Brave.' There is something strange about them. Some of the men… I feel like I recognize them."

I snort. "You meet one Klansman, you've met 'em all."

"No, it's not that. I don't have a passing feeling of knowing these men in another life. I mean that I believe I've actually met a few of those men before. During a point in my life when men like that could have closer access to me. Their hate tastes… familiar. This is the type of scenario I hoped you'd be able to assist me with, Kevin. My duties require me to be in many different places, much of the time simultaneously. I simply don't have the time to be everywhere at once. I would like for you to be me in places where I cannot, to use your unique skills in ways that my other agents cannot."

"I gathered that by the tricked-out apartment and the new gear," I reply, thinking about the slick white reinforced Vibranium-weave armor, Vibranium knives and sonic spear, Kimoyo beads, and Vibranium-reinforced 9mm sidearm that I have adorning an armor stand in my bedroom. "I accepted your offer. I've given you my final answer."

T'Challa raised one eyebrow.

"Ah," he says. "I prepared that speech in case you needed more convincing. I didn't know that your acceptance of my gifts was also acceptance of my offer."

"You elevated my situation. I abso-damn-lutely accept your offer. Have your techs had a chance to locate the source of that video?"

"Not yet, but they are working. The Brave are not fools. They used secure servers, randomized their IPs and uploaded it to darknet forums for distribution. Still, using visual and auditory data from the video, we were able to pinpoint about thirty-four different processing plants or warehouse spaces that the original video could have been recorded in."

My holoscreen leaps back to life, projecting my own three-dimensional map of Washington, D.C., right over the large wooden desk that dominates my living room. Thirty-four red dots spring to life all over the city.

T'Challa leans over the table, his elbows resting on the edge.

"I performed some further analysis and was able to remove twenty-three of these locations from consideration. They all had minor inconsistencies with the video. But these eleven locations—"

He waves a hand, and most of the red dots blink out, leaving, yep, eleven red dots left. They're not even spread that far out. They all seem to center on Ivy City, a formerly industrialized area.

"So this is the area I have to cover? Eleven locations spread across a smaller area looks more like my speed. I'm not Spider-Man, you know. I still gotta pay for gas."

"Yes, I agree this is much more manageable. I can't give you any additional information other than my people have been in one of these warehouses in the last twenty-four hours."

After a few seconds of studying the map on the table, I have a pretty good mental map of it. It would take me a while, but I could give each spot a good search, given enough time.

"How much time do I have for this?"

T'Challa is a bad dude. It's never easy to forget that he's a genius, or that he's regal as hell, or that he could definitely kick your ass up and down the street.

But see, T'Challa has a weapon greater than Vibranium. My guy is bad because he has ice in his veins. You in his way? Soon you'll be out of it. You threaten his people? He'll put you in the dirt.

I know he doesn't flinch when he delivers bad news, because he looks me in my eye until *I'm* uncomfortable.

"My people only have twenty-four hours. Which means you, Kasper, have twenty. Twenty hours to find my people or they're dead before you arrive."

"Way to put on the pressure," I say, but I don't have any beef with T'Challa. I'm going to save these people come hell or high water. That's all there really is to it.

"UMOYA," I say, studying the holo-map that T'Challa has created for me. He's also provided me with a Wakandan Design Group Quinjet that zips through American airspace like a secret. I'm armed, armored, and ready to roll. "Start pulling up all the info you can find about this group... The Brave. I want general info, case files, anything you can find from U.S. Homeland Security, law enforcement records, whatever."

"And would you like milk for your tea?"

"I... uh..." I swear Umoya giggles at my being flustered.

"I'll search and ping you when I find something."

"Thanks," I mutter, turning my attention back to the map.

Eleven red dots equal eleven shipping houses, trainyards, warehouses, or manufacturing plants where the conditions seen and heard in the video matched the conditions in an area where said video could have been shot. Each location is itself an entire scene to examine, to turn over for hints, to explore. And even though I can see in the dark and smell the exact color and condition of a man's socks from two hundred feet away, it still takes me a while to pick through a whole warehouse. The first one, a two-level paper plant, takes me about ninety minutes in total to search through. And if T'Challa is to be trusted—and he always is—I don't have much more time to find his kidnapped diplomats before they're killed in service to good old American Bullshit.

It takes me less time, only about forty-five minutes, to go through location 2.

Locations 3, 4, 5, and 9 have all been torn down in the last week.

Location 6 has already been converted into high-rise lofts.

My Quinjet lands at location 8 and there's blood everywhere. On the walls, splattered on the floor, dripping from the ceiling. Before I can even kick a little ass, some pimple-faced dweeb shines a stage light in my face.

It's a new horror movie being shot on location. Found the wrong video.

220   That leaves locations 7, 10, and 11.

Now, I was a narc cop for a good little while before I accepted T'Challa's generous offer. And for all those years, my driver was one thing: cash rules everything around me. But now, for taking the same risks I used to take in a hope to get noticed and promoted for free, I'm doing it armed, outfitted, and compensated by the great nation of Wakanda.

My armor comes heavy duty now, with a dark gray Vibranium tactical vest, three times as durable as the microweave beneath it. A Vibranium longknife and a place to keep my Vibranium daggers where I won't accidentally stab myself. It's a welcome change that I'm still getting used to.

I've been to space. I've seen all kinds of things in all kinds of places, but nothing prepares me for what I see when I get to location 10—10 because 7 and 11 were the only other choices and I'm not that lucky. Inside smells heavily of one-shower-per-week bodies, but there's something else, something under all of it that sets my teeth on edge.

Pure fear.

They've been here, Azzin and J'kaya. Past the opening threshold. Into the staging area. Warehouse control center is two flights up and I take both sets in one leap, jumping right up to the balcony jutting from the control center and flipping over the railing.

This close, the smell of bodies, blood, and oil is nearly overpowering. I shake my head, focus on what I can see. Bright lights illuminate everything, including blood spatter on the floor and walls, sweat-stained scraps of cloth, and leftover trash— someone had been eating cheap energy bars and had left torn packaging in a little heap in one corner of the room. They hadn't cleaned but hadn't left much behind either: a couple of long blond hairs on a chair, a smudge of oil wiped across a switchboard, a clipped off shoelace.

Easy to get lost in the cacophony of sensory information. The sights, the smells, the hints of memory that people unwittingly leave behind. In the center of this room, for every question that J'kaya refused or evaded, the Brave beat Azzin. His blood is on the rug. On the wall. Splattered against a chair. That blood is the key.

"Umoya." When on the hunt, she doesn't pop to pixelated life in front of me. Instead, she speaks right into my skull.

"*Yes, Kevin?*"

"Can you see what I'm seeing?"

"*Yes, Kevin.*"

"Will you please, if you don't mind, scan this room and send it to King T'Challa. Let him know I'm on the trail of the two lost."

"*It's good to see that you're learning,*" Umoya says with a tone like she's patting me on the cheek. "*I'll let the king know.*"

"Oh, and one more thing? Connect me to Bailey at the 74th. I'm gonna need his eyes too."

Umoya connects me, but there's a half-second of silence before the sergeant's desk at the 74th rings, and in that half-second, I hear it. A jingling of metal, a scraping boot. Someone—a well-trained someone—is here. Before they can split, I'm out of the control room, following their movement. They're up, on the next level where replacement machine parts are kept. Invisible to my scans and, until now, to my senses. There's a ladder up, but I sprint up the wall, gaining the next level in time to see a dark, armored figure shoulder the roof escape door open, nearly tearing it off its hinges. Strong. This is getting exciting.

"You've reached the 74th Precinct, this is Sergeant Nunez speaking."

"Nunez, this is Kasper. Can you connect me to Lieutenant Bradley's desk? I don't remember his cell."

"Kasper? I thought you'd be enjoying that leave with your girl and kid."

"Trying to, Nunez, but work keeps butting in. Connect me to Bradley?"

"Sure thing, bud. What are you doing, jogging? Lotta static on your end."

"Nunez! Bradley! Please!"

"Yeah, yeah. One second, man."

Whoever this is, they're quick. By the time I get through the escape door, they're perched at the edge of the roof. They look back at me and I have to slow up a second.

Big yellow eyes stare right at me from an armored helmet. He's analyzing me, sizing me up. He's armored too: in all black gear, a vest with overlapping plates that look kind of like feathers, and sturdy combat boots. No fear whatsoever.

But I don't need him to fear me. I need to know what he's seen.

"Hold it right there," I yell. He shakes his head slightly, almost as if he's annoyed, and turns to run.

Drawing a Vibranium knife comes to me as quick as breathing. I pull it, will it to its lowest setting, and fire an energy blast just as the armored guy leaps off the roof.

I can sense more than see it connect with the armored dude. I'm rewarded with a heavy clatter as he loses control mid-leap and lands hard on something. I really hope he's not dead or hurt. Bradley chooses the perfect moment to come on the line.

"What you got for me, Kasper?"

"Shit," I mutter, dashing toward the edge of the roof. The armored guy has landed, alright. On a freaking metal bird glider thing that speeds off with him laying limp across it. Even with panther speed, I can't catch it. I sit on the roof and dangle my legs over the side.

"Not funny, Kasper. Please don't tell me you're prank calling me while you're on leave and I'm stuck here with the city's most interesting citizens."

"Oh, Bradley. My bad, man."

"Everything okay?"

"Yeah, I just... I just caught a guy going through my trash. Chased him but he got away."

"Bad luck. Better cancel all your cards and shit before he buys a thousand dollars' worth of tube socks."

"Thanks for the tip," I say, watching the bird's smoke trail as it disappears into the afternoon. "I wonder if you can give me another. Guy has a tattoo, said he's in some group called 'The Brave?' You heard of 'em?"

Bradley's sigh is long and loud. "Those guys. Pain in my ass is what they are. How much time you got?"

"Not much, Bradley," I say as the bird finally gets too far away to see. "Not much at all. So run me what you got. Quick."

○———————○

KING T'CHALLA'S long arm extends to D.C.: he's set me up with an outpost in a small tourist hotel in the suburbs. It's just shabby enough to make no one care much about it. From my encounter at location 10, it takes me an hour to head back to my room, sneak in unnoticed, reoutfit myself, and download new info from Umoya to compare to the notes I got from Bradley. What black suit homie doesn't know is that my Vibranium dagger tagged him, and now that he's stopped moving, I know where he's holed up: a base in a warehouse district in a city called Lanham. Umoya fills me in as I make my way toward my knife's signal in my T'Challa-issued Quinjet.

"*The Brave is a white-nationalist terror organization originating in Birmingham, Alabama,*" Umoya informs me. "*The Brave was a fringe organization until the early 2000s and their membership increased after the terrorist attacks on September 11th, 2001. They have moved their base of operations to Monroe Island off the coast of Georgia. They operate mostly in secret and have not had many high-profile operations or incidents until this abduction. Most of their online posting revolves around keeping 'America Strong' by closing off its borders and removing immigrants from the country. There seems to have been a recent schism in the organization, which has led to a change in leadership.*"

"Trouble in paradise, eh? Might be a lead for me. Keep searching and keep me posted on what you find. Please?"

"*Of course, Kevin.*"

I pass the rest of the ride putting the pieces together. The Brave has the Wakandans, but they've gone underground. I got a blood signature from Azzin, but no way to track it yet. Whoever this is in the black armor was snooping around the same site I was, which means they might know something, which means they're my next stop.

We fly from Ivy Park south through the city. As we pass the Capitol building, the Washington Monument, and the *freaking White House*, I have a moment of strange hysteria as I realize I'm in a Vibranium-sealed jet stealthed against my country's tracking systems, staring down at monuments I haven't even visited as my civilian self yet. I'm an American citizen, but I'm operating on behalf of a foreign nation, and if I'm caught, who knows where I'll end up—or whether T'Challa will be able to help me get free. I let that strange and terrible feeling roll over me and turn my attention back to the journey.

My Vibranium knife's tracking signature has been pinging me from one location for the past hour: a small office park. It's twenty-two miles from my access point. My remote-piloted Quinjet makes it there in about five minutes. It sets me down about three hundred meters away from the pinging point. I check my weapons and slide out into the afternoon. As I move through the shadows in the direction of my signal, I notice my suit, which was its kinda standard white and gray on the Quinjet, start to dapple a little bit—its biocloaking engaging to keep me all but invisible to most conventional forms of detection.

This office park is pretty routine: a couple of six-story office buildings surrounding a small, man-made park with enough room for a couple trees, a walking trail, and a pond with fish darting around in it. In Building 2, on the fifth floor, the signal pulls at me.

After thinking about giving a good scare to the employees screwing-off time in the park, I make my way around the rear of Building 1, and, steeling myself, take a running leap onto one of the brick walls that cover the sides of Building 2, counting on biostealth to shield me from nosy neighbors. I stop at the fifth floor and listen. There's thumping coming from one of the windows on the upper floors: I trust in my suit to let me run along the windows, until I find the one that's cracked open and slide into an empty office where someone is playing Air Supply's "I'm All Out of Love" at an embarrassingly high volume.

I hop to the other side of the office, take a step out—

And then, I catch a quick glimpse of three bird-shaped orbs before they explode around me. None of them are strong enough to put a dent in my Vibranium armor, but they're loud, smoky, and disorienting. If this had been a few years ago, they would've overwhelmed my senses, but I've had time to acclimate to the changes that the Heart-Shaped Herb has made to my body.

The bombs came from the stairwell opposite. I cover the distance in a short wall run and kick through the door to the stairwell just as the black-armored guy leaps down a flight.

He bursts out onto the fifth floor with me close behind. Before I can grab him, he spins and blasts a kick into my chest that sends me stumbling. I'm back into the chase almost immediately, but this time with adjusted expectations. This dude is smart and quick, but I'm not bad at foot pursuits, either. Out on the fifth floor, I catch a glimpse of him rounding a corner, and I chase.

"Umoya," I call. "This bird guy is starting to be a problem. Can you get me info on him?"

"*Just a moment,*" she responds. "*According to the armor design, your quarry appears to be Nighthawk, an alias for Raymond Kane, a Chicago-area businessman and costumed vigilante. According to my records, he hasn't been seen doing vigilante work in at least six months.*"

"He ever involved in villain work?"

"*No,*" Umoya chirps, "*but his methods are usually lethal. Take care, Kevin.*"

I round the corner in time to see Nighthawk run straight toward the fifth-floor window. I cover the distance between us in three big leaps, getting close enough quickly enough to strike out and grab his leg as he crashes through the fifth-floor window. And then we're airborne; my grabbing his ankle sends us spinning.

I hear the bird before I see it—it emits the faintest electrical whine as it slices the air. I have to time this perfectly. He turns himself in midair to grab the bird glider, and as he grabs it, I snatch at his leg again. The glider carries us for a couple hundred feet before it skids to the ground, sending the both of us sprawling across the parking lot. He's up on his feet almost as quick as me, but he wavers a bit. That fall took a bit out of him. Score one for Vibranium armor.

"You tell me what I want to know and this doesn't get ugly," I say as I advance on him. He reaches around, pulls out a wicked looking pair of owl-inspired grenades. "Oh, so that's how you want to play it. Fine. I'll beat the ambassadors' location out of you."

He holds up his hands, a grenade in each, and I slow up.

"Wait. I recognize you. You're not with The Brave," he says. Not a question, but a statement. His voice is mechanical, hollow.

"You're not either?"

The bird guy's helmet tilts slightly to the side. For some reason, I'm detecting annoyance, though the voice stays flat. "I'm hunting them."

"Oh word? It never hurts to have backup. Think we can compare notes?"

He drops his hands, replaces the grenades in the belt pouch he pulled them from. "You can tell me what you know."

"That's not what I meant," I say, returning my Vibranium knives to their sheaths. The parking lot has cleared out, the few people who had been loitering having had the good sense to disappear. "You got somewhere we can hunker and talk about next steps?"

Nighthawk doesn't say anything. He just turns and motions for me to follow. He leads me back into the building we crashed out of. As we walk past the reception desk, the security guard stares slack-jawed at us mid-phone call to the cops. I toss him a wave. Nighthawk walks past the desk nonchalantly, to the elevators. He waves a hand in front of an otherwise normal looking panel and a section of the wall slides open, revealing a different elevator. This one is darker, less office-park chic and more *Mission: Impossible*.

We enter the elevator, which is much roomier than it looks on the outside, and from the time the doors shut until they reopen I don't even notice that I'm moving.

"Smooth ride," I say as the doors slide silently open. Nighthawk glances at me, then steps off the elevator and into the kind of room that I've been in one too many times in my life. Big monitor, blinking lights on tech in various states of disrepair, and a weapons rack stacked tall with nasty looking rifles, grenades, and rocket launchers, all bird themed.

"Is your glider going to be alright? You just left it out there."

"It'll make its way back," Nighthawk says. He reaches up, grabs the sides of his helmet, and gives it a little tug. It disengages from the neck armor with a hiss and he pulls it up over his head, revealing buzzcut-short stubble, then… kinky black ringlets fall down out of the helmet, over her face as the woman formerly known as "bird guy" turns to me.

"Well?" She glares at me with hard eyes, two silver fangs glistening from her snarling mouth. "Don't make a production out of it. T'Challa send you?"

I pull my own helmet off, take a seat on one of the less cluttered desks. "Nightshade—Tilda?" I can't believe I'm standing in front of Dr. Tilda Johnson, formerly known as Deadly Nightshade. Full-time villain, genius inventor, and rogue extraordinaire. She'd had a couple run-ins with King T'Challa, but no one had seen her in a little while.

"My God, I had no idea that was you under that armor. I haven't seen you since, uh… since you were running with that knockoff crew of Misty Knight's! What are you doing here? And what's with the getup?"

"I switched teams," she says, sighing. "Joined the good guys, for all the good that did me. Hooked up with the original owner of this armor."

"Nighthawk? What happened to him?"

She looks down, away, and doesn't answer my question. "Why are you here?"

"You tell me," I reply, crossing my arms over my chest. "I'll bet you already got it figured out."

228   "Of course T'Challa sent you. You're after those missing

Wakandan diplomats. I'm after The Brave just because they need to go, but you being here must mean The Brave got 'em? For what, though? Surely they're not after Wakandan tech or secrets?"

"Nope," I cut in, "nothing so complicated. It's just plain old racism."

"Say what now?"

"Umoya, display video. Please."

"*Okay, Kevin,*" Umoya says, and plays the video against Nightshade's oversized computer monitor. We watch it flicker and fade.

"I mean, it makes sense," Nightshade says, frowning. She turns hard eyes to me. "Must suck being T'Challa's do-boy. Even if it does get you a sweet AI companion."

"*I like her,*" Umoya croons in my ear.

Ignoring Umoya, I shrug. "It's a living. So, there's one thing the video or your responses hasn't cleared up for me. Why are *you* here?"

"I got reasons."

"Mind sharing one?"

"I don't like racists."

"That's fair. But..." I motion for her to continue.

"The Brave are just the latest in a long line of ineffectual, hyperviolent bottom feeders who have no better purpose than to ruin the lives of good, innocent people who are just trying to make a halfway decent life in a system that despises them. Scum like The Brave are better off not being here. I'm fulfilling that."

"Pretty solid reasons. Still feel like you're leaving something out."

"You're as smart as you look."

I swear, Umoya giggles. "You know where The Brave are now?"

She sits down in her special computer chair, swivels it around to face the monitor. She waves again, and it blinks to life. The image on the screen shows a farmhouse and big red barn sitting in the middle of a brilliant green grassy field, surrounded by thick tree cover and rolling hills.

"Drone footage," she explains. "You probably got intel saying The Brave operate out of Georgia. That's old, useless. They're currently holed up in a farm outside Eaton, New Hampshire. Nothing much out there, nobody to bother them. Perfect for them to get up to a whole bunch of no good."

She flips a switch, and the screen goes black, switches for infrared. A big white ball glows inside the barn.

"What the hell is *that*?"

"That, my pantherish friend, is no good."

There's a clatter and whoosh as the elevator doors open. Before I can even pull a Vibranium knife, the bird glider hobbles in, smoking and sparking. Tilda looks at it, then at me.

"I'm sure T'Challa gave you and your sweet AI partner a ride. Saddle up, buttercup. We're going to New Hampshire."

WE TOUCH down near-silently in a clearing about twelve miles outside of Eaton, but still west of I-93. The Wakandan craft is smooth, quiet, and because we've made our journey here after dark, nearly invisible thanks to its cloaking tech. Nightshade is armed and armored up again, her black bird glider silently self-repairing in the Quinjet's hold. We land and Umoya powers the ship down.

"*We'll be here on standby until you return, Kevin,*" she announces through the ship's speakers.

"Gotta get me one of those," Nighthawk mutters before pointing off east, farther into the forest. "Barn's that way. Let's do this quiet."

"Before we go," I say, activating my helmet, "I gotta know your reasons if we're gonna do this whole team-up thing. I remember you having beef with the king once upon a time."

"That's history," she whispers harshly. "The people ahead of us are much more horrible. My time with Nighthawk showed me that."

"Yeah," I say, hoping she'll keep going.

Instead, she fixes the helmet's yellow eyes on me and leans in close. "Let's go."

I can barely hear her moving through the trees, even though I can make out the dull glow of her eyes in the darkness. It's not long before we reach the fencing separating the farm proper from the woods. I scan for sensors or traps, and after finding none, we hop the fence and continue in the direction of the farm's soft lights. There are trucks, and farm equipment, but no people in sight. Most of the light we can detect comes from the dark red barn. We move a bit closer, then dive behind a tractor as a blade of light splits the night, spilling across the grass. The barn door squeals as someone pulls it shut, inviting the night back to its rightful place.

It's then that I catch it. From the barn, a scent. Ambassador J'kina's scent.

"Let's move," I rasp, and we split off the tractor, slicing through the grass in low sprints. There's no moonlight to speak of to give us away as we press up against the side of the barn. There's a window behind me, high up.

I nod at Nightshade, then move, leaping up to the window, grabbing the sill, and pulling myself up. The window's locked—a Vibranium knife makes short work of that, and I'm in. Easy-peasy.

You know how you're never really prepared for what you're gonna find behind a locked door?

There's nothing normal inside the barn. There's a workbench, a bunch of tall metal canisters of gas, and cages. Rows and rows of cages. The soft light doesn't obscure much from me. Almost all of them are empty. All except one. I glance down, where Nightshade is waiting, and motion that I'm going in. She's shaking her head and waving me back down to her. Instead, I drop in and down, landing softly on the sawdust-covered ground.

Ambassador J'kina is here, in a steel-wire cage large enough to hold a man. Alone. She's dirty, tired, her once pristine clothes ripped and grimy with sweat. Her breathing comes slow and shallow, and hers is the only breath in the room besides mine. In fact, the only sound in here besides the hum of the floodlights is the low-grade noise of high-powered tech.

Staying low and quiet, I creep over to Ambassador J'kina's cage. Fury boils up in my chest. Caging a whole human, for nothing but having the audacity to not be born in the right place, or not look a certain way? Not on my watch. A Vibranium knife will cut through these bars no problem.

"Ambassador J'kina, you with me?" Her responding wheeze isn't reassuring. "Hang in there. I'm going to get you out of here. But first, I need your help finding Ambassador Merkeba."

"My king…" she manages. "They are… prepared for you…"

I'm to my feet with knives in hand as soon as the roof of the barn implodes from a sudden impact. There's a thump, a deep thud and tremor, and what seems like twenty minutes of rattling. Dust billows in the enclosed space, and before it can settle I see two slivers of light—mechanical eyes—staring right at me.

"I knew you would come… Panther!"

He explodes through the hazy barn, claws outstretched. He's quick. I barely block his slashes with my knife before spinning away and dropping to a low crouch. As the dust clears, I get a good look at him. It's unsettling, really.

He's a panther too, a star-spangly, more high-tech version of me. His armor is thick, heavy, reminiscent of something Tony Stark would build. It's plated, dark but not black, and a star is pasted right on his forehead. A white stripe framed in red slashes down his torso, stopping at the star symbol on his belt. The armor plating on his knees and elbows is starred as well, but the biggest change to the panther ensemble is the large white mane surrounding his head and shoulders.

"Wrong panther, bruh." I rise, pulling my gun from its hip holster. "And you're the pot right now, man. What kind of cat are you? Umoya?"

"*If I'm correct about this, his real name is unknown, but the insignia on his armor has been encountered before,*" Umoya beams into my head. "*During one of the king's stints as an urban crime fighter. This one may be connected to a former minion of the Hate-Monger, codenamed the American Panther.*"

"I am The Lion of Columbia, protector of this great nation."

"*The American Panther was an anti-immigrant criminal who crossed the king several years ago. He stirred up mobs in Hell's Kitchen.*"

"I protect the rightful inhabitants of this land from people like you, and the man you represent."

"He is a former NYPD police officer and was last seen in the custody of the New York City Department of Corrections."

"People like me? You don't even know what I look like."

"You look like prey." He rushes me again.

His claws tear through the worktable, ripping the steel to shreds. I dodge the slash, block a knee that lifts me off my feet, but I manage to free my gun and squeeze off a couple shots at him. He dodges, the Vibranium rounds burying themselves in the dirt.

He's on me, slashing, striking. He lands a kick to my midsection that sends me sprawling. Before I can recover, he drives his fist into my shoulder—would have been my skull if I hadn't twisted. I need room, space. I draw my legs up, deliver a double-legged kick to his chest that knocks him back a couple steps.

"I thought I would face the Panther himself, not his pale carbon copy." He's pacing when I gain my feet. "Still, you remind me of *him* in more than the way you dress. The way you move, your weapons, all of it. You, your kind, you're all a stain on this country. You weaken us with your presence. The spies you sent, they thought they would weaken us further by spreading secrets and lies. But my Brave and I, we discovered them. And after we found the sickness, we cut it out."

"Where's Ambassador Merkeba?"

"The man? Insignificant garbage. We buried him with the rest. You'll join him soon."

He rushes me again, but this time, instead of meeting him head-on, I dodge backward, send knives flying at his vitals, then immediately switch direction and weapons, busting a couple of shots at the joints of his armor. This is all over.

Or so I think. He pulls up, raises his hands in front of his face. His eyes glow for a split second, and then he throws his arms wide, releasing an energy blast out in an arc in front of him. The blast sends my knives skittering, my bullets harmlessly off target, and me flying. I'm able to catch a glimpse of the ambassador shielding her eyes before my body demolishes the barn's doors and skids across the soft earth. Everything's a quadruple-time blur, which keeps me from seeing or hearing the Lion's approach. But I do feel his armored boot spiking into my skull. The darkness comes quick.

○———————○

FIRST THING I notice when waking up: it's dark, and I can smell my own blood. My armor's gone. Which means no weapons. Which means no Umoya. I'm alone. Nightshade never showed. The ambassador? I sit up quick, which makes my head spin painfully out of control. A sharp buzz builds inside my brain, and I grab my head. It all comes back. The ambassadors. T'Challa. The Brave.

It's then I notice the bars. I'm caged. Trapped. I leap up, grab at the mesh, try to rip it away from the bars, but it's strong. It holds, keeps me stuck here. This isn't good. There are other smells, other bodies. Some are dead. Ambassador J'kina's scent is here. Ambassador Merkeba's is as well. Both alive. Were I the man my armor signified, I'd thank Bast. Instead, I settle for a sigh of relief. If I get the ambassadors out of this alive, I'm asking T'Challa for a raise.

"Don't struggle," the Lion says from outside the cage. "This is the rightful place for you. Out of your armor, you're no more than another strain of the virus damaging our country. Another weak-blooded mutt stain on this nation's greatness. My Brave and I are going to stamp you all out and wash our country clean. You'll have the honor of being the first among the cleansed."

"You said Ambassador Merkeba was dead."

"He will be, soon. Along with you."

"Why? I know that you used to be a cop. I served, too. You have to know, these people you're keeping caged, they have families. People who love them. Your men, your 'Brave?' You're endangering them. Once the axe drops, all of you could face jail time, or worse."

He steps close to my cage, jabs an armored finger at me. "I have already committed crimes for the sake of my nation. The things I did when I was on the force. Swallowing my pride and what I knew to be right and true. Serving and protecting scum like you… we have nothing in common. My Brave and I will rule this country from sea to shining sea. We're ready to die for the future of our nation. All of us. Are you ready to die for yours?"

"This *is* my nation!"

"Your armor says otherwise." He flexes his fingers, and dark claws unsheath themselves. "Maybe my cleansing should begin with you."

Before he can reach the cage, our conversation is interrupted by two members of the Brave. These men are dressed in their normal jeans and t-shirts but hide their identities behind dark masks with white forehead stars reminiscent of the one their leader wears.

"Sir," one of them butts in, and leans close to the armored bigot. I make out "…disturbance… may have had an accomplice… several men lost already."

The Lion stands up ramrod straight and looks over at me. "Your kind are tricky. I'll be back to continue what we started. You two. Stay here and watch him."

He leaves, and all the tension I'd been holding in drains from my body, leaving me sweaty and tired. I study the bars of the cage, the door, the supports holding it up. I'm locked in some kind of magnetic pattern lock, maybe accessed with an electromagnetic pin? Meaning there has to be a master switchboard for the cages. That was why I couldn't pry it open. T'Challa could have picked this lock in his sleep. I'm not T'Challa, but I can think like him. Every cage has weak points. My next step is to figure out where this cage's weak points are.

"Spook looks like he's thinking hard," one of the Brave members says to the other. It's just two of them, alone. By their scents, unarmed. Bingo. Found the weak points.

"Bet you have no idea what that feels like," I bite back.

"Big words from a monkey stuck in a cage."

"You wouldn't know a big word if it slapped your mama across her mustache, bootlicker."

"The hell you say about my mama?!"

"Uh," the other Brave guy interjects. "Calm down. He's for the Lion to deal with."

"I'm of a mind to deal with him right now. Since he's so smart."

A whispery metallic voice splits the darkness. "Let's go to school, then."

At that second, both the air and the Brave members' throats are split by four dark silver quill knives that come flying out of the shadows. The two go down, gurgling on their own blood. Damn. the cop in me recoils at the way Tilda casually murders the two Brave goons.

"Dammit! You didn't have to kill 'em."

"Don't be so sweet polly purebred," Nighthawk scolds, dropping to a gentle landing in front of my cage. "Nobody's gonna cry for these guys."

"You don't know that. And besides, body counts complicate things."

"Not in my experience."

"Look, man, where were you? I could have used your help."

She begins to rummage around the room. It's almost a replica of the barn that the Lion and I crossed claws in, with several workbenches, racks with farming tools hanging from them, and cages. Lots of cages, and all of them this time are full.

"You were thinking with your heart and not your head. I made the safer play. Now, I gotta get you outta here and to your armor."

"But these others? The ambassadors. We can take them if we can get them on my Quinjet."

"Why do you always have to complicate things? Let's go one step at a time and get you out of here first. Ah. Found it."

She jogs over to a panelboard mounted on the rear wall of the room we're in. From where I sit, all I can see are colored buttons and a touchpad. Nightshade plays around with it a bit.

"Can you hurry? The Lion will be back soon."

"No, he won't," she says as an enormous explosion reverberates through the room. "When I do distractions, I go big."

She taps out a quick button sequence, then presses the touchpad.

The lock to my cage clicks open. "Good money," she jogs back over to me. "Whew, you need a bath."

"Just help me find my armor. I can track it by scent. It's not far from here."

The barn door blasts into the room. The Lion steps forward through the smoke, my armor slung over his shoulder.

"It's right here," the Lion says, tossing my armor to the ground. "I see everything that happens in my den. Neither of you can outsmart me. Now, both of you will be cleansed."

Nightshade doesn't say anything. Instead, she raises her arm and fires a salvo of dark silver knives from a wrist-mounted blaster at him. The knives bounce off the Lion's armor as he charges her. I meet him with a shoulder check that clearly hurts me more than him. He skids to a halt and glares down at me, raising a fist to swat me away. I roll with the blow and follow with a spinning kick to the side of his helmet that painfully jars my ankle and leaves me hobbling away. The Lion laughs at my efforts. My ankle hurts, but I've drawn his attention away from Nighthawk. She reaches around her back and pulls out a silvery pistol and a couple of bird grenades. She tosses the grenades at the Lion's feet, and I roll away just as they explode beneath him. As he trips over from the blast force, Nightshade leaps and fires at him. The gun's bullets glow gold in the dark room, and explode against the Lion's armor on impact, creating an acrid scent as they eat through his armor plating.

"It's not gonna be enough," I call to her, moving to reengage the Lion as he pushes himself off the ground. "Be careful. He has weapons—"

He raises his arms to activate the energy blast, but is knocked off balance by another grenade. When he stumbles in my direction, I give him a strong shove that sends him stumbling in the other direction. Nightshade moves in, knives at the ready, but the Lion is fast, and almost completely undamaged. He grabs Nightshade by the arm and tosses her across the room, sending her crashing into the far wall.

Before I can move, he turns and plants his boot in my chest, sending me hard to the ground. "This is the best you can do?" he roars.

I leap up, striking at him. My blows come quick, and some land, but even with the enhancements from the Heart-Shaped Herb, my bare fists bounce off his armor.

"We gotta get through to him!" I shout.

"On it!" Nightshade says, ducking between the workbenches. He whips around to find her, to fire a blast in her direction. A quick kick to his shoulder redirects his shot, and he blasts a hole in the wall opposite us. He catches me with a backhand but I absorb the blow, even though it makes me feel like I just ate one of Tilda's grenades. Gritting my teeth through the pain, I lash out, landing an elbow to his armored cheek.

"That is the final time you'll strike me," the Lion growls, and extends his claws. Being almost completely naked, I'm not excited about this part of the fight. I brace myself as he leaps at me, but he suddenly jerks and goes rigid, then clatters to the ground.

Nightshade comes back into view, the panelboard that controls the cages in her hand. "They power it using a local intranet. That's how he knew we were here. Efficient, but dumb." She taps a couple of buttons and the armor segments open along the spinal seam, exposing the man inside. When the armor is open enough for him to emerge, she reaches down and pulls him out of it. The shock of the sudden disconnection makes him groan.

"You chump! You almost killed me," she yells, shaking him. His head rolls limp on his shoulders. "And you definitely killed some people who look like me. Let me return that favor."

"No! Come on. We need to focus on getting the ambassadors and the other immigrants out of here."

"We need to focus on keeping this from happening again."

"You're not making the smart play." I toss her words back at her, hoping to take her mind off murder.

"This has been my play the entire time. I thought you would have caught on by now. Didn't know you were such a Boy Scout."

"So his life is a good trade for all of theirs?"

She considers me for a long moment. I can feel her hard eyes behind her helmet's visor. "Get your armor and call your ship. We're getting out of here."

All the way down the cages, the doors disengage and pop open. I climb back into my armor.

"Umoya?"

"*Welcome back,*" she greets. "*I am moving the Quinjet to your location now and alerting the appropriate authorities. Would you like to call the king?*"

"No. Let's focus on getting everyone out of here."

It's gonna take the Quinjet a few minutes to arrive, so Nightshade and I focus on getting the immigrants on their feet, tending any major injuries, and readying them to run if the situation demands it.

"Come on," Nightshade calls. We line up about twenty-five kidnapped immigrants in all, all in various states of undress and injury. The Quinjet's lights pierce the night sky, and a couple of stray Brave members, their outlines illuminated by a huge fire visible in the distance, take potshots at the Quinjet. Their bullets can't pierce the ship's Vibranium shields, and it swoops in to land.

"Brave members inbound," I yell. "Let's get these folks on the ship!"

Bullets crack into the wooden barn around us. The Brave are getting close. Our released immigrants are moving as quickly as they can, but they're tired, hungry, and can't load on the ship any quicker. Then, a different sound cracks the night. Brave members go down from gunfire from Nighthawk's glider, which flies around like a giant bird of prey, only with mounted guns instead of talons.

"Well," she says, shrugging at me as she helps an older gentleman onto the Quinjet. "You said I couldn't kill *him*. These guys are asking for it."

I glance back at the Lion, who is on his hands and knees, glaring at us.

"You won't win!" he screams. "It is my divine mandate to purify this country of the immigrant sickness and I will not be deterred! If I can't win through my own skills, I will win through sheer destructive power. Armor, engage self-destruct sequence, authorization code—"

His command dies as he does, from a dark silver blade in his throat.

"There," Nightshade shrugs. "Done."

The only sounds left in the night as we load the immigrant prisoners is fire crackling in the distance, and the remaining warning shots of Nighthawk's glider. I take Ambassador J'kina by the arm, and hoist Ambassador Merkeba on my shoulder. Both are tired, dirty, and alive. That has to be enough for now.

I'M BACK in my slick apartment, watching King T'Challa visit the ambassadors in the infirmary on video. I've been checked and cleared for bed rest in my own place, thankfully. There's a knock at the door.

"Umoya, open the door. Please."

"*I knew you had manners,*" she quips. My apartment door slides open. Standing there is Tilda, sans armor. She walks into the room, looking lovingly at a Kimoyo bead bracelet.

"I really, really hate I spent so much time beefing with T'Challa. All the good tech is here in Wakanda." She looks up at me. "How you coming?"

"Getting there. My check hit my account this morning. More zeroes than I've seen in my whole life. Sending the majority of it back to Gwen—in installments, of course. Maybe I'll be able to make a visit home after this, see my kid."

"That's sweet. You know, I got a chance to talk to T'Challa. He invited me to join you in… whatever this is."

"What'd you say?"

"Maybe. I still got some reasoning to do." She walks over to my window, looks out over the royal city. "You know, we made a good team. And there's still so much out there to fix. The king, shocker of all shockers, agrees with me."

She turns back at me, an excited gleam in her eyes. "Once you mend, want to keep going? Do a classic team-up run?"

I walk over to the window myself and stare out over Wakanda. It stretches out over the horizon. I look over at Nightshade—a lethal Nighthawk now, who plays with her Kimoyo beads as she waits on my answer.

I take a deep breath and let it go. Time to decide. For the million-and-first time:

Who am I?

THE UNDERSIDE
OF DARKNESS

GLENN PARRIS

HOW DOES one describe blinding pain?

For a fleeting eternity, T'Kayla's world had no color, no sound, no sensation at all. Reality invaded that timeless moment of bliss with definition as his right arm hung limp and numb. Flesh-ripping torque exerted by the Jabari adversary had wrung the Prince's shoulder like a chicken's neck. The arm lock wasn't sporting in ritual combat, but nor was it officially deemed illegal. The Panther Clan's champion faced his third challenge of the day and he was losing.

"Ruling!" T'Kayla groaned an objection. Strong fingers sought to massage life back into the injured shoulder as T'Kayla awaited a response. He raised his eyes to the elders for their decision. "They Who Judged the Contest" remained stone-faced, but their eyes shifted for only an instant to the offender. Oriku, the Gorilla clan's challenger, knelt clutching his own throat and sucking the wind for every labored breath.

One spoke for three among the elders. "Combat will continue without quarter."

Oriku splayed knees wide in the sands of battle. Sweat poured from the Jabari prince's brow as his hands dropped from throat to brace desperately against hips in support of his heaving chest's effort. Lungs filled slowly as air trickled in past clenched vocal cords. Painful and deliberate, each successive wheeze whistled from Oriku's gaping mouth with a lower pitch. He contemplated the Panther Prince's tactic.

T'Kayla's improvised counterattack had proven as unexpected as it was effective. The would-be Black Panther grabbed his own right wrist, obviously in agony from the wrenching maneuver. But instead of cradling the damaged limb, T'Kayla used his left hand to suddenly thrust the forearm upward like a spear, striking with the elbow just above the sternum as Oriku closed in for the kill. When the thump shut Oriku's windpipe, the heavily muscled contender nearly passed out. A lesser opponent *would* have lost consciousness and the battle would have been over. This was no common soldier. Like T'Kayla, Oriku had been cultivated and hardened from the seed of generations of warriors.

Slowly, Oriku recovered from the sharp blow to the throat. Soon he would rejoin the assault. T'Kayla's forecast for battle readiness looked less optimistic.

The burden of previous matches took their toll now. T'Kayla's inventory of injuries revealed bruises covering half his body, the price of hundreds of blocked attacks and unchecked strikes. He had acquired more lacerations than he had fingers. As tingling gave way to torrential pain, he tested functionality of the limb girdle.

At least three rotator cuff tendons torn, T'Kayla counted. *No mind-over-matter tricks this time.* He knew human anatomy just didn't work that way, not even when one fought for his life. *I rise to face Oriku as a one-armed man!*

Although swelling held his left eye nearly closed, T'Kayla's vision finally settled on a single image. Jaw locked from his first challenger's knee to the chin, the Panther Prince beckoned Oriku through gritted teeth, "Come on!"

Oriku lifted his gaze from the ground. His drooling ebbed as he finally caught his elusive breath. A smile reluctantly crossed Oriku's face as the Jabari prince took stock of the vulnerable champion. He watched T'Kayla's right arm swing loose and helpless.

Short work.

The throne was within Oriku's grasp. Like T'Kayla's life, he had but to reach out and take it.

T'Kayla surveyed the theater of combat for advantage. Clearly spent, the movement of his every muscle broadcast bone-deep anguish. Leaning on a lone rock with his good arm, misery dragged T'Kayla up to one knee, wide open to the inevitable.

For a brief instant, time again stood still for both fighters. Oriku closed the distance in three measured steps then struck with an open-handed downward blow. T'Kayla's head bobbed once and recoiled from the unanswered slap. He grasped the rock as if it were the only vestige of reality: an anchor to life itself.

"Good night, dark prince," Oriku's hot breath whispered in his victim's ear with both hands clasped together. He swung his leg up to trap T'Kayla's good hand underfoot against the rock. He had tested T'Kayla. His adversary was unable to raise the wrecked right arm in defense, Oriku was sure the Panther Prince could not respond to an overhead attack.

"The reign of the Panther Clan ends today." Oriku savored his moment, then whispered, "And they thought you were the best…" Oriku raised clenched fists overhead for a neck-snapping blow.

There are six muscular attachments to the humeral bone's head. In his appraisal of his injuries, T'Kayla had realized that although he couldn't raise his arm, he could still rotate his shoulder backward and up, albeit at great cost. The maneuver would tear what little was left of his rotator cuff. The Panther Prince watched sidelong, timing his next move.

Come down just a little closer… T'Kayla slowed his breathing and hung his head in apparent resignation. Oriku adjusted his stance to deliver the optimal deathblow to the lower target. T'Kayla swung his elbow up and under, right into Oriku's crotch. The Gorilla prince crumpled and folded head over heels.

"Low blow!" the Jabari cried from the grass. "Foul!"

"Oriku used an unconventional arm hold to disable T'Kayla," the Panther Clan countered. "We did not cry foul then."

246

T'Kayla pivoted against the rock to catch Oriku in a leg-scissor around his ribs.

"Yield!" he asserted to Oriku, then looked to the elders to end this travesty gone wrong.

"Despite facing an opponent who has just fought two previous matches," the elders observed, "Oriku failed to offer T'Kayla the traditional opportunity to yield when he was helpless."

Their expressions remained impassive. "The contest continues."

T'Kayla locked his feet together and squeezed. Oriku's ribcage erupted with a crunching sound and the challenger gasped.

"Oriku, yield! This contest need not end in death," T'Kayla rasped, struggling to speak past his broken jaw while keeping up the constricting effort of his legs.

The Gorilla Clan's challenger looked out, wild eyed, at the assembled peers of the realm. Suddenly, he was losing. Oriku's pride, combined with five years' seniority and a twenty-pound weight advantage, demanded that he break free of the young champion and finish this farce. The pain in his loins lingered as he fought once again to draw breath. Wedging an arm in to break the scissor, Oriku rose up in a crouch to throw T'Kayla off balance.

T'Kayla had been waiting for that move.

He smoothly executed a twist, flipping Oriku over. Oriku's head struck the rock and his body's impact knocked the wind out of the man for the second time in his first contest. Dazed, Oriku had surrendered his leverage against the maneuver, but still had not won a single breath.

"Slap your free hand down twice on the sand if you give up, Oriku." T'Kayla offered a third chance to concede. Oriku struggled and braced his head along the rock to gain purchase against the viselike thew of his opponent's legs. T'Kayla still fought with one arm. Disadvantaged. Vulnerable.

Prying T'Kayla's legs apart, Oriku gained a reprieve and his first breath in over a minute. With it, he vowed, "I'm going to kill you, panther cub!"

Oriku braced his head against the rock to raise both their

combined weights upright with his sinewy neck. T'Kayla reapplied full pressure and exacted a crack from Oriku's ribs, followed by a softer *pop* from the man's exhausted neck. The Jabari challenger's body went limp, his eyes glazed over and rolled up under sagging eyelids.

T'Kayla took a well-deserved respite before rising to receive his accolades as victor. Among cheers from the spectators, the Panther Clan retained its traditional hold on power in Wakanda. Triumphant over a record three challengers in one day, T'Kayla had become the undisputed heir apparent of Wakanda, and remained the Black Panther.

○———————○

THE CENTRAL African sun set on a day filled with unprecedented trials. Bone weary and injured, a victor prevailed. Today belonged to the Kingdom's youngest prince in the end. The Heart-Shaped Herb swiftly healed T'Kayla's body and restored his vigor.

Night finally swaddled Wakanda with a blanket of stars and a warm, welcomed darkness. Lazy locusts sang without a care in the world. Memory of this combat would always serve to remind him that no one ever really *wins* a fight. Some might come out with fewer scars than others but that's all that could be hoped. For survivors, scars emerge inside and out. This day, the taking of a Wakandan life would leave T'Kayla's soul forever scarred.

The Prince stood at the balcony. His still nude body remained on edge, despite an indulgent massage and soothing bath. As he surveyed his realm, the royal palace rested with the peacefulness of a newborn babe.

Asalatu woke. "My Prince, you are troubled."

T'Kayla half turned to his lover as the crescent moon rose late in the evening. Its light brushed a reflected frost along flawless, black skin with his first words to her. "Statement, not question even in the darkness," stern words offset only by the pearly glint of teeth in his smile.

248   T'Kayla crossed the chamber in four feline strides. He

acknowledged her words with a loving embrace. Her own bare skin glowed with earth tones reminiscent of red clay and a softness that melted with ease into his steely arms.

T'Kayla kissed her forehead. "You, too, are restless, my Asalatu."

That literal application of her name always made Asalatu miss her home. She squeezed his waist and chided him, "You call for Dawn in the darkest of night and heat of our love even as it still burns. Why, my Lord? Do you rush *Asalatu*, 'the Dawn'?"

"We have yet to finish the Daré. I only await renewal of your strength."

T'Kayla's command of both Hausa and deep Bantu languages was flawless. He enjoyed the linguistic wordplay in which Asalatu engaged him. T'Kayla knew in his heart that Asalatu missed her family and her own subjects. But for a life in Wakanda, any free, Bahaushiya princess of the outer kingdoms would sell her soul even to play the role of courtesan at the court of Wakanda. "You are forever my Dawn and my Night; Asalatu and Daré."

"You should sleep well," she smiled. "Despite boasts of physical prowess bestowed by your 'Heart-Shaped Herb', I've wrung you dry. Admit it, Alafin!"

Alafin; owner of the palace. A title earned, not given. Wakandan primogeniture had been abandoned long ago. Unlike the European kings who bred within the aristocracy, Wakanda sought the best traits of the original men. Daughters of surrounding lands were expected to submit. Wakandan law obliged that fruit of the Black Panther's loins be shared, mating with as many bloodlines as possible. The heritage of the Black Panther had to remain strong.

That breeding program spawned in T'Kayla, the finest specimen of intelligence, passion, and strength beyond comparison. The four noble houses of Wakanda questioned the wisdom of conferring the title of *Chosen One* upon the king's third son. Challenges ensued. Oriku, the Jabari prince, rose as last of the champions. Cunning guile concluded that, surely, bereft of the enhancement of the Heart-Shaped Herb, and after vanquishing two powerful rivals, twenty-one-year-old T'Kayla would be no match for a third challenge. Oriku, bigger, stronger and more experienced in battle, could not lose.

Disbelief persisted beyond the final offer to yield. Oriku lay in a failed heap to be removed like a sack of grain. The Jabari clan spurned the cheering crowd, but to their credit, they bore the broken corpse of their fallen champion to the snow-topped mountain with a dignity befitting a noble house.

All Hausa and Bantu kings had kept the existence of Wakanda sacred for centuries. The Hausawa had always regarded Wakanda as the Jewel of the Continent. Paucity of open water supported sparse wildlife in contrast to the vast roaming zebra herds to the south that characterized the Serengeti. Only Wakandan Kings were privileged to ride the sacred, striped horse. It was said that the gods allowed no other men to bridle the zebra. So that mortal men should never forget, the Celestial Orishas shaped the whole continent to resemble the zebra's head. It was a point of consternation among recent Wakandan kings that zebras were stolen from the motherland and placed in captivity.

What were they called again...? T'Kayla thought for a moment. *Zoos!* His private herd rested in its corral, secure in the knowledge that no lion, hyena, or barbarian from overseas would dare approach the Wakandan capital.

"Our War Dogs report progress in the New World and Europe." T'Kayla stared off into the near distance as he spoke. "But the Beacon of Freedom once called *Moses* approaches her life's end."

"So this is the source of your troubles," Asalatu concluded. "The decision to seed the New World with our diaspora was a painful one for all. Only the royal families knew that slavery served as our wedge. Guided by Wakandan War Dogs, they secretly leveraged the direction of Western civilization. Prevented consolidation of power and the ultimate destruction of civilization. We contained the Mongols from extending their reign across Eurasia, we'll steer these new Americans, too. They're the sleeping giant we have to watch in the decades to come."

250   "But the suffering..." T'Kayla hesitated in his response. "That

we did not expect. Slavery was never like this… abomination *they* created. Even the Mongols used slaves to the top of their abilities. Treated them like—well, like people.

"Americans. They may actually progress beyond colony to a coalition of equals, both foreign and domestic, eventually," T'Kayla mused. "They're remarkably innovative."

"I hear they've developed limited flight capacity," Asalatu offered.

"You mean those propeller-driven death contraptions?" T'Kayla laughed. "They're as likely to crash as fly every time they launch. Those horseless carriages they're promoting are safer."

"Maybe they should resume use of those hot air balloons," she said. "At least there, they can just float to ground when something goes wrong."

"These people can't go a single generation without a major war," T'Kayla said. "And their technology is getting better."

"Not as fast as ours," Asalatu reassured him.

"Maybe, but fast enough to threaten the five continents. There may come a time that we cannot stop them before they wake the threat from the deep."

"Alafin, Wakanda owns the skies, from low fog to the stars. There is no feat beyond you."

"May the ancestors give me both strength and wisdom to accomplish my first mission." T'Kayla's chin dipped low in the darkness. "The Black Panther leaves at sunup, Daré. A dawn I would delay many moons if I could." He caressed her face. "To be with you, my Asalatu."

BEFORE THE sun rose high in the morning sky, the *Dora Milaje* assembled on the flight deck. T'Kayla inspected his elite guard and special task squad. The women stood in formation as statues, eyes fixed, fierce as the storm that they were. To all who faced them in battle, the *Dora Milaje* represented a force majeure. They came alive as the prince nodded his approval with the traditional

Wakandan salute. These women were his, blood and bone. He hoped he would not waste this precious coin.

"Odobale, your troops appear fit for battle," T'Kayla called, suppressing a smile.

"You offend me, my Prince," she said, matching his expression. "Your *Dora Milaje* are ever ready!"

"We have a mission, Odobale. A mission every Wakandan King has dreaded."

The general of the *Dora Milaje* knew no fear, yet there was only one danger to spark dread in the heart of a Wakanda protector. "Atlantis?"

"Possibly," T'Kayla whispered.

Odobale's voice became a rasp. "But the Treaty…"

"Not the Atlanteans." He shook his head. "The French."

"The French, my Prince? Seriously?" Odobale laughed a breath of relief.

T'Kayla sobered her with a glare. "Does it appear to you that I jest, General?"

"Forgive me, my Prince." Odobale bowed deeply in contrition. "You spoke of the French."

"The French and the Germans, actually." T'Kayla grimaced. "Madam Marie Curie and this young German clerk, Albert something. They're both playing with the atom. They have no concept of what consequences may come from such folly."

"Our War Dogs are aware of these efforts, my Prince. I'm told that we can either stop—or at least delay—nuclear fission for a hundred years. With luck, we'll be able to introduce safe, renewable energy options that will induce them to abandon this foolish research all together. You should not worry about such things."

"It's not an atomic war I fear, General. It's exploration."

"My Prince?" Odobale asked, confusion returning to her countenance.

"An archeologist, one Jean Baptiste Batroc, has a dangerous notion." T'Kayla walked with his general as he briefed her away from the prying ears of the *Dora Milaje*. "He follows in the footsteps of Schliemann. Only instead of Troy, he seeks the Atlantis of legend. He's started from ancient texts. Few papyri survived when we burned the Library of Alexandria. This Dr. Batroc found one. He's starting at the historic Pillars of Hercules and tracking south to the River Styx. He's convinced Africa is the starting point. He's using Madame Curie's radioactive isotopes to tag migrating fish in the jet stream that leads deep into The Zebra's Throat."

"The entry to Atlantis," Odobale concluded with bleak understanding. "Poisoned fishes flowing into Atlantis's waters. They'll blame us first for the act, at worst." She always started with the worst-case scenario. "At best, they'll blame us for not keeping our pale brothers in check and out of their realm."

"Our War Dogs tell me this Batroc has commissioned an experimental ship." T'Kayla leveled his gaze at Odobale. "A ship he can sail under the water."

"The Sub-Mariner will never endure that breach," she finished. "There will be no stopping him and 300 million Atlantean warriors from retaliating. We'll be drawn into a war we'll have to fight with all our resources. We'll have to execute the Rainbow Protocol; an entire world at war."

"You know what that means for Wakanda, don't you?" T'Kayla asked.

They answered his question in unison, "We break it, we bought it."

"Wakanda will be responsible for the rest of mankind for time without end. Some knowledge is just too dangerous for mankind's ken. There's no burning this information out of their collective memories." T'Kayla's shoulders slumped in resignation.

"We are wasting time contemplating failure of a battle we have yet to fight, my Prince."

"*Dora Milaje*!" Odobale shouted.

"Yibambe!" came the answer.

Satisfied, Odobale proudly shouted in chorus with her troops, "Wakanda Forever!"

"WE HAVE passed through the Pillars of Hercules, Dr. Batroc," the captain said cheerily. "And the Sirens have not drawn us to our doom. We're off to a promising day!"

"Others have come this far, in modern times, *mon ami*," Dr. Batroc warned. "We still have to deal with the legend of the Styx. If we can breach that barrier and come back to tell of it, we'll have bragging rights."

The Captain pounded the hull with his fist. "This hull is made as tough as the *Titanic*."

Batroc smiled at the joke. "And that's supposed to inspire confidence?"

"We have the new German-made underwater rockets," the Captain bragged. "Between the depth-detonated explosives and our waterproof Gatling gun, we have nothing to fear on sea, land, or air."

"Nothing but acts of God, *mon frère*." Batroc seemed to force pessimism to squelch his captain's exuberance for supremacy.

"Captain, we've arrived at the release point. The fish tanks are prepared." The ensign appeared unusually nervous.

"Well?" the Captain demanded after a beat. The ensign handed him a sheaf of papers. The Captain's brow furrowed deeply. "All the calculations up to this stage have been correct."

It came Batroc's turn to worry. "But?"

"But the currents flow eastward toward Africa, not west toward the open Atlantic as you predicted."

Captain Aristead looked to Batroc for clarification. "Let's get to the observation deck. I want to see this for myself before we waste a tank of priceless fish."

The three men climbed the ladder to the small poop-deck. Batroc fixed his fists akimbo. "Not only is the current flowing the wrong way, it's an undertow. Look at that whirlpool there." Batroc pointed to a deepening swirl to the port side of the ship. He considered this dilemma for a moment then asked, "How many of the fish will survive the next forty-eight hours?"

"We're down to 60 percent already and we're only three days out of Sardinia," the ensign said.

"Below 50 percent of our original school we won't be able to track the signal," Batroc said. "I say we open the tanks, see where they go. Shall we submerge, Captain?"

"Why not?" Aristead declared. "Down the rabbit hole we go, Doctor. Let's see what's on the other side of the looking glass."

Batroc and Aristead settled in behind the Geigerscope to the welcome sight of a strong signal. A violent jerk wiped mutual smiles clean off each face, and the ensign off his feet. Aristead was first to notice that the ship failed to submerge.

"Chief of the Watch, what's happening? Did we hit a reef?" Aristead muttered under his breath, "Curse the *Titanic*!"

The chief made his full 360 sweep before answering his captain. "No, sir. We're clear all around." He secured the periscope. "We're just not moving!"

"Give me that periscope." Aristead seized the handles, raised the head of the periscope above sea level, and took his own 360 survey.

"There are cables attached to the hull, seaman. Didn't you see that?" Aristead intensified his search. "There's not another ship anywhere on the horizon, though." He hammered the periscope in frustration. "Where are those damn cables coming from and how are they holding us? If they'd punctured the hull we'd be taking on water." Aristead cranked the throttle to full, only to hit another yank back. "Yet we can't pull free."

"Can we turn the ship?" Batroc offered.

"Damn it if we can't." Aristead saw where he was going. "We have two dozen of those underwater rockets. Fire them in all four points of the compass. Before the enemy can respond, we'll slice them to Swiss cheese with the Gatling gun." Aristead grinned.

The gunner took off like a bullet himself. In the turret, seconds later, he fired a volley, but saw nothing. "Captain, the mooring cables are coming from the sky!"

"Fool. There's no balloon big enough to support that kind of pull." Aristead began to show fear.

"An airplane?" Batroc asked.

Aristead shook it off. "The best German biplane can barely get the weight of two men in the air for more than a few hours." He checked the maps. "We're a hundred miles off the nearest shore. No airplane has that kind of range!"

Beads of sweat built along his brow. If no natural explanation springs forth, only the supernatural remains. "I've never believed in the *Dutchman*, but I'll be damned before I yield to a ghost ship."

Aristead opened the hatch to the turret. The afternoon was cold and overcast. The wind blew north from the Antarctic. "There!" The Captain pointed to the mooring cables. "Two of them. They lead up into the clouds. No, not *the* clouds... *that* 'cloud'."

There the object of his bile loomed darker than the rest of the sky. The low-hanging specter was almost opaque on closer examination.

"That's no natural weather system, Captain," Batroc said. "There's something in the middle of it, I'm sure of it."

Aristead, emboldened by a possible scientific explanation, commanded, "Cannon at the ready. Target the center of that halo, ensign." Hand raised like a racing flag, the Captain snapped it down like a midshipman's salute. "Fire!"

The impact clearly struck solid material, but the report didn't sound like steel or iron. It did result in another jerk of the *Neptune*.

"Again!" came the order. This time the cannon reloaded and fired twice without being told. The cloud dissipated to reveal a wide, flat aerodynamic structure, foreign to Aristead, Dr. Batroc, and every seasoned sailor on board.

One of the mooring cables broke off at the source. The Wakandan airship rolled sideways and the second lone cable sheared off, releasing the *Neptune*.

"We're free," Aristead observed. "Dive. Dive. Dive!

"Hard yaw to port, helmsman," Aristead ordered. "Silent running until further notice."

"Good maneuver, Captain. The undercurrents will carry us along with the radioactive fish."

"To hell with your glowing fish, Doctor. I'm trying to save the fifty sailors under my command!" The Captain glared at Batroc's insensitivity before turning to his crew. "Damage report, Chief."

"Amazingly, we're doing pretty good, Captain. A little strain to the number one engine, but we have three others, so I'd say we're at about 96 percent shipshape, sir."

"DAMAGE REPORT!" Odobale braced herself as the Wakandan aircraft recovered from the cannon fire and spinout from the sudden release of electromagnetic moorings.

"General, we have sustained hull breaches on two sides, and the electromagnetic traction on the right is completely ruined. We can repair the second here in the field. We have the parts for it, but I fear we've lost the French ship."

"But we can still fly, correct?" T'Kayla asked.

"We can fly, my Prince, but we are very limited in navigation," the pilot said. "Severe damage to our computing network. The trans resistors are nearly burned beyond recognition. We tried to hold them too long."

"My Prince, I have an idea," Odobale said. "We may not have sophisticated navigation, but we can resort to traditional maritime navigation."

"Traditional? Like hundreds of years ago?" T'Kayla asked, puzzled. "No one in our complement has that skill set."

"No, Alafin, but look there," a familiar voice said from the far deck, pointing out the port window. A tricolor flag with a star in the center. "A Koume fishing vessel."

"Asalatu?" T'Kayla asked. "Daré? Why are you here among the *Dora Milaje*?"

"My Prince, I have been in training for two years," Asalatu answered.

"And you did not tell me?" T'Kayla asked, more surprised than truly hurt as he resisted a craving to caress her newly shaved scalp.

"My Prince, it was my idea," Odobale said. "It seemed to me

that as she has become so close to you over the past few years, she possibly represented a... weakness for the Black Panther."

Odobale bowed her head, penitent for her presumption. "As a member of the *Dora Milaje*, she has the skills to protect herself and her Prince. It seemed best to me."

"To you..." T'Kayla echoed.

"And to me, Alafin," Asalatu whispered. "Soon, you will be not only the Black Panther, but also King of Wakanda. I will not leave your safety to women that I don't know." She reached for his hand but stopped short of contact. "There is no more intimate relation between women than sharing in the service and security of their King. Do you disagree?"

T'Kayla only answered with silence. No more approval needed. Even if it did not please the Prince, he too knew she was right. There would be no playful gloating here. She was now acknowledged *Dora Milaje*.

"Contact the pilot of that ship, Odobale." He turned on his heel and strode for the royal chambers. "I wish to speak with him, and him alone. Am I clear?" His tone was sharp, and Odobale understood his pain. Every *Dora Milaje* pledged her life to block any possible threat to the royal family, no matter how remote. Even if the Black Panther were better matched to face the challenge, the *Dora Milaje* would face that threat first, even to the extent of a suicide mission. And because of this French *Neptune*, they faced Atlantis now. There was no doubt.

"**WHERE DO** you think we are now, Captain?" Batroc asked.

Aristead mopped newborn sweat from his brow. "This is Senegambia. November and it's still hot as blazes."

The *Neptune* surfaced off a sandy beach. Aristead had been topside for an hour on his knees, analyzing the mooring apparatus. His strongest men had finally been able to pry it off the steel hull, with a pile of bent crowbars to show for the effort.

Batroc knelt to see the machine up close for the first time.

He'd kept a low profile since the dressing down Aristead gave him in the pitch of battle.

"What do you make of it, Dr. Batroc?" Aristead smacked the ten-inch disk as he asked.

"It's an EM plate," Batroc said finally.

"EM what?" Aristead asked.

"An electromagnetic plate," Batroc repeated.

"Doctor, I do know something of magnets. There is no magnet on Earth powerful enough to overcome four diesel engines." Aristead passed the strange cord across open palms. "I don't get it."

"Not a magnet, Captain, an electromagnet," Batroc explained. "You see, you can multiply the strength of a natural magnet by wrapping a conductive coil around it and running electric current through it. But you're right. I've never seen anything like this on the Continent or in the Orient. Even those crazy Americans don't have anything like this."

"So what are you saying, Dr. Batroc?"

"Captain," Batroc whispered, "I believe this is our first exposure to Atlantean technology!"

"Now wait one minute, Dr. Batroc, that's quite a leap..." Aristead considered alternatives, but none came to mind. "Atlanteans." Aristead rolled the idea around his mind a moment. "More plausible than facing off with the *Dutchman*."

"I don't think you'd have gotten anywhere with that cannon against a ghost ship, do you?" Batroc offered a wry smile. "Just think about it. History tells us that the Atlanteans were years ahead of us, with unexplained technologies that seemed magical ten thousand years ago. The few scraps of records we've recovered describe feats of engineering that we can't explain, much less duplicate with the best of our modern science. Well, we've just seen another example of it today. We were looking for ruins of a lost continent. What if we're actually on the trail of a hidden civilization?"

"And they're telling us they don't *want* to be found," Aristead said.

"We're getting close to uncovering a legend. Do you want to turn back, Captain?"

"Hell no! There's not a sailor alive who wouldn't give his right arm for a chance to discover Atlantis. Whether those devils like it or not."

Aristead stood and looked down at the disk being carried aboard. "I'm in, Doctor. And let heaven help the better angel *or* sly demon who bars my way."

o———o

"DO YOU know who I am, Daouda?" T'Kayla stood ten feet off the shore of Goree Island on what appeared to be a mesa of water spouting from the sea.

As directed, Daouda stood on the bow of his fishing boat. How many of his ancestors crossed these seas in the bowels of foreign ships, never to be seen again? The Slave Trade had been abolished sixty-five years ago, but men still were not free. Now this apparition spoke to him while walking on water. Was he a ghost? Some returning soul lost at sea decades ago, come to haunt this poor sailor?

Daouda sank to his knees. "Sea spirit, if you have come to finally claim my soul, I am ready. I have raised my family. My sons have learned my craft well. My daughters have proven fertile and borne healthy children. Please allow enough fish from your bounty to support my wives…"

"Stop begging, man. It's beneath you." T'Kayla spoke with impatience and umbrage. "I am—an emissary of the Sky Gods. I need help. My masters seek audience with the sea elves. We have been advised where to look, but I have no way to find the doorway to their realm. If I give you directions, can you employ your skills to navigate us to the portal?"

Daouda hung his head. "So, it *is* my time. You have come to ferry me to the Land of Death."

"I just told you that I am no harbinger of death. Why do you insist on contradicting me?" Royal pique shone through T'Kayla's gentle request.

"I know that when our time comes, merciful gods often present a seemingly innocuous invitation," Daouda said. "I know I have escaped death too many times for the sea gods to forgive. It is my time, and I accept it. Ask of me what you will."

T'Kayla thought through the man's sentiment before reengaging. "I speak the truth to you, Daouda of the Fishers. Show me the way, and I may spare you. As long as you speak no word of this quest with another living soul for the rest of your life, we'll provide you with safe passage back to your village. To your family."

"I have never heard of such a bargain between gods and men before, strange man of the sky. Why should I believe this is anything but trickery of the Orishas?"

"If you do not help me, I will seek the counsel of the sea elves on my own," T'Kayla said. "But if I don't reach them in time, there will be fire and fury such as man has never seen. Not only will you be ushered to the Land of Death, so too will all your family and friends, and even all your enemies. There will be no fishing for your village until the end of time. Can you risk that, fisherman? I cannot."

"I will guide you to the best of my abilities, Lord," Daouda said. "My crew consists of my three sons and five apprentice fishermen, villagers in my debt. May I tell them what I have committed to?"

"No," T'Kayla said with anger. "I offer to spare you from a well-earned death. Tell them, and even seasoned sailors may run in fear. Why tempt brave men? Save your village. Give them the honor of ignorance. Trust them to go blindly on and do that which you have trained them to do so well."

Daouda considered the Black Panther's words.

"This is a leap of faith, Daouda. Will you lead me?"

Daouda touched his chest over his heart and extended his opened hand to T'Kayla. "Anything you wish, Lord. You have my oath of fealty and silence."

T'Kayla led the humble fisherman into the awe that could only be a skyship of the heavens. Daouda looked but touched nothing.

T'Kayla joined his general in the pilot's nest.

"Well?" Odobale forgot herself in her eagerness for the mission. A sharp glare from T'Kayla needed no words to rebuke the familiarity. She added urgently, "My Prince."

"He will guide us. I have sworn him to secrecy. Show him the ancient maps. He will take us right into The Zebra's Throat. How ironic that with all our technology, the threat of Atlantis and the French, our future hinges on the ancient navigation skills of this humble fisherman."

"What if he goes mad?" Odobale asked. "Men fear death more than they fear legends of the gods, my Prince."

"I've seen into his eyes, into his heart, General. This one will not run. Trust my judgment of people."

"We have no choice, my Prince. The fate of the world hangs on your being right on all counts."

The pilot turned to Odobale. "We are getting close, General. There is a good reading on the beacon."

"WE'VE PLENTY of fresh water and food stores," Aristead announced. "The compressed air in the tanks will keep us breathing for three days under the waves, Doctor. Our present location is fifty nautical miles south of the Senegalese border. We're in Portuguese territorial waters. If we're caught..." Aristead spread his hands wide, indicating obviously dire consequences. "We must submerge now or lose the fish to the depths. Are you sure about this?"

Batroc furrowed his brow. "I'm not sure of anything at this point. We've now seen a small taste of Atlantean technology. They've demonstrated superiority to anything we have, but no weapons to rival ours on offense or defense. We may never get another chance. If you ask my vote, I say yes, dive."

"Then we'll face Hades and Neptune on their own terms." Aristead grabbed the speaker horn and gave the order. "All hands, prepare to dive."

The Geigerscope glowed to life and projected its targets on the frosted glass between it and the crew. The sparkling images that represented irradiated fish flowed with the currents down past the limestone cliffs off the coast of Portuguese Guinea, deep into an arboreal maze of forested inlets and coves.

"The fish are diving almost straight down, Captain," the navigator said. "We can follow them at this speed for another twenty minutes before the depth surpasses the *Neptune*'s tolerances."

"The Styx, river of death. I'll push it to the limits, Doctor, but I'll not have this boat become brave sailors' tomb." Aristead nodded. "Just so you know."

"I'm not suicidal either, Cap—" Batroc's answer was lost as the ship bucked and seamen sprawled.

"What the hell was that?" Aristead called, as he realized that he remained on his feet only because his reflexes had clasped the rail fast enough.

"I don't know, Captain, but that was different from the first contact," the Chief of the Watch observed. "But that felt more like a weapon!"

Aristead nodded. "Damage report."

"That will take a few minutes, Captain," the First Mate screamed over the klaxon.

The lights flickered then went out inside the *Neptune*. No light shone through her portals.

Aristead silenced the alarm. "Alright. So they're hostile. Can we see them yet?"

"No, sir." Aristead recognized the navigator's voice in the dark.

"It's black as pitch out there," Aristead noted. "Deploy the phosphorus flares."

"Delay that order." An Amazon appeared from the shadows and spoke with an authoritative air. "Instruct your men to stand down, Captain."

An imposing figure: dark-skinned, shaved head, and as tall as any man on the ship, she stood on lean, long legs fit for an Olympic swimmer.

"Captain!" the Chief of the Watch hollered.

Odobale pointed what appeared to be a solid rod at Aristead, an obvious threat.

The Chief wasn't the First Mate, but he was the most experienced sailor on board and a seasoned soldier. He inched toward the weapons cache until he abutted the end of a similar rod. He turned to assess his own situation, only to find there were five such women on the bridge of the *Neptune*. They were all similarly framed and armed.

"We have your ship, Captain," Odobale announced. "Let's not make this more difficult than it must be. Kneel."

The men complied with the silhouettes outlined in the dim red emergency lighting. All the women wore peculiar googles with darkened lenses.

"The ship is secure, my Prince. Please join us," Odobale asked.

A sliver of light accompanied the hatch opening that admitted T'Kayla to the *Neptune*.

"All right, you people have gone far enough. We'll be taking you back to the surface with us."

Then, in a softer yet more intense whisper, "We need to come to an understanding, you and I, Captain Aristead."

The Chief knelt, as did everyone else, but reached for a flare gun holstered under the navigation console. He fingered the pistol for a moment. Instinct. He fired up into the roof of the compartment, brightening the space like the sun for a moment. The *Dora Milaje* shielded their eyes from the sudden illumination. That's when the Chief moved. He wrestled the woman behind him for her weapon. She dispatched him with little effort but discharged her weapon in the process. The charge hit the console, but not before passing through another unintended target. Asalatu crumpled as she took the burst across her midriff.

T'Kayla rushed to her side and into the waiting sights of Captain Aristead's sidearm.

"This man seems to be their leader." The executive officer stood on the opposite side of the chamber. They had T'Kayla in a crossfire.

One might miss, but not both.

"Target his head as I do. Fire if he so much as flinches. Am I clear, Christophe?"

"Yes, sir." The First Mate met his captain's eyes before barking orders echoing Aristead's command.

Aristead called new orders. "Deploy the flares. Shed some light on these scoundrels."

In the brilliant white light, the gleam of half a dozen shark- and manta-shaped iron craft surrounded the *Neptune*. Turrets with wide-mouthed cannons were trained on the French submarine. All seven ships continued to match course and speed.

"Captain, you-you need to see this, sir." The First Mate relinquished the periscope to Aristead.

"What is it, man?" Aristead panned the scope around at the otherworldly craft, amazed. "What the hell? Are those men... blue?"

"Their ears, sir, look at their ears!" Christophe said. He waited for Aristead to confirm what he had seen, then, "At first, I thought the blue cast was a trick of the light. Then I saw their ears. They're pointed."

"Doctor, what do you make of this?" Aristead passed the periscope control to Batroc. "Do any of your records indicate that Atlantis was populated by blue devils?"

Batroc considered what he saw through the lenses, and said, "No, I've never read that." Reluctantly, he yielded the periscope back to the Captain as the flares died out. Aristead looked up and addressed the weapons duty officer.

"Gunner, activate the running lights and acquire those six targets. Rockets first; if they retreat, go after them with the Gatling gun. I want to capture at least one of those things for analysis."

The gunnery shipman complied, but another sonic assault penetrated the hull as the rocket launchers targeted the ships.

"The hull's vibrating again, sir. But it's different this time. Not like an attack, somehow. Listen."

The harmonic character of the Neptune established, the Atlantean/Wakandan conversation began.

"That's some dialect of Bantu talk, sir." The Chief of the Watch recognized the vibrations as language. "I can't make out what they're saying, but I've heard some of that lingo before. They're talking right through the water at us."

"Not at you, Captain Aristead. At me," T'Kayla said without moving a muscle. He could easily disarm both men, but Asalatu was hurt, he did not know how badly. She did not move.

"Sounds like gibberish to me, Chief," Aristead said. "Anyone aboard speak any Bantu talk?"

Before any crewmember could speak up, similar vibrations issued through the ship from stern to stem. The blue-manned ships shot into motion faster than the gunner could respond.

Aristead snapped a glare at the gunner.

The gunner shrugged his shoulders in frustration. "No shot, Captain. There's nothing but water where I aimed." The gunner tracked the craft along both sides of the ship and directed the steering lights aft. "Look, sir."

The Captain spun the periscope aft and saw what the gunner saw. The Wakandan ship flashed a kaleidoscope of lights at the newcomers. The *Neptune* was all but ignored.

As the ships from the depths convened on the larger Wakandan ship, the vibrating chatter that permeated through the *Neptune*'s hull faded.

"What the devil are they doing out there?" Aristead asked.

Batroc folded his arms. "Talking, it would seem."

AFTER A few flashes exchanged between the two strange ships, the *Neptune*'s hull began to rumble, settled into tones akin to woodwinds, and finally arcane articulation was heard reverberating through the *Neptune*. T'Kayla could hear the Atlantean words through the Neptune's hull as if it were a call box.

"This is one of your ships, Wakandan?" An unseen Atlantean commander spoke in an obsolete Bantu dialect. The crew of the *Neptune* appreciated that a dialogue took place around them, but could not translate it.

"No. It's one of the outsider country's." T'Kayla kept his voice even. "European origin. Not ours, nor under our jurisdiction."

"If that's so, then why are you here?" The Atlantean spoke with deliberate caution.

"They were after you. We got wind of their efforts and tried to intercede. We failed." T'Kayla projected contrition. "I failed."

"Usually it's left to kings to take on the burden of failure—wait, then you are the one called the Black Panther?" the commander realized. "We have heard legends, but we never…"

"I am called T'Kayla. Commander?"

"Pinzir, Majesty."

"Commander Pinzir, these interlopers have seen too much of your culture and mine. We cannot have them return to the Western world with knowledge of either Atlantean or Wakandan technology."

"It would be disastrous," Odobale added.

"Agreed, Wakandan." Neither could see the other, and that by design. "If left up to me, I would execute the whole crew. And sink their craft to the depths of the sea. But there is the radioactive transgression to deal with. What do you propose?"

"Let me—" T'Kayla began, but lost his footing from the quake of a rocket blast.

"What in the name of the ancestors…"

"My Prince. The French gunner, he fired a weapon at the Atlantean ship. The Atlanteans somehow evaded the attack." Odobale analyzed the attack, but she seemed focused on her fallen warrior. Asalatu bled freely. The tremors had ceased, and color faded from her nubile face.

Like lightning, T'Kayla disarmed and subdued both distracted French sailors. When it became clear that their Prince was safe, the *Dora Milaje* again asserted their dominance and re-took the *Neptune*.

T'Kayla cradled Asalatu's head. "See to her when you can, Odobale. For now, we must assuage the Atlanteans before they escalate this situation."

"Before *THEY* escalate?" Odobale was not known as a woman of patience. She spoke to T'Kayla in perfect French to clearly inform the Neptune's crew of its own folly. "These damn invaders are the mad dogs in this arena. How do we contain them?"

"King T'Kayla! Are you injured?" the Atlantean commander inquired.

"I am not harmed, Commander," T'Kayla answered. "But we have one that is… uniquely close to me, who is at the brink of death. We may still have a chance, but we have lost our advantage here. I fear it may take longer than this woman has left to live."

The quality of the transmission changed subtly. Monotoned and loaded with static. The Atlantean commander spoke directly into T'Kayla's body. T'Kayla could hear the Atlantean words through his bones as if he were standing on the blue man's ship. "Speaking here now for your ears only, I believe I know what you are alluding to, King T'Kayla. To grant that favor would release Atlantis from its blood debt. Little more than that has bound Atlantean rulers to abide your people's occasional intrusions. Do you really want to relinquish that leverage?"

"You speak as a wise man of peace, Commander."

"For Atlanteans, those two words don't go together."

The transmission returned to high fidelity and for general Atlantean and Wakandan consumption. "Radioactive fish flushed into our realm, explosives rattling our infrastructure? And you ask favors?" The Atlantean's voice sounded strained. "Atlantis will not tolerate such incursions by your species. If you cannot control them, then I may have to advise the Emperor. We will have to patrol our own waters. Deal with land-humans as we see fit."

"I must ask that you not interfere. We can still salvage this situation," T'Kayla pled.

The Gatling gun found its elusive targets this time. The Atlantean commander's shark-shaped craft quivered, but held its integrity. Wakandan shielding deflected the German-made bullets.

"And now we have a direct attack!" The Atlantean commander's Bantu faltered.

"Commander, Atlantis is a formidable empire to be sure, but if the Imperium pursues this course of action, you will face

Wakanda and its extended forces as well as the combined forces of the industrialized *Homo sapiens* nations. They bicker with one another now, but if you mount an attack with your advanced weapon, you'll unite them across the globe. We won't be able to contain them. Who loses in the struggle? Atlantis and Wakanda. Let us handle this incursion into the shallows of your borders."

T'Kayla made out a single Atlantean word—"Fire"—before the *Neptune* felt the hull-ripping vibration of otherworldly weapons.

The missile pierced the *Neptune*'s hull but did not explode. Nor did the puncture leak water. T'Kayla squinted at the tip of the projectile, then his grimace inverted into a grim smile. T'Kayla plucked a capsule from the shaft and turned to Odobale. "Get this to your medical officer immediately. Asalatu has no time left."

"If I had the authority to declare war today, I would do it." The Atlantean commander made a strange sound that T'Kayla could not interpret, sight unseen. "So, I am glad today to be a simple commander of a patrol squadron. We have ended our mission prematurely and unsuccessfully. I must make a report to the Imperium. And I promise you, that won't look good for Wakanda, Your Majesty."

"I will contact your Emperor and try to make amends. I will not mention your mission unless he does. I may ask if assisting you in your endeavor will set this right. After all, Wakanda respects the sovereign borders of its neighbors."

"You are a wise and noble king, Your Majesty. I will convey your sentiments to the Imperium."

T'Kayla turned his attention to Odobale. "Disembark the *Neptune* and deploy the Tsetse gas. When the Frenchmen go quiet, we'll tow their ship to open waters and set them adrift deep in the western ocean. Perhaps they'll be salvaged by marauders heading to the New World."

"You did not kill them," Odobale observed. "Why such mercy, my Prince?"

"The gas will induce retrograde amnesia. They won't remember the last day or two." T'Kayla spoke with an air of resigned wisdom.

"The failure of so expensive a mission should dissuade France and Germany from commissioning future expeditions in search of lost empires. They will also have no knowledge of Wakanda's intervention here. In so acting, we protect Atlantis from future incursions; Wakanda from discovery; and the French from themselves, at least for a while. And we preserve Atlantis's tacit access to our Vibranium, which powers their economy, technology, and infrastructure."

"Not to mention all of their advanced weapons," Odobale said. "They won't jeopardize such a resource that they think they secretly siphon from our mound."

"Agreed." T'Kayla struck two sharp raps on the console. "As the Atlantean forces turned, did you not ask why they were in the shallows? The commander returned to Wakanda that which is ours. An illegal thing that may yet save my beloved's life."

A communique came in for Odobale from the medical chamber of the Wakandan airship. She shook her head as if it could be seen by the other woman.

"There is one thing, my Prince." Odobale bowed her head in sorrow. "Asalatu will live, but her blood is forever tainted. The extract is a single ounce of fermented, discarded leaves of our Heart-Shaped Herb. I'm told that no common human should ever be exposed to it. Any exchange of bodily fluids will make scion between you and Asalatu, or any woman you seed thereafter, immune to the benefits of the Heart-Shaped Herb. Your legacy to the Black Panther line would end. I—"

"Everything that has been done has been done in the right time and for the right reasons, General. No King could ask for more. We cannot predict the course of such events." T'Kayla understood the ramifications of the Atlantean potion. *Always my Day, but never again may we share our Daré.* "Asalatu will be a fine *Dora Milaje*. Perhaps even a general someday...

"The development of Heart-Shaped Herbal extract to make super warriors is illegal and would cross the line of peace for Wakanda. Between you and I, the Atlantean emperors have become… restless in past decades. Some might describe the sentiment as ambitious, eh Odobale?"

"That Atlantean commander knew the consequences of his discovery. Pinzir offered all of it, knowing it was Asalatu's only chance of survival. He also knows that his Emperor must never have this super-warrior elixir. I am in his debt, and Pinzir is in mine. Neutrality maintained."

"Do you trust him, General?" T'Kayla asked, with a wry smile.

"Yes, my Prince. I trust you, the fisherman, and the Atlantean *explorers*. You are ever an excellent judge of character.

"We have attached a grappling magnet to the *Neptune*, my Prince."

"Just one, Odobale?" T'Kayla asked. He hid the grin from her.

"Yes, my Prince. This time we reel in a sleeping whale. We should have no problem hauling them."

"Then let us go home," T'Kayla said as the doors closed behind them.

"How do you think the Sub-Mariner will take the news of Western invasion, my Prince?"

"I don't know, but this onslaught of technology is making a once-large world so much smaller. We live in explosive times, Odobale. Ground zero is beneath our continent, where all men began. Even for those legends once called elves. Atlanteans have both knowledge and access to Vibranium, too.

"Wakanda must tread carefully. Forever."

RETURN OF THE QUEEN

TANANARIVE DUE

YOU CANNOT *truly know any nation unless your feet have touched its soil*, T'Chaka had often said on long foot treks he had forced his son to endure as a boy, answering T'Challa's complaints about walking so many kilometers when hoverbikes were plentiful. As a prince, he could have chosen from a fleet of hoverbikes!

His father was less stern during their long walks, one of the reasons T'Challa secretly had looked forward to those journeys despite his blistered feet. Over the years, it seemed they had walked Wakanda from end to end, one tract at a time. As his father had expected, T'Challa learned to value the difference in the texture and color of the grasses in Birnin Azzaria and the Alkama Fields, the crispness of the mountain air in the Jabari-Lands, the grasslands drenched with the rich golden strawberry hues of dusk. When reporters and researchers asked him to describe his attachment to his homeland, he did not think first, as they did, of the valuable stores in the Vibranium mines, the mystical legacy of the Heart-Shaped Herb, or the wonders in his laboratory—he thought of the unparalleled coffee crops and plentiful cape crows and the beauty of the mighty cascading froth at Warrior Falls he had gazed upon at his father's side.

You cannot truly know any nation unless your feet have touched its soil. T'Chaka always finished his adage by saying, *Just as you cannot know another's heart until you have walked at their side.*

Today, after only a short afternoon's walk in the midday sun with the Queen of Canaan, T'Challa had learned a lifetime's worth about the neighboring monarchy—not from the woman's grief-drenched words, but from her soil. And from the aged queen's weary walk.

The land in the Kingdom of Canaan was dead. Dark veins of shadow traversed the soil like uncountable gnarled fingers, making the plain appear as rows of stones. Queen Sojourner Truth, an American expatriate like many of this nation's citizens, at times stumbled across the uneven soil, but even at her advanced age, she was too proud to accept the assistance of T'Challa's subtly outstretched arm. No land in Wakanda had ever been so parched, had ever known drought. As a boy, T'Challa had not realized how little Wakanda resembled the rest of the world, even the nations closest to him. The mopane trees that shared their border did not know if they were Wakandan or Canaanite. But Wakanda's soil sang with fertility. Here, dust floated as if the nation itself might blow away in a breeze.

"Shoot—we saw the drought in South Africa and pitied their dilemma," Queen Truth said. "How's that for irony? Shared resources. Loans. And then, nearly overnight, we have the same problem—and worse. Even when it rains, the ground soaks it up so fast there's no water left for the crops. It evaporates. Farming is in ruins, of course. But worse, our water supply is dwindling as if it's being sucked beneath the soil. It's just not natural."

"Of course not," T'Challa agreed. "It is an attack."

But who was responsible, and why? The Kingdom of Canaan had a history of turmoil, but Queen Truth's sweeping reforms in recent years, reversing her late father's neglect of health and education, had won it high regard from its neighbors. So this act of war—however it had been achieved—likely had not sprung from close to home. And with the manipulation of water content deep in the soil, even Wakandan technology would have struggled to strike such a devastating blow.

T'Challa's Panther suit slipped into place across his body as he knelt to touch the soil with his sensor glove. He considered it disrespectful to hide his face behind his suit upon his initial meeting with the queen, but now he was glad to have it—and not just to analyze the soil. His instincts told him that danger was close.

"I already have soil samples, Brother," Shuri's voice teased in his earpiece. "We can compare the sample you take today to the one I have had since last week. And the week before that." The chide in her voice was obvious: she believed he should have taken more of an interest in Canaan's drought and was late to make a personal visit. He felt a jab of shame at his earlier response to her: *How can Wakanda stop a drought?*

His Council was deluged with entreaties from around the globe as seekers and diplomats hoped Wakanda could fix everything from plagues to job crises to civil unrest. And T'Challa had grown uneasy with the implicit promise that intervention would give Wakanda outsized political influence, the beginnings of the "superpower" notion his father had warned Wakanda to avoid at any cost. T'Challa confessed to himself in Canaan's blazing sun that the drought had not moved him nearly so deeply until he had seen the molested soil with his own eyes. Shuri was right: he should have come sooner. Surely he had power to help Canaan, starting with underground Vibranium nets that had helped preserve the groundwater in Wakanda's dry regions.

His soil reading from his suit's computer came with a mild ping: **0.00**. The Fractional Water Index was no doubt zero for the topsoil, which was to be expected, but this deeper probe at 60 centimeters, then 120 centimeters, should have found some evidence of stored water!

Queen Truth was right: it was as if the water were somehow being sucked away.

"But by whom? And how?" he whispered. His voice-triggered computer suggested a familiar hologram face.

"Moses," he whispered.

After all, Moses Magnum had once seized control of Canaan.

Under his leadership, many more American expatriates—like the current queen, named for an American hero who ushered so many from slavery—had moved there.

Beside him, Queen Truth sighed. "Yes," she agreed. "As I feared. An old enemy returns."

Naming Moses Magnum was akin to a conjuring. A tremendous cracking sound assailed them, vibrating T'Challa's feet as the soil twenty meters before them parted like two halves of a canyon. Queen Truth gasped and took a step back on the unsteady ground, and T'Challa nudged her back farther still. The queen's security forces shouted behind them but T'Challa doubted that those armed men, or even the *Dora Milaje*, would rid them of the threat they had stumbled upon. Or been led to. If it were not too late, he would have advised the queen to run.

"Tell your men to hold their fire," T'Challa said, and she dutifully shouted the words back to her men in Swahili, the sole language her nation had adopted at its creation.

Okoye's voice came to T'Challa's earpiece this time: "You should pound Magnum to dust, since he enjoys dirt so much."

General Okoye and the *Dora Milaje* in his royal guard were watching from a cliffside perch, far enough away to give T'Challa privacy with Queen Truth but close enough to watch for trouble. Okoye's breathy voice told him she and the Dora were scrambling to move closer to them. But it was too late for that, too.

"First, we will talk," T'Challa told Okoye. She made a sarcastic sound he barely heard. A figure rose from the soil as if climbing a staircase from deep underground—and Moses Magnum stood twenty meters before T'Challa, every inch of him caked in red-brown soil except for his wide smile.

Like a giant, grinning worm, T'Challa thought. A giant worm with a Mohawk haircut, his body encased in Kevlar.

SOIL INSTABILITY, his suit's computer warned him inside his helmet.

"Brother—" Shuri began in his ear, alarmed.

"Yes," T'Challa told her. "I know."

Diplomacy first, T'Challa reminded himself. He inclined his head in greeting, since he had no plans to get close enough to shake Magnum's hand—and once he *did* get close, it would not be for niceties. "How fortunate for you that you are not dead after all, Magnum," T'Challa said, the politest words he could muster. "I keep hearing reports."

"Ah—you've faced a few of your own trials, King T'Challa," Magnum said. "But what's the saying? You can't keep a good man down." Impossibly, his grin widened.

"You are banned from this nation!" Queen Truth shouted. "We order you to leave at once! And you will immediately cease your unconscionable sabotage against us!"

Magnum's laughter convulsed his belly. "I'm sorry," he said when his fit had passed. "It's just so ridiculous—this unarmed old woman trying to give me orders." He gestured to invite T'Challa into the joke. "I mean, look at her, man! She's a flea giving orders to—"

T'Challa reached Magnum with a suit-powered vault before he could complete the vile insult. Magnum barely had time to comprehend, his eyes widening with surprise as T'Challa gave him a powerful shove in his chest with the heels of both hands.

Despite Okoye's advice, T'Challa did not release his full power for fear of snapping the man's ribcage and stopping his heart cold: he had to know more about his process of evaporating water or Wakanda might not be able to reverse it. But T'Challa also misjudged Magnum's Kevlar, which could absorb bullets... as well as a Panther blow. Magnum flew end over end, landing with a pained howl thirty meters away, but the blow itself had not even rendered him unconscious.

"T'Challa," Okoye said, "you must stop him before—"

T'Challa vaulted again, this time falling short by less than an elephant's length as he watched Magnum sit upright and shake his head, dazed, barely out of T'Challa's reach.

That damnable grin came again, Magnum's teeth painted in fresh blood this time.

Magnum held up his index finger, mocking T'Challa, and then lowered his finger to touch the ground. His grin was locked like iron.

"Magnum, NO—!" T'Challa shouted. An odd popping sound assaulted T'Challa's ears, a deafening tone that vibrated his ear drum.

The earth trembled and flung him away... and then sucked him down. Then, for a time, only the dark.

No light. His ears still rang, but there was no sound. Even in his Panther suit, T'Challa could not move. T'Challa tasted soil in his mouth. For an instant, he wondered if he had returned to Death's Domain. He had always known he would soon return, as all people must.

Only Okoye's voice in his ear, slightly distorted, told him that he was alive: "Don't worry—we'll dig you out!" Okoye said.

T'Challa mustered his suit's energy stores and felt himself bob slightly. He could at least clench his fist for a moment, but then he was trapped again: if anything, he might be deeper underground. He might as well be encased in iron. He did not dare try to use his suit for extraction again. T'Challa saw the blue light inside his helmet indicating that his oxygen reserves were running, as he had carefully designed for water emergencies. The air feeding his nostrils was cold and sterile. His suit would produce oxygen for at least twelve hours, which would give the *Dora Milaje* plenty of time to dig him out.

Magnum's tutelage under mad mutant dictator Apocalypse had given him much greater powers than he had during his days as an arms dealer hoping to overrun Wakanda. In those days, he had tried to destabilize the Kingdom of Canaan to get closer to taking Wakanda. Since then, T'Challa had heard talk of Magnum's ability to move the earth, but this was his first personal demonstration. It was a terrible and enviable ability indeed.

"The queen?" T'Challa inquired, anxious.

"She's alive," Okoye said. "Luckily, she was just beyond the worst damage. Magnum meant only to assassinate you, it seems. The drought might have been a trap. At least in part."

OXYGEN RESERVES – PLEASE REFRAIN FROM SPEECH, his sensor said.

"Brother, save your breath!" Shuri echoed.

The oxygen stream thinned, and T'Challa's lungs clenched, uneasy. But he had to ask. "Where is Magnum?" T'Challa said softly, expending little of his breath.

"Gone," Okoye said. "We've mapped a warren of underground tunnels, but he's not showing on our sensors."

"Do not chase him," T'Challa said.

In the long silence, T'Challa wondered if his comms had failed.

"I'm wasting breath to say it twice," T'Challa said. "Let him go. For now."

"Yes, my king," Okoye said, although he could imagine the irritation creasing her brow.

After such a brazen assassination attempt, the *Dora Milaje* would not rest until Magnum was captured, or, more likely, dead. But a direct confrontation was too risky, especially with such a small contingent, not even a dozen. The Dora were fierce, but they were human.

But a man who could swallow you into the soil with a touch was not entirely human.

T'Challa would need more planning for Moses Magnum. To chase him without research and strategy would be grave folly. He was lucky he had not been killed.

Trapped in his intended grave, helpless against the weight of the soil, T'Challa felt small for the first time since he could remember; smaller than in his boyhood days, walking in his father's shadow. He was the flea Magnum had laughed at and probably was laughing at still. But Magnum would not be laughing long.

In the soil's prison, T'Challa's hidden thoughts whispered the real reason he'd remembered his long walks with his father, the single memory he had tried to bury beneath all the rest: when he was a teenager, as part of more rigorous training for the crown, his father had sent him out to walk alone. And that walk had led to an unforgettable meeting.

Shuri's voice chirped in his ear, nearly hidden in the audio feed as Okoye and the king's guards gave orders from the frenzied digging above him. "Brother," Shuri said. "Do you promise not to be angry? Silence means yes."

T'Challa did not answer, but he was making no such promise.

Emboldened, Shuri went on: "When I saw the earlier soil readings the queen sent us, I knew we needed help. I also knew you'd be too proud to ask. Since you are pinned under the ground, this is a good time to tell you that I've already called for help…"

The Avengers? T'Challa wondered. *We might need the entire army of them.*

"…and she is flying to Wakanda as we speak," Shuri went on.

Only one helper? But the note of mischief in Shuri's voice gave away the answer!

T'Challa's heart flurried against his breastbone as if it could free itself, a sensation that would have felt like fear if he had not understood its true origin. He did not have to ask Shuri whom she had called. Her name came to his lips in a whisper: "Ororo."

AS SHE soared high, Ororo raised her body temperature so her eyelashes would not freeze and her hair would not whip her face like the ice its pale strands so closely mimicked. Clouds fanned in mist across her skin as she made a playful loop through a mountainous cumulonimbus cloud's gaping hole with a shriek of delight. She built the clouds as she flew, hardly aware of how they bloomed behind her as she streaked the sky. She would never tire of it! Of all her gifts, none brought her joy like flight.

For years, spoiled by worship and effortless talents that were feared even by her most powerful foes, Ororo had taken her gifts for granted. But when Forge had stripped her of her powers, betraying both her love and her allyship, she had missed none more than her ability to take flight high above the world, away from the chaotic din, free of confinement in rooms, or buildings, or nations. Or obligations. Being grounded had felt like death. And, after a time, her gift of flight had been the first to return—long leaps at first, then rocketlike dashes straight up for longer and longer intervals. Her greatest love had returned to her even before she rekindled her mastery of weather that had earned her code name: Storm.

She would never take flying, or freedom, for granted again.

Ororo did not worry for T'Challa's safety after Shuri's report—his suit would protect him—but she couldn't imagine enduring his fate! Nothing had erased the paralyzing claustrophobia that gripped her when she was trapped in small spaces, the long shadow that had trailed her since childhood. *Even a goddess must have a weakness*, a seer in a shopping mall in Nairobi had once told her with a sly wink of her eye.

Ororo's joy shrank as she descended, the earth's myriad colors piercing the clouds.

Below her, Wakanda was a verdant jewel. No other nation seemed to *gleam* from the sky. As Storm, Ororo could toss away opponents like paper, but memories were harder to fight.

Once, she had been the Queen of Wakanda, serving at T'Challa's side.

Once, they had both been foolish teenagers seeing themselves in a mirror for the first time: his royalty and her powers blending from the moment they had met when he was abducted in Kenya during a ceremonial walkabout. Instant love neither of them had forgotten.

Once, their wedding served as a joyous truce in the midst of a civil war.

But so long ago. Now she was a visitor to Wakanda—or worse, a stranger. He childishly had blamed her for destruction she had not caused, believing she had betrayed Wakanda when she allied herself with her X-Men team rather than the Avengers. T'Challa's cold words that terrible day still raked her belly: "Please don't come here again."

Well, she *was* coming. Shuri and Ramonda had begged her to return. But not soon enough. The parched lands in Canaan were visible from above too, stark grays and browns stripped of the colors of growth and life. A petty monster like Moses Magnum had no right to suck any nation's land dry! But Ororo was especially incensed that he had done it to try to hurt Wakanda, where once she had reigned as queen.

To try to kill T'Challa.

Storm let out another shriek, this time to direct her clouds with even more speed, to bloat their darkening bellies with moisture, to bid lightning bolts to flare a fiery duel in the sky.

Below her, the Kingdom of Canaan sang with the sound of driving rain.

"...AND WE will *root them out,"* T'Challa's voice came, forceful, floating through the corridor leading to his War Room with the *Dora Milaje.* Ororo could not keep the smile from her face as she approached the doorway with Shuri and Ramonda. Flanked by her sister and mother (with so little family, the term "in-law" held no meaning, and her heart would never "annul" this bright, fierce girl or her wise, regal mother), Ororo felt once again a part of a royal processional. In her mind, she was draped in a two-layered, peacock-colored ceremonial robe like the one Ramonda had worn to greet her.

Ramonda held up her hand to halt Ororo's entrance before she would be visible.

"He will want the reunion to be private," Ramonda said. When Shuri started to object, Ramonda leveled the sharp gaze Ororo remembered well, as powerful as a lightning bolt using only the angle of her eyes. "We won't create a spectacle, Shuri. Not in front of the *Dora.*"

"What spectacle?" Shuri whispered. "She's here to help us plan the counterattack."

"This one," Ramonda tsked-tsked, indicating Shuri with feigned irritation. "Shuri, do you know your brother at all? You saw his mood when he returned from Canaan."

T'Challa's voice rose with anger: "...scour from end to end, no matter where he emerges from his lowly hiding place!"

T'Challa did not often sound so angry. Ororo shivered with the memory of T'Challa's eyes when he had sent her away: beyond anger to cool indifference. Shuri and Ramonda had invited Ororo to Wakanda without T'Challa's blessing, and for the first time she doubted a happy reception. Ororo never would have done anything to harm Wakanda, but her allegiance to the X-Men had torn her and T'Challa apart after he blamed her team for flooding and incalculable damage in Wakanda. Ororo had known T'Challa since they were both practically children, and his eyes that day had been foreign to her. Since he sent her away, Ororo had matched his anger with her own: How dare he not trust her! How dare he blame her for the actions of others! But today… Ororo felt only a novel nervousness speeding her heart, as if she were a young girl again. She sorely missed the freedom and power she had felt in the skies.

"Brother? She's here. We're just outside." Shuri's finger was pressed to her ear's communications device.

T'Challa's voice stopped cold. His quick footsteps approached.

"Deep breath, Daughter," Ramonda said quietly, knowing Ororo's heart. "He needs you." Ororo smiled at the word *Daughter*. She had been called Storm, Goddess, Angel, Demon.

So rarely, so briefly, had she known the title *Daughter*. Ororo returned Ramonda's squeeze, although a bit more tightly.

Ororo was hand in hand with Ramonda when T'Challa ducked out of the doorway and saw her. He could not hide his startlement, the anger etched in his jaw melting to slack… awe. As if he could not believe his eyes. He looked at her first, then at Ramonda, as if for confirmation that he had not imagined the sight of her. And then at Shuri, who was smirking.

"I've brought you a one-person army," Shuri said. "You're welcome."

"I think we have business elsewhere," Ramonda told Shuri.

"What business?" Shuri said, then smiled playfully. "Ah— 'Elsewhere.' Of course."

Shuri slipped into the War Room to join the *Dora*. Ramonda

cast an encouraging smile over her shoulder at Ororo as she turned to leave them alone in the corridor, which was adorned with Vibranium-enhanced spears in decorative colors.

T'Challa's gaze returned to Ororo. He might be the one called Storm, the way his emotions swam so furiously across his eyes: admiration, longing, shame, regret. But no disappointment. No fury. That past was gone. She noticed a small clump of soil tangled in the coils of his hair and gently brushed it away. Habit.

"Ororo," he said, his voice a mere breath. He cupped her elbows in his warm palms. "Welcome home."

A HUSH fell over the *Dora Milaje* as T'Challa returned to the War Room with Ororo at his side, walking with him pace for pace down the center aisle as she had at state functions as his queen. Okoye could hardly keep her eyes in her head, staring with such scrutiny. In the days after T'Challa annulled his marriage to Ororo, Okoye had been his voice of encouragement to drown out the endless objections from Shuri and Ramonda: *You did the right thing, T'Challa. She was never wedded to Wakanda. You cannot predict which way a tree split in two might fall.*

But now T'Challa's stomach churned with the acidic doubts that had stolen his sleep in the weeks after he sent her away. A dozen times he had nearly summoned her, until the churning finally stilled and he convinced himself he had been right to sacrifice his heart for Wakanda. But he had not realized how flimsy the wall around his heart was until Ororo returned, her mesmerizing silver hair framing her face... and those enchantress's eyes. Time swept away, and he felt like a boy in the presence of his first, his only, love again. No other existed like Ororo.

Ororo walked with confidence, ignoring the gazes of wonder and shock. "Please continue the meeting," Ororo said. "Don't let me interrupt."

Instead of joining Shuri and the fully assembled *Dora*, Ororo kept her place beside T'Challa as he faced his royal guard. Okoye's chin was lowered in a pointed stare at him at the break in protocol. Watching, Shuri struggled to keep the grin from her face.

"As I was saying…" T'Challa began and cleared his throat for a deeper timbre. "…as I was saying, our intelligence reveals that Moses Magnum has assembled an army of his own, hidden in underground tunnels along Wakanda's border—not unlike the tunnels between the ancient churches in his homeland of Ethiopia. I assume he planned to assassinate me and then take advantage of the leadership vacuum to try to mount a larger attack. I also assume he has developed a new weapon to try to take Wakanda."

"Agreed," Ororo said. "In his dreams, he's Tony Stark. Always bringing new toys."

"Their apparent encampment may only be another trap," T'Challa said. "So we will identify his capabilities. And we will wait until dawn to counter."

"Your Highness!" Okoye objected. "We are ready to counter now. This attack is the talk of the world! The video of you being dug out of the soil like a dinosaur bone has gone viral. Our enemies are rejoicing! A late response makes Wakanda—and you—look weak."

"The truly strong have no fear of looking weak," Ororo said before T'Challa could answer, mirroring his own thoughts. "Wakanda does not make decisions based on appearances and silly social media. Let them rejoice! Our enemies will be quaking again soon enough."

The *Dora Milaje* stirred and grumbled, shocked, even as they kept their voices low to avoid disrespecting T'Challa. Ororo speaking for Wakanda! And she had used the term "our enemies" as if their marriage had never been annulled. T'Challa gently patted the small of Ororo's back to caution her to be more diplomatic.

"Your objection is noted, Okoye," T'Challa said. "All such talk from our enemies will cease in the light of day."

RAMONDA'S ROYAL feast welcoming Ororo was hastily planned
and held at a late hour, but most of the Council members were

in attendance, it seemed, only to gawk. T'Challa sat side by side with Ororo at the head of the table as he always had, their fingers entwined. For the moment, thoughts of Moses Magnum gave way to delight over Ororo's touch, both discovery and treasured memory in this odd moment that lived in both the present and the past.

And what of the future? The thought came unbidden, surprising T'Challa so much that he glanced at Ramonda as if she might have planted the thought herself. Ramonda seemed to know, smiling at him with her eyes as she sipped her Nigerian palm wine.

And what a feast it was! The Wakandan specialties of lamb and spiced rice were aromatic on the table, of course, but his chefs who had studied throughout the continent had also prepared jollof rice, plantains, goat, fufu, collard greens, Kenyan crunchy bananas, Ramonda's favorite Chakalaka relish from South Africa—and, of course, Egyptian specialties like pigeon and the national dish of Molohia soup, honoring Ororo's birthplace. Even with short notice, Wakandan chefs did not disappoint.

Ramonda rang her glass with her spoon and rose to her feet. The hum of conversation vanished. "A toast," she said, raising her glass. "In honor of the return of my... other daughter, Ororo, known to the world as Storm. I could not be prouder at how she has lived up to her name."

All eyes went to T'Challa first, to see if he would honor the toast. He gave Ororo a quick glance and saw her fragile smile as she waited too. Ororo was fearsome on the battlefield, but she seemed as tentative as he at navigating her heart. To put her at ease, T'Challa also stood up. He turned to Ororo with his glass raised.

"Yes," he said. "To the return of Ororo to Wakanda. We have missed you."

Shuri let out an amused chuff at the word "we," a deflection, but the sound mostly was lost in the affirmations as the rest of the Council felt obliged to join the toast. Several members wore tight smiles that betrayed their objections. The Council, like the *Dora Milaje*, had supported his annulment of his marriage; in fact, some believed he never should have married her at all.

"I have missed you," T'Challa corrected himself. He clinked Ororo's glass.

Ororo's entire face seemed to glow as brightly as her hair. "And me you," she said. "Your Highness."

With her eyes on him, the rest of the room seemed to vanish.

T'CHALLA INVITED Ororo into his chamber as he pored over the intelligence spouting from his computer: troop locations, body scans, geological disturbances in Canaan. His mind never left the screen, but every inch of his skin was aware that Ororo stood close to him. A warm blanket seemed to have fallen over both of them; even their breathing was synchronized.

Magnum's troops seemed to be confined to Canaan, which was good—but implied that sympathizers within that nation had allowed his presence. T'Challa's suit had detected no lies from Queen Sojourner Truth, so for now he must believe she had been caught by surprise as much as he. Perhaps Magnum had triggered the drought so the Canaanites would feel dissatisfaction with her leadership, softening up Canaan for a coup to bolster his plans to try to take Wakanda again. Magnum had ruled there for a time—and surely would like to regain his power.

"But what is his actual weapon?" T'Challa mused aloud.

Ororo moved beside him, only slightly, but his arm felt aflame near hers. He was aware of her every motion and gesture. "Whatever he used to parch the land?" she guessed.

"That would be enough to destabilize Canaan, yes," he said. "But not Wakanda. He would need a much more powerful force."

He turned his eyes to Ororo then, as if he had called her by name.

"You are a distraction, Ororo," he said. "A greater one than I've ever known."

She pinned her lips; part hurt, part irritation. "Then I'll leave your chamber," she said. "Wake me for the fight."

"I have another idea," he said. "Most of what distracts me is… not knowing."

"Not knowing what, T'Challa?"

Instead of answering, he touched her chin. "Not knowing… if I may kiss you."

Ororo's face softened again, her smile turning girlish. "I was wondering the same thing."

"But… you have entanglements." T'Challa refused to bring her reputed lover's name to his lips. Over the years, T'Challa had trained himself to avoid any thoughts of him, or any of the X-Men in the family she had chosen.

"Do I?" Playfully, Ororo examined the chamber, which was emptied except for his bed and the Wakandan fabrics and treasures he had decorated every inch of the space with. "I see no entanglements here. Do you?"

They kissed. The sensation was like tumbling headfirst back into his boyhood. Even his palms were sweaty as they had been the first time he kissed Ororo. He saw the sensations mirrored in Ororo's face.

"And what of your… entanglements?" she said. "Is there another Ororo?"

"That would be impossible," he said. "There is only one."

They kissed again. Hardly aware, they passed a precious hour in each other's arms. An hour closer to dawn.

LONG AFTER midnight, T'Challa sat up with his mind afire. Inspiration!

"Magnum's troops are a distraction," he said. "That's where he wants me to focus. But I've scanned their weapons, and they are unremarkable. Nothing like the Dome he once used against Wakanda. The troops themselves are ordinary, hardly a hundred of them. No match for the Dora, whether I was dead or alive. They're not the invading force—they're for show. They're meant to march in only after…"

"After what? Wakanda is too well fortified for his earthquakes."

"Yes, and with an earthquake too powerful, he would be

worried about burying the Vibranium stores. Vibranium is all he truly wants."

"All the world wants," Ororo mused.

T'Challa went to his computer again; it was synched to his suit, but when he wasn't armored, he sat at his desk to type in a flurry on his keyboard. Had he missed something in his scans? Without questions about Ororo jamming his fevered mind, T'Challa noticed unusual sonic fluctuations as he reviewed the data from his confrontation with Magnum. Hadn't he felt a strange popping sensation in his ears, even with his suit—?

"It's sonic," he realized, sharing his thoughts aloud. "He triggered… a tone. The earthquake made it seem trivial, but… if I felt my ears pop even inside my Panther armor, imagine what such a tone might do to—"

"Of course!" Ororo said, joining his side again. Her hand slid across his shoulder as if it had never left. "With you dead, he might expect a sonic weapon to overwhelm your fighters."

"And he knows we will go back to face him. There is nothing to stop him from using both earthquakes and his new weapon to try to thwart our counterattack. Nothing except…"

"Us," Ororo said.

Their minds were one.

They would not summon the *Dora*, or even Shuri. They would not wait until dawn. They would answer Magnum's attack tonight—alone.

Together.

T'CHALLA HAD forgotten how love, or even the memory of it, lightened the heart and spirit. His heartbeat seemed to propel his flight as he soared high over Wakanda's Great Mound, hand in hand with Ororo. But the power was hers, of course: she was manipulating the electromagnetic field to propel him as if he shared her ability to fly, and they rose and dipped as one. The full moon glowed across Ororo's wildly billowing hair as if the strands had captured its light. What a wondrous sight they must be to a sleepless child staring at them high above through his window! She glanced at him, sharing his nearly giddy joy.

He could barely remember the man he had been when he sent her away, so devastated by the damage to Wakanda, blaming himself… but he only knew how to channel his rage toward Ororo, whom even the Panther God had blessed as his mate. Did he believe he had known better than the Panther God? Had he any right to annul a union that had been blessed? In his cowardice, he had told Ororo that the high priest had annulled the marriage, when they both knew he himself wore that mantle, as well as king. He had shorn himself in two the day he sent her away.

And now…?

T'Challa's comms inside his armor lit up in red from an emergency message. "Brother!" Shuri's voice came. "Why does my scan show you've left the Golden City? And you are… ten thousand feet in the air without a jet?"

"You know why," T'Challa said. His smile was obvious in his voice. "You called her."

"I called her to *help*, not to lead you to—"

"I am leading myself," T'Challa said. "We know what Magnum is up to. We will make sure he never troubles Wakanda again. Don't wake Okoye—"

"You think I'm sleeping?" Okoye's voice broke in. "After Magnum buried Wakanda's king like a pile of rubbish? We'll meet you—"

"No one will meet me," T'Challa said. "That's an order. I'll tell you when it's done."

He silenced the communications channel so he wouldn't suffer through complaints.

Instead, he activated his holographic map of Canaan that showed him the system of tunnels Magnum had created near his border. Magnum glowed as a green dot on the map: he was on the surface after all! Apparently, he preferred the comfort of a bed rather than however his troops were being forced to sleep underground. He had created a shelter and was so sure of his new weapon's capabilities that he dared to sleep in the open.

"He must not see us approach," T'Challa told Ororo.

"Of course! Do you think I'm a child again?" Ororo said. Even her mild irritation was a happy, familiar memory now. "To his sensors, we only look like a large bird."

"You fly like a child," T'Challa teased her. "As if we are on our way to play, not war."

"War *is* play," Ororo said. "When it's done right."

With a laugh, Ororo began her steep descent, plunging them nearly straight down like an amusement park's rollercoaster. If not for his suit's equilibrium, his stomach would have plunged into his throat.

A cement cottage with a steel roof came into view below them. Newly constructed. T'Challa offered Ororo two Kimoyo beads he had fashioned into earrings for her.

"Here, wear these. Your hearing won't be impaired, but they should block any sonic waves."

"'Should'?" she said, hesitating.

"Absolutely... without a doubt... should."

With a mock frown, Ororo slid the earrings in place and parted her hair for him to inspect them. "How do they look?" she said.

"Not as beautiful as the woman who is wearing them," he said. "But they look perfect. They are Wakandan, after all."

"Mine to keep, I hope."

"Of course."

Satisfied, Ororo stopped their descent; they still floated high over Magnum's rooftop. "Then it's time to huff and puff," she said, and raised her arms. "And blow his house down."

A sudden windstorm below them stirred the brush and soil still damp from Ororo's earlier rainstorm, rattling the cottage's windowpanes. Rapidly, the winds screamed to hurricane intensity, until the Jeep parked outside turned over and Magnum's roof whipped away in sheets. Clothing, papers and other items inside danced wildly in the gale. Magnum stood in the shell that remained, his arms raised to protect his face.

Then, just as quickly, Storm's wind died away. Magnum's arms dropped down as he stared up at them.

"Come out, Magnum!" T'Challa called down. "You're hereby charged with an attempt to assassinate the King of Wakanda."

T'Challa shone his spotlight down on Magnum, who was ready for them, fully armored.

His grin gleamed in the light. "Back for more, T'Challa? Did you see? Your video's had fifty million views—and in only a few hours!"

"Tell your men to surrender. Lives need not be lost."

"You mean… these men?" Magnum said.

A hole opened in the soil behind the cottage and Magnum's troops ran out, guns ready. Column after column emerged, not unlike ants.

"I'm gonna make you a star, T'Challa," Magnum said. "Let's see if we can get even more hits with *this* video." He raised his voice for his troops. "Ready… aim… fi—"

Before he could finish, Magnum let out a startled yell as he found himself floating on the wind, yanked upward toward T'Challa as Storm levitated him.

"If they fire at us, they fire at you," Storm said.

"Up here, you are helpless," T'Challa reminded him. "You can't shake the earth without touching it. Now you will stand trial in Wakanda."

"Oh no—I'm not helpless," Magnum said, and he pushed a button on a handheld device T'Challa could only see now that Magnum was so close to him.

Again, T'Challa's ears popped and a ringing sound squeezed his eardrums. Ororo let out a cry, and suddenly they were all diving toward the ground fifty meters below.

"Fool!" T'Challa said. "If she falls, we all fall!"

His Panther suit would protect him from the fall, but he must take pains to protect Ororo. If Magnum perished, so be it.

"No one will fall," Ororo said, her teeth gritted as she regained control. She shook her head as if to clear it, and they floated steadily again, then rose slightly.

She glared at T'Challa. "These Wakandan earrings, though? They are not yet 'perfect.'"

T'Challa grabbed Magnum's shoulders—harder than intended, his Panther claws sinking past Magnum's armor to his skin… and beyond, to tendons. Ororo's cry of pain had enraged him, and now Magnum's cry answered for it as he writhed in pain.

"You will never have control of Canaan or Wakanda!" T'Challa told Magnum. "You'll be locked away so long, no one will remember you!"

T'Challa headbutted Magnum, leaving the man floating limply, unconscious. Or could he be dead? T'Challa was not certain at first, but his suit's sensors read Magnum's feeble heartbeat. T'Challa yanked the handheld control from Magnum's hand, careful not to press the button. He and Shuri would study it to learn how Magnum had harnessed the power to try to disable Wakandan forces.

Gunshots rang out below, and T'Challa angled himself so the troops' bullets grazed his suit, missing Ororo. One errant bullet bloomed red on Magnum's sleeve.

"You're shooting your own man, you fools!" T'Challa shouted down.

"Enough!" Ororo said, and she summoned a new wind. Below them, a hundred troops were tumbled, scattered and helpless. T'Challa wished he had not wasted so much of his evening with Ororo, plotting how to defeat such worthless paper dolls. They were not worthy of this fight.

When she and T'Challa were low enough to avoid killing Magnum, Ororo allowed him to drop in a tangled heap, another human tumbleweed. That left only the two of them still airborne, two warriors with no battle to fight—except perhaps one.

T'Challa retracted his Panther mask so Ororo could see his face. "I've missed this."

The words lay just beneath his tongue: *Come back to Wakanda.*

Take your rightful place as queen. I was impetuous and short-sighted. No other woman belongs at my side.

But it was Ororo who spoke first. "You were right, T'Challa. Somehow, you knew even before I knew myself."

T'Challa's unspoken words withered. "I was right about what?"

Moonlight revealed grim lines in Ororo's face despite her smile. "You always knew who you were born to be. You told me when we were young, and I envied your confidence. But me?

"I… have had many lives. Many nations. Never a *home*. I could not have been a proper queen—not the queen Wakanda deserves. I see that now. Maybe it's a curse that comes with the gift of flight—I can never stay in one place long. I only dreamed I could… because I love you so."

If the stone in T'Challa's stomach had actual weight, it would have driven him to the ground, separating them. Soon, that stone would melt to acid and burn him while he slept. But not yet. In a corner of his mind, he wondered if Ororo was truly speaking her heart… or only telling him what she thought he needed to hear.

"Then… I made a wise choice," T'Challa said, his words more certain than his voice. "But it is best if it is *our* choice, Ororo."

Not past tense—present. Now. Tonight.

"Yes," Ororo said at last. "A mutual choice is always the best choice."

Ororo clasped his hands. They probed each other's eyes until each of them was certain they could find no hidden glimmers of truth, and no more questions except the ones that neither of them could answer. The future was a mysterious and unknowable territory they might, or might not, travel together. Ororo's eyes were dancing gray flames, hypnotic.

A year might have passed before a few of Magnum's men half wakened, groaning below them. Magnum would sleep much longer.

"Thank you for your help, Ororo," T'Challa said. "The *Dora* can clean up the rest."

Still clasping hands, they floated face to face, framed before the liquid moon.

"The *Dora* would have been fine without me. You could have given them all earrings… or something better. But I could not resist a chance to see Wakanda. It's lovely this time of year."

T'Challa quirked an eyebrow at her. "Hey! Every time of year."

Ororo smiled, although T'Challa thought he might see a tear in the corner of her eye. "No lies detected. But do Wakandans have to be the cockiest people on the planet?"

"You know…" T'Challa began. "I am a very important king. My obligations keep me busy. A king never has a day of rest. And then you add the distress calls… this ruler here, another ruler there. The Avengers always calling on me to help save the world."

He paused. "But I can't think of a single reason I need to go back home tonight. Or… tomorrow."

Her pause was endless. Who was the cocky one now? She was thinking it over! "It *is* a shame to waste such a pretty moon," Ororo said finally.

"Where shall we go, my queen?"

"Wherever we land." She smiled, holding him captive with her eyes. "My king."

As rain drummed across Canaan's thirsty soil, Ororo and T'Challa flew.

IMMACULATE CONCEPTION

A "What If?" Tale

NIKKI GIOVANNI

Oakland, California, 1978

DURING A community outreach visit to an after-school program, King T'Challa of Wakanda and five diplomats visiting as a delegation arrive at Washington Elementary School to meet with a group of students and their tutors.

The group exits a pair of black Rolls-Royce Phantoms, accompanied by two SUVs. The hood of each vehicle is adorned with small flags from their homeland. Entering the building, they walk down the hallway and all eyes follow the dignified group.

Mrs. Saunders, the school's principal, escorts the royal entourage into a classroom and announces the special guest to the children.

"WHY IS a king from Africa visiting our school? Are we in trouble?"

The seven-year-old girl with bright eyes and a curious disposition poses the question to her teacher. King T'Challa just laughs.

"Of course not, young scholar," he says. "Many years ago I lived in this very same Oakland neighborhood with my adopted mother. I very much enjoy coming back to visit whenever my schedule allows. If you have time, I would like to tell you a story about it."

"Yes!" one of the young students shouts. "Please stay!" Others join in the chorus.

Smiling broadly at the enthusiasm of the students, the king thinks back to a story he had been told when he was that age. Over the years he came to realize that it was fanciful, yet held many truths. With a few adjustments, it will speak to these youngsters as it did to him.

As the king begins his story, some of the children from the after-school program are clearly fascinated. Others appear suspicious, perhaps because T'Challa and the five men with him, all members of his royal delegation, "look like money," as the saying goes.

The king begins.

"MANY YEARS ago, in the town of Almeda, a bald eagle found in its nest an egg that did not belong there," T'Challa says. "The American eagle is a very strong bird, with a proud history. This eagle was the father of the nest and he rejected the egg. It had a small crack in the shell and intermittently a faint blue glow radiated through the flaw.

"Father Eagle took to the air with the egg in his talons. In a most deliberate manner—eagles rarely do anything by mistake—the eagle dropped the egg into a stream. The current from the stream carried the egg to a nearby town called Oakland..."

IT WAS evening in the springtime, and a woman sat next to Lake Merritt writing a poem in her journal. From the corner of her eye she spotted an object drifting very slowly and with a blue glow surrounding it. She stepped into the lake, then felt frightened and stepped out, but curiosity took her feet back into the water.

The blue glow felt familiar to her.

The woman scooped up the egg quickly and dried it off on her dress. After gathering her journal and sandals, she took the egg home to her small house nearby. Mariam was a petite and lovely woman with honest eyes and beautiful skin. She felt a growing connection to the egg, so it seemed very natural for her to build a warm nest using scraps of beautiful fabrics that came from her homeland, Africa.

"WHY WAS *she* in Oakland?" a little boy blurts out.

"She left Africa because she could not have children of her own," King T'Challa answers. "Sometimes in Africa, when a woman cannot have children, the people in her tribe can make her feel less important than the other women in the tribe."

The boy nodded and T'Challa continues.

SO MARIAM migrated to Oakland, California, where she worked for years as a nanny. One of the children in her care could not pronounce her name correctly, and Mariam adopted the name "Mary." Living modestly, she was happy to raise many children as if they were her own.

Mary knew that her newly adopted egg was not a regular one. What she *didn't* know was that this egg was a small machine made from a very rare mineral called Vibranium, and held what is called nanotechnology.

A very brilliant scientist from Africa had put inside of the egg DNA taken from a king who had lived two hundred years before. He did this because he believed that, one day in the future, this king would need to be reborn in his beloved homeland. The DNA would be the key to make this happen. This same scientist spent a lot of time learning about magic, the mystic arts that allowed him to see things that escaped the human eye.

As the weeks passed, Mariam's egg began to move and then change shape. This scared the shy woman, for she had no idea what was going on, but she decided to just love it. She sang songs from her native land and sometimes she kept the egg in the bed with her as she slept.

Within thirty days the egg changed shape three times. At first, its shape resembled a baby eagle, a chick. After a few more days it resembled a small black cat. Finally, what she originally found in the form of an egg began to take the form of a human infant with very sharp African features.

When the infant opened its eyes, Mariam was in shock. She didn't know what to do with this child except to feed him, clothe him, and most importantly continue to *love* him. He was, in fact, everything she had wanted in her former life in Africa but could not have. It was almost as if this child had been delivered specifically to her.

She gave the child an African name. As he grew, the neighborhood children could not pronounce it, so naturally they teased him.

For the next nineteen years of her life Mary made certain her adopted son was educated. That he was polite. As he got older, it became clear that he was different from the other kids on his block. Though taught to be kind, he defeated any bully who invited him to a fight. In fact, it bothered Mariam that her son fought so easily, and without fear, other boys who were much bigger than he.

The young people in Oakland came to respect him and stopped teasing him about his name. Instead, they gave him the nickname "TC."

In high school, TC excelled at football, gymnastics, and academics. In his free time, he obsessed over martial arts, borrowing every library book on the subject, and he spent hundreds of hours practicing every move displayed on the pages. His success in school earned him a scholarship to the University of California in Santa Cruz. For the first time in his life, TC lived seventy miles from his home.

There some of his most meaningful relationships began in the classroom. While studying engineering and social sciences, TC befriended a fellow student from Oakland, a young man named Huey. He also caught the attention of a professor from Africa named Dr. Mwambi. This teacher guided him away from sports and encouraged him to develop his mind.

Whenever they visited home, TC and his friend Huey began to see the town of Oakland changing. Where before it had been a close-knit community and everyone felt like friends, it had turned more hostile. Eminent domain displaced many local families from their homes as land was taken from them for development. The tension in the air was fueled by the relationship between many Oakland residents and police officers who had migrated to California from the deep southern states, like Alabama.

"Oaklandites" came to believe the police department was racist in nature, a feeling fed by the fact that *only sixteen of the city's six hundred and sixty-one police officers were black.* To add to the tensions, the Oakland chapter of the Hells Angels were growing quickly, taking over Oakland's Foothill Boulevard and claiming their equity in the streets. Law enforcement agencies considered the Hells Angels to be nothing more than a nationally organized crime syndicate.

Huey began to hang out with a new friend named Bobby.

In response to what they felt was racial profiling and harassment from the local police, Huey and Bobby decided to form a group of their own to defend themselves and the neighborhood. Of course, Huey, Bobby, and the others tried to recruit TC because of his strength, intelligence, and fearless nature.

Mary was dead set against this idea. She felt as though young Americans had too much freedom and that everyone should be humble. TC was unsure of which direction he should go in, so he brought his concerns to Dr. Mwambi.

Instead of trying to stop TC from joining the young revolutionaries in the streets, TC's mentor suggested that the young man accompany him to Africa on a school internship, where he could learn more about a country called Tanzania. But TC had little interest in visiting Africa. He was more motivated to travel to places like China, where he could study martial arts.

The truth is, TC had never been outside of California. In the movies of that time, Africa appeared to be a place full of savages and disease. At least, that was the Hollywood version of the continent.

Nevertheless, TC found himself curious about the land that gave birth to his mother and decided this might be an opportunity in disguise. He talked about the internship to his friend Huey, who agreed it could be a magical adventure for him.

"We were kings in Africa," Huey said.

FOR THE weeks that followed, while her son prepared for his trip, TC's mother was terribly anxious. Despite being nervous, she still felt that a trip to Africa would be good for a young man who was so preoccupied with another people's culture, more so than his own.

It was the Tuesday evening before TC's adventure was to begin. Huey and the homies from the neighborhood took TC to some neighborhood dive bars and a rib joint for a send-off celebration. TC was not a drinker, and even after many beers and a lot of pork, he remembered his mother's rules about drinking and driving. He fell asleep in his rusty-but-reliable 1961 Chevy Impala.

He was awakened abruptly by a police officer banging on his driver-side window at 8 a.m., six hours after he had nodded off and an hour past the time of his departure flight to Tanzania. The police officer barked at him in a harsh, gravelly voice.

"Let me catch your black ass here when I come back, and you'll be sleeping in a cell, boy!"

TC was too hungover to argue. As he realized that he had missed his flight, he felt shame and embarrassment set in. How could he disappoint Dr. Mwambi like this? After the man had taken the time to mentor him, even paying for his airline tickets and lodging in Tanzania.

This was *bad*.

HIS MOTHER was waiting for him on the front porch when he pulled up and parked.

"Child, are you possessed by the devil himself?" she asked. "You smell of booze and you look like you woke up under a bridge."

Before he could explain himself, his mother shoved an envelope into his right hand. It was a letter from Dr. Mwambi.

"I waited for you for more than an hour, TC," the letter read. "You have scared your mother and me. I sincerely hope that you did not change your mind about the internship. When you receive this, please take the next flight out of Oakland and meet me in Tanzania.

"Please find the address below," it continued. "You will find me at the residence of my colleague, Dr. Abasi, about whom I have spoken many times. Remember, the deadline for your orientation is on Monday.

"I will pray for your safe arrival."

With great relief TC realized this was a second chance. Rather than allow him to drive in his condition, his mother instructed him to take the #4 bus to a close-by muffler repair shop.

"Take the doorway on the right side of the building and go upstairs, where you will find a travel agency." She shoved some money into his hand. "Give them this, and they will book you on a flight to Tanzania. It may not be a fancy plane, but they will still get you there."

THE TRAVEL agency looked as if no one ever actually did any business there. It smelled of incense and strange animal musk. An elderly man sat behind a big wooden desk that was covered with exotic wood carvings, so intricate that from certain angles they seemed to move almost like water.

The old man was wearing a dashiki and jewelry with a lot of blue gems that glowed almost like Christmas tree lights. These gems seemed to flicker when TC entered the dusty office. Almost like a carnival trick, he thought, to fool him and help them take his money.

"Welcome to Transpacific Travel, young man." The elderly gentleman spoke in a familiar tone. "And how is your mum these days?"

His mother was the only other person that TC had ever heard use the word "mum."

Annoyed and suspicious, TC asked, "How do you know who I am, and how do you know my mother?"

"Everyone in Oakland knows everyone else, young man," the older fellow replied. "Now tell me, what is your destination today?"

"I need to be in Tanzania by Friday or Saturday."

"That is unfortunate, son," the travel agent said. "There are no airline departures from the West Coast to Mother Africa until next Tuesday." Undaunted, TC went on to explain that he needed to be in Tanzania by Saturday to prepare for orientation at a university.

"My apologies, young man, I wish you had planned this trip thirty days ago. It's simply impossible." As TC turned and dropped his head in defeat, the travel agent spoke up again. "There is another way to get this done, but you may not have the fortitude to handle it."

"Are you serious?" TC asked.

The travel agent nodded, stood and walked over to a beautiful wood-and-brass trunk. He opened it and pulled out what appeared to be a fancy blanket.

"What is that, a flying carpet?" TC asked in a sarcastic tone.

"Son, some things cannot be explained in science class," the old man replied. "Tomorrow morning at dawn, be at the Port of Oakland. Be there right before the sun rises. Wear this cloth on your shoulders and find a comfortable place to sit. Keep an open mind and your transportation will arrive within the hour."

TC rolled his eyes and shook his head in disbelief. "This sounds crazy," he said, "but I'm desperate, so I guess I don't have a choice, do I?"

"You will find your way, son," the elderly gentleman said confidently. "And please send me a postcard."

TC shook the travel agent's hand, said thank you, and made his way home on the next bus.

WHEN HE arrived at home his mother was excited. A telegram had arrived from Dr. Mwambi. It read, "TC: do not worry about bringing luggage for this trip. Everything you will need for the next few months will be provided for you. I look forward to having you join me here soon."

With great anxiety, TC explained to his mother about the travel agent and the weird fabric shawl that he had been given.

"I am familiar with this type of fabric," his mother said, looking it over, "and the gentleman was telling the truth. As strange as it may sound, the fact that he didn't take your money should tell you that his intentions are honorable, and he wants to help you reach your destination."

The next morning, TC arrived at the Port of Oakland at 6:30 a.m. It was about fifty degrees on the waterfront, so he was happy to wrap the fabric around his shoulders. He closed his eyes to pray that he could correct his mistakes and receive the gifts that his mother and professor were both extending to him.

Within minutes, he felt... *intoxicated*. His first assumption was that there was still alcohol in his system, but then he began to feel a trance-like state, somewhere between a dream and unconsciousness. Soon he was practically comatose.

"WHAT DOES 'comer toast' mean?" a young boy asks, back at Washington Elementary. King T'Challa picks up a piece of chalk and writes out the spelling of the word on a blackboard.

"Comatose is like being in a very deep sleep, and almost dead," he says. "But still breathing, and still alive."

This causes a murmuring among the students, but they accept what he has said, and King T'Challa continues his story.

AS TC fell into a very deep sleep, it seemed as if he entered a dream. He no longer felt the cold of a fifty-degree morning, and the weird African blanket began to take the form of...

Feathers.

These feathers were familiar—American eagle feathers—and when TC moved these wings they took him instantly into the air. Within the dreamlike state, his entire body took on the appearance of a proud and powerful eagle.

As he flew, he heard a voice. It explained that while the fabric which TC viewed as a "weird blanket" originated in Africa, at some point it had been anointed by a tribe of Native Americans called the Ohlone. These Native American people lived along the coastline of the San Francisco Bay, some in the Oakland area. After they anointed the fabric it was returned to its original owner, a visitor from Africa.

"The eagle did not reject you when you were in that egg," the mysterious voice said. "The eagle delivered you to where you needed to be, to be safe. And the eagle was used to smuggle you from point to point without allowing the wrong people to discover your location. Your very existence would be intimidating to some people and even threatening."

After hours in flight, TC in the form of an eagle began to feel fatigue. From the corner of his eye he spotted a sparrow with no color, an albino. The sparrow spoke to him without making a sound.

"Shall we race?" the sparrow asked.

"I've been flying for three hours," TC answered, "and I'm looking for a place to land and rest."

"But an eagle can fly for much more than that," the sparrow said. "So perhaps you're just lazy?" When TC didn't answer, the sparrow continued. "No worries, you are approaching a small group of islands and you can rest there. You would've lost our race anyhow." And the albino sparrow fell into a dive at an amazing speed, disappearing into fog.

Even though the sparrow's words were insulting, TC the eagle felt energized by them. As he approached the islands he did not stop and continued for a little more than eight hours before he stopped to rest on a large coral reef, part of which poked above the water.

There was a loud ruckus as a group of sea lions fought over a large tuna that was still moving. Suddenly, a majestic bird swooped down out of the mist and snatched the fish with his razor-sharp talons. It was another eagle, and it landed near TC.

"Such a meal is much more deserved by one of our kind," the eagle said. As TC responded, he realized that he wasn't really hungry, and he said so.

"That is because you are traveling on the spiritual plane, my friend," the eagle replied, "not the physical one." Strangely, this began to make sense. The other eagle departed.

After a short time TC took flight once again, and shortly found himself approaching South East Asia. He encountered some very aggressive winds and anxiety took hold. Instinctively, he positioned his head and wings to harness the wind's overwhelming power. This took him to a speed so great that it caused him to black out.

When he awakened, he was back to human form, lying in a fetal position on a bed and gripped by a humidity that felt like the sauna in his school's locker room. A soft female hand placed a warm cloth on his forehead. A very dark-skinned woman with beautiful features and no hair spoke to him in a foreign language.

A familiar figure stepped into the small, humid hut.

"Welcome to the motherland, young scholar!" Dr. Mwambi said. "It is time for you to meet the Maasai people."

IN A flurry of activity, TC registered for his study program at the Muhimbili University of Health and Allied Sciences. He began weeks of learning about the Maasai people and quickly felt a connection to them. Indeed, all Africa felt familiar to him.

One morning when he was getting dressed to go study in the university library, Dr. Mwambi came to find him and was holding a camera in his hands. The professor instructed him to take the camera and go out exploring.

"Bring back many photos, because I will be grading you on what you capture," the professor said. "First take the bus to Lake Victoria, then when you arrive there go to the market and hire a tour guide. For about a dollar a guide will show you the beautiful nature reserves. Those are your objectives."

Though he thought it strange, TC did as he was told and took a seat on a crowded bus—one without the air conditioning he was used to on public buses. His disposition made him stand out, as he looked lost. Children stared at him as if he were an alien.

His bus let him off very close to a market next to Lake Victoria, one of the African Great Lakes. While walking through the market he bought and ate a mango, and heard the voice of a woman speaking in English.

"Are you ready to see the most beautiful natural wonders of this earth?" the woman asked. On her face she wore tribal paint, and on eight of her fingers she wore beautiful rings that resembled the gems the travel agent had worn back in Oakland. For whatever reason, he felt as though he had known this woman for years and found himself to be comfortable with her immediately.

Reaching into his pocket, he pulled out an American dollar.

"Yes, ma'am. I'm ready."

HIS NEW travel companion led him along the banks of Lake Victoria and he marveled at what was one of the most beautiful sights he had ever witnessed. Once he had become used to the heat, Africa felt like a different planet to him. The air was cleaner, the food made him feel strong, and even the garments he wore were more comfortable.

The woman introduced herself as Imani. It was a Swahili name, and she explained that it meant Faith. Knowing this helped TC feel relaxed... but this did not last. The two travelers followed a trail for about an hour, when TC started to notice things that he had already seen and photographed.

"Is there a reason why we are walking in a circle, Imani?"

Imani replied by saying, "Sometimes a straight line is not the answer, sir."

TC had no idea what she meant by this but did not press it.

As they descended a steep hill for about half a mile, the landscape began to change. The trees and plants looked less inviting. The path disappeared and the sky was less bright and clear. Much of the foliage had long aggressive thorns, berries that did not look edible, and the biggest hornets that he had ever seen.

"Where are we?" TC asked.

"You are standing in the Valley of Thorns, my friend," Imani replied.

As TC started to feel dehydrated, he asked, "How long before we reach somewhere that I can find some water?"

Imani reached in her travel bag and handed him a ceramic bottle. "Drink this," she said. "It will hydrate you and make you feel as if you just had a meal."

"What's in it?" TC asked, and Imani explained the mysterious drink to him.

"It's mostly local green plants, and a fruit that is very hard to find." As TC poured some of the liquid out to see what he was about to ingest, Imani snapped at him, "This is not America, and we do NOT waste food here!"

TC apologized and took a swig of the beverage. The consistency of it was heavy, but it was true that the drink was hydrating, and with just one sip it felt like a meal supplement. Whatever the cause, TC wanted to continue on their way.

"Please excuse me," Imani said, "so that a lady can find a private place to relieve her bladder."

As she disappeared behind some bushes, TC looked for a place to sit where there were no thorns or hornets. He continued to drink, and soon his body was tingling. His hands shook as all the hair on his six-foot-two-inch frame stood up, and he got goosebumps.

Then he realized he was losing track of time, and Imani has been gone for close to thirty minutes. He yelled out her name and received no response. As he stood up to move in the direction she had gone, he began to hear drums in the distance. They seemed to be coming from above him.

While TC felt surprised, it was with no anxiety. Instead, he almost felt as if he wanted to beat a drum himself. The sound was *exciting*. The percussion pattern seemed confrontational.

Finally dismissing the drums, TC walked toward the bushes where Imani had disappeared. While walking he brushed against a vine full of thorns that looked poisonous. Looking down at his white linen sleeve, he saw blood and eight long thorns piercing his bicep and forearm.

He pulled these bloody thorns out of his skin and found it bizarre that none of this hurt. If he had been back in Oakland, he'd have been tearing up the bathroom to find peroxide.

The sound of the drums became louder but he was still preoccupied with finding Imani.

With no sign where he had last seen her, TC turned in the opposite direction—and there she was standing. Imani was holding a long metal pole with a glowing blue blade at the end. To his eye, it resembled an axe with a light bulb inside it.

"What kind of tour guide are you?" he asked, realizing he had to raise his voice over the sound of the imposing drums. "Leaving me in the jungle alone for close to forty-five minutes?"

"I never told you that I was a tour guide," she replied. "I simply asked if you were ready to see nature."

"Then, what's up with you pulling a weapon on me?" TC responded. "And these crazy drums that keep getting louder and faster?"

Imani's response would change his life forever.

"This blade belongs to you," she said. "In fact, it was built for you! The drums you hear are communicating. They are letting you know that hostility and pain are approaching."

Imani handed TC the weapon.

The pole fit into his hand like a leather glove. "What am I supposed to do with *this*?" TC asked.

Before she could answer, however, the staff *moved*. It was as if the metal was embracing him. It vibrated and shone an even brighter blue and lavender. Imani responded as she stepped to the side as if to avoid being run over by a bus.

"Sometimes we have to stop speaking," she answered, "and let our third eye lead us."

The next thing TC knew, it was nightfall. He hadn't noticed the sun setting. Between the drink Imani had given him and the staff in his hand, his body was different. It was as if his muscles had grown, and he found he could see in the darkness.

There was a scent, and his nose told his brain that six men were moving in his direction.

Quickly.

TC barked at Imani, "So you brought me into these thorns and a giant hornet's nest to get me *killed*."

Imani just closed her eyes, bowed, and began to walk backward in a bent position, as if he were the Queen of England.

There was motion, and TC saw six African warriors carrying exotic weapons running toward him. It would be a normal reaction, he knew, to panic.

But not today.

TC felt like a quarterback carrying a football. As the warriors came closer he bowed his head and thought to himself, *It would ruin my mother's life if I died while getting my education.* At that moment his blade began to vibrate like an alarm clock, as if to say, "Showtime."

As the six warriors surrounded TC, it became clear very quickly that this fight was not a fair one. Nevertheless, they appeared nervous, and he attacked them on the offense. One of them swung a sword, and the metal point that touched his blue-illuminated blade shattered. What followed was a whirlwind of combat, and three of the frightened warriors were downed with flesh wounds.

The other three warriors actually dropped their weapons so that they could run away faster.

As TC gave chase to finish the remaining three, a force of about two dozen more warriors appeared out of the darkness, running toward him. Some of these warriors were women with shaven, gleaming heads. The thought of fighting a woman

312

made TC uncomfortable, and in his hesitation a female warrior knocked him to the ground and stabbed him in his kidney.

Once again he thought about the possibility of breaking his mother's heart.

Fighting back this thought, he closed his eyes and stepped outside of himself. In a blinding storm of metal, sparks, and blood, the young American warrior felt as if he were in a ballet, moving in slow motion. He choreographed every strike and kick he delivered.

At one point he became so comfortable that he dropped his weapon and relied instead on his random, unorthodox, self-taught martial arts moves. He loved to deliver blows with his hands, feet, and elbows. He also realized that with each blow he struck, his opponents flew several feet into the air. This was not his normal degree of strength.

When the outcome of the battle became apparent, the five remaining warriors dropped their weapons and dropped down to one knee in submission. In less than thirty minutes, it was over.

Imani returned to his side and gave a verbal command that caused the five defeated warriors to stand and disappear in the direction from which they had come.

"Why would you set me up to be murdered?" TC asked in a hurt tone. "Did I offend you? I don't have any money."

"We needed to verify your capabilities," Imani replied apologetically.

"Who is 'we'?" TC asked. Rather than answer, Imani grabbed his arm and began to lead him in the same direction as the warriors who had disappeared into the darkness. By now the drums, which had been playing the entire time, sounded submissive. She walked him through the Valley of Thorns.

After about an hour of awkward silence they approached what appeared to be a riverbank. Tied to a dock was the most beautiful boat he had ever seen, yet the vessel had no sail, no visible motors, and no one to row it. This boat was at least a hundred feet long and resembled those that TC had seen in paintings from Ancient

Egypt. It was the type of vessel that Osiris or Ra the Sun God might ride in majestic works of art.

They both stepped onto the boat and Imani walked up a flight of stairs in the center. TC followed. At the top of the steps was a luxurious, cushioned seat that felt like velvet, which wrapped itself around him. As soon as they were seated the vessel began to move.

Where is the captain? he thought. *And who's driving?* He raised his questions to Imani. "How is this boat moving on its own?"

Without replying she stood up, walked back down the flight of stairs, and continued to another flight that led down and into a lower-level cabin. TC followed and watched, and she slid open a door to reveal a computer unlike anything he had ever seen before. The state-of-the-art computers at his university were huge cabinets with reels of spinning tapes. In the center of this computer was a circle that housed a bright, glowing blue marble.

TC began to realize that these blue gems were reoccurring, and perhaps beginning to steer his life.

"This boat is propelled by a turbine engine, and directed by a computer," Imani explained. "Both are powered by Vibranium— this blue pebble."

TC was fascinated. "That marble is the fuel source?"

"That stone could power utilities for about half of New York City," Imani replied.

TC shook his head in doubt. "No way."

Imani turned and walked back up the stairs. "I am taking you to where all of this will make sense," she said as they moved to the deck. Elegant purple and gold tapestries adorned stone columns that held a roof over their heads. The columns looked too heavy to allow a boat to float, but clearly this was no ordinary vessel.

AS THE regal boat approached a waterfall, TC said to Imani, "We need to stop this boat before we die!"

Imani made a slight and casual hand gesture, as if she were

drying nail polish, and the vessel raised up about six feet from the water. The boat very gracefully hovered past the cascading waterfall and the giant rocks below it.

"Wow. So you're a witch?" TC remarked.

"Well… I have been called a witch before, but I'm afraid I can't take credit for this boat's capabilities. Everything that you are experiencing goes back to technology and the blue stone that I showed you below."

The vessel hovered and proceeded for a quarter of a mile over a stream below, before it reached another waterfall. After passing this one it descended and returned to sitting in the water—but this water was different. It was a beautiful clear blue color and was full of exotic fish that made up every color of the spectrum.

"What kind of fish are these?" TC asked.

"I'm afraid that I cannot answer you," Imani answered, "because I don't share your ability to see in darkness. I can see some things, but I cannot see the fish below the surface."

"Well, this place doesn't look like anything I've seen in the encyclopedia or *National Geographic*," TC remarked. "What town are we in—what part of Tanzania?"

"You are no longer in Tanzania, sir," Imani said, and he stared. "You are now in Wakanda."

Sir? TC thought to himself. *Why is she calling me 'sir' now?*

He felt the beautiful ship slow down, and TC could see the lights of a city in the distance. Before long, the horizon was made up of skyscrapers and flickering lights. The skyscrapers were taller than any building in Oakland, and most cities he had only seen on a black-and-white television.

"Did we leave Africa?" he asked. "Because Wakanda is not on any map that I've ever seen."

"You are in the heart of Africa," Imani replied. "Wakanda is not on any maps because the King will not allow such. Most Africans believe that Wakanda is a fairytale place, like Candyland, and we prefer it that way."

The boat docked, and TC followed his travel companion off

of it and across a lush purple carpet. The carpet soon turned dark with gold streaks in it.

"This looks like we're walking on marble and gold," he said.

"You are close," Imani replied. "You are walking on onyx and gold—marble is cheap and not worthy of the King's feet."

He wondered what she meant by that.

The duo soon arrived at a grand building that reminded TC of an opera house his class once visited in San Francisco. Two huge guards stood in front of the building. Both appeared to be about seven feet tall and he thought they were just shy of two hundred and seventy-five pounds. Both men recognized Imani and made no effort to stop her as she led him along another lush purple carpet.

Two castle-like doors swung open in front of them. As they entered the luxurious chamber, TC could see a balcony ledge with eight older African people seated above him. Each was dressed as if they were in an African version of a Shakespeare stage production. There were a lot of feathers, gems, ivory, long beautiful gowns, and other exquisite garments.

The eight seats looked like thrones, and in one of them, layered with high-backed cushions, was none other than Dr. Mwambi, perched proudly and beaming like a father at a graduation ceremony.

A thunderous voice came from one of the dignitaries seated above him.

"Welcome to Wakanda, T'Challa!"

No one had ever called him that, TC thought, except his mother. She had also given him the nickname "Your Highness."

The gentleman speaking introduced himself as Lord Amari of the Plains, then he introduced each of the others. They included a lord, a scientist, a female military general and, of course, Dr. Mwambi. Lord Amari explained to TC that the task of bringing him from Oakland to Wakanda had been assigned to Dr. Mwambi and Imani.

"We have been watching you since birth," he said. "I am sure that you are confused as to why we brought you to this land and even subjected you to violence.

"You were brought here for us to test you before grooming you for leadership. Some of the people in this room believe that you are the future king of this country. And some of them think that all of this is a *joke*, because you weren't born here.

"What do you think, T'Challa?" Lord Amari asked.

"I think I need to talk to my mum about this," TC replied. "She is from Tanzania and knows more about Africa than I do."

"That is not entirely true," Dr. Mwambi said quietly.

He explained that both he and T'Challa's mother were from Wakanda. "She left because her husband was from the royal family who now rule the country. He was abusive to her because she could not bear children, so she requested permission to leave. The conditions of her being able to do so were that she could only take $10,000 and the clothes on her back.

"She also had to agree to have some of her memories erased," he continued, "so that she couldn't compromise her place of birth by bringing westerners to our borders. With that said, your mother will be arriving shortly from California."

"Everything that is discussed between you and this governing body must remain confidential," Lord Amari explained. "If repeated outside of this group, it is punishable by *death*. We are a secret and self-appointed parliament formed to steer the future of this nation in a more dignified direction."

T'Challa replied, "As I was taught in school, this is what's called a 'coup.' So, as I see it, you are all a group of well-dressed revolutionaries."

"We have recently learned that our king is planning to sell Vibranium bullets to some countries who are on the brink of warfare," the professor responded. "He is planning this in secret, to make billions of dollars to hide in offshore accounts. We believe this is his exit strategy if he loses the throne. He know that his leadership is questionable to many of us."

With that—and even though TC had many more questions—Dr. Mwambi indicated that the discussion was over.

OVER THE next few weeks T'Challa—who was formally known as TC from Oakland—was taken back to Tanzania, where he was joined by his mother to begin his royal grooming. Their lodging was a thirty-room chateau that belonged to Lord Amari.

Amari wanted T'Challa to get used to a lifestyle of luxury, so that his eventual transition would not be culturally shocking. For reasons of security, his training and grooming could not take place in Wakanda.

Accepting this reasoning, he actually began to believe that he would inherit the crown in Wakanda. What he didn't understand was how *he* had been selected for all of this. His mother and Dr. Mwambi explained that almost one hundred years before he was born, the most powerful mystic in the country had voiced a prophecy from the gods, directly and in detail.

The divine mission outlined by the mystic had included the instructions for taking DNA from a specific king, to be placed in an incubator and smuggled out of the country.

Though he found the entire story fantastic, T'Challa felt as though it was pointless to argue. So he accepted his responsibilities, and succeeded beyond everyone's expectations.

AFTER TWO years of extensive and sometimes grueling training, T'Challa became well-versed in the arts of warfare. He was also educated in the history of Wakanda, including its technological advancements and the value of Vibranium.

No matter the nature of the conversation, things always seemed to point back to Vibranium. It was as if this precious mineral was the sun and everything revolved around it.

When the day came that the council felt T'Challa was ready to fulfill the prophecy, Lord Amari turned his training over to the newest member of the secret council: Grand General Bakari.

General Bakari put T'Challa in the royal army on a detail guarding the different palaces that the king occupied. T'Challa kept to himself and spoke as little as possible, for fear of being exposed as an American when he spoke.

A civil war was brewing in Wakanda, and sometimes conflicts within a family can be the most treacherous, T'Challa knew.

○━━━━━━○

PRINCESS OLU stood close to seven feet tall. As the eldest offspring of King Kamali, she should have been next in line to inherit the throne—but this was not the king's wish. Despite her powerful appearance and bearing, she was very sensitive, and resented her father's prejudice.

Yet another clandestine committee was formed, with the goal of severing the king's head from his shoulders, with his crown still attached.

Princess Olu was very much aware of which global leaders wanted a piece of the Wakandan pie, and with this knowledge she organized a secret meeting in the Canary Islands, where they all hoped to eventually hide their stolen wealth. Various kings, presidents, and military leaders decided unanimously to support Princess Olu's plan in exchange for Vibranium. Each leader involved agreed to release some of their most vicious war criminals and terrorists, all of whom would fight based on the lie that they would be freed after they had disposed of the king.

None of the released killers would ever return to civilian life, as all of the council agreed that they were to be assassinated because of what they knew.

All of the foreign war criminals were brought to the Valley of Thorns. The standard protocol for dealing with uninvited visitors on the Wakandan border was to dispatch an elite unit of the royal army, who carried the nickname "the Headhunters." General Bakari instructed T'Challa to join the Headhunters in their skirmish, though to act as an observer.

What followed was known as the Battle of Thorn Valley. The conflict dragged on for nearly thirty days, and most of the original troop of Headhunters was killed. The mercenaries fought without fear, seeming quite at home in the Valley of Thorns, and the Wakandans had never before experienced such unorthodox guerilla warfare.

T'Challa contacted General Bakari to share his personal strategy to eliminate the foreign soldiers. With the general's approval, T'Challa led one hundred female soldiers from the royal army into the valley to engage more than two hundred terrorists and war criminals.

This confused the foreign attackers greatly. In a genius plot on the level of the legendary Chinese General Sun Tzu, seventy-five of the female soldiers *surrendered* to the mercenaries.

As the mercenaries began fighting over who would possess the female soldiers, T'Challa led an additional fifty female killers to the valley. Together his forces overwhelmed the enemy, and the battle that had dragged on for a month was over in a single day.

The female soldiers proved to be even more vicious than the male soldiers. They were patient and fought without ego. T'Challa knew this would be the case, because he had read about the Kunoichi of Japan, who were female ninjas.

"I should have sent my wife, it would have been over quicker," General Bakari was heard to remark.

NO ONE in Wakanda knew that Princess Olu had orchestrated the assault on the border of Wakanda. The surviving mercenaries were interrogated but the foreign leaders had sent criminals and terrorists who knew nothing about the princess.

The battle validated T'Challa's point about female ferocity. General Bakari was so impressed by the way he had used strategy to claim victory during warfare that he and the other Wakandan dignitaries who made up the council decided that it was time to oust King Kamali. In just three days Grand General Bakari assembled a thousand of his troops to surround the palace, so that he could pay King Kamali a visit.

The general drank wine with the king and explained that

some were aware of his plan to hide money and Vibranium outside of the country. King Kamali digressed and used the excuse that Vibranium was so intoxicating that, like too much wine, it could make a man lose his good judgment.

Bakari then "explained" to the king that he was to announce his retirement. The new political lie would be that Kamali was going on a spiritual journey to become a priest. The truth was that the king and his family would be banished to a beautiful island off the coast of South Africa, where they would live out their days under the watchful eye of a satellite forty thousand feet above them, armed with sophisticated weapons to deter anyone from leaving the island. Edward VIII of the British royal family had lived out a similar fate in the Bahamas—without the satellite full of weapons above his head.

This banishment was a lifestyle that Princess Olu would describe as that of "privileged hostages." She made it known that, one way or another, she would find a way off of that island… eventually.

During his "State of the Kingdom address," King Kamali brought forth Abu Ra, the most respected mystic in the country. Abu Ra was said to be two hundred and twelve years old, the same mystic who delivered the prophecy from the gods that T'Challa would be the genetic manifestation of an ancient king. Abu Ra was respected in Wakanda the way that Moses was respected by anyone who read the Bible, so no one suggested—or could even imagine—that politics were in play behind the scenes and that King Kamali had been seduced by greed.

KING T'CHALLA'S coronation celebration lasted one week. Everyone in the country was invited to meet him. The mystery of his background quickly faded, as people were hypnotized by the fact that he was willing to take a photo with everyone who asked for one. Never before had a king been so approachable.

Mariam, the queen mother, found it amusing that he had mastered a Wakandan accent. He could turn it off and on at will.

Following a military parade, an air show with acrobatic jets, and an opera with war drums, King T'Challa settled into his new royal profile with the queen mother by his side. One of his first royal orders was to appoint Imani his new minister of culture. She was responsible for bringing him to Wakanda, and the king felt that she was a good representation of the country. He also felt that her nature was that of a leader.

Perhaps more so than himself, even.

King T'Challa was a progressive king as soon as he took the throne. He downsized the military and he began to display more of the country's music and art in foreign countries. Wakanda did not need ever be concerned with his greed, because King T'Challa was not intoxicated with wealth.

He *did* enjoy the luxury of having everything at his command, yet he could also be just as comfortable riding the bus in Oakland. Eventually, however, T'Challa grew anxious and sad.

He felt as if he had lost control of his own life. He had never asked to be the King of Wakanda, and it began to feel like a burden. One night he had a dream that he was an eagle flying over Oakland, California.

After only three years of royal service, he summoned the great mystic Abu Ra for counsel. When Abu Ra arrived at the royal palace, King T'Challa had already rehearsed what he was going to say to the elderly wizard, but Abu Ra took the lead in the conversation before T'Challa could even speak.

"You miss your home in America, Your Excellency," the mystic said. "I am already aware. It came to me in a dream where I could see you in the form of an eagle, flying over the place where we sent you to begin with."

The powerful mystic had seen T'Challa's dream and understood it to be prophecy.

King T'Challa began to explain himself. "It is a tremendous burden for me to feel as though my heart is rooted somewhere else, and yet I am ashamed of the idea of disappointing you and the council.

"I have been watching my birthplace, Oakland," he continued. "It is changing quickly, and not all for the best. The United States in general is having a cultural awakening and I feel like I should have a voice in the new world."

"You are the descendent of legendary bloodlines," Abu Ra explained. "The prophecy stated that you and one other would lead Wakanda to peace and tranquility."

This response brought T'Challa some peace of mind, and he had a déjà vu moment.

Imani was the second person to share his bloodline. They were kin, and this is why she felt familiar to him. They found each other at that market—not randomly, but instinctively.

Abu Ra continued, "You have done what you were brought here to correct. King Kamali was not good for the people of Wakanda. You came here and made your introduction by defeating our attackers on the border. You also changed the culture nationally, by showing us that life is more peaceful when we focus on art and less on warfare.

"That is a big statement, coming from a warrior and a combat veteran," Abu Ra said. "You are leaving Wakanda better than you found it, and that is a historical accomplishment. I only ask that you help us to identify a new king, someone who shares your values and principles."

IMANI WAS shocked and nearly overwhelmed when King T'Challa explained that he was selecting her to be his bride, and the next ruler of Wakanda. The two of them had no romantic interest in each other, but this was the only way that he could put her in power before he returned to his American homeland.

Historically, Wakanda had never had a female ruler on the throne.

"I think you are about to lead Wakanda like a nurturing mother," King T'Challa explained to Imani humbly, "and not lead like a warlord."

He also explained that they were both descendents of previous kings, as decided by a prophecy.

Imani revealed that the first time she saw T'Challa, she felt as if she was speaking to someone whom she already knew. He knew it was true.

Mariam was happy when he asked her to return to California with him. She also missed the simple life, and it was she who had left Wakanda in the first place because she had been made to feel disrespected when she was becoming a young woman.

They did not, however, give the people of Wakanda the huge royal wedding that they might have wanted to see. He felt as though this would be hypocritical, as he knew that he was transitioning back to the United States.

KING T'CHALLA spent the next year helping Queen Imani to get comfortable with her new duties. At the same time, he and his mother began to make arrangements to return to Oakland.

His mother returned before the king and had their home renovated. Abu Ra made a national announcement that the king was leaving Wakanda to explore foreign lands—for the potential of building a colony outside Africa. Queen Imani assured King T'Challa that she would rule the land in the same dignified manner that he had. She also established a $1 billion diplomatic endowment for T'Challa, so that he could develop any projects he found to be worthy abroad.

Abu Ra, the great mystic, asked to visit King T'Challa. The king always wanted to converse with the old wizard, and this time the man brought him a gift. T'Challa immediately recognized the "fancy blanket" that the travel agent had given him back in Oakland. It was the same African cloth that granted him the ability to take the form of an eagle and fly to Africa. This same African fabric also gave T'Challa his first glimpse into the mystic arts.

Queen Imani arranged for a grand feast as a farewell gathering for the king and the council that had groomed him for leadership. Although everyone regretted that he was departing, they also felt a great appreciation for the influence he had brought to the national culture in Wakanda.

The following morning, by himself during a grand sunrise, T'Challa draped himself in his fancy blanket and transformed. He took flight in the form of an eagle, and this time the flight path was not at all stressful. He had a much better understanding of the spiritual plane.

After three days of peaceful flight, he found himself back on the waterfront of the Port of Oakland. He gracefully sailed to a rooftop where he could land and resume the form of a human. It took him a few minutes to digest the fact that he was actually back home, as he felt like he had just stepped out of a movie. For the first time in years, T'Challa felt like TC again.

Oddly enough, he had missed the smell of bus fumes and fast food. When he visited his childhood home and spent time there with his mother, the home felt much smaller, despite her renovations. His needs had changed. T'Challa didn't need a palace but he did need his own space.

So T'Challa settled in a chic apartment in downtown Oakland. As he moved in, he organized his thoughts about what direction to take his life in, and soon found himself inside a coffee shop, writing random thoughts on a napkin. This hobby of writing about things that he felt were meaningful turned into poems. And through the art of poetry, T'Challa found he could vent, or even express, thoughts that were difficult for him to speak out loud.

While watching television and reading newspapers, T'Challa realized that he had political aspirations. He wanted to become involved in the political process of the land that was his birthplace, but he did not seek the spotlight.

Substance abuse and prostitution plagued T'Challa's old neighborhood. An election was coming the following year for the next Mayor of Oakland. T'Challa met a young man who had some great ideas about countering crime by giving young people jobs.

The young man's name was Andy, and he owned the coffee shop where T'Challa liked to sit and write poetry. Andy had given jobs to a lot of young people in the neighborhood. In fact, he struggled to make a profit because he had more employees than he actually needed. As his friendship with Andy grew, T'Challa convinced Andy to run for mayor, and he made Andy a deal.

T'Challa purchased the building next to Andy's, renovated it, and knocked down a wall to make Andy's coffee shop bigger. More seating meant more potential for turning a profit. T'Challa's building had four floors and he decided it would become the home of Black Eagle Books.

○──────○

ALL OF the children know the bookstore, a place from which any child could take a book home with them, as long as they promise to return it in good condition. They could see T'Challa isn't really concerned with making money by selling books, but instead provides a place to connect with young people and feed their interest in reading and writing.

○──────○

T'CHALLA ASKED Andy to focus on his campaign, and T'Challa helped to run the business operations of the coffee shop and bookstore as his silent partner.

Andy convinced T'Challa that he should share his poetry with the people of Oakland. He felt like the poetry was consistent with what was going on in an ever-changing community and country. He introduced T'Challa to a customer who hosted a local radio show. The customer asked T'Challa to be a guest, and this one visit to a radio station resulted in him returning every week to recite a poem, broadcast from an AM radio tower. At the time, AM radio was listened to the most.

Then T'Challa found himself having a conversation every day with an elderly gentleman named Mr. Oscar. Mr. Oscar liked to read T'Challa's poetry, and he loved to talk about the local sports teams. T'Challa never told people that he was a roaming king from Africa, and most people wouldn't have believed it anyway.

Mr. Oscar found a piano abandoned in an alley and repaired it, then donated it to the bookstore. He often played the piano in the background while T'Challa shared his poetry with customers drinking coffee. One Friday evening he invited some musician friends to join in, and this grew into a regular event every Friday consisting of music, poetry, and community bonding.

T'CHALLA'S BACHELOR days came to an end when he accepted an invitation to visit Mr. Oscar's church. Mr. Oscar invited him because he wanted T'Challa to meet his beautiful granddaughter, Erica. Erica was studying at a local university to become a librarian, and she had been impressed with what she had heard about T'Challa and Black Eagle Books.

Andy won the election to become the next mayor. Most of the town agreed that he had proven himself to care about people and not personal gain.

When T'Challa invited Erica to his apartment, so he could cook dinner for her, she turned him down. Then, just two weeks later, she accepted an invitation to meet his mother and have dinner at her home. She immediately hit it off with Mariam, who adored Erica so much that T'Challa started thinking about his future.

One year later, T'Challa and Erica were married.

T'Challa and Erica moved to a quieter suburban street, and his mother lived with them there for the next year as Erica prepared to give birth to T'Challa's son. Soon thereafter T'Challa bought an even bigger home on a hill, and he trained a group of security personnel to guard his family around the clock. He wasn't naïve, so he knew that if the general public learned that he had sat on a throne, it could be dangerous for his family.

He became less public as he spent more time with his family, and less time at Black Eagle Books. His time was also redirected as he and his wife decided that they wanted to buy enough land to build a public library, a theater, and school of literature and art.

His life had changed dramatically since the Battle of Thorn Valley.

AFTER AN hour of telling this story to the young students in Oakland, King T'Challa looks at the clock and readies himself to turn his attention to other financial matters in other parts of California. But he smiles and waits, of course, for the children and staff who wanted photos with him for Instagram and Snapchat.

As was his practice, he did not refuse.

While they were exiting the school, the Wakandan Minister of Arts, Jarobi, asks a question.

"My Lord, forgive me, but was all of that story true?"

The king replies with his own question.

"Jarobi, have you forgotten about Anansi the Spider? Were you not a child when the elders told you that story? And did you not believe that the fairy tale from the Ashanti people was historical fact?"

Jarobi nods, so T'Challa asks, "And what did you learn from this flying spider?"

"I learned that adversity is inevitable," Jarobi replies. "And that with perseverance, great things are possible. Slaves who left Africa carried that story around the world."

King T'Challa says, "Thank you, Jarobi. Remember this— feed their imaginations and they will figure out the rest."

Later that evening T'Challa reclines at home on his living room couch, watching the Golden State Warriors play basketball on television, his son sleeping on his lap. His wife sits next to him reading an *Ebony* magazine when Wakandan technology interrupts the television transmission. Suddenly, Abu Ra is on the television screen.

Abu Ra speaks in a disappointed tone. "Forgive me for interrupting you, my King, I don't care much for politics, but I always find myself in the middle of them. The council is putting pressure on Queen Imani to make a declaration of war. They wish

328

to overthrow the government in Tanzania to conquer them and make them a colony under our flag."

T'Challa's wife, Erica, stands up and walks out of the room.

Abu Ra continues, "If the Queen does not concede, the council will likely find a way to remove her quietly. She was not their chosen leader to begin with, she was yours. And like you, she never asked for the throne."

Before Abu Ra could finish, T'Challa gets distracted when his wife returns and hands him his fancy blanket.

ERICA IS not happy about what she had just overheard, but she is strong, and she knows what T'Challa needs to do...

Mwisho (Swahili)
The Beginning

LEGACY

L.L. McKINNEY

ERIKA RAN her fingers over the print on the plane ticket resting against her palm. *Destination: Birnin Zana, Wakanda.*

The familiar swell of excitement that had wrapped itself around her when she opened the card and found this very itinerary rose again. It was the only thing she'd asked for, for her sixteenth birthday, and now it was finally happening.

And she could hardly believe it.

"You okay, baby?" Mom's voice rose over the sound of Normani serenading them with her latest single.

Erika lifted her gaze to catch her mother's in the rearview mirror. "I'm... better than okay!"

She slipped the ticket back into the envelope and tucked it away in her bag, which she set on the seat between herself and her brother, who was too enraptured in something on his phone to be bothered with anyone else in the car.

Mom smiled, the expression crinkling her eyes. "This is gonna be epic. Ain't that what the kids say?"

"Not really." Erika shook her head but continued to smile. There was nothing that could dampen her spirits today, not even her mother's usual corniness.

Erika turned her attention back out the window, her gaze roaming the veins of traffic heading into and out of the airport, people coming and going on their own travels.

Briefly, she wondered if any of them were headed to Wakanda as well. Or maybe some of them were arriving from there, like her grandmother had all those years ago.

Grandma May had often spoken of the first time she came to America, how everything was so big and loud and dirty!

"So much smoke," Grandma would say, pinching her nose. "So much trash. What a waste! It didn't make for a good first impression."

"But Papa had." Miles, Erika's little brother, had smiled big at the preemptive mention of their grandfather. They'd both heard the story enough to know what came next.

"Oh yes." Grandma chuckled and rolled her eyes shut as she basked in the memory. "He was big and loud, too, but in a good way."

Grandma always told stories like that, about Papa and about Wakanda. She painted pictures with words, telling them of the glittering towers and the bullet-fast trains that snaked between them. About the dancing lights that lined the streets, and the screens that would pop up from your very fingers to show you the way. She spoke of the food and the people, the festivals and gatherings, the shops and markets, so much so her stories almost felt like home.

Almost.

"I hope I get to show you, someday," Grandma had said, with a crinkle in her eyes that was so much like Mom's.

Erika swallowed thickly as a sudden swell of emotion closed off her throat. Her eyes burned with the threat of tears, and she concealed a sniff by coughing into her fist.

When her arm lifted, the sunlight streaming in through the window caught against one of the black, metallic beads wrapped around her wrist. Grandma's beads. The bracelet had been hers before…

Before.

The bracelet was the second half of her present. First came the ticket, then came a peculiar little box neatly wrapped in gold and silver paper. Tucked inside was a note written in the familiar tight but elegant letters her Grandma managed to write perfectly every time she picked up a pen.

> *Erika,*
> *I always wanted to take you and your brother back to Wakanda, so you could see where I come from. Where you come from. Even though I couldn't, I want you to have this, so you'll always have a part of home and a part of me. I know it's hard now, but have courage, baby. Yibambe.*
> *Love you long as the sun shines,*
> *Grandma.*

The bracelet had been in the package, tucked away in a little satin cloth that shimmered even in shadow. Erika had put it on that day three weeks ago, and had worn it every day since.

There were a couple other tickets, as well. One for Miles, and one that would have been Grandma's but now Mom was going in her place. She'd never been to Wakanda either, so it was the perfect opportunity.

Dad had elected to stay behind. He was in the middle of a big project at work and didn't want to walk away from it so soon, but also didn't want the family to wait on him to finish since that could take months. Plus, someone needed to keep an eye on the twins. At two years old, no one was keen on taking them on a round-the-world trip just yet.

"We'll all go back together, sooner rather than later," Dad promised.

In turn, Erika had promised to bring him back a souvenir to make up for it until then.

So, plans were made and tickets were confirmed. While Mom and Miles had digital copies, Erika had asked for a physical one, and kept it in Grandma's card. Just about every night leading up to the trip, she would take the ticket out and stare at it, still not able to believe it was real. She told herself she wouldn't until she was standing at the airport, and now...

Now she could barely contain herself as Mom pulled up beneath a sign marked 'Departures.'

The car had barely stopped before Erika threw open her door and climbed out, rushing around to the back as the trunk popped open. She started hauling suitcases out and setting them on the ground, one of them toppling over with a loud *smack*.

"Whoa, what's the rush?" Dad came around from the passenger side, reaching to help with the last bag, which was caught between the side of the trunk and a spare tire. "You've got plenty of time."

"She's just excited." Mom leaned in toward him for a quick kiss. "You got the emergency numbers?"

"Yes," Dad said.

"The meal plan?"

"Yes."

"The play date schedule?"

"Yes..."

"The groc—"

"I know how to take care of my own children, woman," Dad said before closing the trunk. "I got this."

Mom arched an eyebrow, her expression amused. "Oh, you got this, do you?"

Dad grinned then, his hands snaking around Mom's waist. "I got something."

She laughed and swatted him in the shoulder before leaning in for a lengthier kiss, her arms going around his neck.

"Gross," Miles muttered, not looking up from his phone.

"How you think you got here?" Dad snorted, then reached to snag Miles by the back of his head, pulling him in for a hug. "Have fun, listen to your momma."

"Yessir." Miles tried to act disinterested but returned the hug, briefly, before promptly pulling away and turning for the door, dragging his suitcase behind him, his head still bowed over his phone. He stayed glued to that thing. Most ten-year-old boys would be into video games or football or something. Not Miles. He liked making videos, which meant he liked watching videos. All. The. Time.

Dad shook his head before looking to Erika. "Your turn," he said, holding open his arms.

Erika pressed into his hug, shutting her eyes as he squeezed her. Excited as she was, she was gonna miss him. A week wasn't that long, but could seem like forever at the same time.

"Take lots of pictures to show me when you get back," he murmured into her braids. "And eat enough for both of us."

"I will. Love you, Daddy."

"Love you, too." He gave her another squeeze before letting go and moving around toward the driver side of the car.

Erika took hold of her bag and dragged it up onto the sidewalk after her.

Mom was bent over into the car, saying goodbye to the twins, who were both still too asleep to really know what was going on as she slathered their faces in kisses.

Soon Dad pulled off, leaving Erika and her mother waving after them.

Mom sniffed and wiped at her face. "Okay. Let's go find your brother before he ends up causing an international incident."

"Unless there's an app for that, it ain't happening." Erika followed her mother into the airport. Her face crinkled when hot air blew into it as they stepped through the doors. Ugh, she hated when they did that. What was the point?

Sure enough, Miles stood just to the side, headphones on, fingers still moving across the screen. He didn't seem at all bothered by the fact that people had to step around him and his stuff to continue on their way.

Mom flapped a hand to get his attention, and the three of them headed for the counter, weaving between people and groups as they went.

This wasn't Erika's first time flying, but coming to the airport—where people shuffled around, grunted at each other, and were herded into this area or that space—always reminded her of going to the zoo, except the airport was indoors and air-conditioned, thank God. And the lines, man, the *lines*. Thankfully, this one to check their luggage didn't look too long, and they had plenty of time, so she wasn't worried.

The one to get through TSA, though, was a doozy. It flowed out of the roped-off area and along the side of the ticket counter, a snake of people who looked irritated to be here, but knew they really didn't have a choice, so no one complained. Mostly.

"It… doesn't look that long," Mom offered, though she didn't sound convinced.

"Uh-huh," both Erika and Miles answered at the same time.

Forty-five minutes, one searched bag, and five trips through the metal detector later—Mom kept forgetting bits of jewelry she was wearing—the three of them emerged carrying their bags in one hand and their shoes in the other.

"See, that wasn't so bad!" Mom settled onto a bench to tug her boots back on, like she hadn't cussed Daddy the whole time for not buying Pre-Check for the family this year "because they didn't travel enough to need it."

"What's with your bracelet?" Miles made a face, his brow furrowed.

It took a second for Erika to realize he was talking to her. "What?" She straightened from tying her Converse and lifted her wrist, glancing at the beads.

At first, she didn't know what he was talking about, but as she twisted her wrist, she saw it. One of the beads pulsed gently, a faint blue hue wrapping around it and fading with a soft trilling sound every few seconds.

"Wow, that's… weird," she murmured, turning her hand over to look at the others. "Maybe the metal detector set it off?"

She pitched a glance in the direction of the scanners they'd wandered through. The bracelet was definitely made of metal, but she'd forgotten she was wearing it, and… nothing happened.

Really weird…

"Okay." Mom scrolled through her phone as they stepped out of the way of other people hobbling along shoeless and beltless toward the benches. "Our gate iiiiiiiiis this way."

She led them off through the terminal, discussing food options, which, funnily enough, had Miles's rapt attention. Erika, however, kept being drawn back to her flashing bracelet. It looked like it was starting to glow faster… or maybe that was a trick of the light.

"Hey, Mom?" Erika called.

"…though I'm not in the mood for pizza—what is it, baby?" Mom asked.

"Has this ever happened before?"

Mom finally stopped walking and turned to look at her, then down at the bracelet when Erika held her arm up.

"Huh." Mom reached to finger the pulsing bead. "Not that I know of." She made a face, lifting her brows and turning her mouth down as she shrugged. "Maybe you should put it away, if it's bothering you. Someone in Birnin Zana can probably tell us what's wrong, if anything is."

"No, it… it's okay." Erika lowered her arm. "I want tacos."

"You *always* want tacos," Miles complained. "I want a burger."

"And I want peace, so how about this. The taco line wasn't that long. Here—" Mom produced a twenty and offered it to Erika. "—you go get your tacos, then meet usssss over there at that cluster of tables. I'm gonna grab a chicken wrap while he gets his burger. We'll be right there. I'll have eyes on you the whole time."

Erika rolled hers. "I can handle getting food."

"I never said you couldn't. Be careful, baby. Come on boy, stop acting like you ain't ever been fed in your life."

Snickering, Erika turned to head for the taco line. She could see Mom and Miles slip into the crowd in front of Biggie's Burgers.

Prrlrlrl, prrlrlr. Prrlrlrl, prrlrlr. Prrlrlrl, prrlrlr.

Erika looked down at the beads. Not only was the one blinking faster, it was getting louder, too. Enough so that nearby people started glancing around, then at her for the source of the sound. Her face heated, and she slapped her hand over her wrist. "Sorry! Sorry."

When the couple in front of her looked back to the menu they'd been discussing, Erika peeked at the bracelet between her fingers. Her heart jumped and her eyes widened when she saw that not one, but three beads now flickered and pinged, louder, and louder, and LOUDER.

Glancing around, she spotted the sign for a nearby restroom and—with one quick glance in the direction of Biggie's—hurried across the food court and pushed through the door.

PRRLRLRL, PRRLRLRL. PRRLRLRL, PRRLRLRL. PRRLRLRL, PRRLRLRL.

The trilling echoed even louder in here. What was going *on* with this thing!

She hurried over to the counter that stretched in front of a long mirror, stepping in between two white women while one curled her hair and the other applied mascara. Both looked at her like she'd farted or something after she snatched the bracelet off and set it down.

It kept trilling.

"Sorry," Erika murmured to the women as she turned the bracelet over. The darn thing had to have an off switch or something.

"There you are," a voice called from nearby, the accent thick, and familiar.

Erika glanced up and into the face of a Black woman she didn't know filling the doorway, eyes on her.

"E-excuse me?" she asked.

The woman's eyebrows lifted in surprise. "American. Interesting." She looked from Erika, to the bracelet, then back again. "Where did you get that? If you don't mind my asking."

Erika snatched the bracelet up, the trill muffled by her hand. "It was a present."

"How lovely." The woman's eyes moved over Erika, from the top of her head to her feet, then back again. "Who gave it to you?"

Fighting the urge to squirm under the scrutiny, Erika looked away briefly. "My grandma," she explained.

The woman *hmm*ed to herself as she strode forward. Her heels clicked against the tile. The red of her dress made her light brown skin glow where it was visible. She looked like a model, but something about the way she moved told Erika she was more than that.

After more than ten years in karate, Erika could spot a fighter in a crowd. It was the way they kept their shoulders back, hands at the ready to block or strike at a moment's notice. It's how Erika carried herself without even thinking about it.

"May I ask who your grandmother was?" The woman drew closer, but not uncomfortably so. Not yet.

The white women pretended to be caught up doing whatever, but kept stealing glances at Erika and the Black lady in the mirror.

Erika swallowed thickly, her heart thumping in her chest.

The woman smiled, the expression easy. Genuine. "It's all right."

She lifted her wrist and revealed a set of beads identical to those currently clutched in Erika's hands.

The relief that moved through her was instant and almost strong enough to drop her to her knees. The shock that followed, thankfully, locked her legs. Erika felt her eyes go wide. *That's* why the accent was familiar. It sounded like her grandma.

Erika pointed. "You're from—"

"Yes," the woman interrupted, lowering her arm. "And I thought you were too, for a second, when I first saw you in the food court. But when you didn't turn off the beacon, I wondered if something was wrong."

"Beacon?" Erika opened her hand and eyed the bracelet resting against her palm. It continued beeping and blinking rapidly. Beacon. Of course. Now that she heard the word, it made so much sense she felt silly for not realizing before.

"Mmm. The Kimoyo beads are able to track one another, if you know the right frequency." The woman folded her arms over her chest, looking amused. That's when Erika noticed another bracelet on the woman's opposite wrist. More than one—she counted three at least. One of the beads blinked in time with Erika's.

A chill traced the length of Erika's spine like an icy finger. She frowned. "You were... tracking me?"

The woman chuckled, and her smile sharpened. "Don't worry, little *Dora*. I promise to make this quick."

"Dora?" Erika asked. "My name's not—" That was all she managed before a fist came at her face.

She dodged to the right, bringing her hand up to swipe it aside, just in time to block a second blow.

"Ah!" Pain danced up her arms when a fist connected with it. Better than her face.

The white women screamed and ran for the door, leaving their belongings behind.

Erika backpedaled as the woman stepped into her space and aimed a knee at her gut. She twisted around, but caught the business end of a roundhouse kick square in the back. The pain was quickly overpowered by panic as she brought her hands up to catch herself against the wall, but rolled with the momentum.

It was a good thing she did, because the woman's heel drove into the tile with a loud *CRACK!* Right where Erica's face had been.

The woman's lips curled in a snarl and she yanked her foot loose, adjusted her stance, then came at Erika faster than anyone she'd ever faced, on or off the mat.

A flurry of blows rained down on her, fast and decisive strikes. Erika stayed on the defensive, ducking and dodging where she could, blocking when she couldn't get out of the way in time. Fire danced through her limbs. Her heart thundered in her chest, fear stampeding through her limbs. *Scream!* she shouted at herself. *Call for help!* But she couldn't. Her throat was tight, her attention fixated on staying outside of the woman's grasp, but she was so fast.

A haymaker nearly took her head off for the second time. She lifted her knee to block a snap kick with her shin, then threw herself around, aiming to drive the heel of her shoe into her attacker's temple.

The woman withdrew, barely managing to dodge, surprise flickering through her gaze before she smirked. "Well done, little *Dora*, but you can't evade me forever."

With a flick of her wrist, something glinted in the cold glow of the bathroom lights.

Erika barely had time to register the edge of a blade before the woman slashed at her with it. Erika felt the weapon catch in the fabric of her jacket, then felt the white-hot burn as the skin along her arm split.

She finally screamed, clamping her hand down over the wound. Blood welled up slick and warm beneath her fingers.

The woman brought the weapon back around. This time Erika ducked under the swing, letting her momentum carry her through into a side kick to the woman's stomach. It drove her back a few feet, but she was still between Erika and the exit.

Panic and terror surfing her veins, Erika spun and raced deeper into the bathroom. She didn't know what to do, where she could go, there *was* nowhere to go! Her arm throbbed. Her heart felt like it was going to jump right out of her chest it beat so hard. She felt the drumming in her temples.

The sound of those heels clicking sent another spike of dread through her body. She reached the far wall and threw herself around the corner... and right over a bucket and mop.

Her feet slammed into it, sending dirty water splashing across the floor. She landed in a heap, water splashing into her face and soaking her clothes. Scrambling to get up, she slipped on the now slick floor. The sharp click of those heels came up behind her. Red flashed at the edges of her vision—the woman's dress as she lifted the weapon overhead.

Erika's fingers slipped in the water, brushing up against something hard. The mop. She snatched it up and brought it around just in time to deflect the blade. The surprise on the woman's face quickly melted to anger. She lifted the blade again.

Erika twisted the mop around, swinging the blunt end at the woman, who managed to pull back but not before the handle connected with a *crack!*

"Ahh!" The woman shook out her wrist. "You little..."

Stunned, but only for a second, Erika scrambled to her feet, brandishing her makeshift weapon. It wasn't a bo staff but it would have to do. She threw a frightened glance toward the exit.

"There's no escaping, little *Dora*," the woman purred.

"M-my name's not Dora!" Erika shouted, her voice cracking. The familiar burn of tears filled her face and stung her eyes. "Please, just… leave me alone!"

The woman chuckled and stepped slowly toward Erika, who drew backward to keep space between them. If she made a break for it, could she reach the door before the woman was on top of her?

"This is what the *Dora* have come to? Even in training, you shouldn't simper so." The woman lifted her weapon, a long, impossibly thin blade made from a metal that looked to bend as she moved. "Take your warrior's death with pride, if you can."

The next jab came faster than the last, and if it wasn't for the mop it would have likely taken Erika's arm clean off. Instead, she managed to knock it wide, though the blade cut through the top of the mop like a hot knife through butter.

The woman swiped, lunged, struck with both weapon and fist, driving Erika back steadily, keeping her on the defensive. It was all Erika could do to stay outside of her reach, especially since she kept losing pieces of her mop. Tears blurred her vision. She blinked rapidly to clear it as she scrambled backward.

"Keep moving," her sensei had said during sparring sessions. "Always keep moving. If you can't attack, retreat. It takes more energy to swing and miss. If your opponent is stronger than you, tire them out."

But it didn't look like this woman would tire any time soon. In fact, it felt like she was moving faster. Or maybe Erika was moving slower.

Her arms burned, especially the wounded one. Blood ran hot against her skin and slicked her fingers, made her grip clumsy.

The next blow sent the mop flying from her hands completely, and sent Erika stumbling over backward, landing on the floor.

The woman advanced, weapon lifted. "One more for my collection."

She brought the blade down.

Erika shut her eyes and threw her arms up.

Clang!

The sound made Erika's teeth rattle. Her eyes flew open just in time to see how close the blade had come to splitting her face open before something got in the way. A... spear?

She couldn't get a good look before the woman stepped back, her face drawing up with a healthy dose of shock and barely controlled rage. But that anger wasn't aimed at Erika.

Instead, her attacker glared at another Black woman, who held the spear that had saved Erika's life. This woman stepped between the two of them, shielding Erika with her body. "Not today, Ysra."

The woman, Ysra, scoffed. Then chuckled, straightening from her fighting stance. "Maybe not, Ayo. But you can't protect them all. Not forever. Not from me."

Ayo started toward Ysra, but the latter was quicker. She stepped back, lifting her arms to take hold of her bracelet and twist. Light filled the room, so bright Erika had to look away.

When it finally faded, Ysra was gone, and Erika was left blinking away the spots in her vision. Ayo hissed something in a language Erika didn't recognize, but she knew cussing when she heard it.

"Ahh." Ayo twisted her wrist and her spear snapped... shut? It drew in with a series of clicks until it was small enough for her to slip it into a pouch strapped to the outside of her thigh.

Any other time, Erika would've thought that was the coolest thing she'd ever seen. She was into that sort of thing, different weapons and fighting styles, and would've probably asked if she could get a closer look. But she didn't really care about that, in the moment. Couldn't think past the fact that some random woman had just... tried to *kill* her.

Oh god... oh god... Her heart continued thrashing in her chest. Her breathing picked up. It was like she couldn't take in enough air, no matter how hard she tried. Pain burned hot along her arm and she clutched it to her chest, shaking and whimpering. Her body felt like it was too small, too tight for her. Everything went sort of fuzzy, and a sob tore free from her throat. Then another.

And another. She curled in on herself as her body worked through the lingering terror, leaving her dizzy with it.

"Hey," came a soft voice, and Ayo knelt in front of her. "Breathe, child." Ayo drew a slow breath in through her nose, then let it out through her mouth. "Like this." She repeated the action. "Breathe. With me. Come on." And again.

For a second, Erika stared at her, not fully comprehending what was happening, but then it clicked and she started to mimic the slow inhale and exhale demonstrated for her.

"That's it," Ayo coaxed. "There you are. Breathe. It's all right. You're safe. Let me see."

Fingers curled around Erika's injured arm, their touch gentle. She released her hold on it, sniffling and whimpering as Ayo inspected the injury. The tears wouldn't stop, but she didn't feel lightheaded anymore.

Ayo pulled at the bloodstained cloth of the split sleeve. "A clean cut. Not deep, but probably still painful." Her accent matched Grandma's, and that Ysra woman's. Ayo pulled a deep green scarf from around her neck and started wrapping it around Erika's arm like a bandage.

It *hurt*, and she jumped with a hiss, her fingers clenched. "A-ahh!"

"Breathe," Ayo repeated.

Erika took a few more shaky breaths while Ayo worked until the binding was finished.

"There. That should do, for now." Ayo looked up from the scarf, her gaze catching Erika's. "You crossed swords with Ysra, and this is all you walked away with?"

Swallowing thickly, Erika cast a quick glance at what remained of the mop.

Ayo followed her gaze. "Ahh. Not even swords, then. Impressive. Or lucky." A smile curled her lips. "Maybe a bit of both. Come, up you go." She gripped Erika's elbows and helped her to her feet. "Why did she attack you in the first place. Do you know?"

Erika's legs shook, like the rest of her, but held. She sniffed, and wiped at her nose with her good hand. "S-she thought I was someone else," she murmured. "Some chick named D-Dora."

Ayo's eyebrows drew together. "Why did she think that?"

Erika hesitated. The last time she showed her Grandma's bracelet to someone, they tried to cut her head off.

"I promise you're safe now," Ayo insisted.

Still wary, Erika drew the bracelet from where she'd shoved it in her pocket and held it up. It was still beeping and blinking, but slower now.

Ayo stared at it, surprise clear on her face. "Where did you get this?"

Erika edged back a step. Ysra had asked the same question. "Why?"

"Because I think it's why Ysra attacked you."

That didn't make any sense. "...It was my grandmother's." She quickly tucked the bracelet away again. "Her name wasn't Dora, either."

"I imagine it wasn't. What's yours?"

"Erika..."

"Well, Erika. *Dora* isn't a person. It's a title. A position someone holds, like a warrior. Or a bodyguard, that's closer. Because of that bracelet, Ysra thought you were one of these guards, a *Dora*. Or at least one in training, given your age."

"Guard?" Erika blinked rapidly, not understanding. "Wait, the bracelet? Grandma said everyone in Wakanda had one."

"They do. But the ones the *Dora* wear are a bit special." Ayo presented her arm. Wrapped around her wrist was yet another one identical to Grandma's.

Erika stared at the beads, her thoughts tripping over themselves as her mind worked through this new information. Ysra attacked her because she thought she was a *Dora*. She thought Erika was a *Dora* because she saw Erika's bracelet. No, not *hers*...

Erika's eyes went wide. "Wait... Grandma was... a *Dora*??"

The faintest of smiles touched Ayo's lips. "So it seems."

"And... you're a *Dora*..." Erika said, pointing.

"I am. And so was Ysra, once. But that was a lifetime ago." The way Ayo's face twisted slightly, the pain that played over her features, sent a tremble through Erika. "Now, she's an assassin for hire, who kills and collects the bracelets of her former allies in her spare time. I was tailing her to what I thought was her next target, but it seems your grandmother's bracelet caught her attention."

Something in Erika's chest tightened. She took another deep breath. "Her bracelet." She shoved her hand into her pocket to clutch at the beads again. "Does that mean you knew my grandmother?"

Ayo shook her head. "No, I'm sorry."

Erika hoped she could keep the disappointment off of her face. "Oh…"

"But," Ayo said, "I know someone who likely did."

Ayo looked like she had more to say, but they were interrupted by a shout at the bathroom door.

"Erika? Erika!"

Erika's stomach nearly dropped to her shoes as her mom whipped around the corner, eyes wide, expression wild. "Erik—oh god." The relief on Mom's face bled into her words, and she swept forward to snatch Erika in against herself. "Oh thank you Jesus… you're all right." She squeezed Erika tight enough she couldn't breathe for a second, then drew back to level a look at her that could've melted her face clean off her skull. "Where the hell have you been! I've been looking everywhere for… hello?" Mom finally caught sight of Ayo standing just behind Erika, and turned that look on her instead. "Can I help you?"

For her part, Ayo managed to look unbothered, despite being on the receiving end of one of Mom's death glares. "My apologies. I was—"

"Talking to me about grandma's bracelet," Erika cut in, the words racing across her tongue before she could stop them. "She has one, too. She's from Wakanda, like Grandma. They're from Wakanda. We were talking about Wakanda…" Her heart was beating so fast and loud she was sure everyone could hear it.

"O-oh." Mom's glare fell away as she glanced back and forth

between Erika and Ayo. "So that's what was taking you so long."

"Y-yeah. Sorry." Erika pressed her teeth into her lower lip.

Mom sighed heavily, her face full of understanding as she smoothed a hand over Erika's braids and kissed her forehead. "It's okay, baby. I was just worried about you."

"I'm sorry," Erika repeated.

"And worried we was gonna miss this flight. Tickets to Wakanda ain't cheap."

"You're traveling to Wakanda?" Ayo asked, her eyebrows lifting. "I think we may have the same flight." Ayo reached to take up Erika's bag, offering it to her. "Mind if I accompany you to the gate?"

Erika took the bag with a murmured thanks.

"Sure." Mom rolled her shoulders in a shrug. "Maybe you can tell us what we should do while we're there. It's always best to ask someone who knows the neighborhood." As they exited the bathroom, she snapped to get Miles's attention.

Without looking up from his phone, he fell into step beside them as they walked.

"I'd be happy to," Ayo said. "And to continue our earlier conversation about your bracelet, Erika, and the legacy tied to it."

The tightness that had taken up space in Erika's chest and threatened to push her out of her skin earlier finally eased. She drew her hand out of her pocket and uncurled her fingers from around the beads. They lay dark and silent against her palm, but the promise of the story they held, the legacy Ayo talked about, burned bright in Erika's heart.

Grandma May had always been supportive of her with her martial arts. In the beginning, when her parents were scared she'd get hurt, Grandma May was the one who signed Erika up. She took her to practice and matches until, eventually, Mom and Dad got on board. And even then, she was her loudest cheerleader.

Looking back, it made a strange sort of sense. Her grandmother was a warrior, and had shared that with her, even in that small way.

"Legacy." Erika swiped at her eyes. "I'd like that."

"Aww, baby." Mom wrapped an arm around Erika's shoulders and squeezed.

"Good." Ayo nodded. "But, first things first, we need to find the nearest medical kiosk and get that wound properly bandaged."

Mom stopped dead in her—and Erika's—tracks. "I'm sorry, *what?*"

Erika flinched, though it had nothing to do with her injury this time. "About that…"

THE MONSTERS OF MENA NGAI

MILTON J. DAVIS

CHIEF GAKURE jumped from his bed, grabbing his shield and spear when the wailing began. His wife and children woke as well, startled by his actions.

"What is it?" Njoki, his wife, asked.

"Probably a simba attacking the herd," Gakure said.

Njoki picked up her spear and shield as well. She turned to Gathu, their eldest son.

"Run to the village and get the others," she said. "Tell them a simba has come."

"Yes, Mama," Gathu said. He grabbed his knife, then fled the hut.

"Mukami, watch your brother and sister," Gakure said to their second eldest daughter. "Do not leave the hut."

Mukami nodded. "Yes, Baba."

Gakure and Njoki hurried to the cattle pen. Together they had amassed one of the largest herds in their village, if not the entire land. They were not about to lose their wealth to the hunger pains of a stray simba.

When they reached the pen, their anxiety increased. This was not the first time a hungry predator had invaded their holding, but there was something strange about the cattle's behavior. Gakure expected to see the herd running about and pushing at the fence, but instead the bovines stood still as they wailed. They were almost to the gate when one of his largest bulls sailed through the air toward them.

"Move!" Gakure shouted.

He shoved Njoki away. The bull crashed to the ground near Gakure, its long horns tearing his shield away and raking his arm. He yelled in pain, dropping his spear and grabbing his wound. Njoki rushed to his side.

"Husband!" she shouted.

Gakure's eyes were not on her. He stared at the pen in fear. Njoki looked up to see the source of her husband's terror. A thing in the shape of a person loomed over the cattle, a misshapen giant unlike anything she'd seen. It threw back its head and yelled before jumping from the pen and landing beside the broken bull. But Njoki did not run in fear. Every person of her tribe was a warrior. She stood between her husband and the monstrosity, her shield and spear raised. Gakure stood beside her, his spear lifted over his head with his good hand. They whispered to the ancestors who they would soon join, asking for the strength to battle what stood before them.

Shouts rose behind them as the other villagers arrived. The monster glanced at them and emitted another yell. It grabbed the bull's legs then threw it onto its shoulder as if it was a broken doll. With another cry, it bounded into the bush.

Njoki lowered her shield and spear. Gakure dropped his weapon and fell to his knees, grabbing his wound again. Gathu was the first to them, falling to his knees before his injured baba. Njoki tossed her weapons aside, then briefly hugged her family before tending to Gakure's wound.

"What was that, Baba?" Gathu asked.

"I don't know," Gakure replied. "But I know where it came from."

The others gathered close to them. Their healer, Gatimu, knelt before them.

"Once again Mena Ngai curses us," he said.

Gatimu laid his hand on Gakure's shoulder. "What will you do?"

"The only thing I can do," Gakure replied. "I will send for Bashenga and the Panther Clan."

"There is no need for that."

The village folk turned their heads to the unfamiliar voice.

A group of unknown warriors emerged from the bush, following a man who stood at least a torso taller than the tallest man Gakure had ever seen.

"I am Oboro," the man said. Oboro reached behind him and took an object from one of his warriors. He tossed the thing toward Gakure; it hit the ground then rolled to the wounded warrior's feet. It was the monster's head. Gakure leaned forward to get a close look at it before looking at Oboro.

"Are you of the Panther Clan?" he asked.

Oboro spat. "No. Our people come from beyond the mountains. You no longer need to put your trust in warriors that are too far away to save you from the dangers that lurk within the shadows of the mountains. We will protect you."

BASHENGA FACED off against a dozen of his best warriors in the training circle. His opponents wielded blunt swords and spears, but that would not stop the pain they could inflict without breaking his skin. Bashenga, the Panther Clan's best warrior and leader, carried no weapons. He crouched, his muscled legs taut as he turned with the warriors to keep them before him. When they attacked, it would be face to face as warriors should. But in the real world, advantage always trumped honor.

The drummers played and the fight began. A pair of thick arms appeared at Bashenga's sides then pinned his arms against his body. Bashenga threw his head back, smashing it against his unknown attacker's nose. He pitched his body backward, pushing the warrior down and falling on top. The warrior's arms flew wide on impact, releasing Bashenga. Bashenga rolled backward off the warrior and came to his feet in time to meet the others' charge. He ran at them then jumped, his bare foot striking the shield of the closest warrior and forcing him into the others.

Bashenga caught the spear aimed at his ribs, wrenching it out of the warrior's hands and throwing it into the face of the warrior behind him. The warrior dodged the spear but fell to Bashenga's elbow smashing into his jaw. The attack became a confused melee, Bashenga working his way through the warriors as he used his feet, hands, elbows, and knees to fight his attackers. When the drummers finally played the cadence ending the training, only Bashenga stood, the other warriors groaning as they rubbed their wounds.

Inspecting his body, Bashenga frowned. Although he sported few bruises, some would have been crippling wounds had the warriors' weapons been real. He glanced at the defeated fighters; some of them smiled back at him, but others studied him with blank faces. Every one of them was a potential challenger for his position. They would return to their homes, analyzing this fight and seeking advantages in their next encounter. Though they were loyal to him, they were not his friends. They never would be.

Bashenga walked back to his home in the center of his village. The people cleared a path for him, nodded in respect. Bashenga returned their attention, stopping to play with the children along the way. He took his position seriously, but not so seriously that he did not have time to share some joy with his people. He was approaching his home when he heard his named called. He turned to see Chipo, the elders' herald.

"What is it, Chipo?" he said.

"The elders request your presence," Chipo replied. "There is trouble at the mountain."

Bashenga's eyes went wide. He ran past Chipo and through the village until he reached the meeting tree. The elders congregated there, dressed in their ceremonial robes. Their faces were not pleasant.

"I came as soon as I received the word," Bashenga said. "What is going on at the mountain?"

Elder Chana, the matriarch of the elders, used her staff to stand.

"For months, we have not received any tribute from the villages near the mountain despite our alliance, our agreement to protect them from harm," she said. "We suspected they had decided they no longer needed our protection. We sent our messengers to discover the truth. They returned with disturbing news."

"The monsters have returned," Elder Kimbo said. "The villages are being devastated by their attacks."

Bashenga glared at the elders. "Why am I just hearing of this?"

"It is not for you to question our knowledge and when we share it," Elder Kimbo said calmly.

"I will gather my warriors and set out immediately," Bashenga said.

"There is no need for that," Elder Chani said. "The northern tribes have found a new champion."

"Impossible!" Bashenga blurted. "There are no warriors in the valley that can handle the monsters except the Panther Clan."

"Apparently there is one," Elder Maana said. "He calls himself Oboro. Not only has he defeated the monsters, he claims the mountain as his."

"We will depart in a week, after we construct more weapons and consult with Bast," Bashenga said. "I will confront this Oboro and take back what is ours."

"We must discuss this," Elder Maana said. "Do we wish to be saddled with this burden?"

"The mountain is ours," Bashenga said. "It was given to us by Bast. You all know how valuable it is."

"We also know the cost of protecting it," Elder Cama said.

"We are willing to pay that cost," Bashenga responded.

"Are we?"

Bashenga could see where this discussion was leading. The elders had summoned him once they had made up their minds. This meeting was only meant to give him their decision.

"I will speak no more on this until I return from the mountain," Bashenga said.

"We have not given you permission to go," Elder Chani said.

"I did not ask you," Bashenga replied.

Bashenga ignored the angry protests of the elders as he walked away. He was the leader of his people. Although it was customary to consult the elders, it was not required to follow their recommendations. The situation at the mountain was much more serious than they could perceive. They did not fight the monsters that the metal from the mountain created. They did not witness the terror firsthand like he did, nor did they suffer the pain of watching so many good warriors die. But there was some good to come of it: the discovery of how to tame the metal that caused the sickness. Whatever these other leaders were doing would not last. There was only one way to stop the monsters, and Bashenga knew how.

Bashenga entered his home. Luckily, his wife and children were not present. He moved his bed aside then dug into the packed dirt with his hands until he uncovered a medium-sized ironwood box. Despite its thickness, Bashenga could feel the vibration of the sky metal in his palms. The Panther Clan learned early the transformative effects of the metal; they lost many warriors attempting to discover its secrets. He had saved this portion in case a time came that he would need it again. Now was that time.

Bashenga set out for his destination alone, a heavy blanket thrown across his shoulder to hide the box. His destination was secret. He traveled to a site known only to himself and those like him, men who were entrusted with the secret of metals and the skills to mold them. He journeyed the rest of the day until nightfall, setting up a perch in a tall acacia to protect himself from predators that stalked in darkness. After securing the box between branches, Bashenga found a spot in the tree to rest for the night.

The sun's warmth stirred him from slumber. He opened his eyes and was greeted by the intense stare of his totem. The panther had apparently slipped into the tree during the night, seeking the same respite as Bashenga. It took Bashenga everything in his power not to cry out in joy. Bast had sent her servant to protect him during the night, a sure sign that his journey was true.

"I see you, brother," he whispered.

The panther yawned and stretched, its deadly claws extending from their sheaths. It stood on the branch, leapt from the tree, then sauntered away.

Bashenga gathered the box and continued his journey. His stomach grumbled with hunger, but he could not stop until he reached his destination. It was almost noon when he found himself staring down into the valley of iron. The steep gorge was known only to the blacksmiths, its hills abundant with the ore used to make the weapons of the various tribes in the region, including the Panther Clan. Bashenga picked his way down the slope, making sure he placed his feet properly to avoid falling into the canyon. Halfway down the slope he found his final terminus, a small opening that led to the sacred cave.

Two men turned their heads toward him as he entered. There was no secret word to say, no special gesture to gain entry. Only blacksmiths knew of this cave, a testament to the oaths and initiation of the forgers' cult.

Bashenga went first to the blacksmith's shrine, pouring libations to the spirit of the forge and offering sorghum and five kola nuts. After asking for the forge spirits' blessing for a successful smelting, he approached the men sitting near the kiln.

"Welcome, Bashenga of the Panther Clan," the kiln master said. "What brings you to the Breath?"

"I'm here to forge weapons of war," Bashenga said.

The kiln master looked over his shoulder to the shrine.

"That is a paltry offering for what you wish to do," he commented. "You should go and bring back something more suitable."

Bashenga's face became stern.

"Something more for the spirit of the kiln, or you?" he asked.

"It makes no difference," the Elder said. "You will not use this kiln until you do so."

Bashenga's first instinct was to kill the man, brotherhood be damned. But that would serve no purpose. He could not work the kiln alone when smelting the sky metal, so he needed the man's help.

"I will return," he said finally.

Bashenga left the cave and climbed out of the valley. He wandered into the bush in search of something that would make a suitable sacrifice. His search was soon rewarded when he came across a herd of antelope drinking at a shallow waterhole. Bashenga the warrior became Bashenga the hunter. Using his shield to hide his features, he crawled toward the waterhole until he was close enough to throw his spear. Bashenga rose onto his knees, took aim, then threw the weapon. His aim was true; the spear pierced the side of an antelope. He jumped up to claim his reward and the other antelope fled. He was almost to his prize when he discovered a contender for his kill.

Bashenga didn't see the crocodile closing in on his kill until he was almost upon it. He ran faster, hoping to reach the carcass before the beast. Bashenga grasped the antelope's antlers just as the crocodile clamped its powerful jaws onto its hind quarters. A desperate tug of war ensued with Bashenga being pulled to the water's edge. He had come too far to lose his kill to a crocodile or any other beast. He raised his spear then threw it. The spear sank into the crocodile's eye.

It opened its jaws in pain and Bashenga fell backward with his prize. But the crocodile did not give up. It charged onto land, spear protruding from its eye. Bashenga threw the antelope behind him then turned to face the attacking reptile. He was a Panther; he would not flee a battle of any kind. As the crocodile opened its jaws, Bashenga jumped. He cleared the crocodile's gaping maw, descending toward its head, and caught the spear shaft as he landed, driving it deeper into the water lizard until it reached its brain. The crocodile shuddered then fell limp. Bashenga stood then pulled his spear free, a broad smile on his ebony face. This was a much better offering.

He dragged his kills away from the waterhole and went about his work. He skinned the crocodile then butchered the antelope to make it easier to carry. When he returned to the cave his brethren were astonished.

"The iron spirit is pleased," the eldest man said.

Bashenga nodded. "Are you ready to work?"

He revealed the box then handed it to the old man. He felt the vibrations and gasped.

"Sky metal!"

The younger man's eyes went wide. "I will fetch the others!"

Bashenga assisted the kiln master in preparing the kiln. The brethren appeared as the kiln was readied, their talking drums tucked under their arms. Long ago the Panther clan realized the vibration of the sky metal caused the sickness of those who came into contact with it. They attempted many ways to control it, but it was by chance that they discovered the solution.

During the treatment of a warrior, the village healer noticed an improvement of the warrior's condition whenever a certain note was played by the drummers. The vibration of the note matched that of the sky metal, negating its lethal energy. The blacksmiths adapted the drum playing to their forging process, enabling them to render the sky metal safe as they mixed it with iron to create an alloy that, while stronger than any metal known, was safe.

His brothers arrived. They feasted on the antelope and crocodile before setting about their serious task. The drummers played and the box fell still. Bashenga opened it, taking out the sky metal and giving it to the master forgers. He assisted in blending the sky metal with the proper amounts of iron before pouring it into the kiln. When the time was right, the kiln was opened and the bloom removed. It was time for Bashenga to display his skills. He hammered the bloom to the proper thickness, then passed it on to his cohorts to shape it into spearheads and blades, enough to arm the warriors and hunters Bashenga needed to carry out his plan.

Bashenga returned to the village two weeks after his secret departure. When he entered his home, he met the relieved smile, then the angry glare, of his wife, Aminali.

"Where have you been?" she scolded. "No one knew where you were. We all thought you had gone to the mountain alone."

Bashenga embraced his wife then they kissed. Small arms

hugged his legs; he looked down at their twins, Azizi and Amani. He knelt and hugged them both.

"Baba, where have you been?" Azizi said. "Amani said a simba ate you!"

Bashenga narrowed his eyes when he looked at Amani and his mischievous daughter laughed.

"I was just playing, Baba," she said. She shoved Azizi's head. "You'll believe anything!"

Bashenga sat on his bed and his family crowded around him.

"I went to the valley," he said. "There was something I needed to do that could not wait."

"Not even long enough to tell your family?" Aminali asked.

"Yes," Bashenga answered. "And now I must go again."

Aminali pulled away from him. "Where now?"

"I must go to the shrine," he said. "The Panther Clan must march soon, and we must be prepared."

"So, you are still going to the mountain despite the elders' advice?"

"Yes," Bashenga said. "The elders don't understand how important it is to us."

"To us, or to you?" Aminali asked.

"I will tell you as I told them," he said. "What is important to me, is important to our clan. I do not make this decision selfishly. I am guided by the wisdom of our ancestors and the blessings of Bast. It is to Her that I will go now."

Aminali stood. "Now?"

"Yes," Bashenga said.

"Can't you at least share a meal with us before you leave?"

Bashenga stood and hugged his wife again.

"I will return tomorrow, I promise you," he said. "I must do this today."

"Take someone with you," she suggested.

Bashenga shook his head. "I must go alone. Whatever Bast shares will be for me only. It has always been this way."

Bashenga kissed his children then left his home again. Many of the warriors gathered around him as he strode through the village, curious about his intentions.

"Be ready when I return," he told them. "We have much work to do."

Once again Bashenga found himself alone on an important journey, but unlike his trip to the valley, the outcome of this sojourn was unsure. It had been a long time since he'd prostrated himself at the feet of Bast and begged for her wisdom. He had failed to honor Her over the years, instead listening to the elders, so he was not sure she would hear him out. His doubts were eased when he remembered the panther that visited him during his journey to the valley. At least he knew She watched him.

Reaching the base of the sacred mountain at sundown, he set up camp then relieved his hunger with dried antelope meat he'd brought from the smelter's cave. He thought of his family, how he could have been in their company enjoying a delicious meal, his children filling his ears with wild stories and his wife sharing her soothing words and companionship. He shook his head to clear it of such weak thoughts. There would be time enough for comfort. For now, he had to do what was best for the clan.

AT MORNING'S light he broke camp and climbed the mountain to Bast's temple. No one knew when the sacred building had been constructed or what hands had cut and raised the stone. The edifice existed long before the memory of any of the people that now inhabited the valley, and the language inscribed on the stones had long been forgotten. Yet the structure remained, a testament to its power.

Bashenga checked his bag of blades before beginning the final leg of his journey. The stone stairway leading to the temple was incredibly steep, so much so a person could place their hands on the steps before them without bending. As he took the first step a figure burst from the nearby foliage, placing itself between Bashenga and the way up. Bashenga recognized it as the panther that had shared his perch. As their eyes met, Bashenga was not sure the beast recognized him. Instinct urged him to lower his spear and defend himself, but he knew that was not prudent. This was Bast's messenger. She would either let him pass or kill him where he stood.

The panther approached Bashenga, coming face to face with the warrior, nervous in the face of his god. Its nostrils flared as it sniffed about him, as if confirming he was the person it had encountered before. The panther emitted a short roar then turned away and climbed the stairs. Bashenga did not move, watching the beast as it loped away. The panther stopped, turned its head to him, and roared again. Bashenga climbed the stairs toward the panther. It remained still for a moment then continued to climb the stairway.

They reached the crest of the stairway. The panther disappeared over the rim and Bashenga followed. The temple appeared before him, looking exactly as he remembered. The grounds were free of foliage, as if tended by invisible hands. At the far end of the courtyard stood Bast. She radiated power in her regal pose, her human body straight and rigid, her arms pressed against her sides. Her panther head crowned her regal neck, her eyes staring outward into the heavens. Bashenga's panther companion sauntered up to the statue then lay at its feet. Their eyes met once again and the panther growled. Taking the sound as a sign, Bashenga approached the statue. He halted a few feet away then prostrated himself before Her.

"Goddess," he said. "I come before you as your servant. I ask your blessing on that which I carry."

Bashenga took the basket of blades from his back. He took out the blades, spreading them before Bast then stepping away.

"These blades are forged from your gift," he said. "We have discovered the power of the sky metal and how to harness it. I ask only that you share your blessing with what I bring to ensure our victory in the coming battle."

What has taken you so long, Bashenga?

Bast's voice rang clear in his head, startling him.

I gave this to you long ago, and yet you hesitate to claim it.

"Forgive me," he said. "The sky metal carried a sickness we had to overcome."

And you have, yet you still stay away, Bast replied.

"Is that why you have given the mountain to Oboro?"

I have given nothing to anyone other than the one who kneels before me.

"But the elders—"

I do not speak to the elders, Bast interrupted. *I speak only to you and those of your blood. You are my Panther.*

The sky metal blade glowed to an intensity that forced Bashenga to look away. Moments later the spiritual light subsided. Bashenga gazed upon them.

"By the ancestors," he said.

The blades shimmered, their surface polished to perfection. He reached out to touch the spearhead close to him then jerked his hand away. It vibrated like the raw material, yet it felt different.

The blades you have created will last countless generations, Bast said. *They will be handed down from warrior to warrior from clan to clan. As long as they exist, the mountain will belong to the Panther Clan.*

Bashenga gathered the blades and put them back into the bag.

Go, Bashenga of the Panther Clan, Bast said. *Claim what is yours.*

○———————○

"SOMEONE IS coming!"

The goat herder ran as fast as his narrow legs could manage, an unexpected vanguard of the ranks of warriors close behind. His cries alerted the village and the villagers spilled out of their huts, shields, spears, and swords at the ready. When they saw the warriors following the goat herders, their hearts dropped in despair. There was no amount of bravery that could stand against these people.

The warriors halted at the village edge. A man continued forward, wearing a head ring of panther teeth.

"Do not fear," he called out. "I am Bashenga of the Panther Clan. We have come to protect you from the beasts of the mountain."

Gakure, the village chief, stepped forward.

"We need no protection, especially not from the Panther Clan," he boasted. "We have Oboro, which is almost worse than the demons."

"This mountain wasn't given to you, who cannot defend it. It was not given to Oboro either," Bashenga said. "It belongs to us, and I will fight Oboro for that right."

"What does that mean for us?" Gakure said. "Do we exchange one tyrant for another? Better we run both of you away and face our fate alone."

"What has he done?" Bashenga asked.

"He says he protects us, but the demons still come," Gakure said. "Yes, he kills them, but not before they do their damage."

A smirk came to Bashenga's face. "The people missing from your village are the very demons that ravage it."

"What are you saying?" Gakure asked.

"Oboro is exposing your people to the raw sky metal and transforming them into demons. Then he kills them and says he is protecting you. He is using your fear to control you."

"And what will you do?" Gakure asked, his anger etched on his face.

"We will show you," Bashenga said.

Bashenga returned to his warriors. He raised his spear and they ran through the village then into the bush, toward the mountain.

"Where are they going?" his wife asked.

"To the mountain and to their deaths," Gakure said. "If the demons don't kill them, Oboro will."

BASHENGA GAZED at Mena Ngai filled with apprehension. Bast's words were true, but still he worried. He looked at his warriors, their spears tipped with sky metal, their sword blades fashioned from it as well. The drummers milled among them, sky metal knives hanging from their waists. Their task was the most important of all. Bashenga broke the sacred oath among the blacksmiths by teaching them the rhythm that soothed the sky metal's fire, but it was necessary. Bast's words overruled all others. Mena Ngai had been given to the Panther Clan and they would claim it.

"Drummers!" Bashenga shouted.

Calloused hands struck the cowhide drumheads, pounding out the once secret rhythm. The Panther warriors struck their shields in time, following Bashenga into the bush surrounding the mountain. Unlike his warriors, Bashenga did not possess a shield. He carried a stabbing spear in his right hand, a warclub in his left. He watched the bush and grasses, his hands tight around his weapons. After only a few minutes' progress a shrill cry rose over the voice of the drums. Bashenga spotted the monster to his left, running toward his warriors. The drummers fell back as the warriors stepped forward and formed a shield wall. All eyes fell on Bashenga and he sprinted toward the beast. The first kill would be his.

The beast crashed into the shield wall. The warriors pushed it back and the creature stumbled away. The beast yelled and charged the shield again, but this time its attack was interrupted.

"Come to me, monster!" Bashenga shouted.

They charged toward each other, Bashenga running in a crouch. When he reached the beast, he spun to his left. The creature stumbled by him as he struck it in the back with his club. As it arched its back in pain, Bashenga stabbed it behind the knee, severing its hamstrings. The beast fell to its knee and tried to pivot around, but Bashenga struck it again with his club. The ball of sky metal cracked its skull, sending it face first into the grass. Bashenga dropped his spear and club then pulled his machete free from its wooden scabbard. With two chops the monster's head rolled free. Bashenga gripped the beast's hair then lifted the head for all to see. The drummers played a victory rhythm, the warriors dancing with their shields and spears raised. He had shown the way; the others would follow.

The hunt began. The creatures unaffected by the sky metal sickness fled the drummers and warriors; those infected attacked. Despite their discipline, warriors were lost. Bashenga took each death personally; he had made this decision for them all, so he was responsible. Yet Bast's promise pushed him on. At the end of two days, the lands in the shadow of Mena Ngai were free of the monsters.

The Panther warriors were celebrating their victory when Oboro and his warriors arrived. Bashenga sat on his stool enjoying a bowl of goat stew when he saw them crest the eastern horizon, their feathered head rings bouncing in time with their gait. Oboro ran at the lead, beating his shield with his spear to set the pace. Kabongo appeared at Bashenga's side with his weapons.

He sat down his bowl, took his club and spear from Kabongo, and sauntered toward Oboro, his warriors falling in behind him. The groups halted a spear's throw away from each other. Oboro and Bashenga continued walking toward each other.

"What are you doing here, panther man?" he shouted.

"Protecting what is ours," Bashenga shouted back.

"You gave up your claim when you did not answer the Bandele call for help."

"We cannot answer a call that was never sent."

Bashenga and Oboro stood an arm's length from each other.

"Go home, panther man," Oboro said. "Or I will make your wife a widow."

"You will try," Bashenga replied. "It is your right to challenge me for the right to rule. At least this way your claim would be legitimate, instead of stealing it."

Oboro yelled then lunged at Bashenga with his spear. Bashenga knocked the spear aside with his club then stabbed at Oboro's ribs. Oboro blocked the stab with his shield. The two exchanged thrusts and blows, spurred on by the chants of their warriors. Bashenga battered Oboro's shield with his club, the sky metal wreaking havoc on the cowhide and wood frame. The shield finally shattered; Oboro cursed and tossed it aside.

"Yield, Oboro," Bashenga said. "I don't want to kill you."

Oboro answered with a glare. Bashenga nodded in response.

He tossed away his spear. Oboro grinned and resumed his attack. Bashenga fought with the agility of his totem, dodging Oboro's powerful strokes, his club battering the warrior's arms and legs. Oboro's spear finally reached its mark, the blade cutting a crease across Bashenga's ribs. The Panther chief responded by slamming his club against Bashenga's wrist. The bone snapped; Oboro cried out as he dropped his spear and fell to his knees, grasping his broken arm. Bashenga moved in, standing before Oboro, both hands gripping his club as he raised it over his head.

"I yield!" Oboro shouted. "I yield!"

Bashenga lowered his club. He turned to his warriors then nodded.

"Panther Clan! Forward!" Kabongo called out.

The Panther warriors advanced to Bashenga's side. Oboro's warriors fled, leaving their defeated leader in the hands of their enemies.

"It is done," Kabongo said.

"Yes, it is," Bashenga replied. "Time to go home."

THE PEOPLE of the village went about their daily routine, despite the tension from the Panther Clan's visit. One day, Gakure found himself awakened by shouting and cheering. He stepped out of his hut to find the streets filled with villagers.

"What's going on?" he shouted.

"The Panther Clan has returned!" someone shouted back.

Gakure gathered his family and hurried to the village meeting tree. When he arrived he saw an amazing sight. The Panther Clan warriors were gathered under the massive tree canopy; their stern faces focused on their leader, Bashenga. To the left of Bashenga were the heads of demons, so many Gakure couldn't count. On his right was Oboro. The warrior was on his knees, his head hanging and his hands tied behind his back.

Gakure approached Bashenga.

"You are a man of your word," he said.

"I am," Bashenga replied.

Gakure glanced at Oboro and frowned.

"What will you do with him?" he asked.

"What do you wish for me to do?" Bashenga asked.

"Let him go back to his people," Gakure said. "He has been humiliated. I doubt they will return."

"You are generous," Bashenga said. He handed Gakure a knife. Gakure went to Oboro then cut his bonds.

"Leave us," he said.

Oboro stood, rubbing his wrists. He glared at Gakure, but that arrogant look transformed into a subdued expression when Bashenga looked upon him. He ran from the village, pelted by refuse.

"Do you claim to be our masters now?" Gakure said.

"No," Bashenga replied. "All we ask is that which was given to us, and that you join us in reaping its bounty."

"That mountain has been nothing but trouble," Gakure said.

"Not anymore," Bashenga replied. "Together we will prosper, and the Panther Clan will protect our land from those who dare otherwise."

"Like Oboro," Gakure said.

"What is your decision, Gakure?" Bashenga asked. "Will you join us? Will you become part of Wakanda?"

Bashenga extended his arm. Gakure considered his decision. He glanced at his people, then to the stern warriors beneath the meeting tree. He grasped Bashenga's forearm.

"We will join you, Bashenga of the Panther Clan."

Bashenga pulled Gakure into a hug.

"So be it," he said. "So it begins."

The Bandele wasted no time in organizing a grand feast. Gakure gave three bulls as offering to the ancestors and Bast, providing much meat for the celebration. The villagers and the warriors gathered at the village center, enjoying good food, good drumming, and excellent dancing. For two days they feasted; on the third day Bashenga gathered his warriors on the outskirts of the village.

"Kabongo, I leave you in command. Make sure you send patrols to the mountain. Keep everyone away, and deal with those who come down with the sickness."

"I will, Bashenga."

"I will return soon with the others," he said.

Bashenga set off alone, a provision bag strapped to his back. He made good time, running at a warrior's pace following well-worn trails between his village and the highlands. It was when he neared his homeland that his easy mood dissipated. Smoke columns rose from encampments near the village, the camps filled with warriors from nearby tribes. Bashenga slipped into the bush, using all his stealth to cover the remaining miles to his village. When he reached it, he could feel the tension among his friends as they went about their daily chores. He decided to wait until nightfall before going any farther.

Bashenga slipped into the village as soon as the sun disappeared below the western hills. He avoided the occasional villager enjoying the cool night, reaching his home without incident. He crouched then tapped on the door.

"Who is at my door at such an hour?" Aminali challenged.

"It's me, Bashenga," he said.

Bashenga looked about as Aminali unfastened the door then set it aside. She grabbed Bashenga's arm then pulled him into an embrace.

"Husband!" she said. "You're alive!"

Bashenga held his wife tight.

"What would make you think I was dead?"

Aminali led him to their bed.

"The elders called a council the day after you and the warriors departed. They said you defied their commands and spoke against the ancestors. They said you were no longer worthy to lead our people."

"That is why the others are here," Bashenga said.

"Yes. They mean to choose another chief from among the lineage candidates tomorrow. There will be a challenge match."

A wave of fatigue swept over Bashenga. He lay down on the cot, and Aminali lay down beside him.

"What will you do?" she asked.

"I must rest for now," he said. "Tomorrow, I will go to the challenge."

Aminali sat up. "You can't! Not without your warriors!"

"If I wait until Kabongo and the others find out what happened, it will be too late. I must go, and I pray that Bast will be with me."

Morning came and the villagers gathered at the meeting tree. The elders sat under the canopy, the seriousness of the moment expressed in their faces. A circle of drummers formed a ring in the clear space before the meeting tree, the people gathered behind them. Elder Chana entered the circle, sweeping all with her eyes.

"We are here to choose a new chief," she said. "Bashenga has defied the ancestors. To placate them, we must choose a leader who will regain their respect. Who wishes to compete for this honor?"

The ring parted as the contenders entered. Each person was a supreme warrior of their tribe and possessed the proper lineage to serve as chief. The warriors prostrated themselves before Elder Chana in respect.

"Is there anyone else?" Elder Chana asked.

"Yes."

Bashenga entered the ring and the crowd let out a collective gasp. Elder Chana's face twisted as she stabbed her finger toward him.

"You have no place here!"

"I do," Bashenga said. "Like the others here, I am a warrior and I possess the lineage. And the last time I looked, I was still chief."

"You have disrespected the ancestors!" Chana shouted.

"If I have, then I will be defeated," Bashenga said. "I will make it easy for you. I will fight all the contenders at the same time."

Elder Chana grinned.

"So be it," she said. "Begin!"

The drummers played and the contenders attacked. Bashenga ran toward them, his eyes and mind focused. As his assailants converged, he changed direction, veering to the right to confront the closest warrior. He drove his fist into the man's gut then kneed him in the face, knocking him backward into the ground unconscious. A second contender smashed into him, wrapping his thick arms around Bashenga's waist. Bashenga headbutted him on the bridge of his nose then brought his elbow in the same spot. The man cried out then released him. The other attackers converged on Bashenga simultaneously, striking him with fists, feet, knees, and elbows. Bashenga fought back, but each blow took its toll. He fell to his knees, covering his head under the deluge of hits. He finally curled his body into a ball, his consciousness slowly leaving him.

Bast, he thought. Have you abandoned me? Were your words truth?

YOU ARE MY PANTHER. RISE AND CLAIM WHAT IS YOURS!

Energy burst from his chest then rushed into his limbs like a swollen river. Bashenga sprang to his feet, flinging his attackers away. He was among them before they recovered, beating them as they beat him, sending them into momentary oblivion. The last challenger lost his bravery and fled through the drummers' ring and into the throng. A stillness gripped the village; even the elders were silent. The calm was shattered by a loud roar from the nearby bush. People ran in every direction as a black panther emerged from the thicket. It loped into the challenge ring and up to Bashenga. The panther rubbed its head against his leg then lay at his feet, licking its front paw.

"Bast has blessed us with Mena Ngai, and She has chosen me as her guardian," Bashenga said. "As I have defeated all challengers, the ancestors are pleased as well. Our future lies at the mountain. There we will learn the secrets of the sky metal and we will share the bounty with every tribe that stands here. Will you follow me?"

Aminali entered the circle, their children in tow. She stood by her husband as their children surrounded the panther, playing with it as if it was a pet.

"I will join you," she said.

The families of his warriors came, then others. The last to enter were the elders. Elder Chana walked up to him.

"Our fate is in your hands," she said.

"It is in Bast's hands," Bashenga replied.

The drummers played and Bashenga looked to the north.

SHADOW DREAMS

LINDA D. ADDISON

DERA HAD never traveled so far from her village in her fourteen years except in her dreams. But this was no dream; she was on a train to the capital of Wakanda. As excited as she was about training to become a *Dora Milaje*, Dera was also very nervous. Everyone in the village was excited, especially her parents and sister. Dera was going to do everything she could to make them happy.

More than anything, Dera wanted to make her grandmother proud. It was her passing that made Dera two weeks late to begin her training. Her mother had tried to get Dera to leave sooner, but once it was clear her grandmother wasn't getting better, Dera wouldn't leave her side.

The last words from her grandmother were, "Be the best you can for Wakanda."

The train pulled into the main station, where most of the passengers got off. Dera was waiting on the platform with one bag slung over her shoulder when a tall girl about Dera's age, dressed in a white tunic and pants with a red scarf, walked up. She had a short sword in a waist belt and looked strong.

"Hello, you must be Chidera! I'm Uto. Welcome to Birnin Zana, the Golden City."

"Everyone calls me Dera. You are a trainee also?" Dera asked with a smile.

"Yes, I hope you aren't disappointed that a full *Dora Milaje* didn't come to take you to the training facility." Uto stood with her hands on her hips. "They do have more important things to do."

"Oh no." Dera shook her head. "I didn't know we were allowed out of Upanga as initiates."

Uto laughed and patted Dera on the shoulder. "Well, it's not a jail. Although with all the training we do, a jail might be more relaxing."

Dera wrinkled her brow.

"Don't worry, you'll be fine. Only the best are given a chance to train. Now, let's get you to your new home."

Dera tried not to look like a tourist but it was hard. There was so much to see, so many people wearing intricate, colorful patterns representing different tribes. The enticing aromas of spicy minced meat and vegetables sold by street vendors offering samples made her mouth water. The streets of the Golden City were crowded, but Dera stayed next to Uto as they walked to the *Dora Milaje* training facility.

People made space for them as they walked, out of respect and because no one wanted to bump into the trainee warrior. The Upanga building rose high into the sky. Before they stepped through the entrance, Uto faced Dera and put her hands on her shoulders. "Your village is now Wakanda, you are from Wakanda, all villages. You understand?"

Dera looked into her eyes and nodded.

"Answer out loud."

Dera took a deep breath. "Yes."

When they walked through the entrance Dera glanced to the right, where the Royal Palace could be seen through the large lobby windows. "May I ask a question?"

"Of course."

Dera nodded to the palace. "I didn't realize we would be so close."

"How better to protect Wakanda?"

"And the King?" Dera asked.

"The King is Wakanda, but you know that," Uto said.

Dera lowered her head. "Yes. I'm sorry."

Uto gently lifted Dera's head. "We never bow our head for anyone, except the King. Okay?"

"Yes," Dera said.

"You must be tired from traveling," Uto said. "What would you like to see first, where you will sleep or the training area?"

"I want to see the training area," Dera said, brightening up.

Uto smiled. "This way."

They took the elevator up three floors and walked down a long hallway until they were in the entrance area of a large open room. Each of the corners was set up for a different type of training from hand-to-hand, weaponry, and martial arts. There was a rock-climbing wall to the right, and a running track around the edge of the room.

"Leave your bag here and pick a weapon." Uto pointed to the open shelves to their left.

Dera stuffed her bag onto a shelf and selected a short blade from the wall, before following Uto into the training room.

All the trainees were dressed in white like Uto. Dera felt out of place in the green and gold-trimmed tunic and pants of her village. They approached a group sitting on the edge of a padded area, watching two young women spar with short blades while the teacher talked them through moves. Dera and Uto stood nearby, and Dera could barely make out what the teacher was saying because she was talking so fast. In the end, one of the young girls used a wrist block to dominate the other, causing her to drop the blade. They sat down with the group without a word.

The teacher motioned for Dera and Uto to come to the front of the group.

She tapped Dera's blade. "So, you are the new arrival?"

"Yes."

"I can barely hear you." The teacher leaned down. "Did you actually speak?"

"Yes," Dera said, louder.

Several of the others sitting on the ground tapped each other's blades in support.

The teacher walked around Dera, taking her in. "What is your name?"

"Chidera, but I am called Dera."

"And where are you from, Dera?"

Dera opened her mouth to say the name of her village, but instead said, "Wakanda."

"Good, you have learned your first lesson." She nodded to Uto, who sat on the floor with the others.

"Let's see you disarm me." The teacher grabbed Dera's blade wrist, applied a nerve lock, and swept down with her own blade, stopping within an inch of Dera's neck. When Dera didn't move, she released her, causing Dera to stumble back and fall to the floor.

"I-I wasn't…" Dera stopped talking, realizing what had just happened.

The teacher leaned down, grabbed Dera's hand, and pulled her to her feet. "You weren't ready?"

"The *Dora Milaje* are always ready," Dera said.

"Yes, even in our sleep." The teacher pointed to one of the seated trainees with her blade.

"With every inhale and exhale," the student said. "Ready to defend, ready to die for the King, for Wakanda." The other trainees tapped their blades and shouted, "For Wakanda."

"You aren't *Dora Milaje* yet, that's why you're here," the teacher said. "Show me the first form for knife disarming." She stood with her blade pointing at Dera, then closed her eyes.

Dera went through the form she had been taught since she was eight years old as fast as she could, and bowed when she finished.

"Very pretty flow." The teacher opened her eyes and smiled slightly.

Dera's heart dropped.

"Your blade made a lot of flat noise. Listen." The teacher raised her blade and swiftly swung it in front of Dera's face, close to her nose. "Which is fine, if you wish to slap your opponent."

She swung her blade again. Dera couldn't see the difference in the angle, but she could hear it as it whistled through the air. "What is that sound, Dera?"

"The killing sound," Dera said, looking the teacher in the eyes.

"Good, at least you know the difference." The teacher nodded to the seated trainees, who stood. "After dinner you'll return here to begin blade training."

Dera waited for the other trainees to leave. Somehow, she lost sight of Uto.

The teacher came up to her. "Those are lovely clothes, but you need to change into trainee clothes. Did you go to the dorms before coming in here?"

"No, teacher." Dera walked with her to the exit area.

"My name is Okoye. Come, I'll show you."

"Thank you, Teacher Okoye."

Okoye pulled Dera's bag off the shelf, handed it to her, and smiled. "Just Okoye will do."

"Thank you, Okoye."

Dera put the short blade back on the shelf but Okoye returned it to her. "Let this be your first weapon." She took a leather sword belt from the top shelf and gave it to Dera, who tied it on her waist and put the blade in it.

Okoye crossed her arms and smiled. "Yes, that's better."

THE TRAINEE dorm was on the fifth floor. One large room with bunk beds and the head of each bed had two narrow closets.

Okoye pointed to the third lower bunk bed. There was a change of clothes folded neatly on the bed. "I'll wait for you in the hallway."

Dera changed quickly, stuffed her bag and clothes into the closet with her name on it at the foot of the bed, and rushed into the hallway.

She walked with Okoye to the dining room one floor below. There were rows of tables; the food was in a separate room, where they served themselves from trays of vegetables and spiced meat. Dera followed Okoye's lead, taking the same food and drink, and sat at the same table.

She did more listening than talking, although everyone was pretty quiet as they ate. Dera saw Uto at another table across the room, who waved and went back to her conversation with the others. Even though she was tired after dinner, Dera went back with Okoye to the training room. There were a few trainees who also went back to practice different hand-to-hand styles, some with weapons, some without weapons doing martial arts.

Dera didn't know how long they practiced side by side, doing the first short blade form over and over again, first slow and then faster until she stumbled, almost falling.

"Time for you to go to bed." Okoye helped Dera stand. "I'll see you after breakfast."

Dera made her way back to the dorm, barely saying good night to the other trainees. She lay on her bed and went to sleep without even taking off her clothes.

She dreamed she was doing the form, over and over again. The sun had barely risen when someone shook her foot. It was Uto.

"Good morning. I'm above you." She pointed to the bed above Dera's. "Don't want you to miss breakfast. I could hear you moving in your bed all night."

Dera sat up, rubbed the sleep out of her eyes. "I think I dreamed I was still doing the short blade form."

"Well, that's one way to get extra practice time in," Uto laughed.

Standing up and stretching, Dera winced. It felt like every muscle in her body ached.

Uto pursed her lips. "That's not going to go away real soon, but you'll get used to being sore. After lunch some of us are going to do a hot tub soak, it'll help."

"Thank you."

"You've got a few minutes for a quick shower and to change clothes. The bathroom is to the left out the door. See you in the dining room." She left the room.

Dera got to the dining room minutes before the food trays were removed.

THAT DAY and many days after went by quickly. Once a week they didn't train. Half the day they did charity work by helping in shared gardens, public parks, or senior centers in different neighborhoods of the city. The other half they were free to explore the city in groups of two or three. There was so much to see, vendors selling products from all over Wakanda, food prepared in ways Dera had never seen or tasted. They were given a small allowance to spend, but never had to worry about paying for food, since the vendors were always happy to give them a sample of anything they wanted. They didn't buy jewelry or clothes, because as trainees, they were discouraged from accumulating items that didn't fit a function of their training.

Dera practiced all the drills as long as her body would allow, often pushing past its limits. She felt she wasn't gaining speed and stamina at the same rate as the other trainees. Uto was in one of the more advanced groups because of her strength and agility.

"We each develop at our own rate," Okoye said when she saw disappointment on Dera's face at not advancing to another group. "If I thought you could do more, you would know."

More nights than not, Dera dreamed she was doing the drills. It didn't seem to help when she woke up tired. She had gotten to the point that she knew when she was dreaming and could direct which exercises she wanted to practice.

"Lucid dreaming is something few can naturally do so well," Okoye said, when they sat in her office to review Dera's progress.

"But it's not making me better when I wake up."

"It has to be doing something. Everything has a purpose. Be patient."

Dera agreed, but didn't feel it in her heart.

SHE SPENT as much time training as her body could handle. The thought of not being one of the best fighters took over her mind. The more she directed her sleep time to do certain training practices, the easier it got to dream it. In her dreams, she could perform better without getting tired, but she woke to find it didn't make her run faster, jump higher, or fight any stronger than she could the day before.

By week three, Dera decided if she didn't make it through training she wasn't going back home. It was better to get a job and stay in the Golden City than return home in shame.

"Dera, why are you thinking that way so soon?" Uto said as they walked to dinner after training.

"I know, I know." Dera shook her head. "It's because I'm one of the worst in the class."

"That's not true." Uto put her arm around Dera.

Dera pulled away from her and ran back to the empty dorm room, slammed the door and slid to the floor, punching the carpeted floor. If she couldn't be *Dora Milaje*, what was the meaning of her life? This was all she had thought about, all she had worked for since she could walk. Was she only a pretty form dancer?

Dera decided to skip the optional evening training time and went to bed. Falling into a familiar dream, she was in the training room, but for the first time she wasn't alone. A young girl, very similar in body to Dera, was climbing the rock wall, scrambling up and across faster than any human Dera had seen in real life.

She walked over to the rock wall and looked up at the girl. Who did she put in her dream? The girl scrambled down the wall like a spider and leapt to the ground in front of Dera. She stared at the girl's face, but it was blurred. The girl's body was a copy of Dera's.

No matter what she did, the girl's face wouldn't come into focus. That had never happened. This was the nightmare her life had become.

"Who are you?" she blurted out loud.

"I'm here to help you, Dera."

"What?" She stepped back, away from the blurred girl. Was

this how having a nervous breakdown began, dreaming a faceless version of herself?

"I can help you become the best Adored One, even better than your teachers, if you want."

Dera shook her head. "Now I've made a faceless copy of myself to convince me I can do better."

"I'm not created by you, but if you need to believe that, so be it." The girl stepped closer to Dera, her face still a smeared image. "You can call me Iyawa. I live in a parallel universe that's a version of Wakanda, except we're sick and dying. In our Wakanda, we used Vibranium to increase our powers and defeat our neighboring enemies, but we didn't realize its radiation was also destroying our genetic structure.

"We've lost so many, and even though I won't live long, I was able to use my power to contact you in your dreams because we are related through DNA. I can't heal myself, but I have felt your pain in my dreams and I can help you."

"A parallel universe?"

"Yes, you must have read about multiple realities."

"Yes, but there's no proof—"

"The top scientists in your reality are investigating the concept. What proof they have found hasn't been shared with regular people, but it exists. I exist."

"This is the strangest dream I've ever had." Dera rubbed her neck and closed her eyes. She was tired. In her exhaustion, she had created this weird dream to make herself feel better.

"Wouldn't you do anything to be better?" Iyawa asked.

Dera opened her eyes. "Yes, I've tried, when I'm awake, when I'm dreaming. Still I'm one of the lowest performers."

"So now, let me help you," Iyawa pleaded.

"I'm definitely losing it." Dera shook her head. "What can I do differently that I haven't already tried? I've done all the exercises here, only better. No matter how well I do in my dreams, I wake the same, not stronger. Training with myself won't change anything."

"There's something in the genes that helps our bodies decide how much muscle to make. It holds back the body from making more muscle. If this inhibitor is released, then your muscles can grow."

"Okay, that makes some sense, but how can I change my body from here?" Dera gestured at the room.

"We can do it—together." Iyawa held Dera's hand. "Your body and mind can make any adjustment needed with my guidance. The mind can control every part of the body, even down to the smallest parts."

Dera looked at the two hands—exactly the same hands, her hands.

"How?"

"Go to sleep. I will teach your body how to change. You will wake stronger and get stronger each day."

Dera shrugged. "I give up. I'm tired anyway. Sleeping in a dream. I've done that before." She closed her eyes and surrendered to the exhaustion.

DERA JERKED awake in her bunk bed.

Uto leaned over from the top bunk. "That's the quietest you've slept in days."

Dera laughed. "I had the craziest dream."

Uto jumped to the floor. "What was it about?"

"You wouldn't believe me if I told you."

"Hmmm, I don't know. I've had some strange dreams in my life." Uto stuffed her mohawk into her night headscarf. "I'm going to shower. We can do dueling weird dream stories over breakfast."

Dera sat up. At least she felt more rested than she had done in a while, and hungry. Whatever her mind did to create the dream wasn't all bad. At breakfast Dera ate almost twice what she usually did, then she rushed to the practice room to get there on time.

Over the next week Dera's performance in all areas began to get better. Each day she could run a little longer, jump higher, spar with the short sword and spear faster. Her dreams at night were of practicing with her blurred self but giving herself corrections.

The corrections stayed in her body and mind memory when she was awake.

The second week her teachers began to notice and moved her into a more competitive group. The fear she would end up leaving in disgrace dissipated as Dera began to excel.

After breakfast of the third week, Dera and Uto were walking to the practice room. Uto playfully punched Dera in the arm. "Your muscles are really showing. I guess the extra food you're eating is turning right into muscle."

Dera laughed and punched Uto back, knocking her off balance. She quickly grabbed Uto so she wouldn't fall. "Oh, I'm sorry. I didn't mean to hit you so hard."

Uto rubbed her arm. "Uh, that's okay. I guess you don't know how strong you're getting. What's your secret?"

Dera shrugged, deciding the dream explanation was too ridiculous to repeat. "I don't know. I guess I'm catching up with all the exercising I've been doing in my dreams."

Once they entered the practice room, Okoye assigned Dera to run track. She ran one lap at an easy pace to warm up. Her legs and arms pumped effortlessly, as if she wasn't running at all. On Dera's fifth time around she wasn't tired or out of breath, it was like flying in the air. She felt like she could run all day without stopping. Wondering how fast she could go, Dera moved to the inside lane reserved for the fastest runners and picked up her pace until she was going around them, lapping them. A couple others picked up their speed to try to catch her but no one did.

Dera settled into an easy pace, feeling she could run faster if she wanted but there were others on the track.

"Dera!" Okoye yelled from the center of the room.

Dera started slowing down and moved to the outside lane until she was jogging. When she stepped off the track, she couldn't believe how energized she felt. Not out of breath, not tired. She had never experienced anything like it in her life. Others were staring at her, including Uto, who walked over with a container of water.

"What in the world was in your breakfast this morning?" Uto handed her the water.

"Nothing unusual." She gulped the water down.

"Dera," Okoye said again.

Dera gave the container back to Uto and ran over to Okoye.

"Let's walk. Even though you don't seem to need much more of a cooldown," Okoye said.

"I could use more," Dera answered. She felt like she could use more running.

They walked around the outskirts of the track.

"That was very impressive. You've never run so fast. I'm not sure anyone in your group has. It seems you've found a way to increase your performance. I've noticed a huge improvement in all your work."

"I thought for a while I wasn't going to be able to complete my training and become *Dora Milaje*, but now I see it's possible."

"Yes, more than possible. At this rate you could become one of the strongest we've trained."

Dera didn't know what to say. These words reminded her of what her blurred self had said in her dreams. "Thank you, Okoye. I just want to serve Wakanda the best I can."

"Yes, I know that has been a driving force for you, for all of you. I'm curious, what do you think has changed for you?"

Dera stopped looking ahead and turned to Okoye. "I-I think my work in my dreams has finally started helping my body when I'm awake."

"Nothing else?"

"I haven't taken anything, if that's what you're asking." Dera glared at Okoye.

"Hmmmm, I believe you."

They stopped in front of the short sword corner. "Let's see how your dreams have helped your sparring." Okoye pulled out her sword.

This reminded her of her first day at Upanga, but she wasn't that same girl anymore. Dera pulled out her sword and lunged at Okoye, who stepped to the right and swiped the flat part of her blade at Dera's legs. This should have made Dera flip on her back onto the ground, but instead she somersaulted and landed on her feet, twirled to face Okoye in a lower stance, and faked a right lunge.

Okoye saw the fake and jumped over Dera's swipe to the left. They kept at it for a couple more minutes with no one gaining a winning point, until Okoye said, "Enough."

Neither of them were out of breath. Okoye said, "Let's see your dual wielding." She nodded at two trainees watching. They each gave a sword to Okoye and Dera.

They both started in defensive stance, with one sword behind their backs. The sound of their blades dancing against each other drew attention from others. Again, after a short time with neither gaining control, Okoye stopped them.

"How do you feel, Dera?"

"I feel—good."

"Yes, I see." Okoye sheathed her sword, handed the other back to the trainee. "I would like you to go for a checkup."

"But I've never felt better."

"Yes. I want to make sure you keep feeling good."

Dera returned the sword to the other trainee. "You want me to go after training?"

"I want you to go now, Dera."

Dera put her sword away and walked out of the room without looking at anyone.

Okoye pressed the communication bead on her Kimoyo bracelet. An image of the main doctor at the medical center came up. "She's on her way."

THE DOCTOR finished in time for Dera to go to the dining room for lunch. She sat down with her food next to Uto. Some of the others looked sideways and then away.

"So what did they say?" Uto asked.

"Nothing. They did a lot of tests, took samples of everything, then told me I could go."

"Oh." Uto continued eating.

"You seem upset. Is it because I'm doing better than you?" Dera tapped her fork on the plate.

"No, Dera, it's not that." Uto held Dera's hand. "I want you to do well. If you're the best of all of us, that's great. I'm worried about you. That you're all right."

Dera stood up. "Why wouldn't I be all right? I've never felt— stronger." She shoved the chair aside and rushed to the training room.

When she entered, Okoye met her at the entrance. "I need to talk to you."

They went to the office behind the bleachers. Instead of sitting at the desk, Okoye sat in one of the chairs and motioned Dera to the other chair.

"We got the results of your tests."

"Yes?"

"There are no foreign materials in your body, no nanites, except the same things you came here with. However, when we compared your body stats now to when you arrived, they found a big difference. Something in the genes related to your muscles. They think this may have something to do with why you've been getting stronger suddenly."

"Do you think…" Dera said slowly. "Do you think a person can change things in their body with their mind, if they want it very badly?"

"You know about this gene?" Okoye asked, leaning forward.

"I know a little." Dera looked down at her arms. They were more muscular than even Uto's arms.

"If you're asking if someone could change their body with their thoughts alone, then yes. In general, we do all the time, usually through situations that cause stress and result in a lowering of our bodies' defenses, making us sick. But to make this particular change involves understanding on a level of scientific detail that few have. It would take years of training the brain, mind, body connection to access frequencies outside the normal."

"Would using Vibranium help increase this control?" Dera asked.

"That's an interesting question. Why do you ask?"

"We've been taught Vibranium can increase powers in humans."

"The use of Vibranium is strictly controlled because of its side effects. It can be very dangerous, depending on how it's used." Okoye stood up. "We don't know at this point why yours has changed. Since you are performing so well, I'm going to put you in the highest-level group. You can return to practice."

"Thank you, Okoye." Dera stood to leave. Glancing once at Okoye, she couldn't decipher the look on her teacher's face, but it was disturbing.

THAT NIGHT Dera dreamed, as usual, of being in the practice room. Iyawa, the blurred girl, appeared within seconds, carrying a spear. Dera had gotten used to her dream self being there.

"Today was more excitement than I'm used to," Dera said, walking up to Iyawa.

"I hope exciting because you're doing so well in your workout." Iyawa twirled the long throwing spear in the air.

Dera cocked her head to the left. Why would her copy not know what happened today? "There was more than that."

Iyawa tossed the spear to Dera, who caught it easily. Another spear appeared in Iyawa's hand. "Tell me."

"You don't know?"

Iyawa slammed the foot of the spear into the ground. "I told you I'm not you, not your imagination. After all this time, still you don't believe me."

Dera stepped back.

"What happened today?" Iyawa asked.

Playing along, Dera said, "Okoye sent me to medical for a checkup. She wanted to make sure my increase in performance was natural."

390   "Sounds like something she would do."

"How would you know?"

"Like I explained, my reality is a copy of yours, we have our own Okoye also. Had. She died from her mutations. Like so many of us, especially the *Dora Milaje*. We used the Vibranium in everything, our weapons, shields, until it was too late."

"What did the tests show?"

"Nothing introduced from the outside to my body, but they found that the muscle inhibitor is different. They don't know why."

"Did you tell them about your dreams, about me?"

Dera shook her head. "Why would I tell them about you? I thought you were just my imagination, but now—"

"Now you're starting to believe me?"

Dera nodded slowly.

"Good, because we need your help."

Dera tightened her grip on the spear. "How can I help you?"

"Our King is dying, Dera. We've done everything we can to help him, but nothing is working. We need you to get a sample of your King's DNA, so we can use it to try to correct our King's damaged genetic code."

Dera went into attack stance with both hands on the long spear. "Now I know either I've lost my mind or you really aren't me. I would never even think of something like this, something that could put our King in danger."

Iyawa walked into the blade of the spear. "How can taking a little DNA put your King in danger?"

Dera felt no resistance as the girl walked up to her, the spear passing through her chest.

"Do you really think you can hurt me here?" She waved her hands.

Dera let go of the spear and it disappeared. "I-I don't trust you, whoever—whatever you are."

"Then trust yourself. I told you my name is Iyawa, but it's not. I used that name because the truth would be much harder for you to accept, until now."

"What do you mean?"

Iyawa's face and body morphed until she looked like a mutated version of Dera with four arms—two normal, two shrunken—missing fingers, and legs made of a metal material.

"No—"

"Yes," Iyawa said, "I'm you in my reality. How else could I know exactly how to shift our DNA? My enhanced abilities allow me to communicate with you from my universe when you sleep. There's no one else who has this ability."

"No," Dera said, shaking her head. "That's impossible. No matter what universe I come from, I would never do anything to put Wakanda or the King in danger."

"Like you, I would give our life for Wakanda," Iyawa said. "That is exactly what I'm trying to do. To save Wakanda, my Wakanda."

"But-but you're asking me to help you use our King. I can't. I won't."

"No, I'm not asking you to put your King in danger. There is only one King. For all the infinite realities, we are all connected. We are one. Our King is dying. Our King is your King. We can connect the two of them and they will both live."

Dera shook her head. She squeezed her eyes closed, willing herself to wake. The last thing she heard before waking was her own voice, Iyawa's voice, whispering: "What danger there is, you carry in your genes back to your universe. You can't escape me. You have to sleep eventually."

Dera sat up abruptly. "No—no!"

Uto leaned over the top bunk. "Are you all right? Bad dream?"

"Yes," Dera whispered.

"Well, there's still time to get more sleep, Dera." Uto flopped back on her bed.

Dera shook her head. "There's no time for sleep."

She got out of bed, put her slippers on, and rushed out of the dorm room. Running up the stairs to the sixth floor, she tapped on Okoye's apartment door until she opened it.

"Please, I have to talk to you."

"Can't this wait until the morning?"

"No—no, either I'm losing my mind, or the King may be in danger."

Okoye opened the door and let Dera in.

They sat on the couch and Dera told Okoye everything. Okoye let her talk without interrupting.

"Whether I'm going crazy or this is real, I think I've become a danger to Wakanda. I would throw myself off our highest building, but I don't know what Iyawa meant that I carry danger in my genes. I'm afraid she did something to me that even my death wouldn't stop." Dera covered her face with her hands.

Okoye gently removed Dera's hands from her face and held them. "I don't believe you're going crazy. Wait here."

Okoye went to the bedroom. Dera could hear her talking, no doubt on her Kimoyo communication bead. She came out and said, "Someone from our advanced research team is coming to talk to you."

Within minutes there was a knock at the door. Okoye opened the door to an older woman in a purple jumpsuit.

"This is advanced researcher Zira. Dera, please tell her everything you just told me," Okoye said.

Zira sat next to Dera. "Do you mind if I put my hand on your arm? It helps me feel the truth of what you say."

"Okay." Dera looked perplexed.

When she was done explaining everything again, Zira nodded at Okoye then said, "Dera, you must go back to sleep and find out more about why this other you said you were a danger to Wakanda."

"You think she's real? I'm not crazy?"

"Sometimes what seems crazy is explained with the unexplainable. What you have said makes sense out of the changes in your body and fits some emerging research we've been doing on parallel universes. We know raw Vibranium radiation can cause mutations.

"Whatever this version of you said, there's more to their plan than they shared. It's possible more was done to your genes than suppression of NCoR1, so your muscles could increase."

"Suppression of what?" Dera asked.

"It's the inhibitor we found changed in you," Okoye said.

"You said she doesn't know what goes on when you're awake?" Zira asked.

Dera shook her head.

"Good, then go back to sleep. See if you can find out what else she did to you, but say nothing about talking to us." Zira handed a Kimoyo bracelet to Dera with two beads on it.

Dera recognized one bead as a communications bead. She slipped the bracelet on. "What is this one for?" She pointed to the odd bead.

"To track your bio-signs."

Dera looked at Okoye. "Do you want me to go back to the dorms? I don't know if I can sleep now. I'm—"

"Afraid?" Okoye asked.

Dera looked down.

Okoye sat next to her, lifted her head. "Not everything we do to protect the King is in a battle. You can do this, Dera. For Wakanda."

Dera took a deep breath and stood up. "For Wakanda."

Zira said, "It would be better if we go to my lab. We can give you a very light relaxer and monitor your sleep to see when you're dreaming, and any other changes in your body."

The three of them went to the lab, which was empty. Dera lay down in a special pod, took a light sedation, and went to sleep.

DERA WAS in the training room alone. "Iyawa! Iyawa!" A blink later the blurred-face version of Dera stood in front of her.

"What did you mean, I am a danger to Wakanda?"

"Thought that might get your attention. Glad you're finally believing this is real."

"I don't know how much of this is real but I know you aren't my imagination."

"Good." Iyawa walked closer to Dera.

"What did you do to make me a danger?' Dera asked louder.

"I programmed a virus in your genes." She shrugged. "It's dormant now but can be activated by me. We learned much about how the human genome works while trying to save ourselves, to save Wakanda, more than scientists in your reality know. It's a very lethal virus, spreads quickly, lies seemingly inactive for a few days—to give it more time to spread."

Dera stumbled backward. "You would destroy us to save your dying Wakanda."

"We can't just sit and wait to die out." Iyawa raised her voice. "We don't want either Wakanda to be destroyed. We want both to live."

Dera shook her head and slumped to the ground. "I don't have any access to the King as a trainee. I've only seen him from in a crowd since I've been here. How can I get this DNA to you?"

"You don't have to be near the King. Find something he has worn or touched, like a container or hair shed from his head. If you can't take something he's touched, then rub it on your hand or arm, to transfer his DNA to your skin."

"I don't understand how you'll get it to your universe."

"Don't worry about that, just do it." Iyawa caressed Dera's head. "I know it's hard to trust me. But trust yourself. Even in another universe, your commitment to Wakanda is complete."

Dera looked up. "How do I know you aren't planning to have your King do the same thing to our King as you've done to me?"

"Because I'm the only one who—" Iyawa stopped and tilted her head to the left. "Did you tell someone about us, and now you're trying to get more information out of me?"

Dera scooted away from her. "No! Who would believe me anyway? I would rather die than be part of something like this."

Iyawa was suddenly next to her, on the floor. She poked Dera's shoulder with her finger. "You should take very good care of your body. Don't think dying would protect Wakanda, it would just release the virus sooner. The only one who can dissipate the virus is me. Who did you tell?"

"No one!" Dera yelled.

Iyawa grabbed Dera's right wrist. "I don't believe you. I didn't want to do this the hard way, but you have left me with no choice." She grabbed Dera's other wrist.

"What are you doing?"

"If you won't do what is needed, then I will have to do it myself."

Burning pain entered Dera through her wrists. She screamed, tried to pull away, tried to imagine being somewhere else in the dream, but couldn't. The pain entered her veins and began to creep through her hands.

Through the pain, Dera saw what looked like Iyawa's hands melding into her wrists. She had to wake up but couldn't. Dera pulled her hands up into the air, throwing Iyawa off balance. Dera pulled away with everything in her, feeling like she was ripping her wrists open, and fell backward away from Iyawa. She envisioned herself across the room holding two short swords.

"What are you thinking?" Iyawa walked toward her, short swords appeared in her hands. "You can stop me here, by fighting me?" She laughed and threw the swords into the air, catching them easily as they twirled down, assumed an attack stance, then ran at Dera.

They fought for what seemed like hours. Neither got tired, neither won or lost. When Dera knocked one of the swords from Iyawa's hands, all the swords disappeared and Dera couldn't make hers come back. They began fighting hand-to-hand, kicking, striking and whirling faster and faster.

Until Iyawa yelled, "Enough!" Putting Dera in a twister lock, the burning pain began again, flowing into Dera's spine, thighs, shoulders at the same time. Dera screamed as Iyawa merged into her body, until she had no voice, no body, no pain.

Where am I?

"So, you're still here? Wasn't sure any part of you would survive. You'll get to see how a true *Dora Milaje* protects Wakanda."

A true Dora Milaje *wouldn't put the King or Wakanda in danger, no matter what reality they are from.*

396   "Let's wake up and see."

Iyawa woke in a lab with two women standing over her. She recognized Okoye immediately, but the other woman was only vaguely familiar.

"How do you feel?" Okoye asked.

She tried to lift her head but couldn't move her body. "I'm fine, except I can't move."

"Your bio-signs are good, although there were spikes, like you were having a nightmare. Did the Other come in your dreams as before?"

"Yes," Iyawa said slowly. "Why can't I move?"

The other woman put her hands on either side of Iyawa's face. "We gave you a deep body block. For your own safety, until we were sure how your meeting went."

Suddenly Iyawa recognized the woman. She tried to shake her head. "You're Zira. A mutant."

"Yes, Dera, but how did you know I'm a mutant?"

"I—I was guessing."

Zira closed her eyes. *Dera, are you there?*

Yes, she took over my body, she's here too. She put a virus in me that can kill everyone, which she can activate. I think they want to transfer their King to ours using DNA to link them, like she did with me.

We were afraid of something like that happening. I was called in because I can sense and communicate directly with others' minds. Stay calm, Dera.

Zira looked up at Okoye. "They are both here."

"Is Dera safe?"

"Yes, but Iyawa is controlling her body."

"So she did tell you everything," Iyawa said with resignation.

"Yes, we know you adjusted her NCoR1, but what of this virus?" Zira asked.

"There's no virus. I told her that to force her to help us, but when I realized she could have told someone else, this was our last thing to try."

"How can we know she's telling the truth?" Okoye asked.

"I would know if she's lying. She's not."

Okoye came into Iyawa's line of sight. "You must return to your universe and release Dera."

Iyawa closed her eyes before answering. "There's no point in returning. The body I left behind will only live a few more days." She opened her eyes. "We weren't sure Dera would survive the merging, but she did."

"And this one-way trip is what you had planned for our King?" Okoye asked angrily. "If our Dera wasn't living in this body, I would strangle you with my own hands."

"I'm the only one with the ability to cross over," Iyawa said. "We only wanted the King's DNA to see if we could heal our King and give our people hope. Our scientists are working day and night to find a way to help those who aren't as sick. I've failed. I will return control back over to Dera."

Iyawa closed her eyes.

Dera found herself surfacing from the place of no body. She opened her eyes. Tears filled them.

Zira looked at Okoye. "Our Dera is back."

"For good?" Okoye asked.

Zira nodded, giving Dera an injection to reverse the paralyzing effect of the body block.

"The other is locked deep inside me," Dera said.

Dera looked at Zira. "I felt Iyawa's Wakanda, when she released me. The people are suffering and have given up. Is there anything we can do to help their King?"

Zira sighed. "I also felt the sorrow of that Wakanda when in contact with Iyawa. The question of interfering with another reality is something we three can't answer. It would have to be discussed in a meeting of our scientists, the elders, and the King."

Dera sat up slowly. "Maybe we were meant to help. As wrong as my other self was to do this to me, what is done is in the past. Now both our realities are changed, maybe there's no right or wrong going forward, only futures that grow from here."

398   Okoye helped Dera stand up. "Sounds like it's not only the

muscles of your body that have gotten stronger. That's advanced thinking."

"And not wrong," Zira said. "I'll contact everyone needed to arrange a meeting today."

Dera yawned. "I think I need some sleep. Real sleep, without sharing dreams."

Okoye frowned. "Will you be safe while she's still with you?"

Zira held Dera's hand and said, "Iyawa has no power from where she's locked inside Dera."

"I am strong enough to stay in control, even while asleep," Dera said. "Iyawa waits with real hope for the first time."

BON TEMPS

HARLAN JAMES

SHURI WANTED to scream and scratch T'Challa's eyes out.

But the look on her mother's face… combined with the fact that it would be treason to attack that emotionless, smug, overbearing, and oh-so-confident-in-every-decision-he-made brother of hers, made the crown princess clench her fists so hard she was sure her nails were drawing blood from her palms.

She swallowed hard and narrowed her eyes at T'Challa, who stared back at her wearing that damnable neutral expression that she hated. She took a deep breath, gritted her teeth, and spat out her response, trying—and failing—to hide her emotions.

"May I ask, o' mighty King, *why* I can't go to Ibiza for my conference? I go every year, and each year I bring back vital intelligence about the ruling families of Europe and America. Intelligence, I might point out, that would be of value as Wakanda strides more forcefully into the outside world, as you commanded."

T'Challa looked almost amused as he reclined back, eating grapes during this rare quiet moment in the throne room.

His always-present *Dora Milaje* had cleared the royal court, until only they and the royal family remained. T'Challa's royal attire was relatively casual, a green turtleneck with a black silk suit and loafers, a dark purple scarf drawn tightly about his shoulders and waist. Shuri was dressed casually as well, with just a T-shirt and jeans, and her favorite black Chuck Taylor sneakers.

As usual, the Queen Mother's presence ruined everything. Ramonda, just like always, looked every inch a queen in one of her flowing Kente cloth dresses. She exuded restraint and confident grace, her long gray hair flowing down her shoulders. Shuri sighed as she watched her mother out of the corner of her eye, and felt all of her usual inadequacies.

The Queen Mother, of course, never believed in Casual Friday. Nor had she agreed when T'Challa allowed Shuri to go with her friends to Spain in previous years. After last year's fiasco, however, instead of confronting her daughter, she'd poisoned the much more easily swayed T'Challa, and left the decision to the one person she felt Shuri wouldn't defy.

Exactly like T'Challa was about to do. He shifted on his throne, looked down at her, and popped another grape into his mouth. Bast, she hated when he looked at her like she was still some precocious little girl-cub, instead of the crown princess and next in line for the throne of Bashenga.

"Intelligence, you say?" Ramonda commented. "Last year, you brought us the personal cell numbers of Harry and Meghan." She stood off to T'Challa's side, in her usual spot. "And if I remember correctly, there was an incident with Idris Elba that we had to have smoothed out."

"That—" Shuri pulled her shoulders back and stuck her chin out, refusing to meet her mother's eyes, keeping her gaze directly on T'Challa. "—was not my fault, brother."

"It's never your fault, is it?" Her mother sighed. "When are you going to grow up, girl? You are a princess, for Bast's sake."

T'Challa just stared with that piercing gaze of his, the one he used when Shuri felt he was trying to judge her soul to see if she was worthy of her crown and position.

"Regardless of past years, you may not go, little sister," T'Challa said at last, using a voice she had come to recognize. "It is a waste of your time... and ours."

That was the final straw. *Decorum be damned*, she thought.

"You may sit on our father's throne, brother," Shuri hissed, "but that doesn't make you *my* father! You can lounge there and preen, but don't forget that I know you're an arrogant, emotionless... *emnweni*, pretending to be a king!"

"Shuri!" Ramonda said, her voice rising. "Apologize to your king *right now*!"

"I will not, Mother! I do not ask for much from my king, but I *do* ask that my itinerary be mine alone, outside my royal duties." She glared at the nonplussed T'Challa, who continued eating grapes.

"You asked me, brother, to tone down my extracurricular activities and concentrate on my royal duties," she continued. "I have done as you've asked. You asked me to increase my training regimen with Zuri, and I have. You've asked me to mentor at the Science Academy, and I have—even taking on a professorship and teaching advanced seminars. I've done everything you've asked of me, so I don't understand why you're all of sudden acting like you don't trust me."

T'Challa shifted on his throne again.

"I do trust you, sister," he said calmly. "That is why I have made my decision, despite your current breach of etiquette."

"But T'Challa..." their mother started hesitantly.

"My decision is final, Mother." T'Challa looked calmly at his mother, who shrank back almost imperceptibly at his unspoken communication. Shuri had no idea what they were talking about, but couldn't stop her temper from flaring again.

"Haven't I warned you two about planning my life without me?" She'd already had a roaring blowout with them over dinner, not that long ago, about their intention to send her to a meeting of African royalty in Nigeria. It just *happened* to be scheduled for the same time as another of her "can't miss" events, her annual safari getaway with some friends from T'Challa's court. The Nigerian gathering was well known as a matchmaking event for unwed royalty. She wouldn't be caught dead with the spawn of some of those jacked-up dictators who attended, and had refused to attend, then stomped out.

T'Challa hadn't stopped her then. This time he was couching his demands as a command from her king, putting her in an untenable situation.

"There is something I need you to do for me, Shuri." T'Challa raised himself smoothly from his throne and walked down the few steps to stand in front of her, placing one hand on her shoulder. Abruptly, Shuri realized that T'Challa hadn't physically touched her in months. They'd been so close before he became king.

What had happened?

"There is a mission that I need for you to take on," T'Challa whispered to her. "I have some experience in this area, but this may be the one time where… you're the best choice for this. It should be an easy task, but just in case, keep your wits about you and keep your hands on the prize. You never know what plans others might have." Looking up at his throne, he nodded toward a young, oddly pale *Dora Milaje* guard on the left, who walked out of the throne room, then quickly returned to hand Shuri a silk-covered lockbox.

"Inside that box is one of our nation's greatest treasures. It is not dangerous, but it is valuable to me and possibly to others." T'Challa spoke loudly as he walked back up to his throne and sat on the edge. "I entrust the delivery of it to you, Shuri, my beloved sister. It must make it to its destination, no matter what."

Shuri turned the box over in her hands, easily hefting its slight weight. She turned questioning eyes toward her brother.

"Just in case there is any trouble, I am sending Bolanle Zidona along with you," T'Challa continued, indicating the light-skinned, slim-built *Dora Milaje* still standing at attention. "There will be Hatut Zeraze who can find you if necessary, but Zidona will serve as your close-quarters support for this mission."

The diminutive Bolanle didn't look a day over sixteen.

"Her spear is bigger than she is!" Shuri protested, prompting a glare from the insulted *Dora*, whose cheeks turned a deep red. "Wherever you are sending me, I don't need any of your precious bodyguards with me, T'Challa. I can take care of myself. If it's dangerous, I'll call for some of the local War Dogs."

"Oh, really?" her mother said, hands on her hips. "As with the men you tricked in a rubber dinghy, and left abandoned in the middle of the Mediterranean on your last debauched expedition?"

"Or," T'Challa added, "like the ones you abandoned at the gathering in Mykonos, after ducking into a bathroom complaining of 'women's problems'—which coincidentally seemed to vanish a few hours later, according to the paparazzi photos that appeared the next day."

"Or," her mother continued, "the War Dogs you ousted by ordering them to drink with you in Gstaad, abandoning them in a hotel bar crying in their beer?"

Shuri looked down at her shoes, scuffing the floor with the rubber soles.

Her mother glared at her. "The point is, you've taken advantage of male bodyguards in the past, so this time, there will be someone who goes where you go, and has no reason to give you one iota of privacy."

"And who—" Ramonda peered at T'Challa, who nodded in confirmation. "—has been ordered to not let you leave her sight in that wicked city."

That caught Shuri's attention.

"What wicked city?" She looked up. "I've been around the world, Mother, and handled myself just fine."

T'Challa tilted his head. "You've never been to Mardi Gras."

SHURI REFUSED to talk to Bolanle the entire journey, staring out the window of their private jet as the baby-faced warrior typed on her laptop. Just as Ramonda had ordered, the *Dora Milaje* shadowed Shuri's every move, from the point the crown princess left the throne room to when they entered the limousine in front of the palace to the second they stepped on the jet.

If Shuri went to the restroom, a cheerful Bolanle was right there, either humming to herself outside the stall or, the one time Shuri found a single-stall bathroom at the airfield, placing a Vibranium net over the window to make certain Shuri wouldn't have a head start if she tried to escape.

As they walked out to the royal jet, Bolanle handed her a thermos of what smelled like her favorite flavor of Jamaican coffee from a local coffeehouse. Shuri stared at the peace offering for a second, then took it with a nod.

That doesn't mean I have to talk to her, Shuri convinced herself. *But this is really good coffee*, she thought as she drank it down gratefully before nodding thanks to the young warrior.

As they went through Customs at a private airport in Mississippi, they were met by a relatively nondescript car. A short time later, Shuri balanced the precious box in her lap as their driver maneuvered them through the heavy traffic into downtown New Orleans, then to the private luxury villa Bolanle had rented for them for the weekend.

The pixie-like *Dora Milaje* effortlessly lugged their bags into the massive multi-bedroom villa but dropped her own in the room next to Shuri's master suite. The two women proceeded to wash up from the trip before meeting again on the wooden patio, which surrounded a heated pool and waterfall.

Drying her hair with a fluffy white towel, Shuri plopped down on a lounge chair. Bolanle followed a few seconds later, a matching towel wrapped around her head, and finally broke the silence.

"Your Highness, are you ready for your debrief?" Her tiny high voice seemed the perfect fit for her delicate features, which she completed with a short American-style wig of braids selected for this mission.

Shuri sipped on a sparkling water. Her friends were probably in Ibiza by now, sipping champagne in one of the largest hot tubs to be found—especially that cute Winthrop. Instead of joining them, she was here in New Orleans with a pint-size *Dora Milaje*, and the only comfort was that she had already been invited to a party.

On the downside, it was being thrown by one of the older black super heroes in America. T'Challa really had it in for her.

"No," Shuri said, and she pouted. "Here I am, at the greatest party Americans have come up with in their short history, and instead of going out to enjoy myself, I'm stuck playing delivery woman with you and a box."

Bolanle didn't respond.

After an uncomfortable silence, Shuri peered over the top of her sunglasses.

"Well, we might as well get to know each other," she offered glumly. "It seems as if we're going to be close together for the next few days. If I know my brother, he wouldn't have sent you with me if you weren't good at trailing people.

"And why?" Shuri threw her hands up in the air. "They seem convinced that I'm going to get into some kind of trouble. No one ever considers that I might know *exactly* what I'm doing.

"Instead," she huffed, "everyone expects me to be the trouble-maker, the one who embarrasses the royal family. Wakandans think they know everything about me, but put them—*anybody*—in the same spotlight… put all of their business out in the street, and see how they look."

She crossed her arms and leaned back sulkily into the chair.

"Well, we're going to start on a different foot, Bolanle," she continued. "You're going to tell me something personal about yourself, and we're going to find an equal footing. It's not fair that you know everything about me, and I know nothing about you. Before we go any further, I want to know who you are, and why you're here."

Bolanle grinned.

"A very nice speech, Your Highness," she said, emphasizing Shuri's title. "No matter what I say, one person here will always be a little more 'equal' than the other. Only one of us will be able to give orders, instead of making requests."

Shuri smiled at the girl's impudence.

"I do not mind telling you, because there is not much to tell." Bolanle looked down at the ground, scraping her sandals back and forth across the marble floor. "This is my first overseas assignment as a *Dora Milaje*, so I don't know why General Okoye gave me this assignment. I don't have any specialized knowledge that will make delivering this package any easier. I've just been given the basics of *Dora Milaje* training and the advanced urban infiltration training…"

She trailed off as she noticed Shuri's look and sighed.

"That is not what you want to hear. It's not what anyone wants to know about. You want to know about this." She pointed to her hand, turning her pale hands over and back. "How does a daughter of Wakanda end up with almost white skin, green eyes, and what would be long straight black hair if I grew it out?

"The story my family tells is that a white hunter wandered into Wakanda a couple of generations ago and loved it so much he decided to stay," she continued. "He did so with the blessing of the king, or so they say. That is probably a polite lie about what happened, but none of us have ever been eager to understand what happened that far back." She looked up at the blue sky and the dappled clouds passing by.

"How… how could that have happened?" Shuri sat up and stared at her companion. "Wakanda was never conquered by colonizers."

Bolanle looked over and rolled her eyes. "Really, Princess? Is that what they taught you? And you accepted it entirely?"

Shuri dropped her gaze. "I'm more about the hard sciences than history, to tell the truth."

"Well, think it through, Your Highness. There is one Black Panther, and a whole lot of Wakanda. You don't think anyone has made it an inch inside Wakandan borders… ever?" Bolanle stared. "Not to be impolite, but consider how many times a Black Panther in the past stopped Wakandan invaders. It's always at the border, right? Has any king ever lived on the border? No, it always takes time before the king arrives from the capital. Do you think they treated the Border Tribe villagers kindly during that time? That they didn't take any… advantage of the women they encountered?"

Shuri sat silently, as Bolanle looked down at her hands.

"The truth is, it's a recessive gene that comes out in my

mother's line every once in a while. I have dark-skinned brothers and cousins who look just like you, Your Highness, but for some reason, I got stuck with a freckled complexion, elfin features, and long straight hair."

Bolanle shrugged. "It just meant I had to work a little bit harder, deal with a few more jokes, and smack around a couple of jerks before I graduated. Then, when they came around looking for someone to represent our tribe as one of the king's concomitants, well, I was just as good as anyone else." She looked at Shuri with a challenge in her expression. "You know something about having to prove yourself, do you not?"

"That's about all I seem to be doing these days," Shuri muttered quietly. She sat up and looked at Bolanle. It had been so long since she'd had someone she could just... talk to. Court politics meant she couldn't confide in anyone around the palace, and talking to the Queen Mother, well, that was a recipe for having her feelings hurt.

And T'Challa? He was the king... and the problem.

"Sometimes, I feel like I'm wasting my life," she said finally. "I bounce around, one month the genius inventor saving Wakanda with her brains, and the next month I'm the national embarrassment for being seen in a hot tub with Idris Elba."

Bolanle raised an eyebrow. "You *will* tell me about that later."

Shuri laughed for a second before coming back down.

"It's just... T'Challa and I are so different. He's quiet, I'm loud." She ticked off on her fingers. "He's a wait-and-planner, I'm a jump-off-the-cliff kind of girl. He's basically a monk, and me, well, everyone's seen the paparazzi photos.

"He's muscular and I'm..." she waved her hands down her slim frame. "Our god even speaks to him, while she's never bothered to appear to me. I'm supposed to believe because my older brother tells me to, the same man who I played blocks with as a child. I'm a scientist, and I'm supposed to have faith simply because I'm told to by my brother and I'm a princess?

"And none of this matters, because he sits on the throne. He's the king, and I'm just a spare, in case something happens to the person in charge. That's my life, just waiting around to see if they need me." She sighed. "A life unextraordinary."

"Filled with dances, foreign junkets, the best education money can buy, and a fortune that rivals all the royal families in Europe put together," Bolanle noted sarcastically.

Ignoring her, Shuri looked over at the pool.

"I think about challenging T'Challa for the throne every Challenge Day." She watched a small fly struggle in the water, kicking its legs and flapping its wings. "He'd have to accept, you know. And I know we're different, but I can't help but think that one day, I'd take him. That would prove to my mother that I'm just as worthy as her sainted son."

Shuri looked over at Bolanle.

"Would you accept me as queen?"

Bolanle glanced down. "The *Dora Milaje* would accept anyone as the rightful ruler of Wakanda who is blessed by Bast to win a sanctioned battle for the throne," she said carefully.

Shuri shook her head. "No, I mean you, Bolanle Zidona, citizen of Wakanda. Knowing what you know, could I be your queen?"

Bolanle smiled wistfully.

"Ask me again, later, after we've done our duty. As for a fight between you and your brother… I mean, *Beloved*," she corrected quickly. "I'm not going to answer. Honestly, I don't know why I'm here, and frankly, Your Highness, I don't know why you're here. Anyone could have delivered that." Bolanle hitched herself up and gestured to the box sitting next to her. "Yet for some reason your brother wanted you here, and they sent me along with you. I suggest we make the best of it."

Shuri pulled the box up onto her lap and jiggled it slightly, hoping to hear a rattling that might identify it. "Do you know what's inside?"

"I do, Princess," Bolanle said with a challenge. "You didn't ask?"

"T'Challa and I weren't exactly on speaking terms when I left, Bolanle, if you didn't notice."

"I noticed that you were angry with him. He looked more amused than anything else." Bolanle cut off Shuri's retort. "Yes, yes, Princess. Let's just say you're right and move on. Your job is to deliver that box to Jericho Drumm at 11716 Dauphine Street, and place its contents in his hands before returning to Wakanda." Bolanle grinned. "My job is to make sure you do your job."

"Is there a time constraint for this," Shuri asked, "or do I just need to make sure that it gets there before I go home?" She opened the box and found a shimmering silvery necklace nestled in a foam seat. Picking it up, she placed it around her neck. At the center of the necklace was a Bast icon, a snarling panther's face.

"Well, it's Vibranium, Princess. It's not going to spoil or any such thing, but according to my brief, this batch has absorbed some energy it normally shouldn't, and Beloved wants an outside opinion."

"What kind of energy?" Shuri poked the necklace with one of her nails. Nothing happened.

"Magic, Your Highness. That's why we've been sent to Doctor Voodoo's Mardi Gras ball tomorrow night."

"Another ball?" Shuri sighed. "Yippie."

"I don't know, Your Highness. It sounds fun to me. A costumed Mardi Gras ball? A magic necklace? And one of the foremost practitioners of the mystical craft outside of Africa? Indeed, it sounds rather awesome."

Shuri sipped from her drink. "A normal Tuesday for me, Bolanle." Sitting up, she smiled. "There's nothing that says we have to sit around here tonight, though, is there?"

The young *Dora Milaje* shrugged. "I have to check in, but given the time difference, that won't take long. What did you have in mind, Princess?"

"What else?" Shuri clapped her hands. "Bourbon Street!"

BY THE time they'd made it down to the famous venue at the center of the French Quarter, the sun had set and the party had begun in earnest. Thumping music poured out from the bars, balconies, and street musicians, all competing with one another for the crowd's attention.

Bourbon Street was a solid mass of tourists and partygoers, some dressed in expensive costumes, others who threw on whatever they could find and called it a costume. Many wore regular street clothes, but they all had some kind of beverage in a plastic cup, and kept offering to share with Shuri, who politely declined. There were some interesting sights, though.

Shuri laughed as she circled one voluptuous white-wigged woman dressed as Ororo, yet with much less costume than her friend would ever be seen wearing in public, especially since she became leader of the X-Men. She spotted a couple of Black Panthers strolling through the streets, as well. It weirded her out a little bit. Her brother filled his costume with muscle, while the last Panther she saw was short, white, covered with foam muscles, and had a bit of a stomach hanging out the black tights. Still, she thought, the effect was… nice, especially the white eyes and the little ears.

Bolanle frowned at the imposter.

He caught Shuri looking. She gasped as the imposter chugged down a beer, blew her a kiss and gyrated his hips suggestively. T'Challa *never* moved like that.

Bolanle pushed her down the street before she could say anything rude to the man. It might have made her feel better to tell the fellow what she really thought, but Bolanle was insistent that there was plenty more for them to see.

White, black, Asians—everyone seemed to be joyous, amorous, and exuberant, with not a care in the world other than getting to the next bar or to the next drink. People danced and swayed, shaking their hips and waving their arms. They were in doorways, on balconies, wherever and whenever the mood struck them, and whether or not they could stay upright.

Without even realizing it, Shuri found herself dancing as a young black boy drummed a rhythmic beat on a large plastic bucket, while a small crowd gathered around his gratuity can on the sidewalk. She tossed a few dollars into the can and wandered on down the street, wide-eyed and amazed, Bolanle close behind.

A couple of blocks farther along, the crowd grew denser, with screaming, dancing, drinking women and men looking down from festooned second-story balconies onto a massive crush of people inching their way down a single block, all adorned in some kind of beads and looking for more. Men waved strands of them at young college-age women, some of whom bounced up and down yelling, "Me! Throw them to me!"

Shuri gawked at the bawdy signs carried by some of the American revelers; "Cougar Patrol" read one set, waved in the air by some drunken college boys. Bolanle frowned at another that said, "Beads for… Considerations."

People were getting a little too close for her taste, starting to bump Shuri as she tried to maneuver through and around the close-quartered crowd. Behind her, she could glimpse Bolanle pushing her way past some drunken fraternity types, trying to stay a step behind. So Shuri reached back, grabbed an arm, and pulled her close, locking elbows with the young warrior.

She was elbowed in the side, and began gagging at the smell of alcohol, wet trash, and urine. She pinched her nose and looked over at Bolanle.

"Does no one smell that?"

Bolanle just shrugged and gestured toward an open door.

"Perhaps we should duck inside?"

Just as she spoke, it seemed as if the whole street came to a standstill, with bodies locked up against one another trying—and failing—to move farther along. Shuri and Bolanle, not the tallest of women to begin with, couldn't see what had happened. Yet all of a sudden they couldn't move an inch, and they were surrounded by tall, sweaty, drunk Americans.

The crowd's attitude began to change, becoming desperate as more and more people tried to push their way into and out of the struggling standstill.

Someone ahead of her shouted, "Get your damned hand off my butt!"

Then the same person said, "Thanks, man. I don't know why his momma didn't teach him to keep his hands to himself."

There were shrieks and cheers as someone ahead of her apparently got a drink poured on them, and a scuffle broke out. Pressed up against Bolanle, Shuri tried to adjust her arms by raising them up above her head, but that only made it worse.

"I think we'd better get out..." she said, then she felt an offending hand wandering up her leg. With the tightness of the crowd, Shuri couldn't tell if the hand came from in front, from behind, or to her side. She shoved her body in the direction of the hand and glared, hoping to get it off and still stay upright in the throng.

A sickening *snap* cracked in the crowd, followed by another drunken cry of pain. All of a sudden, a man screamed.

"She broke my finger," a drunken voice howled.

"And I'll do worse to the next person who touches me or my... friend," Bolanle snarled loudly. "I can do this all night."

Behind her, Shuri could sense the crowd shifting and pushing them toward the outer edges. Bolanle grabbed her hand and dragged her toward a doorway. Shuri looked down to see the *Dora Milaje* warrior's hand locked in some stranger's, a young man who was using his massive body to run interference and push his way into a dark bar. Behind her, someone put his hands on her shoulder blades, urging her forward.

"Y'all okay?" A ruggedly handsome young man behind Shuri looked concerned as they stumbled into the bar, which was crowded but not the pure chaos of the scene outside. "Your friend there was about to start a riot, seemed like."

Ahead of her, Bolanle was twisting the other man's arm, forcing him onto one knee. Around the bar, patrons looked on amusedly as the tiny woman forced the much larger man's bulk down to the filthy floor.

"Hey, ow, ow, *ow*! That hurts, lady." The big man grimaced.

"Listen, you've got the wrong guy. I was trying to get y'all out of there."

Bolanle just narrowed her eyes, twisting his thick wrist even harder.

"I did not need your help," she said.

"Yes, you did… *ow*, dammit, that *hurts*. Jay, you gonna help me here?"

The young man circled Shuri and stepped toward Bolanle, hands up.

"Listen, friend, I promise you, my brother's a blockhead, cheats at spades, and still owes me five hundred dollars, but he'd never do something like that." Jay looked from Bolanle to Shuri. "We were trying to help. Really. Let Rick up, and we'll be on our way."

Bolanle glanced over at Shuri, who gave an almost imperceptible nod. The *Dora Milaje* warrior threw Rick's arm down to his side and stepped back to watch the bulky man shake his wrist back and forth, trying to get some circulation going again. The one called Jay reached out to grasp his brother's good arm and drag him erect.

Rick glared at Bolanle before turning around and grabbing an open seat at the bar, still shaking his right wrist.

"Let me look at it," Jay said calmly.

"I'm okay," Rick muttered.

Jay squeezed in near the bar, garnering a nasty look from the lady in the next seat. He grabbed Rick's wrist.

"Ow, man, I told you it's okay."

Ignoring him, the smaller man flexed the offending wrist back and forth, side to side, watching his brother's grimaces at each movement.

"Yeah, you'll be okay," he said finally, then he smiled. "Next time, let 'em go once you've saved 'em."

Rick grinned back. "But her hand felt good." Then he frowned as he looked back at the two women. "At first."

Shuri watched them as they bantered back and forth, and Jay asked a pretty young bartender for some ice. They both wore jeans, tennis shoes, and black American football jerseys. The younger one, Jay, tall and slim, had a blue-and-silver-trimmed one that proclaimed "Panthers," while the larger, more muscular one, Rick, wore one with "Saints" trimmed in gold.

Despite their different builds, she could see the familial resemblance—the same brown eyes, the same wispy beards, the same crooked smile. They both spoke with light Southern accents and mannerisms, though it seemed more pronounced in the older brother. There was also more mischief in the older one's eyes, a little more of the troublemaker spirit, while Jay seemed somewhat serious, polite and, frankly, more handsome.

The young man caught her appraisal, grinned, and waved her over. "Can my brother buy y'all a drink to make up for his foolishness, and the stupidity of that crowd out there? I don't want that to be your lasting impression of Southern hospitality."

"A drink?" Rick sputtered. "The chick almost rips my arm off, and now I'm supposed to buy her a drink?"

"First of all," Jay said patiently, "it wasn't this one—" He pointed at Shuri. "—it was that one." He gestured at Bolanle. "Second of all, you can take it out of what you owe me, so it's really me buying the drinks, not you.

"Third of all," he continued, "your mamma taught you to do good deeds for their own sake, not for reward, not for thanks, and even in the face of punishment."

"Bruh, enough of the lectures," Rick said. "I get them from Momma enough as it is." He turned back around toward the bar and raised his massive hand to hail the bartender. Looking over his shoulder, he asked, "Whatcha want?"

Shuri and Bolanle looked at each other. Bolanle nodded and squeezed up tighter to the bar.

"I'll take a mineral water, and she'll have the same."

"Will she?" Jay looked at Shuri, raising his eyebrows slightly. "Does she have a voice of her own?"

Shuri cleared her throat. "A mineral water will be fine."

"Ah, the beautiful one speaks," Jay proclaimed in a teasing voice, eliciting a surprised frown from the *Dora Milaje*. He turned.

"Bartender, three bottles of your most expensive water, on me!"

"Don't tempt me," Rick said. He chuckled as he took a swig from a cold beer.

Bolanle grinned as well, adopting the spirit of their teasing. Affecting a British accent, she curtseyed.

"Am I not beautiful as well, young master? Do I not deserve your favor?" she asked Jay as she accepted the glass bottle of water from his brother.

"Ah, my Lady." Jay jokingly bowed. "Your countenance is like the morning sun, and your eyes like the freshest dew, but they doth pale before thy companion, the morning star of the west, the evening star of my heart."

The four of them looked at one another... then burst out in laughter.

"Damn, bro," Rick said, tears running down his cheeks. "I know you were into medicine, but that theater streak? Didn't know you had that in you."

"I think I'm flattered," Shuri chuckled as Bolanle punched Jay's arm in protest. It seemed like a light tap, but Shuri wondered. Jay waggled his eyebrows at her.

"I got a million of 'em," he said proudly.

"Do any of them work?" Bolanle replied.

"I'll let you know later," Jay said confidently, peering at the now blushing Shuri. "Would you ladies like to join us for a real N'Awlins meal? I'm Jason, by the way." He reached over and took Shuri's hand in a gentle shake. "This big lug is my older brother Richard. And you..."

"I'm Sh—" Shuri started before Bolanle stepped forward and cut her off. "She's Shia, and I'm Tawny," she interjected.

Jason scratched his head. "Shee-ah? That's an interesting name. How do you spell that?"

"S-h-i, accent mark, a." Shuri caught on quickly and added a slight French accent. Americans, she had been told, couldn't tell a Nigerian from a Haitian when it came to voices. "It's means 'Gift from God' in my home country."

"Well, you certainly are," Jay said dreamily before a sharp elbow from Rick brought him up short. "Anyway, we know this great neighborhood restaurant that serves the best po' boys around."

"That is," Rick added as he glanced over at Bolanle, "if y'all are done breaking fingers for tonight."

She shrugged. "I'm done. How about you, Shia?"

"Only if you insist…" Shuri laughed. "…Tawny."

With the boys taking up flanking positions, the four of them headed out into the night and caught cabs to the Garden District. At a restaurant called Julie's, Rick and Jay treated them to jambalaya, shrimp, and oyster po' boys, and alligator gumbo. Then they returned to the French Quarter for late-night beignets from a place called Café Dumont.

As they ate, the two young men regaled Shuri and Bolanle with their antics in college, where Jay was pre-med, a theater buff, and a budding columnist at the campus newspaper, while Rick held down an engineering major topped off with chemistry minor. They expressed some surprise at that, but Rick shrugged.

"I may be big, but that doesn't make me dumb," he said.

"No, goofing around makes you dumb, bro," Jay said teasingly.

"Work hard, play hard, bro."

Bolanle and Shuri then began inventing stories of their own. First they claimed to be "almost in-laws," with Tawny the new fiancé to Shia's brother. Struggling not to laugh, they made up outrageous stories about misspent childhoods, first crushes, and wayward vacations to exotic locations which led them to become lifelong friends, now on their first trip to America and the South.

A couple of hours passed and they found themselves at an upscale bar in Uptown near Tulane University, where Rick swore he knew one of the bartenders. It turned out that she had dumped him a few months earlier, but the woman, Roxanne, was still willing to comp them a couple of drinks, wryly saying she had dated "the wrong brother."

"So, what do you do back home?" Jay looked over at Shuri as he handed her a drink while glancing over at Bolanle and Rick, who seemed to be getting along famously. Bolanle was showing the larger man the arm lock she used earlier. Shuri took a tiny sip and pursed her lips at the strong liquor.

"I am a scientist," she admitted, knowing how that normally went over in her flock of friends. Jay started to speak, but she quickly held her hand up to stop him. "I know, I know, not very exciting," she said. "I don't tell many people outside my family, but it's who I am."

Jay gave her a confused look. "Why would you want to hide that?" he said quietly. "Beauty and brains? That makes you the catch of the century, not someone who's going to end up an old maid at home with twenty-eleven cats."

Shuri eyed him suspiciously, not believing his reaction, but Jay calmly took a pull of his drink and leaned over to her.

"What is your main field of study?" he asked. "I'm training to be a doctor, but I'm focusing on laboratory research and immunology, rather than actual patient care. I'll do that when I'm old and tired." Then he paused and added, "How about you?"

"No one's ever really asked exactly what I do," Shuri said thoughtfully, scratching her chin. "I guess you could say that I'm mostly metallurgy and computer science." She brightened. "Lately I've been getting into African folklore and legends, and trying to discover—or more accurately *re*cover—some of the ancient knowledge that our ancestors possessed, to see if I can apply it to the more technological ways of today."

Jay nodded. "People forget that the Ancient Egyptians had aspirin, and used sutures to close wounds. If we could take ancient knowledge, and supplement it with our modern technology…"

"You get it!" Shuri said. "A melding of the old and the new, the ancient and the modern, all to make futures we can be proud of! In fact, I was just telling my brother T—"

Bolanle was there.

She slapped her hand over Shuri's mouth.

"We agreed not to talk about my fiancé this weekend, remember, Shia," she gritted through her teeth, as Rick grinned at

Jay. "We swore this would be a girls' trip, *right*?" Then she removed her hand.

"You are right, Tawny." Shuri looked embarrassed. "Forgive me, Jay. I did not mean to bring up familial arguments."

"No worries, beautiful," Rick jumped in before Jay could say a word. "We're imposing our wonderful familial relationship on you, so you can talk about your knuckleheaded brother all you want to, if you ask me."

"Yes indeed," Jay agreed. "Don't stop talking on our account, but—" He stood up. "—you can hold the thought until I get back from the little boy's room. Rick?"

"What?" Rick was still grinning at the two women. "Oh, sure, yeah, I need to go, too. Ladies, we'll be right back."

"I thought only ladies went to the bathroom in packs," Bolanle teased.

Rick shrugged. "Eh, it's just an excuse for my brother to discuss with me whether it's worth it to continue to squire you ladies around town, especially—"

"Come on, man." Jay slapped his brother across the back of the head, then he dragged him away.

"What?" Rick rubbed the back of his head as they walked off. Shuri and Bolanle looked at each other, and began laughing again.

"They're amusing!" Bolanle admitted. "And cute, especially the one who's stuck on you."

"He is rather… interesting, isn't he?" Shuri said noncommittally, but she couldn't keep the slight grin off her face. "And aren't you supposed to be guarding my every move?"

"You've shown me that you can handle yourself in situations like these. It seems as if we should deliver the box as quickly as possible, and you can see what develops in the couple of days before we head home. Besides…" Bolanle placed her hands beneath her chin, and looked at Shuri. "…all work and no play…"

"…keeps a beautiful lady alone at night."

The silky voice was male.

Shuri and Bolanle looked up. Standing next to their table,

flanked by two overbearingly obvious bodyguards, stood a slender, handsome, yet severe-featured man, smiling down at them. *As a lion would an antelope*, Shuri thought. His silk suit, ascot, and black spats signified wealth, as did the gaudy rings on his pale fingers. European royalty or gentry, perhaps, but his eyes bothered her. They were a hunter's eyes: steely blue and intense, matching his slicked-back brown hair and his at-the-ready stance.

This was a man trying to cloak himself in charm and civilization, Shuri thought to herself. A dangerous man.

"Excuse me?" Bolanle glared up at him. "This was a private conversation."

"Ah, but when one is given such a perfect opening line, one must take advantage," the man said, his accent giving Shuri and Bolanle a slight glimpse of Southern heritage. He took Shuri's hand and kissed it.

"I am Elijah DePortes, at your service," he said smoothly. "I apologize for eavesdropping on your conversation, but I could not help but overhear that you two lovely ladies will be in our fair city for only a short time. I would like to present you with the opportunity to see our fine city at its best, during the greatest party it has to offer."

"I think we'll do fine on our own," Bolanle said, pulling Shuri's hand back down to the table.

"I believe you would," Elijah's voice remained smooth despite Bolanle's hostility. "But there's just something about you ladies... I can't quite put my finger on it, but it intrigues me. May I?" He gestured to the table, but Shuri shook her head, fingering the Vibranium necklace.

"We are with someone," she said politely, "so we have to decline your gracious offer."

Elijah smiled with his mouth, but his eyes seemed to change, becoming narrower, with hints of red veins bulging on his pupils.

"I insist." He started to pull a chair out, when it was blocked by a muscular leg.

"I think the ladies told you they were with someone," Rick

said, his voice sounding deeper and meaner than before. "Move on, before things get out of hand." Standing at his side was Jay, who looked at her to see if they were okay.

Shuri nodded, and Jay visibly relaxed.

The bodyguards started forward and Elijah held up his hands to stop them.

"I was only offering my hospitality to a pair of visitors who seemed to be on their own." He took a step back to allow Rick and Jay to pass. Then he smiled again at Shuri.

"There's just something about you that… I can't place it, but it's going to bother me until I do," he mused. "If I may make a suggestion, ladies, there's a gathering—a sort of soirée—that I think you might enjoy. Something uniquely New Orleans. Please come as my guests, tomorrow night."

"Their schedules are already full." Jay looked murderous at the blatantly disrespectful invitation. "They don't need your… companionship, Foghorn."

"Ah, insults." Elijah looked amused. "The sign of an immature mind. Ladies, if you want to see the adult New Orleans, where the magic truly lies, you can join me at the mansion at 11716 Dauphine Street tomorrow after dark. I'll leave your names and descriptions at the door. I promise, it will be a night you will never forget." Elijah bowed to the table, then turned and began to walk away. "Oh, one last thing." He stopped and looked back. "Wear something pretty. I'm sure women of your… stature, can conjure up something during Mardi Gras."

He looked disdainfully at Rick and Jay, and walked off, his bodyguards at his heels. As soon as they were out of sight, all four exhaled.

"That was weird, even for New Orleans," Jay said.

"Aw, we could've taken them," Rick boasted.

Shuri and Bolanle looked at each other. "I don't know," Bolanle said skeptically. "Those bodyguards had some impressive gear."

Shuri glanced over at Bolanle, who shrugged.

"You want to hear something even weirder?" Shuri whispered

to their companions. "We already have an invitation to that ball."

Rick and Jay glanced at each other. "A party at a mansion on Dauphine Street?" Rick said. "You're on the guest list?"

"What? You don't rate?" Bolanle smiled, enjoying the looks on the brothers' faces.

"Not for that crowd," Jay said softly.

"Oh." Shuri reached across and took his hand. "We didn't mean anything by it, it's just that we have an obligation to go to that ball. If you had tuxedos…"

"Not my normal wardrobe for Mardi Gras," Jay said.

"And finding one for rent now?" Rick added. "Impossible."

Shuri held on to Jay's hand, its warmth invitingly comfortable. He gripped hers a little tighter.

"How about this?" she said. "How about you two meet us when we're done at the party, and we'll join you for another fun night. We'll bring a change of clothes, and go from there. Are you interested?"

Jay began to smile again. "That sounds wonderful. Right, Rick?"

"Ow! Dude, stop kicking me under the table," Rick grumbled. "Sure, I'll play third wheel and hang out with the soon-to-be married chick, instead of going out to find my own date."

"You assume I'll be there." Bolanle looked at Jay and Shuri. She put on a British accent. "Seeds of love blossoming on the savannah… I won't be able to stand this much longer."

"You're going to have to," Shuri smiled. "Because we have a date."

A RENTED black Suburban SUV, armored, slid past the historic mansions on Dauphine Street. Shuri had wanted a limo. "Why not show up in style?" she'd argued. "And who needs to worry about parking?" But Bolanle argued that they didn't have time to clear a limousine service, much less one that could provide an armored vehicle.

424

"What would I tell your handsome beau if I let you get

kidnapped?" she teased, looking over at Shuri as she navigated the rented SUV into a parking spot a couple of blocks from their destination.

Shuri grinned as she smoothed her black evening gown around her legs. It was one of her favorites, made of a soft, silky fabric, tight around her chest and waist but loose and flowing around her legs. Sleeveless, of course. In the palace, Zuri might thrust a spear at her from around any corner and call it "training." This had taught her to keep her arms and legs free of entanglements. The Vibranium necklace rested on her chest in prominent view.

Bolanle wore a similar dress, but in green. She had wanted them to deliver the silvery necklace in the box, but the princess successfully argued that no one knew what they were delivering.

"And," Bolanle had been forced to agree, "it does look good on you."

Shuri touched up her makeup one last time in the sun visor's mirror before getting out of the SUV. "Hey, Bolanle, should I worry about wearing this necklace out in public, if it's so important?"

Bolanle shrugged. "No one else is supposed to know that we're bringing it here to Dr. Drumm," she said. "Beloved said it wasn't dangerous, and it goes perfectly with that dress. And what? Did you plan to make your grand entrance into the ball carrying a box? Or did you plan to make me carry it?"

Shuri laughed. "I guess not. And T'Challa did tell me to keep my hands on it."

The two women gathered small clutch purses and walked down the tree-lined streets of the Garden District toward the home of Dr. Drumm, their host for the evening. Shuri walked purposefully in the dwindling daylight, her heels clicking on the sidewalk. Thoroughly back on duty, Bolanle scanned the few people on the sidewalk, alert for any peril that may arise to endanger the princess.

Shuri slowed down as she neared her destination.

"Is that it?" she gasped.

Bolanle frowned as she halted before the gate.

"You mean that dump?"

Shuri looked at her in amazement. "You don't see it?" Her eyes returned to the mansion. "Okay, tell me what you see."

Bolanle furrowed her brow and concentrated. "I see an old, white, moss-covered Victorian-style mansion that has seen better days, *not* a place where you have a fancy Mardi Gras ball. It looks more like a condemned haunted house than the home of one of the foremost practitioners of the mystical arts."

Shuri looked again with her eyes wide. "I can't believe you don't see it," she said. "It's *totally* where a master magician would live."

Before them stood a gleaming black mansion with tall two-story columns, tucked away in the evening shadows of a beautiful garden. Green moss hung from sycamore trees that led down a lighted path past lush topiary cut in shapes she didn't recognize. A trio of bonfires crackled and snapped in the garden, with people in tuxedos and evening gowns laughing and drinking in the ever-changing lights and the incense-scented smoke.

Visible through the full-length windows, colored lights danced and flickered from inside as faint strains of New Orleans jazz floated through the evening air.

"Why can't I see what you see?" Bolanle pondered, keeping Shuri from entering the gate. "A spell, perhaps?"

"One way to find out." Shuri pointed to a small intercom hanging on the entrance gate. "Maybe we're supposed to announce ourselves."

"Let me, Princess," Bolanle instructed warily. Slowly, she pushed a rickety button on the rusty intercom. A deep voice, gravelly, gruff and with a slight French lilt, responded.

"May I help you?"

Shuri smiled. "Princess Shuri of Wakanda and Bolanle Zidona. I have something for you."

"Shuri! Your brother has told us so much about you. Please, enter and be welcome." Shuri could hear the smile in the voice as the gate swung open. She and Bolanle slowly stepped through, their heels clicking on the cobblestone path. As soon as they stepped beyond the gates, Bolanle gasped as the mansion's true form revealed itself to her.

"Told you!" Shuri laughed, and bumped her with her hip as they walked through the crowd toward the mansion's double doors. "Magic."

The doors swung open as they approached, and they stepped into a grand foyer that rivaled any room in the Wakandan royal palace. A single staircase, black carpeted with gold filigree, dominated the center of the room. Dark, almost blue-black wood paneling covered every wall, and a huge crystal chandelier swung from the ceiling beneath a massive skylight that let the night's full moon shine directly into the foyer, where its light reflected off the polished wood. Several of Dr. Drumm's guests wandered from the foyer into different rooms, many wearing small Mardi Gras masks that coordinated with their evening wear. Several stopped at the statues and curios scattered throughout the foyer and hanging on the walls.

Shuri hooked her arm around Bolanle's and ventured into the main room, gazing up at the paintings and wooden masks displayed on the wall. Bolanle ran her hand across a black stone statue of a long-necked, two-headed man with his fists clenched to his sides, while Shuri stared at a blue wooden pointy-headed figure holding out a basket and chains, white eyes staring hungrily at anyone who dared approach.

Bolanle tugged at Shuri's arm, and they walked across the room to a massive display case and stared inside. Placed on a platform in an obvious place of honor was the largest black cat either of them had ever seen, green eyes ablaze, teeth bared but frozen with its hackles raised as if eternally ready to attack. Shuri placed her hand on the glass window and gazed into the cat's lifeless eyes, trying to feel a connection.

All she felt was the cold.

"Interesting, isn't it?" A deep voice with a Caribbean accent spoke from behind her. It was the voice from the intercom. "Both in Bast worship and in Voudon, black cats are considered lucky."

Shuri turned around to find a smiling Jericho Drumm walking up behind them. Tall, with broad shoulders, he was dressed all in black, from his silk turtleneck to his single-breasted suit jacket and pants. His trademark dreadlocks were tied in a neat ponytail, with a silver streak down the exact center. Around his neck he wore several multicolored bead necklaces of all shapes and sizes, and around his shoulders was a red cloak, clasped by a totem of some kind.

In the middle of his forehead he had painted what looked like a small "v" inside a circle just between his eyes, whose irises seemed to flicker and change color every few seconds.

Shuri liked him immediately.

"Ours are bigger than yours," she said impudently, but with a smile as she reached out to shake Drumm's hand.

Jericho laughed uproariously. "Too true, too true, young lady. Gods, a Wakandan royal with a sense of humor. You are a breath of fresh air, Shuri, compared with your brother." He turned his gaze. "And this young one?"

Bolanle bowed formally. "Bolanle Zidona of the *Dora Milaje*, Dr. Drumm—or do you prefer your heroic nomenclature, Doctor Voodoo?"

"Names are important in the mystic arts, Bolanle," Jericho replied as he gestured them farther into his mansion. "Thank you for asking, but for tonight, Dr. Drumm, or even Jericho, will be just fine. Please, come into my study."

He escorted them through the crowd and around the hors d'oeuvres-laden waiters to a securely locked room in the back of the residence. He indicated one platter as it was carried past by a harried waiter, and snagged one of the martini glasses balanced precariously on the plate.

"Be sure to try the gumbo before you leave." He drank down the delicious-smelling concoction before waving a hand over the door's lock. "It's an old recipe, and it's delicious."

He pushed the double doors open and led them into what looked like an everyday office suite, with an overflowing bookshelf, a sturdy wooden desk, and a couch and several chairs positioned around a glass coffee table. On the walls were certificates noting several degrees, and—Shuri grinned to herself—a black-and-white cat poster that proclaimed, "Hang In There, Baby."

Jericho followed her eyes and shrugged. "It puts people at ease," he said as he offered them seats. Then he relaxed back into his chair. "First, our business. I believe you have something for me?"

Shuri leaned forward to speak but a hand on her leg stopped her. "Forgive me, Dr. Drumm," Bolanle said, "but first we need assurances that you are who you say you are. This—" She indicated the room around her. "—does not seem like the office of the Houngan Supreme. This seems like… a therapist's office. As far as we know, you could be an imposter, a shapeshifter, or some other creature pretending to be Dr. Drumm."

Jericho nodded approvingly. "I can see why T'Challa sent you along, Bolanle. Suspicious, concerned, thorough, and willing to speak up, even in front of royalty. My compliments. As for the office, well, I *am* a licensed psychiatrist. For years that was how I made my living, until I was trained in the arts of Voudon."

He closed his eyes, and as he did, a ghostly form rose from his body and hovered above his head. A full-bodied apparition, the man wore little around his see-through chest and torn pants, as if his condition was the result of a great battle he had lost.

"My twin brother, Daniel." Jericho opened his eyes and looked at the two women, whose mouths hung open in shock. "He and I have held back the forces of evil here in New Orleans and around the South for years now, and when my friend T'Challa asked me to examine an artifact for him, well, that was something that piqued both our interests."

The ghostly figure nodded to them, and settled back into Jericho's body.

"Is that enough proof for you, Bolanle?"

She sat back in her chair and gestured for her companion to continue.

Shuri reached behind her head, unclasped the necklace, and silently passed it over to Jericho, who examined it in the room's light. The necklace sparkled, shone, and glittered as he turned it this way and that, examining the clasp, the links, and finally holding it up in the air. He made a quick hand gesture; a green glow enveloped his fingers, and was absorbed by the jewelry.

Jericho made a hurrumphing sound, and gestured again, with the same results. He placed the necklace on the table and looked over at his visitors.

"T'Challa told me that this latest batch of Vibranium possessed some unique properties, and I see that he was right." He scratched his forehead gently. "Instead of absorbing normal energies, it's absorbing magical energy. Even with Wakanda's fabled security, there have been whispers in the mystical world about this new Vibranium and its possible uses in sorcery. I'll want to consult with Stephen Strange and Michael Twoyoungman, but this could be a major breakthrough. The applications... could be endless. Thank you, Shuri, for delivering this so quickly."

Shuri nodded, and looked over at Bolanle, who seemed still in shock at Jericho's ghostly brother.

"You're quite welcome, Dr. Drumm," she said, "but I must ask a question: why you? We have 'mystics' and priests in Wakanda. Why would T'Challa send it across the ocean?"

Jericho smiled. "Your brother owed me a favor," he said. "He knows I love magical mysteries, and this, Princess, is a big one." He stood up, stretched, and handed the necklace back to Shuri, who, with Jericho's nod, clasped it again around her neck. "Ladies, I have another mystery for you tonight, but we can talk about that as we enjoy the party. Shall we?"

He led them back to the door and, with a twist of his fingers, sealed the room with a mystical lock. As he did, Shuri noticed a small ripple in the air above his head as his brother departed again.

"Ah, Monica is here," Jericho said, sounding pleased. "Ladies, come with me. Daniel's on the door tonight, so he'll release the protection spell that keeps the mansion and grounds hidden to those who are not personally invited on the invitations. You'll enjoy meeting her."

430   Bolanle nudged Shuri. "That's why he sounded different

earlier. That was Daniel, not Jericho, who spoke on the sidewalk intercom."

As they wandered back through the crowd to the foyer, the doctor nodded and shook hands with his guests. "Indeed, my brother allows me to be in two places at once, and we rigged up a—well, spectral communicator, to allow normal persons to hear him. Tonight was the perfect night to test it. Normally, we can only talk to each other, but now he will be able to talk with as many people as he likes. I'll expand its uses later. Imagine getting a call from Great-Aunt Matilda after her funeral? We'll be able to resolve so many emotional issues."

Jericho continued to talk as they walked toward the front doors, shaking hands and chitchatting with people as he led his two guests back through the foyer, to stand on the mansion's steps.

"Here she comes." He pointed out into the garden at a figure coming down the cobblestone path. A statuesque woman walked confidently in their direction, a slight smile on her face. Her dark skin and long wavy black hair contrasted with her slinky strapless white dress, which seemed to sparkle and glimmer on its own. Shuri sized up the unknown woman, deciding she was about T'Challa's age, with that same self-confident attitude and flair that so annoyed her about her brother.

On this woman, though, Shuri thought, *it fits.*

The woman seemed to glide up to Jericho, and held her hand out to him. He never took his eyes off her face as he took her hand and kissed it, and then the woman's cheek.

"Monica, thank you for coming. I know this isn't your type of thing, but your presence is very welcome," Jericho said.

Monica shrugged. "When an Avenger asks, there's no question. I was in town for the weekend, anyway." She offered her hand to Shuri, who looked at her questioningly, and back to Jericho. "Monica Rambeau," she said. Her grip was light and warm in Shuri's hand.

"The Sun Goddess," Bolanle whispered, and then immediately slapped her hands over her mouth, embarrassed.

Monica smirked. "Only one person has called me that. Wakandan, right?"

Shuri nodded. "Princess Shuri of Wakanda, and this is Bolanle Zidona of the *Dora Milaje*. And you are Spectrum, aren't you?"

Rambeau smiled wistfully. "My identity's no big secret, Princess, but let's not broadcast it, okay? New Orleans is my home, and I don't need my house or my parents' houses to become tourist stops."

Shuri nodded as they turned back toward the mansion. Bolanle seemed about to burst with questions, and with a grin, Shuri nodded for her to ask away.

"Ms. Rambeau, I hate to ask… You were the first woman of color to lead the Avengers, and your light and energy powers make you one of the most powerful beings on the planet." Bolanle babbled as she waved her hand toward the shining dress. "I know I should ask you something deep or profound, but I have to know. Is this the dress… or is it you?"

As Monica walked, the white dress got brighter and brighter, and then, with a small burst, it changed color to a sparkly warm gold.

"Little from column A, little from column B," she admitted with a laugh. "Reed Richards gave me some of their unstable molecule fabric that Sue wasn't going to use, and Sue suggested a wonderful designer in Manhattan who whipped this up for me. I hadn't had a chance to wear it out yet to see its effect with my powers, so tonight seemed to be a good night to try it."

"And I do appreciate you coming, Monica," Jericho added softly. "I know you feel like you don't belong in the world of magic, but I have a feeling that you're just what I—I mean, we— will need tonight."

Bolanle and Shuri looked at each other. Monica shook her head.

"We used to date," she said, as she took Jericho's arm, "but we decided it would never work, with us being from two different worlds."

"*We* decided that?" Jericho protested softly. "I don't remember being given a choice."

Monica put a finger on his mouth to silence him as they entered the grand foyer. "Let's not tonight, okay? Can't we just enjoy ourselves?"

Jericho smiled softly. "A little business first, and then fun."

She smiled, and they walked into the party.

"How do you know Spectrum?" Shuri whispered to Bolanle.

"First of all, she's Spectrum, one of the most powerful human beings in the world who also happens to be African American. Second, the *Dora Milaje* keeps a list of enhanced people in the world, especially the ones who could end all life as we know it on a whim. Third, we… might keep a list of women, superpowered especially but some who are not, outside of Wakanda that might, *might* be worthy of being a Wakandan queen," Bolanle whispered back. "The Storm Goddess and the Sun Goddess make up the American list."

Shuri looked over at Monica, whose angelic dress made her seem to float next to Jericho. With her flight powers, she might actually be floating, she realized.

"Doctor, you mentioned a mystery," Shuri reminded him as she nabbed one of the traveling glasses of gumbo and licked her lips. Jericho tore his eyes away from his radiant companion and frowned.

"Ah, yes," he said slowly. "There was a gentleman earlier who was asking about you, and mentioned he had invited you and your charming companion to my party."

Shuri looked at Bolanle, who grimaced. "Ah, yes. Elijah. We… ran into him at a restaurant last night. Skinny, intense eyes, bodyguards?"

Jericho looked around the room. "He brought more than a couple of bodyguards tonight. More along the lines of an entourage."

Monica shook her head. "I hate it when people impose upon you."

"Yes, well, he had an invitation. Indeed, I have to admit that I had an ulterior motive for sending you one, as well."

She smirked at him. "Figured. It's been a while since we talked, so when your invitation… *appeared* in my bedroom, I figured that it would be Avengers business." She waited, then added, "Don't keep me in suspense."

Drumm kept scanning his guests. "Well, this is a bit of a story."

"Not another one." Monica sighed.

Jericho smiled at Shuri and Bolanle.

"Everything in the South, and *especially* everything in New Orleans, involves a story," he explained, "a mask that hides its deeper meaning." Still he kept a wary eye on the crowd around them. "There was a man, a street magician in New Orleans, who was charmed by a visiting princess. She gave him a taste of a life much richer than he deserved, but almost immediately the woman left him behind in the same streets where she found him.

"The man couldn't stand the idea of going back to where he started," Jericho continued. "So he began to charm women, including a witch, from whom he learned some minor but real magic. Before he could become a magical threat, however, he was attacked, killed, and resurrected by one of New Orleans' resident vampires."

Jericho gestured to the crowd around them.

"Most vampires in New Orleans are regular people, trying to make it one night at a time. This is the one city in the United States where vampires, demons, witches, ghouls, werewolves, zombies, and all sorts of creatures can feel at home, no matter what culture or city gave birth to them. In fact, several are in attendance tonight." Jericho gestured around the room. "See?"

He waved his hand. A green flash burst behind Shuri's eyes, and instead of a man wearing a tuxedo, she saw the flame-headed creature sample the gumbo.

"Demon," Jericho said.

Shuri looked around, and shivered. There were werewolves, at least one zombie, a few demons with flames of different colors, and other creatures she couldn't identify, mingling with the other guests, chatting and laughing. Jericho waved his hand again, and the creatures disappeared back into their human forms.

Bolanle, having seen the same thing, reached down to her leg, pretending to scratch an itch. She came up with a small

Vibranium dagger in her hands, but Jericho put a hand out to her, urging calm.

"We all get along as much as we can in the Big Easy, girls," the doctor said. "For many of these residents, there are butcher shops, blood banks, and other sources of sustenance that don't require violence. With that said, there's always a… bad element."

Monica looked a little worried. "Jericho, should we be telling them about this? They won't be in town for long."

He shook his head. "They need to know, Monica. Especially considering who they've already encountered."

"Encountered?" Shuri looked doubtful. "Dr. Drumm, I struggle to believe in what you can do, much less fairytale creatures like vampires."

Monica raised an eyebrow. "Yet you're the sister of a cat god's high priest," she said. "How can you be a skeptic?"

Bolanle spoke up. "That's faith, not magic."

"And I can explain everything T'Challa can do through science," Shuri added. "Metallurgy, botany, horticulture, neuroscience, and technology." She looked at Bolanle. "To be honest, I only know Bast through T'Challa. Our 'god' has never deigned to appear to me, only my brother. I am—like the rest of Wakanda—dependent on T'Challa to tell me what our god wants.

"As with any good scientist, if I can't see proof of something's existence, a part of me has to withhold any conclusion, especially if I can duplicate it or come somewhere close with technology." She shrugged. "With more time to study, who knows?"

"That's a line of discussion I'd love to explore with you at a later date," Jericho said. "However, this vampire magician has stumbled across a source of magic that allows him to hide his vampiric nature from other mystical practitioners. The vampires he leads are particularly active during Mardi Gras, in part because the fasting that follows will make humans less… call it 'appetizing.' And so, they seek to gorge themselves.

"Having accepted the mission of protecting this city," Jericho continued, "I've decided to put an end to their hunting. But rather than wasting the time needed to locate them, I've engineered a way to get them to come to me."

Shuri didn't like the sound of that.

"What did you do?" Bolanle's eyes sparkled like her dagger.

The doctor actually looked sheepish. "I leaked news of a mystical object coming to Mardi Gras, an object of sufficient power to lure this particular killer and his brood to this party."

"What artifact?" Shuri asked, knowing full well what he was about to say.

"Why, a mystically charged Vibranium necklace." Jericho smiled. "The King of Wakanda himself had it made for me. T'Challa discovered that it doesn't react to non-magic types, so it's safe for non-practitioners to wear around, like you are now. It does give off a tiny bit of a mystical scent, but it's nothing particularly dangerous as long as it's in the right hands. But in the wrong hands… it could supercharge necromancy to the nth degree. I suspect that's what they want it for."

"You mean, I'm bait?" Shuri put her hands on her hips skeptically.

Drumm shrugged. "T'Challa was confident that you could handle yourself for a day or so, especially if he sent one of his most promising *Dora Milaje* along with you. And since you don't particularly believe in magic, that kept the necklace's mystic signal mostly under wraps. If T'Challa had brought it, his belief in the supernatural would have attracted every necromancer, witch, wizard, and sorcerer in the South down here to get it the moment he touched the soil."

Jericho looked around, and then back at Shuri.

"And, just in case, I've had my brother keeping an eye on you this whole time. Except for the unfortunate encounter at the restaurant, at which time Daniel had me ready to teleport to your rescue just in case. You've been perfectly safe."

"Until now. You can hand that trinket over to me now, mystic," a nearby voice snarled. A blinding flash filled the room.

Jericho, Shuri, and their friends found themselves alone in the foyer, surrounded by Elijah and his cadre. Gone were the guests who had stood close by.

"I'm so very glad you accepted my invitation." Elijah leered at Shuri, licking his fangs as his minions snarled at Bolanle, who pulled a second Vibranium dagger from underneath her dress. Monica looked slightly amused, while Drumm had a broad smile on his face.

Bolanle nudged Shuri and pointed to one of the younger vampires. This one, wearing a T-shirt under his suit jacket, had a finger dangling backward on one hand.

"Dead, and you still can't keep your hands to yourself," the *Dora Milaje* taunted.

"You'll get yours," the vampire hissed.

Next to Shuri, Jericho's eyes began to glow, and she could feel a slight warmth coming from Monica, who began to emit a glow.

"Ahh, Eli." Jericho smiled. "You're still stuck in the past, trying to punish a woman long dead, who forgot your existence the instant she left New Orleans. Though I am impressed with this latest teleport spell." Shuri heard a faint crackling coming from him. "Most magic users can't operate within these walls—not without my express permission."

"Your guests will make good meals," Eli snarled. "I just needed them out of the way while I rip your throat out, and the throat of this pretty princess. I seeded the crowd here with my children, more than you see here in front of you. So surrender, or I'll order them to start the festivities early, and drain every norm in these halls."

"What makes you think I won't just stake you all?" Jericho questioned curiously. A long staff appeared in his hands.

"You won't know who is an opponent, and who is a hostage," Eli snarled. "Our charms will keep your mystic senses from seeing us, and as you said, no one else can use magic inside these walls."

Doctor Voodoo smiled.

"Even in New Orleans, times have changed, Elijah. We have cell phones, Internet, and fewer Confederate statues." With a flourish, he indicated Monica standing at his side with her hands on her hips. "Even super heroes, powered by science. Monica, dear, may I have one pulse?"

A look of concentration appeared on her face, and she emitted a single pulse. Ultraviolet radiation, Shuri thought as she felt a wave of heat flash over her skin. It was as if someone had opened a door to the sun, and quickly closed it. Every vampire in the room screamed, making Shuri want to put her hands over her ears.

Doctor Voodoo *tsk*ed at the weakened creatures.

"There's nothing mystical about the power of the 'Sun Goddess.'" He winked at Bolanle. "You can't hide from her power, and as for my vampire friends, I had Daniel tell them to leave as soon as Monica arrived.

"So, my dear Spectrum—happy hunting."

Mouth open, Shuri watched Monica transform her body into what looked like a glowing gold hologram and shoot off through the ceiling. As she did, Bolanle leaped toward the broken-fingered vampire, slashing at him with her Vibranium daggers. She tagged him with a slash across his cheek, causing him to scream as the wound began to sizzle and burn.

The *Dora* grinned fiercely. "Blessed by the High Priest of the Panther God before we left home," she gloated. "I wondered why Beloved took the time, but the Black Panther is wise, and it isn't my right to question him." She plunged her daggers into the vampire's shoulders, causing him to shriek and scream with every blow.

At Shuri's side, Doctor Voodoo floated off the floor and began to chant. Eyes glowing white, dreadlocks crackling with energy, he began throwing unidentifiable energy bolts at the scattering vampires, who shrieked and burned whenever he connected. Voodoo threw a bolt at Elijah, who managed to dodge and crouch, peering murderously at Shuri.

"I should have killed you last night, Princess," he spat at her. "Ripping your throat out then would have been easy."

438   "Not as easy as you might think," Shuri replied, setting herself

into a defensive stance. "I've dated wayyy worse than you, just in the last few months."

With a roar, Elijah leaped at her and slashed at her throat with his claw-like fingernails, but the princess dodged and kicked out at him with her hardened heels. Missing his eyes by only inches she reset, whipping out her own Vibranium dagger from a thigh holster and weaving it in front of the vampire's face. Suddenly she knew why T'Challa had given it to her.

"Faith-based weapons only work if someone believes, Princess," he taunted. Elijah snarled and feinted, causing her to jab her weapon at him. "Remember, you're a scientist. You don't believe unless you have proof, isn't that right?"

A quick movement and he knocked Shuri's dagger from her hand. It clattered across the floor. She couldn't help glancing at the dagger, and that was when Elijah pounced, using his greater weight to knock her to the ground, landing with his hands around her neck.

Shuri couldn't breathe, and began to panic. The Vibranium necklace was caught under the vampire's hands, painfully digging into her skin. She could feel the Bast icon cruelly digging into her throat, as her sight began to dim from lack of oxygen.

"You lost your greatest weapon when the glowing witch left." Elijah's hot breath smelled of wine and blood. "She can't generate enough energy to kill us—not while keeping you alive at the same time—and your friends are too busy to save you."

Head to the side, Shuri could see Bolanle fighting to get to her, her slashing causing smoky, sizzling wounds. But the vampires blocked her path. Voodoo was struggling with his own opponents, and outside the window bright flashes indicated that Monica was busy with her own enemies.

"All alone, no powers, no faith," Elijah whispered. "Nothing but death, resurrection and obedience to me for the rest of eternity, Princess. I would feel sorry for you, if that emotion still existed for me."

Shuri turned her head back around and stared at Elijah,

reaching deep inside herself. She thought about the things her brother could do, and the wounds that her new friend Bolanle was causing with her blessed knives. She concentrated with everything she had, and then let go.

All of a sudden she could feel heat on her neck, emanating from her necklace, and Elijah began to squirm, then *scream*. The vampire jerked his hands back quickly, letting her go. As Shuri rubbed her neck and coughed to get some air back inside her lungs, Elijah's burned hands shook and smoked, a Panther head burned into them.

Shuri sat up. "It seems my faith is a little stronger than either of us thought, vampire," she noted. Then her newfound confidence faltered as Elijah prepared to leap.

"Princess!" Voodoo threw his pointed staff to her. Shuri caught the staff cleanly and whirled it around, the pointed end toward Elijah's chest. The vampire snarled.

"You don't have the guts to end me, Princess."

Shuri thrust the staff forward, knowing exactly where to find Elijah's heart. Instantly, the vampire began to disintegrate.

"Enjoy hell, monster."

The loss of their master seemed to take the fight out of the other vampires. Jericho, Shuri, and Bolanle eliminated the rest within minutes. Monica floated back through a wall and returned to her normal form, brushing dust off her gown, which was white again.

"This was the best date we've ever had, Jericho," she said, hugging him.

Drumm smiled and looked over at Shuri.

"I feel as if I should apologize for this chaos, Princess," Jericho said. "I know it wasn't exactly why you wanted to come to New Orleans. I hope I can find a way to make it up to you."

Shuri shrugged, looking at Bolanle, who was panting from her exertions. She looked as if she had thoroughly enjoyed herself.

"It answered some questions I had about myself," the princess said, "and it did get my heart rate up." She grinned. "*Now* I'm ready

to party."

Monica laughed. "Nothing like the possibility of death to make you want to live, right?"

Shuri nodded in agreement.

"Unfortunately—" Jericho looked around at the piles of dust, wrecked statues, and torn paintings in his foyer. "—I think this particular party is over for tonight. Though I understand you already have post-party plans, Princess."

Shuri just gaped and Bolanle looked at Jericho with awe as the four of them opened the foyer's double doors and walked down the cobblestone path toward the gates.

"How did you know that?" the *Dora Milaje* asked. "Magic?"

Jericho laughed as they stepped through the gates to the street. "Not everything is mystical, my dear." Standing across the street, Jay and Rick were leaning against a purple SUV, waving at them.

"Dr. Drumm, what's up, dawg?" Rick hugged the older man, and the younger brother followed suit. As they did so, Shuri could see some sort of hidden handshake.

"See you next week?" Jay asked.

"Indeed," Drumm said, and Shuri looked askance at him. The doctor just shrugged.

"I teach 'Intro to Psychology' at Xavier," he said. "It's all about knowing who you are, before figuring out someone else." He looked pointedly at Shuri, while putting an arm around Monica.

"Anyway, gentlemen, be on your best behavior with these two," he continued. "They might be a little more than you can handle." He winked at Shuri.

"We've got it, Doc," Jay said, holding his hand out to Shuri. "A line on a house party in Slidell, with some brothers. We'll have 'em back before too long."

Jericho stepped over to Shuri and placed his hands on her shoulders. "Enjoy yourself, and leave yourself open to new experiences. As we now know, there's still a lot for you to find out. Don't be too hard on your brother, either, and know that your destiny is your own, not anyone else's." He nodded to Bolanle, as Monica gave Shuri a hug and a kiss on the cheek.

"Bolanle, it was very nice to meet you," he said. "Now I should get back to what's left of my guests." There was a sudden sound of drums in the night. Jericho and Monica disappeared in a cloud of smoke. Bolanle stared at Shuri, and then at their two escorts.

"Doc does stuff like that all the time." Jay shrugged. "N'Awlins, you know?" He gestured. "Come on, ladies, let's go."

THE BOYS led Shuri and Bolanle to a massive party in a suburban house with a huge back yard and a pool. Music was pumping, kids were dancing, and no one seemed to care who had invited "Shia and Tawny."

Shuri and Jay ended up with drinks out on the back patio, laughing and talking for hours. Bolanle would wander out, meet Shuri's gaze, grin, and head back inside, where Shuri could hear her high-pitched laugh every now and then. Rick brought them new drinks, eyes laughing merrily.

As the night grew cooler, she and Jay scooted closer and closer together, until by daybreak they were hand in hand. They talked about everything, including living with big brothers.

"Your brother looms large in your psyche, doesn't he?" Jay asked.

"No more than yours." She grinned as Rick delivered them new drinks, this time something he called a blood orange margarita. "But we fight all the time," Shuri complained. "You two seem like you're best friends."

"We are." Jay shrugged. "That doesn't mean we don't fight. Friends and family don't have to be on the same page. We do have to be in the same book, however.

"We tease, we taunt, and yes, we fight, but we can do that because we're family," he said. "We know in the end that when push comes to shove, we'll have each other's backs. Because, when it comes down to it, we're a family. Nothing else matters.

"I'd bet it's the same for you and your brother. No matter what, he's your family. He'll always be there, even when you don't want him to be, and he'll always want to make sure you're safe and yet can stand on your own feet. Just… give him a chance."

Shuri sat silently for a second, and then kissed Jay lightly. She placed her head on his shoulder and watched the first glow of dawn.

"Maybe," she whispered to the light.

BOLANLE WORRIED about the amount of liquor she had seen Rick consume, and talked them into leaving their vehicle in Slidell. They would retrieve it later. So, after a hearty late-morning breakfast, Jay and Rick rode with the ladies back to their residence.

Standing in the doorway, Bolanle kissed Jay and then Rick on the cheek, and took a few steps back to give Shuri some privacy. Rick swept Shuri up into a great bear hug, tickling her neck with his scrawny beard and making her giggle. He gestured to Bolanle, and they walked over to an empty couch.

"I guess this is it, huh, Shia?" Jay looked down at Shuri with tender eyes.

"Yes, I must get home," Shuri whispered. "My brother will begin to worry."

Jay tilted his head. "Yeah, having the King of Wakanda watching your every move can't be fun."

Shuri's jaw dropped, as Jay's eyes danced with amusement. A giggle bubbled out of her throat, turned into an infectious laugh, and within seconds the two of them were holding their sides. Once she had caught her breath, Shuri smacked Jay on the arm.

"How long have you known?"

"Since the bar," Jay said smugly. "Believe it or not, Black people consider y'all to be 'our' royalty, just like Harry and Meghan are 'their' royalty. Did you really think calling yourself 'Shia' was a disguise? You might as well have been hiding behind a pair of fake glasses!"

"Also," Rick added as he and Bolanle wandered back over, "hanging out with folks like Doctor Voodoo and Spectrum isn't exactly conducive to going incognegro."

Bolanle glared. "Did anyone else know?"

"Girl." Rick shook his head. "Everyone at the house party knew. No-one-cared. You weren't asking for special attention, and you seemed cool."

"And you don't have to worry about photos," Jay added. "It's Mardi Gras. Everyone knows to keep the cameras off, unless they've asked. Nobody, I mean *nobody*, needs to have Facebook or Twitter photos come back to haunt them in job interviews in a couple of years. Deck's already stacked against most of us already."

Bolanle looked at Shuri, who nodded.

"Perhaps, you need to set your sights wider," Bolanle suggested. "Africa—and Wakanda especially, nowadays—needs men and women of honor from other lands to help our people... 'acclimate' to the world as it is, instead of as we wish it to be."

"You would be honored guests," Shuri agreed.

Jay took her hand and caressed her wrist. "As long as I get to see 'Shia' at least once while I'm there, I don't see why we couldn't make that work."

Rick slapped Jay on the back. "Dog, you're in."

The other three just groaned. "Way to ruin a good moment, numbskull," Jay muttered.

"What are big brothers for?" Rick grinned. "Kiss her, dumbass, so they can go take a nap."

Shuri pulled him down into a passionate kiss that left them both panting. She could feel Jay's eyes on her as she sauntered into the house, and just as the door closed, she blew him one final kiss.

LATER, ON their private jet, Shuri stared out the window as Bolanle worked on her laptop, most likely writing up some type of report for T'Challa or someone. She broke from her reverie as Bolanle cleared her throat.

"I can leave certain activities and contacts out of my official report, Your Highness, if you so desire."

"Thank you for being so cool about it, Bolanle," Shuri said.

444   "I may have to reconsider some things when we arrive home. I

think… I think T'Challa somehow knew that I would find out some things about myself and my faith in Bast on this trip.

"I'm pretty pissed at him for putting me through this, but I have to admit it when he's right," Shuri said.

Bolanle smiled. "Beloved is pretty smart, isn't he? And it doesn't hurt to be in communion with a god."

"And did you ever figure out why they sent you?" Shuri raised an eyebrow at Bolanle.

Bolanle shrugged. "I'm not worried about it. Maybe Okoye wanted me to learn a little bit about the one royal closest to my age? Maybe I blend in better in New Orleans? Who knows? Either way, I… had fun, Princess. And maybe," she looked down, "I made a friend whom I would gladly follow if she advanced to her proper position in life."

Shuri smiled.

"And while I'm thinking about that…" Bolanle looked sheepishly down at her laptop, which beeped at her. "…you might want to drink a lot of water over the next couple of days. Your trackers have been disabled since before we headed to Bourbon Street, but they're still in your system."

"Trackers?" Shuri looked over at her. "What trackers?"

Bolanle looked sheepish. "The microscopic ones you drank in the coffee I gave you back at the airport, a few days ago. It was your mother's idea. Family, you know?"

Shuri looked her, and they both began to laugh.

STRONGER IN SPIRIT

SUYI DAVIES OKUNGBOWA

CRICKETS. THE sound of home is always crickets.

Whenever I am away—to another country, another planet, another dimension—it is loud insects that always remind me of Wakanda. That and the thick myriad of scents of the rainforest greenery currently around me, with or without the slithering next to me in the swampy undergrowth as I sludge through. But mostly it is the collective chorus of crickets, their restlessness, that reminds me of who I am: T'Challa, King of Wakanda, the Black Panther. It is a reminder not to sleep, to remain, like them, restless always.

A grasshopper that sleeps about will be soon awake in a lizard's mouth. That is what the Wakandan proverb says, is it not? Neither can I sleep until I know I am safe, until I know Wakanda is safe.

"You would think," I say into my earcomm, "that the royal aircraft of the most technologically advanced country on the planet would land in a rainforest without incident." I brush aside the dwarf plantain leaves leaning into the path before me. "You would think, eh, Shuri?"

Shuri, who I left with instructions to plant her bottom on the throne until I returned, but who didn't wait one second after I left before running back to her lab to settle in front of its many screens, scoffs.

"The Talon Fighter is equipped for vertical takeoff and

landing," she says, in that breathless manner that tells me she is working on something as she speaks to me. "Don't blame me if you cannot land a simple plane."

"You know this is not my first time setting it down in a forest," I say. "Perhaps there's something peculiar about this place."

"No, nothing special about Lagos," she says. "That's if you take away the fact that it's the most populous metropolis west of our continent, which possibly also makes it the most dangerous place for you to be visiting in your current condition."

She pauses. "And yet, it is also the only place in the world right now that we may be able to find healing for the thing that ails you. So, sure, yes, I would say there's nothing peculiar about Lagos at all."

"You know I meant the forest."

There is a pause, and I know she's peering into the screen, trying to see if she can warn me of anything the Panther Habit is not currently picking up.

"That's not even a forest, from what I can see here," she says. "It's called the Lekki Conservation Centre. So, like an uncultivated botanical garden."

"Which is exactly why you should leave me alone and stop being an overprotective aunty. I will be fine. Go and perform your duties. It is a bad omen for the people to look upon an empty throne, don't you know?"

"Yes, yes, I've heard you," she says, but I can hear the haptic feedback of screens being tapped. "I will go, but only once I know you're safe and are ready to meet Okoye's contact."

I follow the pathway she has sent to my visual feed. It is a boardwalk, apparently, one used during the day for sightseeing, now closed for dusk. Shuri has marked the area low-security and is right, because I come upon no patrols, nor any life at all, save for a red-butt monkey who doesn't even regard me as I go past. Toward the end of the boardwalk, I branch off into more uncharted territory, scale a wire fence, and soon I am near to the highway, cars flashing by and impatient drivers leaning on their horns.

"I'm going to disengage the Habit now," I say into my earcomm.

"Please, ensure the Talon remains cloaked all the while I'm here. And Shuri…" I pause, so she understands. "…I will be fine. I will get the cure, and then all will be well, okay?"

There is a silence, an exhale. "Okay," she says. "Be careful, T'Challa."

I engage the bodysuit's cloaking, allowing it to rearrange and manifest into regular clothes. Now dressed in lighter material, the latent heat of onsetting night hits me, made more humid by my standing in the tall grass. I trudge upward until I'm on the side of the highway, cars running by at speed. I cross over to the median strip, checking to see that I have nothing identifying me as the King of Wakanda. I take off my necklace—a small keepsake Shuri and I both wear, on which is carved our family history—and put it in my pocket. Shuri believes it is wise to disguise myself completely in a city she calls *carnivorous*. "Everyone there is on a quest for something shiny," she said, "and a king is always shiny."

Perhaps she is right. Unlike most missions I've gone on, it is imperative for this one that no one knows I am the Black Panther.

But even more important is that I do not get into any trouble without the Habit. Because, for the first time in a very long while, I might be unable to defend myself without it.

I cross to the opposite side, where there is an empty bus stop, and stand there. Ordinarily, I would've had someone pick me up and deliver me to Okoye's Lagos contact—she and Shuri would've seen to that. But this fight is mine, one I need to fight and conquer alone in all my humanness. What ails me ails me alone, and if I cannot defeat it, for my survival but also to remain alive for my people, then am I even worthy to be their king?

I pull out a basic mobile phone and order a rideshare. *Fifteen minutes*, the application tells me.

After standing on two legs for five minutes, another bout of sickness hits me. Weak joints, throbbing ribs, splitting headache, pain coming out of my eyes, heart pounding in my ears. All the worst parts of humanness increased a hundredfold. I sit on the bench, trying not to double over, waiting for it to pass.

450

The first time my immune system attacked me, after returning from the trip to the planet Barnard, it wasn't this bad. It's worsened since then, though, happening far more often and lasting much longer. And right before and after these bouts, all of my powers are diminished, and remain so afterward, which means each bout takes my abilities down just a peg. No amount of technology or shamanism can heal this fully, or bring my powers back up to speed so far—we have tried it all. Remanifesting the Habit is now often precarious, because if I happen to get one of these episodes while in it, the secret and legacy of my people may end up lying in the ditch in a foreign country.

I should've listened to Shuri. She *did* warn me not to go off to Barnard, but how was I to resist what European astronomers called, "a second-Earth candidate, with 99 percent confidence?" I have a duty to Wakanda, yes, but also a duty to the world, to ensure that any crucial information passed down by those with less advancements and resources than Wakanda is right and true. I had to go out there and verify it myself.

Returning with a fatal autoimmune disease contracted while walking the planet's terra was not in anyone's plan, but it happened.

Returning with the exact kind of illness that took my mother just after my birth, and now threatens to take me? Even worse.

I clutch my stomach, gritting my teeth until the pain passes. I take in deep breaths, let them out through my mouth. It will be a few hours before the next bout will come. It will be sharper, stronger. With each new bout, I will be less and less Black Panther, and unlikely to remain alive if they go on. And go on they will, because a sickness that once defeated all the Chief Shaman's attempts with the Heart-Shaped Herb and Wakanda's most updated medical procedures, ensuring my mother, N'Yami, did not survive it, is no simple sickness. Perhaps, like then, it is a sickness that cannot be solved on the human plane, which is why I must seek solutions elsewhere. If the realm of man has offered no answers in the past, now is the time for the realm of gods.

The rideshare arrives.

"Oga, are you all right?" the driver asks when I crawl into the back seat.

"Drive." One thing is clear in my mind: I must move fast if I'm to find the cure before it's too late.

"Where to, sir?" the man asks.

"Use your map." I turn to face the window. He continues to ask me, but my thoughts have faded into my plans for my time here. He finally gives up and consults his map for its intended purposes.

SHURI HAS set up everything about my presence here in a manner so discreet, I feel like I'm on an actual clandestine mission. She has handed me a very Lagosian name: *Tunde Martin*. This is what the desk clerk at the similarly clandestine hotel tells me when I present the number I was provided for my booking. I observe the place as she searches for the record and retrieves the keys. This is not a hotel at all, but a large house someone built and probably decided it was too expensive to maintain as a residential abode. Based on what I know about the country's taxes and the government's penchant for milking businesses dry, this must be one of those carnivorous qualities I've heard about.

I have no luggage, but a bellboy follows me to my room anyway, lingering and waiting for a tip just for pointing out directions I could've found myself. Okoye warned that to succumb once to any form of what she described as *Lagos aggro* was to invite more upon myself. So, following her directive, I shut the door in his face.

The room is the barest I've ever been in—just bed, desk, TV and drawer unit—but it doesn't matter because I won't be staying long anyway.

I undress and take a warm shower, then open the wardrobe for the plain, basic clothes sent ahead of me. I put the necklace back on, running my hands around it, feeling its edges and raised parts. As I stand there, in front of the still steamed mirror, it hits me: if I don't take this seriously, I could be gone, just like my mother.

"You will always find help if you open yourself to it," my father, T'Chaka, said when I visited him in Djalia, the Great Veldt of Wakanda's collective memory. "You must know when to lay aside that weight on your shoulders and trust the world around you for a little help."

"But I *have* tried," I complained. "Everything from Shuri's most updated bio-nanites to Bast and the Herb. Nothing has worked so far."

"But you have not tried that which was recommended by Bast."

"Her comrade god of healing?" I shook my head. "I'm not sure attempting to access a foreign, unproven, untested deity while in this state is a good idea."

"Perhaps," my father said. "But you must remember this is not just any deity. This is Bàbálúayé, the god of healing, known to cure even the most obscure of physical and mental illnesses." He paused. "This is N'Yami's god."

I remember being so aghast that the only thing that came out of my mouth was, "Mother's... god?"

"She did once have a deity of allegiance beyond Bast, yes," T'Chaka said. "Remember that before she became your mother, she spent a large part of her time abroad to heal the grief of her family's passing. It was with Bàbálúayé's help that she did so. I believe Bast knows what she is saying when she recommends him." He seemed to look through me. "Our only regret is that we did not attempt to do so in her time."

I let the sad, wistful moment pass, before I said, "I'm sure we cannot access a foreign god from here, though."

"But we don't know that, do we?" my father said. "Just because something is not a part of Djalia does not mean it is not a part of our collective memory, or that you have no access to it. Remember that you always carry us all within you: all of your ancestors, all of your gods, all of the Black Panthers who came before you. *You* are the embodiment of our collective memory, our legacy in the flesh. And you can call on any part of us when in distress, just as you do this Great Veldt. If Bàbálúayé was once a part of N'Yami—"

"Then I can have access to him."

"But it will not happen easily," he seemed to sigh, as much as a spirit could. "You must surmount this distrust of the world out there to do so, as your mother once did. One day, you will have to lead Wakanda to embrace that same world. And if you cannot demonstrate trust in it yourself, can your people in turn trust you to lead them on that journey?"

I exhale and wipe condensed steam off the bathroom mirror.

I never in my life imagined that the one place I would seek a solution to secure my future and that of my country would be with a completely alien and unproven entity, who may or may not have once had dealings with my mother, and who may or may not be inclined to help me. Then, there's also the fact that I can't access Bàbálúayé on my own—not in the first instance, at least. I have to find a local shaman or diviner devoted to the god—called a bàbáláwò in these parts—and access the god through this person. But I can't just look up a bàbáláwò in a local directory, either. The British worked their magic so well during their time here that antipathy toward the veneration of gods or ancestors is now deeply entrenched in their psyche, like most of the rest of the continent. Therefore, I must convince yet another stranger—Okoye's contact, who she has already arranged with on my behalf—to find and take me to a bàbáláwò.

I chuckle nervously at my reflection in the mirror. For the first time ever in my life as king and protector of Wakanda, neither my powers nor my Habit nor my money or might can save me. The future of my people and the survival of their legacy of the Black Panther now lies in the hands of a motley duo of strangers who could choose to care less if I live or die.

When I leave to meet with Okoye's contact, the bellboy is still hanging around, following me with his eyes. I hand him what I think is a small tip—all of the only Naira I have in cash—but he still hasn't stopped thanking me when I exit the building.

OUTSIDE, THE air is muggy with heat, even though it is night. I cross the road and take another rideshare to the agreed meeting point: a waterfront lounge called Farm City that exists somewhere between open-air bar, restaurant, and nightclub. I suspect it morphs from one to the other depending on the time of day. Currently, it's in its transition from late-night bar to nightclub, but still serving food for those just arriving from long shifts at multinational corporations. I order ahead for my contact: a whole fish grilled amongst spices in tin foil alongside a soft drink of bitters. It feels local, so I assume they would like it.

The order takes a while, and my contact arrives before it, while I am people-watching. It takes me a moment to pick her apart from those milling about, their numbers growing with the moon rising over the lagoon. She settles adjacent to me on the table and folds her arms, giving me a long, assured stare that makes me realize she's who I will be meeting with.

Wakanda has eyes all over the world these days. I barely get to meet them unless I absolutely have to, and they only maintain intelligence liaison with teams that report to Okoye or Shuri, who then distill that into whatever strategic or tactical information I need to know. In my head, I've often envisioned these scouts and eyes to be just like Dora Milaje material—fierce, combative, warrior-types. But the woman before me possesses none of these— at least, not on the face of it. She is on the smaller side, looks easygoing and stylish—jeans, blouse, jacket, braids—but remains nondescript regardless. It occurs to me now that maybe this is why she was chosen. If I am to blend in, it makes sense that my contact should too.

"Your Highness," she says, leaning close to speak over the increasingly loud music. Even seated at the table, she bows slightly. "Welcome."

I return her bow, leaning close as well. "At this point, you may simply call me T'Challa. We aim to keep my anonymity, do we not?"

"Indeed," she says, studying me. "You look..." She squints, her eyes small and piercing. "...well."

"Yes, I do," I say. "What ails me is not something the eyes can see."

She nods. "I am sorry. I hope I can do my part to help alleviate it."

The music drops off for a short break, and we are able to lean away from one another and speak clearly.

"What is your name?" I ask.

"LN-3258," she says, and offers a wry smile. "But you may call me Àbíkẹ́."

"Àbíkẹ́," I say. "Wakanda thanks you for your service."

The fish arrives, and the woman gleefully dips into it, eating with small and well-manicured fingers. She is young—thirty, maybe—and wears a wedding ring. I wonder what her spouse thinks of her meeting with a stranger so late. If there's anything I know about our neighbors on the continent, it's that most of their cultural practices frown upon such things.

"This is great, you should try some," she says between mouthfuls.

I wave her offer away. "I'd prefer to be done with this before I try to put anything in my body. Who knows what could aggravate the situation?"

She looks solemn, wipes her fingers. "Can you... tell me about it?"

"I would, but it would make no difference," I say. "Consider it that my body believes it should be fighting something, except whatever it has spotted isn't there. But it keeps fighting anyway, and therefore becomes at war with itself." I shrug resignedly. "Now I must stop it before it's too late."

She nods, solemn again, and does not return to her fish. I wonder if I have put her off it.

Everything after that is more businesslike, as the resumption of the music, louder now, makes further small talk impossible. She leans in and tells me about the shaman—bàbáláwò—she has found, and when he will be expecting us—in the morning. My preference would've been to leave immediately, but she explains

things don't work that way. I request a rendezvous point, and she insists she will come get me. She also insists on accompanying me back to my hotel.

"These streets are not safe for a newcomer like you to navigate alone at this time, and in your current state…" She lets the sentence hang.

A retort rises in my chest. *I am the Black Panther*, I want to say. *I am a king and protector. I am capable of handling myself.* But I push it all down.

Lay aside that weight on your shoulders, my father had said. Perhaps this was one of those times.

"Well, this is your city," I say. "Lead the way."

THE RIDESHARE trip Àbíké́ and I take the next day is the most zigzag thing I have ever participated in in my life. I have visited multiple cities on the continent before, especially since no diplomats are allowed into Wakanda, so I have to meet them in their countries. Often, I move in a convoy and the paths before us are cleared by police or military escorts. But for the first time, I am in a foreign city on a non-stealthy operation, moving as one with the ants of its own people, and nothing prepares me for the madness that is Lagos on a weekday morning.

I've come to understand that most cities on the continent are unlike Birnin Zana—no city in the world is, anyway. I've always understood them to be haphazard and fierce, with a few pockets of decorum, but all underpinned by a relentlessness that would put anyone on edge. Lagos, however, I find is another kind of ferocious. Despite how early it is in the day, every driver—ours included—is already in attack mode. They hiss, curse, belittle, intimidate. Our driver leans on his horn and pokes his body out of the window to yell at someone to *Move, idiot!* The other driver responds with their own horn and a rude gesture. And while all this happens, several cars whip around both, only to settle into the gathering traffic jam a few yards ahead. This scenario repeats itself at every junction with a traffic light between my hotel and our destination, a place Àbíkẹ́ refers to as Mile 2.

As often when I ride through these streets, I think of the stark difference with Birnin Zana's Vibranium-driven transport infrastructure and wonder how it may be of use here. All this energy on display could be put to better use if everyone wasn't so involved in a race for survival, where those who blink for too long get relegated to the background. But the usual worries resurface: what if someone with the wrong motives got hold of this technology? Over the years, I have fought people trying to commandeer Vibranium for their own selfish ends. There is no guarantee that such do not exist amongst those exactly like me— if anything, there is a higher likelihood I could be hoodwinked by kinship.

"Worried about something?" Àbíkẹ́ asks, an eyebrow raised. Today, just like the day before, she is dressed in work clothes and a jacket.

"Not worried, just thinking," I say. "Look at all this bustle. How great would it be to harness it for the right use? Just the right support and technological advancements, and imagine what Lagos could become." I look at her. "Okoye ever tell you what the Golden City is like?"

"Only in bits, but I know enough to visualize," she says. "Lagos is no Birnin Zana, though. Nor can it ever be, regardless of technology."

I find that an interesting take. "How so?"

She tilts her head. "We have a history you do not have. Look, for instance, at how I take you to someone who will connect you to the gods of your own people, yet we do so in hiding. We are a people you have never had to be; we hold on to beliefs suffused with lies and handed down to us by strangers, in a way you've never had to. We have molded fictions to make those beliefs comfortable, and we fight amongst ourselves about who has the best interpretation of them. This is not unique to us, yes, but it is a reminder that our problems are not technological problems. They are problems of the self, of our very being, twisted and now unrecognizable." She cocks her head. "Perhaps, like your illness, it is our own body fighting against us. And we struggle with that because we are forever playing catch-up, always less-than because too much has been shaved off us. That's something no amount of technology can fix."

I ruminate on that for a moment. "You don't think some sort of upgrade, technological or otherwise, could at least help begin that journey?"

"Maybe," she says. "But I think it is a journey we must be ready to undertake ourselves. We must desire it before we can accept any help we wish. Otherwise, it is just another case of someone imposing upon us something we are unprepared for." She looks at me. "And though it may come from a sister nation, if that sister nation has not itself gone through the same suffering and oppressions as we have, then what is the difference between you and our past or current oppressors?"

"I wouldn't be forcing it down your throats if I simply offered it, though, would I?"

"You wouldn't need to." There is a strength and edge to her tone, one that says she has thought about this for a while. "You of all people must know that something offered by a hand that possesses power, no matter the intent, carries the danger of compulsion? It is in the nature of power to impel, even though inadvertently. Which is why, as ungrateful as it sounds, offering what isn't asked for is not always the right choice."

We zip across the bridge over the lagoon separating the city's islands from its mainland. Looking out over the gray-green water, I wonder if this is the same reason Bàbálúayé, who had once helped my mother when she asked for it, did not reach out when she was dying. Or now, when I myself could very well be on the same path. Perhaps asking for help holds much more power than I think.

WE ARRIVE at Mile 2 and the slated house after three hours, most of it spent in traffic jams seemingly caused by nothing but ebullience. The bungalow before us has seen parts of it renovated multiple times, an old frame with patches of new wrapping. The front sections of the low roof are of newer zinc than everywhere else, and the masonry pillars have been painted afresh recently, stark against the was-once-white of the sides. Old elegance trying to stay relevant. A young woman bounces a baby while seated in a plastic chair to one side. Àbíkẹ́ greets her in Yoruba and inquires about someone. They converse for a short, sharp stint, and the woman shouts someone's name, before giving us a final once-over and returning to her baby-bouncing. I ask Àbíkẹ́ about the communal living vibes I'm picking up. She points out that it is a face-me-I-face-you house, many one-room apartments smushed together and rented by strangers who are forced to share everything, bathrooms included, and become closer to family than they would like. This makes sense, because what I truly sense is simply the performance of community, as any familial or neighborly affection is notably absent.

A man emerges from the front door with no shirt on. He wears a long, drawn expression that immediately turns into a beaming, earnest smile once he sees Àbíkẹ́, and particularly once he spots me.

"Àbíkẹ́-Àbíkẹ́," he hails, while giving me a once-over, eyes lingering for a bit over my necklace.

Ooh, my necklace! The one part of my Wakandan identity I completely forgot to take off before coming on this trip. I tuck it into my shirt to hide it.

"So this na the oga, ehn?" He stretches out a hand. "Welcome sir."

I shake it, giving him my own appraisal, remembering what Shuri said about me being shiny. Strong hands, rounded biceps, a bit of belly. Definitely a worker in an occupation requiring physicality. Family man, if I had to guess. He possesses a soft roundness borne by men who eat well, which for an African man means it is more likely than not that he never has to cook his own food. Also, judging by the way he winks at Àbíkẹ́, I am *pretty* sure he is a family man.

460

"Lemme go and wear shirt and we'll be going," he says, disappearing into the house. I lead Àbíké off to one side.

"Are we being scammed?" I ask.

"What do you mean?"

"That man," I say, "is not a bàbáláwò. At least, not from the research I've done on what to expect and the signs to look out for."

"Signs?" she scoffs. "Like?"

"I don't know. Aren't they supposed to be, like, priests?"

"Maybe you've been watching too many old films," she says. "But no, this is Rahim, not our bàbáláwò. Rahim is a middleman."

My eyes widen. "Excuse me, a *what*?"

"Did Okoye not tell you?" she asks. "You don't just find or walk up to a bàbáláwò here. Someone has to connect you with one. That's what people like Rahim do—they connect things that would rather not be, eh, connected. The practice isn't particularly condoned, you see."

My internal alarm begins to flare. I was already skeptical about working with two strangers. A third is one more stranger than I'm comfortable with. This would be a good time to contact Shuri and consult, but there is the small matter of being spotted in the Habit—the only way I can keep long-range, undetectable contact with Wakanda. I could risk it, but what if I fall into one of my bouts, and it lasts long enough for me to be spotted?

I grit my teeth. No good choices here.

"How do you know he's legit?" I ask.

"We don't," she says, mostly unperturbed. "So we shine our eyes." She clicks her tongue. "Welcome to Lagos, Your Highness."

Rahim returns, humming a tune. He screams instructions about where he's going to some invisible person who does not respond, and then we're on our way.

This time, we take one okada each to our next destination, only minutes away. My rider is a teenage boy who wields the motorcycle like an aircraft, weaving between vehicles and human traffic and balancing it on sidewalks. I am windswept by the time all three of us gather at what I believe is the bàbáláwò's place. The gate guard lets us in when he spots Rahim.

Surprisingly, this is a very good-looking house. Veranda tiles polished clean; clearly bulletproof doors—imported, if I had to guess; a small hedge. There's a child watching us through the screen door, who is soon joined by a smallish man who beams upon spotting us just in the same way Rahim did. He greets us, tells me I can call him Aláfiá Orìṣà Ilé Ifà, and then ushers us through a back door to a separate part of the house that, immediately as I enter, smells like mold.

It's a small office with a desk and chair. On one wall are customer reviews, printed off various online listings like Yelp and Amazon, all congregated around a framed photo of him that reads: *Aláfiá Orìṣà Ilé Ifà Limited: Guidance, Elevation, Ancestor Reverence, Physical/Spiritual Readings, Cleanings & Healing!* The adjoining room, which we enter right away, is clearly a divination room, and has all the accoutrements I'd learned about while reading up on practitioners of divination: sacred trays, sacred palm and kola nuts, sacred chain, powder, and a bunch of incantation verses written in Yoruba on a wall.

He asks us to sit in some plastic chairs, and we do.

"Rahim has told me everything you want." He keeps a calm, firm expression. "You wish to communicate with Bàbálúayé. Now, I don't ask my clients what they need it for, as long as you can pay. Have you been told how much?"

Àbíkẹ́ concludes the conversation with him in Yoruba, and they read out a number to her—bank account details—and she sees to payment as instructed by Okoye or Shuri, I'm not sure which, I only know that it's been arranged. I watch it all with interest.

While this is happening, the next bout hits me out of nowhere.

I know it's worse this time even before I crumble to the ground. My knees become useless immediately, ribs feeling like they could crack in contraction. My head pounds so hard I strain my eyes wide. The three gather, asking questions I don't hear. They lift me up, but I only know the feeling of being carried, not of their hands. A sharp pain runs through my chest when they lay me down in what seems like a bath, and then pour water over me. Now it feels like there is something crawling in me, eating through me.

Someone—the Aláfiá—pulls my shirt open and rubs something powdery on my chest. At this point, I feel close to a convulsion, vision slowly clouding, and I can't tell if my body is jerking or not. He opens my lips and pours something between them. The pungent smell of alcohol, mixed with some kind of bitters and whatever else, goes down my throat, but that is the least of my problems, as I'm trying to combat the sudden heat of my body, fire under my skin like a fever accelerating.

Then, suddenly, it's all subsided at once. Except I still feel myself fade, control and feeling leaving my hands. Weightlessness takes over, my vision growing dimmer. I can see all three figures, but they are wobbly now. *A strong drink, that*, I think. *What was in—*

One of the three figures stabs something into the person in the middle—Àbíkẹ́—and she crumples to the ground.

Oh, f—

THERE IS nothing but dark murkiness before me. I am a floating ball of consciousness. Though I can see the events of the divination room, it is a screen far, far away, too far to make out anything but fuzzy movement. All around me is black ink, and I am swimming in it. It isn't too different from the transitory phase I often encounter when the Chief Shaman helps send me into Djalia. But that doesn't stop me from panicking.

Doomed, is the only thing I can think. *I am doomed.*

If I survive this, what am I to say to my people, who rely on me? That the one time their protector's strength and powers had been curtailed to make way for healing, I succumbed to the ways of the world beyond? Not even to a physical element, but to a simple con!

Is this what I get from reaching out? I ask, to my father, but really into the void. This is clearly why Wakanda stays hidden, why we cannot afford to show or open ourselves to the world. Despite knowing how powerful we are, we would always be worried—and rightfully so—that any kink in our armor, any little demonstration of our humanness, would be interpreted as weakness and exploited. If the king and Black Panther cannot survive the outside world without his powers, how can Wakandans ever feel *they* can trust the world more?

Open yourself up, my father's voice echoes in my head. *Trust.*

So I close my eyes and trust.

o———o

THE PROCESS of spiritual connection is the same regardless of where or who one is connecting to: be it Djalia, Bast, or as I soon discover, Bàbálúayé. First comes the sinking, the sense of drowning, but only for a short moment. Next comes the asking: creating a very clear picture in the mind of who it is I wish to connect to or converse with. I have no image of Bàbálúayé, so instead I think of my mother, how I have always imagined her from the pictures I've been shown and stories I have been told. Her grace, her patience, her fierceness, her smile. All of this brings a strong enough sense of presence that I can hold on to.

And the third and final: waking.

I open my eyes and she is there: my mother, N'Yami. Standing before me, in what looks similar to Djalia, but different. This feels like not a separate Great Veldt, but one of my own making, of my own design. It feels like I have opened up a connection that once did not exist, and it unveils before me in real-time. I look at myself—hands, feet, body: *I created this.*

I know it is her, even though she looks wildly different than I have imagined, more *alive* than I could ever conjure.

She nods to me, smiles, her eyes tight and shiny.

"Well done," she says, and it all goes blank.

o———o

WHEN I open my eyes again, I stand before a god.

Bàbálúayé exists as a shimmer, one that never stays in a recognizable shape long enough for me to retain a lasting image. First, he is a woman, tall and large and strong; then a man, tall and large and strong; then both, then neither. Next, a dog's head on the body of a spirit made of smoke and chalk dust; then a tree that speaks, but only through the patter of rain on its leaves; then a sickness, a collection of body sores and diseases amassed over a period longer than my brain can fathom. Finally, as a formation of flies of all kinds—houseflies, mosquitoes, bees—that speak only through their buzzing.

But whichever form the god takes, he speaks. And whichever manner of speaking he employs, I understand, but cannot repeat.

It lasts for a long or a short time, I do not know—time is impossible here. But soon, I know I have all the information I need to cure what ails me: a specific, exact recipe. I know I need one single herb, one that doesn't grow in Wakanda, but does in this city, and, as it seems, I could even pick it up in the very same conservation center where the Talon Fighter is parked.

Thank you, I say into the void, but the god is already gone.

I AWAKE for a third time, wet and furious.

The two men in the divination room have their backs to me, speaking in low tones. I try not to turn my head too quickly, so that the water about me does not give me away, but only so I can look at two things. One: Àbíkẹ́, still on the floor, but seemingly alive and breathing, Bast be praised. Two: my clavicle, at the necklace.

Empty.

They recognized it. Now they know I am Wakandan. Now they probably know I'm the king. Bast knows what they have planned next.

I rise out of the water like a tsunami wronged, moving as fast as I can, so that there will be no time for these two men to respond. My body suddenly feels fresher, more awake, more *connected*.

They whip their heads around, but not in time.

I don't hit them really hard. I'm well aware that even without the Habit, and even with depleted powers due to my illness, I'm still stronger than most men. So, just a *tap, tap, tap,* fists and open palms only. Chest, shoulder, legs—no head blows. They go down easily.

The Aláfiá tries to throw something at me, but I'm able to kick his hand soon enough. Chalk dust spills all over the floor. In his other hand is the necklace. I pick it up.

"You didn't know what this was," I say, showing it to both men, "but you were willing to rob us of it." I toss the necklace in my hand. "Perhaps because you believe you possess some semblance of power, more than we do. Perhaps because you think us seeking help here means we are weak." I will the Habit out of its cloaking technology, remanifesting it into the bodysuit. "But you don't know power, and perhaps I must show you what that is."

The Habit spreads over my chest, hands, legs, face. I stand there: not yet at a hundred percent myself, but still king, still protector, still powerful. Still the Black Panther, no matter what weaknesses I perceive in myself.

"Now, I am going to pick up my friend, and I am going to leave," I say. "If you dare speak a word of this to anyone, I know where to find you." The Habit's mask makes my proclamations come on stronger than I intend. I can see them flinch. "And if she doesn't wake, by Bast, I know who to send for you." I lean in. "You think, by your connection to power, you can swindle innocent people. Let me assure you that my ancestors, my people, *me*—whatever you have, we have it much, much stronger."

ÀBÍKẸ́ COMES to only when I pull her out of the rideshare and onto the pavement.

"Ouch," she says, rubbing her forehead. "Where are we?"

"Back in Lekki," I say, above the sound of the scared driver zooming off.

She wiggles her fingers. "What happened back there?"

"We trusted."

"And?"

"And… it turned out all right."

"We got what we came for?"

I think for a second. "Yes."

She stands slowly, shakes her head. "I feel woozy."

"I can get you another rideshare."

"No, it's okay, I'll get one myself." She straightens her jacket, regarding me head to toe.

"I feel like I had a vision of you in the Black Panther suit, back there."

"Perhaps it was not a vision."

She looks me over, then it dawns on her. She reaches out, tentatively, and touches my now regular clothes.

"Is that—"

"Yes."

"I've always wondered what it looks like, worn."

I offer a wry smile. "That is a show of power. And a wise woman once told me power does not impose itself on friends."

She chuckles. "Good one. I'll see it one day, eventually." She bows slightly. "Your Highness."

Then she crosses the road and is gone.

The route back along the boardwalk is just as mishap-free as it was the first time. The monkey is no longer perched there. The crickets welcome me back as I search for the Talon Fighter's location and find it with ease. As soon as I engage it, Shuri is in contact.

"All done?" she asks over the comm. "How did it go?"

"Better than I expected," I say, engaging the thrusters and lifting the Talon Fighter through the trees. "I have a recipe that, even without trying it yet, I already know will work."

"How so?"

"Because," I say, cloaking the aircraft as I take to the city's airspace, "it comes from a place I can trust."

"Ehh," Shuri says. "I don't know what that means, but it better be good."

"Oh, it's better than good." I shift the plane into autopilot, relaxing into my seat. "It is the best of myself I have ever been and will ever be."

ZOYA THE DESERTER

TEMI OH

"THERE IS no such place," they tell her. First the police officers, and then the physicians and the immigration officials, to whom they refer her case.

Zoya awakes in a hospital in another world. Mist rises from the silty river right outside her window. An old city she's only read about in books, those gothic towers, and steeples, those high-rise office blocks glittering like shark's teeth. How can this place be real? she wants to say.

"Lon-don."

"That's right," the psychiatrist says. A middle-aged man with a kind face. "And do you know what year it is?" She opens her mouth, counting backward how many years it is since King T'Chaka took the throne. "Who is the current prime minister?" She bites her lip, her mind drawing a blank. "The US President?"

Already, regret curdles in her gut. She should never have left. A thought which had occurred to her the moment her plane took off, and the smugglers she had paid to help her escape had shouted, "Hold on tight," from the cockpit. She had braced herself as they flew into a patch of turbulent air and watched the mountains and crowded waterways of her homeland grow dim.

What will they call her now? Zoya the abdicator? The deserter.

"Do you know what happened?" he asks.

"A plane crash." She remembers that much. "Only I survived."

"That's right—" He squints down at the document on a clipboard in front of him. "—and you say that you are from a place that doesn't exist."

"Wakanda," she says. And he nods slowly, a sympathetic look in his eye.

"Are you sure? Is it known by another name?"

Home. She thinks but says nothing.

"Are you here to seek asylum?" the man asks, and she turns to him in confusion.

"From what?"

There is nothing beyond Wakanda, her mother had said. By which she had meant, there is no place better than Wakanda. Zoya curses herself now. Curses that she'd had to see for herself.

"Is there any way," she asks, "that you can help me to get back?"

He looks mournful, says quietly, "We can certainly try to help you to… get better."

SHE'D LEFT in the middle of the night. Climbed down the fire escape of her mother's high-rise apartment, careful not to turn on any lights. She'd taken almost nothing with her. A flimsy hemp rucksack, its inner pockets stuffed with cash to hand over to the smugglers.

That last sight of her bedroom had been moonlit and sorrowful. Posters peeling like leaves at their edges, sun-faded curtains, and, between them, that familiar view of step-town. Those notches on the doorpost that marked almost two decades of growth. Her Kimoyo bracelet, which she'd left on the nightstand with a letter for her mother. Her wrist had felt naked without it.

They treat wanderlust like a sickness in Wakanda. It baffles almost everyone. The countries on the border are referred to with a dismissive wave of the hand. The UK, Europe, and the US, with a wary shudder.

"Do you know what it's like out there?" the teachers and professors had said.

Pestilence and plague, war—and worse, history. History has not been kind to people like us, she had learned. And out there, whole nations of them live and die bound by the heavy shackles of it. Colonialism, warfare, slavery. We alone were saved. We alone were raised up.

But a secret longing to leave had begun to clutch at her. Zoya would pass languorous afternoons in the gilded halls of the great library, poring over foreign maps, pictures, and stories. What if she grew old and died and never sank her soles into the white sand on the beaches of Lampedusa? Would she never see Buddha's light in the Huangshan mountains? The Apollo Salon in Versailles? Or the cave of crystals in Naica? Or the quiet temples built into the moss-furred hills of Nikko?

Her yearning only grew more acute after her friend and lover, Tawanda—a beautiful misfit from the Jabari Tribe—disappeared. Her mother, who had never approved of their courtship, hoped that his disappearance would shake her from her discontent but, if anything, it did the opposite.

One more year of school and feast days, one more year of friends she had grown apart from, staid ceremony and that cold awful restlessness. By the end of it, a plan crystallized in her mind.

Once she'd resolved to do it, events progressed rapidly. It was easier than she thought it would be to come by enough money to bribe the smugglers, and as soon as she managed to, they gave her a date: "Tomorrow night."

Which left her with barely any time at all, to pack what few things it was worth taking, to write that letter, to say goodbye.

She might have said it out loud if she wasn't terrified of waking her mother.

Zoya closed the door to her bedroom carefully and stepped out into the hall of their apartment. How many times had she emerged through that door to the smell of her mother's cooking or her aunts singing or her little cousin racing up the hall with a toy train. Zoya shook the memories away like scales. No time for nostalgia.

472   Would she need a coat? The books she had read warned that it

was cold in Europe this time of year. All she owned was a woolen cardigan which was normally too warm for Wakanda's mild climate. But she grabbed it anyway, and just at the moment that her foot touched the threshold, she heard the sound of a breath behind her and almost jumped out of her skin.

A shadow at the end of the hall, her door ajar.

"Mother!" The outline of her tall figure, glister of moonlight on her silk pajamas, and on her cheekbones. "Are you crying?"

"You're leaving me," her mother said. Too late for Zoya to lie. "I'm…"

"You need to see for yourself."

"Yes."

"And you're hoping you'll find him too." Zoya didn't answer.

"They might not let you back," her mother said. "On the border. If word gets out that you used a smuggler, they may—"

"—call me a deserter and I'll be exiled forever." A heavy quiet in between them for a moment, until finally her mother said, "Wait," and ducked into her bedroom. Zoya could hear the sound of her rifling through the chest of drawers in her dresser. She emerged a moment later with something in her hand. A necklace with a panther medallion that Zoya could only just see in the dim light.

"Jewelry?"

"Your grandmother took it with her whenever she traveled." She presses it in Zoya's hand and then kisses her fingers. "To remind her of home."

"Thanks…"

"Don't thank me. You will see," her mother said, stepping back into the hall, an iron-hard resolution in her tone. "You will see that there is nothing else."

"I BELIEVE you." The nurse's name is Keesha. She's typically beautiful, with a small build and skin the color of raw sienna. Her baby hairs are gelled like a tiara around the side of her face.

Zoya has been in the hospital for almost a week and they are thinking of referring her for long-term psychiatric care as soon as the immigration officers return with an update about her case. Zoya No-one from Nowhere, they're calling her now.

They say they have never heard of Wakanda and their certainty is beginning to rattle Zoya's own sense of reality. One morning she asks one of the nurses if she could find the clothes she was wearing when they brought her into the hospital, and when the woman informs Zoya that all her clothes were lost, she finally breaks down into desolate tears. If only they could find her shoes, then at least she might be able to run her fingers along the treads, loosen the rust-colored dust and hold something from home.

"I saw when you showed the doctor that…" The nurse glances at the neckline of Zoya's papery hospital gown.

"My necklace," Zoya says, reaching in to pull it out. The burnished silver with the worn face of the goddess Bast. "Well," she says as it glints under the hospital's fluorescent light, "apparently it was my mother's. And her mother's mother's."

"Is it…?" The nurse's eyes widen with only half-suppressed glee.

"Vibranium," Zoya says.

"May I see it?"

Zoya hands the necklace over with some reluctance. Keesha examines it carefully, marveling at it. She taps it with one of her acrylic nails and senses the vibration wobble back.

"It is true…" she says in an awed whisper.

She leans into Zoya as if she might be able to find the Golden City behind her eyes. "Is it just the way they say it is? Wakanda? A utopia, almost? People live for years, they don't die of cancer? No war? No history?"

"A different history."

"That's what I mean." There are tears in her eyes now and Zoya is confused by the sight of them.

"I'm sorry," they catch in her long plastic lashes, turning her mascara to mud, "I just—I wanted so badly for it to be true."

TAWANDA HAD told her one night that he believed in nothing at all. A head-spinning blasphemy. Not the panther goddess Bast or Kokou, the god of war. He said no prayers to Mujaji, the god of hunger on feast days. Thoth or Ptah the Shaper, Sekmet, or even Sobek. He hadn't sworn fealty to the fabled White Gorilla who M'Baku, Tawanda's uncle, had claimed he ate the flesh of.

"What do you believe in?" she asked.

"Nothing," he said with a shrug. "I only want things."

"Like what?"

"To be free from this place. To be free of ceremony and tribal tensions. They tell us that the world outside is shackled by history, but I'm shackled by it here. Our tribe are outcasts. That border…"

His eyes drifted away. "It's not just about keeping them out. It's about keeping us in. And that's not the only way they do it. They hardly ever let us see maps of the whole world or films or music from Outside. They want to lock us in, lock even our desires inside."

His words made Zoya shudder. And they lay under the stars for a long while.

"I believe in something," she told him finally.

"Hm?"

"I believe in you. Believe that you can get anything your heart desires. I believe that I love you."

"I love you, too," he said and kissed her.

He'd been a musician. Had lived in the mountains with the rest of his tribe, coming into Birnin Zana occasionally, for events, concerts, and festivals. They'd meet in what little time they could snatch between one or another, and in between, only longing.

He was clever and cautious and beautiful. He was filled with the same restlessness and she loved him with a desperate kind of love.

When he'd disappeared, her heartbreak had crippled her. She'd cried so hysterically that a blood vessel in her face burst. Zoya sank into a depression from which she never properly recovered. "And you're hoping you'll find him, too," her mother had speculated. Of course she was.

ZOYA WAKES before sunrise to the sound of long-awaited rain. Liquid torrents of orange, white and green refracted through the fourth-floor window and onto the rumpled sheets of her hospital bed. The door flies open and Keesha dashes in, breathless, and glancing over her shoulder.

"We have to leave now!" It's 6 a.m. and her face is wild.

"Wait, why?"

"We have maybe two minutes before they get here."

"Who?"

"I just checked in this morning and the nurses in the staff room were saying that some officers are coming today to take you to some kind of detention center. I saw their van parked outside."

"What does that mean?"

"I'm not sure. But you're probably never going back to Wakanda." The word "never" strikes terror into Zoya's heart. In a moment of silence, they both hear the muted rumble of voices coming down the hall.

"That's them." Keesha pushes a trolly in front of the door, hoping to keep it shut.

"How will we get out?" Zoya asks, throwing off her covers and leaping out of bed.

"I have a plan." Keesha pulls off her backpack, rummages inside, and tosses Zoya a black hoodie and a pair of trainers.

"Get those on," she says and then rushes to the window. Her trembling fingers fumble to find the latch just as someone outside the door shouts, "It's locked!"

Zoya pulls on her clothes and then rushes over to help. But the latch is stuck, caked in so many years of dirt and congealed paint that it won't open.

"Someone get security!" Another voice outside and an alarm begins to sound.

Keesha swears under her breath as she fights to loosen the window. "We're trapped."

"No." Zoya leaps to her feet and looks around the room. As a thunder of boots comes along the hall outside, her eyes alight on the red tank of a fire extinguisher fixed to the wall. Zoya loosens it and turns back to the window.

With one quick pitch, the glass explodes and the roar of the rain, the sound of traffic and sirens cascades in.

The door behind them flies open and the police burst through. Keesha vaults over the sill and onto the wide window ledge. No time to wait, Zoya scrabbles out after her, onto the brick and crumbling plaster that is slicked with rain. It's about two handspans wide, easy enough to walk across if she doesn't make the mistake of looking down.

It's a sickening drop, four stories down to the canal below. When she glances at it, the street telescopes below her. If she falls, she'll surely die. Nausea roils in her stomach and Zoya tries to fight it by taking a deep breath.

"Hurry!" Keesha's voice, a meter or so ahead. She shimmies along the ledge and then turns around the corner of the building.

Zoya feels like a tightrope walker, her feet searching for purchase on the uneven surface. The ledge is wet, and for one sickening moment she thinks she feels her foot slip and her heart plunges with terror. Zoya flings her arm out, and her fingers find the cool metal of a drainage pipe which she clings desperately onto until she regains her balance.

Behind her, she can hear the police officers and security guards, leaning out the window, shouting. Zoya closes her eyes and remembers the one and only time she went to Jabari village. The narrow passes made deadly with ice and her hand in Tawanda's. Him telling her not to look back, not to look down. At the memory a calm comes over her, and she musters enough courage to keep going.

Two stories down is a bridge that leads from one window of the hospital to another. Zoya and Keesha make a leap for one of its struts, grab hold of it, then slide like firemen onto the walkway. The friction burns the palms of her hands and Zoya lets out a cry of pain once she's on her feet again.

"Over there!" comes a shout from their left. And Zoya turns to find a crowd of police officers closing in on either side of them.

"What do we do now?" Zoya asks, and her heart sinks. They really are trapped and all their efforts were in vain. Keesha looks between the hospital security staff and the police officers with the panic of a creature struggling in a trap. Then she looks over the side of the walkway, and down at the bottle-black canal below.

"We jump."

TWO FLOORS down, the wind screaming in her ears and then the hard, bruising smack of the water. Zoya knows—from her summer holidays jumping off the bluffs at Warrior Falls—that the best thing to do is not to struggle. She surrenders first to the freefall and to the freezing water as the canal swallows her whole.

It's December in London and temperatures are hovering around 0°C. The cold sears her bones, and when she finally resurfaces, her chest feels almost too tight to gasp.

Chaos everywhere, the shouts and sirens, the headlights of cars thrown in hectic shards across the surface of the water. Keesha is gasping too, coughing up water and shivering so violently her lips look blue. But she holds a finger up to them and silently the two girls swim to the muddy bank, ease themselves out of the water, and wait quietly for a long time in the shadow of the bridge.

THE AIR smells different here, of steel and smoke and gasoline. They wait quietly for almost an hour until they're so cold they can barely feel their fingers and toes. All the while, Zoya thinks back, wondering when in her life she's ever really been cold. Maybe once, that trip up the mountain to Tawanda's home.

Once Zoya and Keesha are clear of the officers they run down the rain-soaked streets and leap onto the back of a moving Routemaster bus. The kind that Zoya has seen brightly illustrated in English children's books. The kind that look like steampunk chariots.

"I'm really here." Relieved laughter spills from Zoya's mouth as she clutches the yellow grab-handle of the bus. "Really in Lon-don."

"No one says it like that," Keesha laughs. "Lon-don," and she mimics Zoya's thick accent.

"Lundun," Keesha says and they both laugh.

Because they are still shivering, Keesha suggests they get off at Tottenham Court Road and buy discounted Christmas jumpers from Primark.

Zoya has fun in the store, laughing at everything. "Why are your clothes so plain?" She picks up a black blouse. "I wouldn't wear these things even to a funeral."

Keesha shrugs. "It's modern, I guess."

They leave the shop in a different direction from the way they came in, via Oxford Street, where the Christmas lights are up. Oversized baubles and stars, lovely palimpsests of light.

"Do they celebrate Christmas there…?" Keesha asks.

Zoya shakes her head. "We don't celebrate the other one, either. That other feast day about the man who was executed and came back from the dead."

"Easter," Keesha laughs, but Zoya is distracted. She is dazzled by everything on Oxford Street. The sweetshops and clothing stores, the brightly lit outlets with "I (heart) London" hoodies in every size and color. The gasoline rainbows making rivulets of yellow and purple in the gutters. The red buses and beetle-black taxis with adverts pasted across them. Everything surprises her. The busyness of the place and the people. She's most fascinated by the cars, the sound and smell of the metal beasts that she's only ever seen scale models of in the tech museum.

"Is it true they eat oil?" she asks as she steps out into the road.

The sound of a horn erupts from one of them. Keesha grabs Zoya's hand and tugs her out of the way as the driver swerves to miss them.

"Watch out!" he shouts.

"Saved your life again," Keesha says. "Don't they have cars where you come from?"

"We do—" Zoya says, looking down at the pavement. "—but they don't have wheels."

"What, no one's invented that yet?"

"No," Zoya says with a shrug, "our cars fly."

ZOYA WANTS to devour the whole city. To see everything. Although Keesha is keen to get home, Zoya pelts her with questions, about everything. About school, about their queen. She wants to know what their country buys and sells if not Vibranium.

She wants to go to their department stores and touch everything. To do the "tourist things"—sit on the brass backs of the lions at the base of Nelson's Column. To peer at the armed guards outside Downing Street. Or marvel at the white-stuccoed buildings along Belgravia that look like iced cakes. She wants to sing every song about the city she's ever heard.

"I love it, too," Keesha says as they walk through Theatre-land and come out in Chinatown. "You know my dad, he was from Ghana, he was a lecturer there in a university. An expert in ecology. But he came to the UK hoping to build us all a better life, and he died here working as a security guard."

"That doesn't sound better," Zoya says.

Keesha shrugs. "All I know is that I love this city. That it's in my bones like a sickness."

As they walk through Chinatown, Zoya thinks she can glean some of what her friend loves about the place. Although there are many different tribes in Wakanda, with their own variations of customs and cuisine, it's nothing like the fierce melting pot of cultures that thrives here. Zoya slows her step as they walk through Chinatown, staring up at the vermillion paper lanterns strung between terraced apartments. In the window of every restaurant are a hundred things she has never seen before, let alone tasted.

By the time they enter the British Museum, she's heady with delight. The kind of joy that comes from finally touching a thing you've always wanted. She can hardly believe it—here she is, with a total stranger in the middle of a real adventure.

480   "My favorite things are the mummies," Keesha says as they

head into the great court of the museum, "although I can never remember how to find them."

This is one place that Zoya did learn about in school. Although, standing here now, in the middle of the quadrangle, it's easy, in the face of its austere beauty, to forget what she'd learned. It's still raining outside and the sky is gun-metal gray through the tessellated glass roof. The voices of the tourists and schoolchildren echo in a white noise roar off it.

The two of them end up walking for what feels like hours through the bright airy galleries that smell of dust. And as they do, Zoya's heart wrestles with them. The museum is a dream, she can see, an attempt to capture the world, to catalogue its history and return it here, neatly polished, to Bloomsbury. Except that all she's ever been taught is that history is brutal. That so many of these treasures were paid for with blood. She hears her mother's voice in her head by the time they reach the Africa galleries, a bitter taste in her mouth, and she has to sit down for a moment on the bench.

"My dad talked about the bronzes all the time, too," Keesha says, and they both stare at the exquisitely carved plaques. "About how the British colonial officers looted them from the royal palaces of Benin and sacked the ancient city like thieves."

"Not 'like,'" Zoya says. She looks away, down at the marble floor, and says, "Don't you find it hard to enjoy any of this when you know things like that?"

Keesha shakes her head. "Obviously, I think they should be sent back. That reparations are owed. But also, history is bloody. Unforgiving."

"Not ours," Zoya says and her friend's eyes flash. "It's true. We've never invaded anyone. Not slaughtered or executed their people. Not sold them like cattle into generations of slavery."

Keesha flinches. "That's true, but who has Wakanda ever helped except for themselves?"

Zoya is startled. This is a point of view she has never heard before.

"You have so much technology, you have a cure for cancer,

and yet you live in your happy bubble while people outside starve or suffer and die. You pay nothing in foreign aid, you host no immigrants or refugees. You say that 'history has not been kind to people like you,' but how kind have you been?"

THE SUN is setting by the time they have lunch. They sit under the florescent lights of a McDonald's and Zoya wolfs down a burger.

"I haven't tasted anything like it," she laughs and takes a long, delicious drag of cola. "This one tastes like syrup."

By this time Keesha has grown distracted and withdrawn. Finally, she tells her companion what is on her mind.

"You might be wondering why I risked my life, and my job, to save you."

"Because you're kind?" Zoya says hopefully.

"Because I need your help," she says. "I need a way to get into Wakanda."

"I don't even have a way," Zoya says, her heart sinking as she comes again to consider the gravity of her situation. She's a fugitive, a complete foreigner in this strange place.

"But you do." Keesha's eyes fall to Zoya's chest.

"This?" She pulls out the panther medallion again. "How will this get me home?"

Keesha looks over her shoulder, leans in, and whispers, "Don't you know what you have? Don't you know what this is?" When Zoya shakes her head she looks astounded. "I thought for sure you were a member of the royal family or something. A princess, or related to one."

"No, my father was… um, sort of like a diplomat. We call them 'Hatut Zeraze,' but he died when I was young and my mother is a professor."

"Well, maybe one of them knew a member of the royal family. Because this—" She eyes the medallion meaningfully. "—this is a token of the royal family. A sign of peace."

482   Zoya examines it again, holds it up to the light and notices, this

time, the engraving along its side that reads, *The friends of our friends are our friends*. "Peace," she says in a low voice. Thinking back to the urgent way that her mother had pressed the thing into her hands.

"How do you know about this?"

"So, you know I told you I have a friend who knows about Wakanda?"

"I don't know if you did."

"Well, okay, I do. I have a friend. Well, actually," a blush rises in her cheek, "more than a friend. He's spent his life finding out about these things. He wants to go. He *needs* to."

"But it's impossible," Zoya says. "The border tribe will capture him and throw him in jail or—"

" —not if he shows them this," Keesha says. "They'll know he's a friend. They'll grant him safe passage into the Golden City. How else do you think the friends of the royal family travel in and out of Wakanda with no problem?"

Zoya's head is spinning all of a sudden, with awe and gratitude to her mother who had the foresight to give this gift to her. A way to return home.

"But, why would I give it to you?" Zoya's eyes narrow. It seems to make sense now, why this stranger would risk her life to save a runaway she met at a hospital. Of course, Keesha wants something from Zoya. How naive she feels for not suspecting this before. Zoya says nothing, too uncomfortable with the sudden tension between them. Keesha takes a deep breath and then says it quickly.

"Remember what we were talking about in the museum. About kindness. About being a good person? A noble woman? How history has so few of them. I believe that you are, though." She leans forward. "I believe *you* are. That you can be. There is someone I love who needs your help. Someone whose life depends on it."

KEESHA LIVES with her grandmother and her three brothers in a rundown council flat off Edgware Road. They take the bus there, and all the way, Keesha tells Zoya about the man she's in love with.

Zoya smiles. "I know how that feels," she says. "How good it feels to be in love."

The two of them disembark on a crowded high street that is sweet with the smell of shisha. Less grand than central London, just as crowded. Fabric stores and phone shops, cracked pavements and schoolchildren.

They turn down a slip road and take an elevator that's covered all over with lurid bubbles of graffiti. Through an uncovered walkway to a chipboard door and, behind it, the noise and squalor of six people living in a flat that was built for two. The sound of the television clashes with the heavy bass coming out of a speaker in someone's bedroom. Behind the thin walls, someone is arguing.

"I'm home," Keesha shouts, her shoulders relaxing as she steps over the threshold.

"You have a friend." The old woman in the hall is her grandmother. She's bundled like a snowman in layers of bobbled polyester. "Boiler's broken again."

"This is my—" Maybe Keesha was going to say the word *patient*, but she stops herself. "—friend."

"Well, welcome friend."

"Welcome," Zoya nods respectfully. "I mean—thank you."

"How is he?" Keesha asks.

Her grandmother simply shakes her head and Keesha looks crestfallen at the old woman's response.

"What's the matter?" Zoya asks.

"My friend," she says, a sob catching in her throat. "He's very sick."

As they walk together down the shadowed hall, Keesha says, "They say waiting for someone to die is like waiting for a baby to be born."

"Who says that?" Zoya asks as they walk.

"Maybe only me."

He's in her bedroom, gaunt and stained with sweat. Half-asleep.

484   "It's worse when you love someone," Keesha says, walking over to his bedside, to take his hand and kiss his forehead. "I keep thinking, 'I wish it was me.'"

"You?" Zoya starts at the sight of him, feeling as if the floor might fall out from under her. The whole room tells the story of the life they live together. Dented takeaway boxes, turmeric-yellow curry stains, the jagged edge of a condom wrapper. The smell of body odor and sick. She's memorized the face of the man in the bed. Kissed every part of it. Skin like hickory wood. Dreadlocks. Sharp lovely features.

"Zoya?" He says, not surprised at all.

"Tawanda?"

THEY'D TRAVELED to the border forest together once, she and Tawanda, and spent a night together sleeping in a tent under the stars. The forest itself was lush with life. Trees she'd learnt the names of in kindergarten; the Bladdernut and the Real Yellowwood, the weeping Karee and African Holly with its fragrant blossoms and bright red fruit. The sound of birds, and the smell of mist rising up from the foliage. Soil black as crude oil and bright spears of sunlight lancing through the verdant canopy.

"I think the last time I came here," Zoya had said, "I was a child."

"That school trip," Tawanda smiled. "I think it's required for everyone."

"'What is our border for?'" Zoya quotes her teacher.

"Someone always says 'to keep others out?'"

"Yes, and our teachers say—"

"—'to preserve what's inside.'" They say together.

That night, it had suddenly occurred to Zoya how happy she was, with him. And she was overcome with a strange kind of nostalgia, for her present moment. A longing to preserve it forever, a terrible awareness of the passing of time. "Why are you crying?" Tawanda had asked.

"Because I'm so happy," she'd said. He'd smiled and kissed her on each of her cheeks.

"I'm happy too," he'd said, then bit on the word. "I'm happy because..." Still neither of them had the courage to say it.

"Happy because...?" she'd prompted. She could see her own face reflected in the jet of his eyes, bent as if in a spoon.

"...I love you." They said it at the same time and then started laughing. Though it wasn't long until a chill of seriousness came upon them.

They were both quiet for the rest of the night, drawn inward with a sudden anxiety.

I love you felt like a promise, Zoya realized with a shudder.

She tried to project her mind forward, ten years, twenty. Would it still be true, these words they had uttered at eighteen? Shouldn't it always be? Shouldn't it outlast even death?

"I never want it not to be true," she'd said finally in a hollow whisper, her hands cold. And she could tell from the look in his eyes that he had been thinking the same thing.

HAD THIS been part of his design? To summon her like a ghost from his past life only to trap her here?

"No," he promises.

"But I've been keeping an ear out," Keesha says. "In my job. Looking for someone, anyone, who might know a way to help him."

"It's a kind of fast-moving cancer," he tells her, "the doctors say I don't have long."

He winces in pain and readjusts himself with some effort in the bed. Zoya can see how much the muscles in his arms have wasted, and some of her old tenderness for him returns.

"You said you would always—"

"I know what I said." His face is a picture of regret. "There are so many things that if I had a chance to... mistakes. Forgive me? I thought I would never see you again."

"But I came after you. I found you. I sacrificed everything, to find you." Zoya can feel a hot rush of tears and fights to choke them back.

"And I'm grateful," he says, with a heavy rasp, "blessed. You're Bast-sent. A hero."

"You can be," Keesha says, looking meaningfully at the panther medallion around Zoya's neck.

Hero, though. The word sticks like a barb in her thoughts. Hadn't she had something like this in mind all those years she spent reading stories in the gilded library of the Golden City? Escape means adventure. Adventure means a chance to be heroic, and what is more heroic than sacrifice?

Zoya considers her mother, something she had once overheard her saying. "I'm so proud of Zoya. It's not even just because she's clever, or talented and respectful, it's because she's kind. Thank Bast, isn't that what all mothers hope for? To create a good thing. A good person. There is more good in the world now, because of her."

"You'll never see him again," Zoya says to Keesha, an edge of spite in her voice. "If I give him my necklace and he returns home."

"I know," Keesha says, "but I'll never see him again if he dies."

A tear rolls down Zoya's cheek. She'd been so heartbroken to lose him, that first time. How much more devastating would it be to lose him forever?

"Okay," she says, unlatching her necklace. "Okay."

THE TRIP to the airport a week later is somber. Rain lashes the windows of the cab and the gray streets melt to nothing behind them. Keesha cries most of the way, gripping Tawanda's hand. Zoya fixes her gaze out of the windscreen. At the endless streets of suburbs, in the gray fields, and suddenly she's repulsed by this place. Sodium streetlamps and drenched pedestrians. The rain gusting up the sidewalks. When she handed over the panther medallion, she'd felt her hope vanish along with it. She's slept on the sofa of Keesha's crowded apartment for almost a week now. There is talk that a friend of a friend can get her work washing dishes in a kitchen—Keesha had told Zoya this news brightly, as if it was supposed to thrill her.

Last night she'd spent what little money she had on a cardboard box of chicken that, halfway through eating, she discovered was still pink inside. A little while later, the sickness had come, heaving into the toilet, crouched on the cold floor shivering. She'd lain back on the rotten bathroom mat and looked at the black speckles of mold growing in a constellation across the ceiling. Homesick. She'd thought. She'd sold her destiny for what?

The taxi drops them off at Terminal Four and they all pile out into the crowded airport departures area. Zoya's only flown on a plane once in her life and she stares at the destinations lit up on the board. Rome, Bangkok, Tokyo, Niganda. She tries to remind herself that this is what freedom means. Now she's left Wakanda she could go to any of those places.

Although—she glances at the boarding pass Tawanda is clutching in his hands with a sudden stab of envy—perhaps there is only one place she wants to go.

"I guess this is goodbye," he says to her, once he's finished making whispered promises and apologies to Keesha.

"I guess," Zoya says. It hurts, almost, not to touch him.

"You're saving my life." He pats his duffle bag where he's hidden the necklace. "I don't even have the words to thank you."

Zoya nods modestly. Zoya the hero, she thinks to herself. To everyone else she's an illegal immigrant, a vagrant. Back home, she's a deserter. But, at least, to these two people, she's a hero.

When he hugs her she realizes that he still smells the same, smells of home. Of dust, and Jabari wood.

"Take care of yourself," he says.

"Can I see it?" Zoya asks on a sudden whim. "One last time?"

"Sure," Tawanda says, opening his duffle bag and handing it to her.

The friends of my friends… This time, when she holds it she imagines her grandmother, who'd been a member of the *Dora Milaje* for many years and then worked to train new warriors. Zoya wonders, now, if *she* was given this medallion as a token of affection from some member of the royal family. If she gave it to her daughter as

Zoya's mother gave it to her. The real gift isn't the exquisite carvings, the way the metal catches the light, the reassuring weight of it in the palm of the hand—the real gift is home.

Her mind balks when she tries to imagine Tawanda's journey. To Niganda—as there are no direct commercial flights to Wakanda—and then across the border. With this royal token that will grant him safe passage, back into the Golden City, where it's summer for half the year. To a hospital where he may be cured, though his path is still uncertain.

So is hers.

"Sometimes I wake up in the night thinking she was right, after all," Tawanda laughs to himself.

"Huh?" Zoya looks up at him, though her thoughts are still far away.

"Your mother. Maybe there isn't anything else. Not for us, anyway."

"Don't say that!" Keesha gasps.

"I feel as if leaving made me sick. The way astronauts return to earth with withered bones, the kind of sick you get from being too far from where you belong."

When she looks up again, he's smiling benevolently.

"I always knew you were the best of them." He reaches to take back the necklace but she doesn't let it go. "The kindest of them."

How kind am I? A thought that flashes white-toothed like lightning in the back of her head. Kind. History hasn't been kind to people like us, as they all say. Except that it has been to Wakandans.

Another thought occurs to her, a wild, selfish impulse, and she tries to bat it away. Looks down at the medallion again. She wanted adventure but she doesn't want any of this place. The cars, the gray weather, the food. She doesn't want to spend her life dreaming of the Warrior Falls, or the Golden City. Or her mother's voice. Or the way the sun looks behind a veil of Wakandan dust. She will tread a circle, she will go from city to city, a nomad, a loner, and when she describes her home they will tell her, "there is no such place." If he leaves her now, how can she return?

"Tawanda," she says, and her grip on the necklace tightens, "I think history is kind to people who are kind to themselves." He sees in her eyes what she's about to do, but before he can reach out a hand to stop her, she is running.

As fast as she can, through the crowded airport, the luggage carousels and uniformed air hostesses, the queues of weary travelers. Outside, she hails a cab with no idea how she'll pay, but as she rides away she feels like the richest woman in the world. Her grandmother's necklace is as heavy as gold bullion in her pocket. She could still have an adventure. She could still go anywhere in the world, could still see Lampedusa, Huangshan, or Nikko—but there is only one place she longs to go.

ABOUT THE AUTHORS

LINDA D. ADDISON

Linda D. Addison is an award-winning author of five collections, including *How to Recognize a Demon Has Become Your Friend,* and the first African-American recipient of the Horror Writers Association Bram Stoker Award®. She has received the HWA Mentor of the Year Award and the HWA Lifetime Achievement Award. In 2020, the Science Fiction & Fantasy Poetry Association designated her a Grand Master of Fantastic Poetry, and she has over 350 poems, stories, articles in print. Linda received her fifth HWA Bram Stoker Award this year for *The Place of Broken Things,* written with Alessandro Manzetti. She's excited about the 2020 release of a film (inspired by her poem of same name) *Mourning Meal* by award-winning producer/director Jamal Hodge. She has fiction in three early landmark anthologies celebrating African-American speculative writers: the award-winning anthology *Dark Matter: A Century of Speculative Fiction* (Warner Aspect), *Dark Dreams I* and *II* (Kensington), and *Dark Thirst* (Pocket Books). Her work has made frequent appearances over the years on the honorable mention list for *Year's Best Fantasy and Horror* and *Year's Best Science Fiction.* She has a BS in Mathematics from Carnegie-Mellon University and currently lives in Arizona.

MAURICE BROADDUS

A community organizer and middle school teacher, his work has appeared in magazines like *Lightspeed Magazine, Weird Tales, Beneath Ceaseless Skies, Asimov's, Cemetery Dance, Uncanny Magazine*, with some of his stories having been collected in *The Voices of Martyrs*. His books include the urban fantasy trilogy *The Knights of Breton Court*, the steampunk works *Buffalo Soldier*, and the award-winning *Pimp My Airship*. His middle grade detective novels include *The Usual Suspects* and *Unfadeable*. As an editor, he's worked on *Dark Faith* anthology series, *Fireside Magazine, Streets of Shadows, People of Colo(u)r Destroy Horror*, and *Apex Magazine*. Learn more at MauriceBroaddus.com.

CHRISTOPHER CHAMBERS

Christopher Chambers is a Washington, D.C. native and a Professor of Media Studies at Georgetown University. He's written the award-winning bestselling Angela Bivens novels from Random House *Sympathy for the Devil* and *A Prayer for Deliverance*; his short story "Leviathan" was nominated for a PEN/Malamud Award for short fiction. He co-edited the popular *The Darker Mask* with author Gary Phillips, published by Macmillan and featuring writers Walter Mosely, Lorenzo Carcaterra, Mat Johnson, Naomi Hirahara, Victor Lavalle, and award-winning artists like Shawn Martinbrough. He is the author of pulp novel *Rocket Crockett and the Shanghai She Devil*, and a contributor to *Black Pulp I*, and *The Bronze Buckaroo Rides Again* (where he penned the Foreword). He is a contributor to the bestselling and Anthony Award-winning political/pulp/speculative fiction anthology *The Obama Inheritance*, published by Three Rooms Press. His "new-noir" crime novel *Scavenger* has been starred by *Publisher's Weekly* as "groundbreaking."

MILTON J. DAVIS

Milton Davis is a Black fantastic fiction writer and owner of MVmedia, LLC, a publishing company specializing in science fiction and fantasy based on African/African Diaspora culture, history and traditions. Milton is the author of nineteen novels; his most recent is the post-apocalyptic adventure *Gunman's Peace*. He is the editor and co-editor of nine anthologies; *The City, Terminus, Blacktastic, Dark Universe* with Gene Peterson; *Griots: A Sword and Soul Anthology* and *Griot: Sisters of the Spear* with Charles R. Saunders; *The Ki Khanga Anthology*, the *Steamfunk!* anthology, and the *Dieselfunk* anthology with Balogun Ojetade. MVmedia has also published *Once Upon A Time in Afrika* by Balogun Ojetade and *Abegoni: First Calling* and *Nyumbani Tales* by Sword and Soul creator and icon Charles R. Saunders. Milton's work has also been featured in *Black Power: The Superhero Anthology; Skelos 2: The Journal of Weird Fiction* and *Dark Fantasy Volume 2, Steampunk Writers Around the World* published by Luna Press, and *Bass Reeves Frontier Marshal Volume Two*. His Steamfunk story "The Swarm" was nominated for the 2017 British Science Fiction Award. You can contact Milton Davis from his website: https://www.miltonjdavis.com.

TANANARIVE DUE

Tananarive Due (tah-nah-nah-REEVE doo) is an award-winning author who teaches Black Horror and Afrofuturism at UCLA. She is an executive producer on Shudder's groundbreaking documentary *Horror Noire: A History of Black Horror*. She and her husband/collaborator, Steven Barnes, wrote "A Small Town" for Season 2 of *The Twilight Zone* on CBS All Access and episodes in SerialBox's *Black Panther: Sins of the King*. A leading voice in Black speculative fiction for more than twenty years, Due has won an American Book Award, an NAACP Image Award, and a British Fantasy Award, and her writing has been included in best-of-the-year anthologies. Her books include *Ghost Summer: Stories, My Soul to Keep*, and *The Good House*. She and her late mother, civil rights activist Patricia Stephens Due, co-authored *Freedom in the Family: A Mother-Daughter Memoir of the Fight for Civil Rights*. She and Barnes live with their son, Jason, and two cats.

NIKKI GIOVANNI

Nikki Giovanni is one of America's foremost poets. Over the course of a long career, Giovanni has published numerous collections of poetry— from her first self-published volume *Black Feeling Black Talk* (1968) to

New York Times bestseller *Bicycles: Love Poems* (2009)—several works of nonfiction and children's literature, and multiple recordings, including the Emmy-award nominated *The Nikki Giovanni Poetry Collection* (2004). Her most recent publications include *Chasing Utopia: A Hybrid* (2013), *Standing in the Need of Prayer* (2020) and, as editor, *The 100 Best African American Poems* (2010). A frequent lecturer and reader, Giovanni has taught at Rutgers University, Ohio State University, and Virginia Tech, where she is a University Distinguished Professor.

HARLAN JAMES

Harlan James is an award-winning public speaker and writer of words who believes a good story is the best way to educate and entertain the world. A born-and-bred Southerner, James has spent most of his life on the periphery of the comic strip, comic book, and literature communities, and is now working on his fourth movie screenplay. When not writing, he can be found tinkering with his precious Mac computers, playing with his beloved mutt, and beating the next level on *Mortal Kombat*.

DANIAN DARRELL JERRY

Danian Darrell Jerry, a writer, teacher, and musician, holds a Master of Fine Arts in Creative Writing from the University of Memphis where he teaches literature and English composition. He is a 2020 VONA Fellow and a Fiction Editor of *Obsidian*. Danian founded Neighborhood Heroes, a youth arts program that employs comic books and literary arts. He also works with special needs students at the Bowie Reading and Learning Center. He was a featured guest at the 2019 Mercedes-Benz SXSW MeConvention at Frankfurt, Germany. His work is discussed in *This Ain't Chicago: Race, Class, & Regional Identity in the Post-Soul South* (University of North Carolina Press), *Hip Hop in America: A Regional Guide* (two volumes, Greenwood), and other publications. As a professor, he taught fiction writing and performance reading at Memphis College of Art, and he teaches literature and composition at the University of Memphis and serves as a Writing Specialist at Rust College. Currently, he revises his first novel, *Boy with the Golden Arm*. As a child he read and drew comics, and as an adult he writes his own adventures. His work appears or is forthcoming in *Fireside Fiction, Apex-Magazine.com* and *Trouble the Waters: Tales from the Deep*.

KYOKO M

Kyoko M is a *USA Today* bestselling author, a fangirl, and an avid book reader. She is the author of *The Black Parade* urban fantasy series and the *Of Cinder and Bone* science-fiction series. Her debut novel, *The Black Parade*, has been positively reviewed by *Publishers Weekly* and *New York Times* and *USA Today*-bestselling novelist, Ilona Andrews. She has been both a moderator and a panelist for comic book and science fiction/fantasy conventions like Dragon*Con, Geek Girl Con, Multiverse Con, Momocon, and The State of Black Science Fiction. She has a Bachelor of Arts in English Lit degree from the University of Georgia, which gave her every valid excuse to devour book after book with a concentration in Greek mythology and Christian mythology. When not working feverishly on a manuscript (or two), she can be found buried under her Dashboard on Tumblr, or chatting with fellow nerds on Twitter, or curled up with a good Harry Dresden novel on a warm Georgia night. Like any author, she wants nothing more than to contribute something great to the best profession in the world, no matter how small.

L.L. MCKINNEY

Leatrice "Elle" McKinney, writing as L.L. McKinney, is an advocate for equality and inclusion in publishing, and the creator of the hashtags #PublishingPaidMe and #WhatWoCWritersHear. Named one of The Root's 100 most influential African Americans of 2020, she's spent time in the slush by serving as a reader for agents and participating as a judge in various online writing contests. Elle's also a gamer, Blerd, and adamant Hei Hei stan, living in Kansas, surrounded by more nieces and nephews than she knows what to do with. She spends her free time plagued by her cat—Sir Chester Fluffmire Boopsnoot Purrington Wigglebottom Flooferson III, esquire, Baron o'Butterscotch or

#SirChester for short. Her works include the *Nightmare-Verse* books, starting with the *A Blade So Black* trilogy, and an upcoming graphic novel for DC featuring Nubia, Wonder Woman's twin sister. Elle is a Gryffindor with Slytherin tendencies.

TEMI OH

Temi Oh wrote her first novel while studying for a BS in Neuroscience. Her degree provided great opportunities to write and learn about topics ranging from "Philosophy of the Mind" to "Space Physiology." While at university, Temi founded a book-club called "Neuroscience-fiction," where she led discussions about science-fiction books which focus on the brain. In 2016, she received an MA in Creative Writing from the University of Edinburgh. Her first novel, *Do You Dream of Terra-Two?*, was published by Simon & Schuster in 2019 and won the American Library Association's Alex Award.

SUYI DAVIES OKUNGBOWA

Suyi Davies Okungbowa is a Nigerian author of fantasy, science fiction and general speculative fiction inspired by his West African origins. He is the author of the highly anticipated epic fantasy series *The Nameless Republic*, forthcoming from Orbit Books in 2021. His highly acclaimed debut, the godpunk fantasy novel *David Mogo, Godhunter*, was hailed as "the subgenre's platonic deific ideal" by *WIRED* and nominated for the BSFA Award. His shorter fiction and nonfiction have appeared internationally in periodicals like Tor.com, *Lightspeed, Nightmare, Strange Horizons, Fireside, Podcastle, Ozy,* and anthologies like *Year's Best Science Fiction and Fantasy, A World of Horror,* and *People of Colour Destroy Science Fiction*. He was named one of fifty Nigerians in the *YNaija 2020 New Establishment*.

GLENN PARRIS

Glenn Parris is the author of *The Renaissance of Aspirin*, his debut novel, *Dragon's Heir: The Archeologist's Tale*, and *Unbitten: A Vampire Dream*. His short story "The Tooth Fairies" heads up the anthology *Where the Veil is Thin* from Outland Entertainment. As a board-certified rheumatologist, Glenn Parris has practiced medicine in the northeast Atlanta suburbs for over thirty years and now writes medical mystery, science fiction, fantasy, and historical fiction.

ALEX SIMMONS

Alex Simmons is an award-winning freelance writer, comic book creator, screenwriter, playwright, teaching artist, and creative consultant. He's written for Disney Books, Penguin Press, Simon and Schuster, DC Comics, and Archie Comics. Simmons is the creator of the acclaimed adventure comic book series *Blackjack*. He has also helped develop concepts and scripts for an animation studio in England. As a teaching artist, Simmons has created and taught creative arts workshops for students and educators in the United States, West Indies, Africa, and Europe. Simmons has served on panels, and delivered lectures on children's entertainment mediums, as well as empowering young people through the arts. His clients range from Random House to the New York Film Academy. Simmons founded the annual family event Kids Comic Con, as well as three comic arts exhibits, which have traveled abroad. He is currently developing a comics and creative arts program for children in the US, Europe, Africa, and India. For over twenty years, Simmons has been a member of arts and education boards for the New York State Alliance for Arts Education, the Department for Cultural Affairs, and the Museum for Comics & Cartoon Art. He has been a panelist at many literacy and arts events, and he has been a guest speaker at numerous colleges and educational institutions here and abroad.

SHEREE RENÉE THOMAS

Sheree Renée Thomas is the author of *Nine Bar Blues: Stories from an Ancient Future* (Third Man Books), her first all fiction collection, and her work appears in *The Big Book of Modern Fantasy* (1945–2010) edited by Ann and Jeff VanderMeer (Vintage Anchor). She is also the author of two multigenre/hybrid collections, *Sleeping Under the Tree of Life*, longlisted for the 2016 Otherwise Award, and *Shotgun Lullabies* (Aqueduct Press), described as a "revelatory work like Jean

Toomer's *Cane*." A Cave Canem Fellow honored with residencies at the Millay Colony of the Arts, VCCA, Bread Loaf Environmental, Blue Mountain, and Art Omi / Ledig House, her stories and poems are widely anthologized and her essays appear in *The New York Times*. She edited the two-time World Fantasy Award-winning volumes, *Dark Matter* (2000, 2004), that first introduced W.E.B. Du Bois's work as science fiction and was the first Black author to be honored with the World Fantasy Award since its inception in 1975. She serves as the Associate Editor of the award-winning journal *Obsidian: Literature & Arts in the African Diaspora* (Illinois State University, Normal) and the Editor of *The Magazine of Fantasy & Science Fiction*, founded in 1949. Sheree was recently honored as a 2020 World Fantasy Award Finalist in the Special Award – Professional category for her contributions to the genre. She lives in Memphis, Tennessee, near a mighty river and a pyramid. Learn more at www.shereereneethomas.com

CADWELL TURNBULL

Cadwell Turnbull is the author of *The Lesson*. He is a graduate from the North Carolina State University's Creative Writing MFA in Fiction and English MA in Linguistics. Turnbull is also a graduate of Clarion West 2016. His short fiction has appeared in *The Verge, Lightspeed, Nightmare*, and *Asimov's Science Fiction* and a number of anthologies. His *Nightmare* story "Loneliness is in Your Blood" was selected for *The Best American Science Fiction and Fantasy 2018*. His *Lightspeed* story "Jump" was selected for *The Year's Best Science Fiction and Fantasy 2019* and was featured on *LeVar Burton Reads*. His debut novel *The Lesson* is a finalist for the Neukom Institute Literary Award. It has also been shortlisted for VCU Cabell Award and longlisted for the Massachusetts Book Award. Turnbull teaches creative writing at North Carolina State University.

TROY L. WIGGINS

Troy L. Wiggins is an award-winning writer and editor from Memphis, Tennessee. His short fiction has appeared in the *Griots: Sisters of the Spear, Long Hidden: Speculative Fiction From the Margins of History,* and *Memphis Noir* anthologies, and in *Expanded Horizons, Fireside, Uncanny* and *Beneath Ceaseless Skies* magazines. His essays and criticism have appeared in the *Memphis Flyer, Literary Orphans* magazine, *People of Colo(u)r Destroy Science Fiction, Strange Horizons*, PEN America, and on Tor.com. Troy is Former Co-Editor of the Hugo Award Nominated *FIYAH* Magazine of Black Speculative Fiction, which received a World Fantasy Award in 2018. He was inducted into the Dal Coger Memorial Hall of Fame for his contributions to Speculative Fiction in Memphis in 2018. Troy infrequently blogs about writing, nerd culture, and race at afrofantasy.net. He lives in Memphis, Tennessee with his wife, Kimberly, and their four-and-a-half-pound beast, Jojo. Follow him on Twitter at @TroyLWiggins.

ABOUT THE EDITOR

JESSE J. HOLLAND is the author of *The Black Panther: Who is the Black Panther?* prose novel, which was nominated for an NAACP Image Award in 2019. He is also author of *The Invisibles: The Untold Story of African American Slaves Inside the White House*, which was named as the 2017 silver medal award winner in U.S. History in the Independent Publisher Book Awards and one of the top history books of 2016 by Smithsonian.com.

Jesse is also the author of the *Star Wars: The Force Awakens – Finn's Story* young adult novel, the nonfiction book *Black Men Built The Capitol: Discovering African American History in and Around Washington, D.C.*, and is one of the co-creators of the late, lamented comic strip, *Hippie and the Black Guy*.

Jesse served as a former Distinguished Visiting Scholar In Residence at the John W. Kluge Center of the Library of Congress, a former Visiting Distinguished Professor of Ethics in Journalism at the University of Arkansas, former faculty at Goucher College's Master of Fine Arts in Nonfiction program, and was a judge for the 2020 Harper Lee Prize for Legal Fiction.

He is currently the Saturday host for C-SPAN *Washington Journal* as well as an assistant professor of Media & Public Affairs at The George Washington University. He is a former Race & Ethnicity writer for The Associated Press, as well as a former

White House, Supreme Court and Congressional reporter. Jesse was awarded a doctorate of humane letters from Lemoyne-Owen College in 2018.

He lives in Bowie, Maryland with his wife Carol, daughter Rita, son Jesse III and dog Woodson Oblivious. You can see more at his website, www.jessejholland.com.

ACKNOWLEDGEMENTS

FIRST AND foremost, I would like to thank my wife and children, without whom my life would not be complete. Thank you, Carol, Rita, and Jamie.

I would like to single out several people whose advice and kind words assisted me in working on this anthology: Jeff Youngquist, who heard about this idea first; Porscha Burke, Claudia Gray, John Joseph Adams, Jonathan Maberry, Chris Golden, Eric Flint, John Lewis, Andrew Aydin, Elana Cohen, Caitlin O'Connell, Timothy Cheng, Adri Cowan, Sheree Renée Thomas, and Stuart Moore.

I can't thank my beta readers and family enough for their support throughout this process: my parents, Jesse and Yvonne Holland; my siblings, Candace Holland, Fred Holland, and Twyla Henderson; and my ever-patient mother-in-law, Rita Womack.

At Titan Books, I would like to thank all the people who take the raw material and turn it into a physical book, including editor Sophie Robinson, Nick Landau, Vivian Cheung, Laura Price, George Sandison, Paul Gill, Chris McLane, Katharine Carroll, Lydia Gittins, and Polly Grice. Without them, you wouldn't be reading these words.

An extra-special thank you goes to Jason Anthony, whose creative mind and strong writing skills helped us with an absolutely great Nikki Giovanni story. Keep your eyes on Jason's work, because he's going to be special one day!

This book would not exist without the efforts of Stephen W. Saffel, who pushed this book across the finish line and kept me going with kindness, civility, and hard work when the night grew dark. Without him, none of this would have been possible.

I can't forget the support I received from the gang at the Kluge Center at the Library of Congress, the School of Media & Public Affairs at The George Washington University, the great people at the Smithsonian National Museum of African American History and Culture, the always supportive Alfred Street Baptist Church and Grays C.M.E. Church, the writers and students at the Goucher College Master of Fine Arts in Nonfiction program, the men of Omega Psi Phi (especially my home chapter of Eta Zeta and my graduate chapter of Chi Mu Nu), the members of the National Association of Black Journalists, and, of course, all my friends and former colleagues at the Associated Press.

Thank you, Stan and Jack.

And we all should appreciate the work done by the writers who kept faith with the legend: Reginald Hudlin, Don McGregor, Christopher Priest, Ta-Nehisi Coates, Evan Narcisse, Roxane Gay, Jason Aaron, Nnedi Okorafor and all the writers and artists who worked on the *Black Panther* comic books.

Of course, thanks goes to the cast and crew of the *Black Panther* movie, including Ryan Coogler, Joe Robert Cole, Chadwick Boseman, Michael B. Jordan, Lupita Nyong'o, Angela Bassett, Danai Gurira, Daniel Kaluuya and Winston Duke. The Black Panther would not have become the international icon he is today without their able assistance.

And finally, there were so many people who helped get this book published that it would be impossible to name them all. If I've omitted anyone, please blame my head and not my heart.

For more fantastic fiction, author events,
exclusive excerpts, competitions, limited editions and more

VISIT OUR WEBSITE
titanbooks.com

LIKE US ON FACEBOOK
facebook.com/titanbooks

FOLLOW US ON TWITTER AND INSTAGRAM
@TitanBooks

EMAIL US
readerfeedback@titanemail.com